AS245418

The ... use

Harlequin (UK) Limited's policy is to use papers that are natural, renewable and recyclable products and made from wood grown in sustainable forests. The logging and manufacturing processes conform to the legal environmental regulations of the country of origin.

Printed and bound in Spain
by Blackprint CPI, Barcelona

MILLS & BOON

Published in Great Britain 2014
by Mills & Boon, an imprint of Harlequin (UK) Limited,
Eton House, 18-24 Paradise Road, Richmond, Surrey, TW9 1SR

THE BABY SURPRISE © 2014 Harlequin Books S.A.

Juggling Briefcase & Baby, *Adopted: Family in a Million* and *Confidential: Expecting!* were first published in Great Britain by Harlequin (UK) Limited.

Juggling Briefcase & Baby © 2010 Jessica Hart
Adopted: Family in a Million © 2009 Barbara McMahon
Confidential: Expecting! © 2009 Jackie Braun Fridline

ISBN: 978-0-263-91194-7
eBook ISBN: 978-1-472-04489-1

05-0714

Harlequin ... use papers that are natural, renewable and recyc... from wood grown in sustainable fore...s. The loggi... ...es conform to the legal enviro... ...ental regulation...

Printed a... by Blackp... ...n CPI, Barcelona

JUGGLING BRIEFCASE & BABY

BY
JESSICA HART

Jessica Hart was born in West Africa, and has suffered from itchy feet ever since, travelling and working around the world in a wide variety of interesting but very lowly jobs, all of which have provided inspiration on which to draw when it comes to the settings and plots of her stories. Now she lives a rather more settled existence in York, where she has been able to pursue her interest in history, although she still yearns sometimes for wider horizons. If you'd like to know more about Jessica, visit her website: www.jessicahart.co.uk.

CHAPTER ONE

LEX drummed his fingers on the table and tried to tell himself that the uneasy churning in his gut was due to one too many cups of coffee that morning. He was Alexander Gibson, Chief Executive of Gibson & Grieve, one of the most popular and prestigious supermarket chains in the country, and a man renowned for his cool detachment.

A man like him didn't get *nervous*.

He *wasn't* nervous, Lex insisted to himself. He had been sitting on this damned plane for over an hour now, and if he had to commit himself to flying at thirty thousand feet in little more than a tin can he'd just as soon get it over with, that was all.

See, he wasn't nervous, he was *impatient*.

Lex scowled at the sleety rain streaking the cabin windows, and then stiffened as he caught sight of a limousine speeding across the tarmac towards the plane. His drumming fingers stilled and the churning that wasn't nerves jerked his entrails into a knot so tight that it was suddenly hard to breathe.

She was here.

Very carefully, Lex flexed his fingers and set them flat on the table in front of him while he steadied his breathing.

He wasn't nervous.

Lex Gibson was never nervous.

It was just that the steel band that had been locked around his chest for the past twelve years had been steadily tightening ever since he had heard that Romy was back in the country.

It had notched tighter when Phin had casually announced that he had offered her a job in Acquisitions.

And tighter still when Tim Banks, Director of Acquisitions, had rung that morning to explain that a family crisis meant that he would have to miss accompanying Lex on the most important deal of his life.

'But I've arranged for Romy Morrison to go with you instead,' Tim had said. 'She's been working with me on the negotiations, and has built up an excellent rapport with Willie Grant himself. I know how important this meeting is, Lex, and I wouldn't suggest her unless I was sure she was the best. I've sent a car to pick her up, and she'll be with you as soon as possible.'

And now here she was, and the steel band was clamped so painfully around his lungs that it hurt to breathe. Lex forced his attention back to the email he had been reading, but the screen kept blurring in front of his eyes. It would be fine. Romy was an employee, nothing more.

He wanted this deal with Grant more than he had ever wanted anything else and if Romy could help him persuade Grant to sign, that was all that mattered. The sooner she got on this plane, the sooner they could get the deal done.

He was *impatient*. That was all.

The car had barely stopped by the steps of the executive jet before Phil, the driver, was out and holding open the door for Romy.

'Mr Gibson doesn't like to be kept waiting,' he had said

anxiously, watching Romy run around the flat, frantically ticking off items on a mental list.

'Nappies…travelling cot…high chair…oh, God, the *car seat*! Yes, I *know* he's been waiting an hour already…I'm coming, I'm coming…'

Travelling with Freya was nerve-racking at the best of times, and Romy had been so flustered by the thought of coming face to face with Lex again that she had forgotten first the pushchair and then the changing mat, until Phil, forced to turn round and drive back to the flat twice, was beside himself.

He was clearly terrified of Lex. Almost everyone who worked for Gibson & Grieve found their chief executive intimidating, to say the least.

Romy wasn't terrified, or even intimidated. But she was very nervous about coming face to face with him all the same. Sitting alone in the back of the limousine as they crawled through the rush-hour traffic, she had swung wildly between wondering what else she had left behind, and wondering what she would say when she saw Lex again.

What she would *feel*.

Best not to feel anything, Romy had decided. Lex clearly wanted nothing to do with her. He had made no effort to talk to her at Phin's wedding, and not once in the six months she had been working for Gibson & Grieve had he found an excuse to speak to her.

Perhaps she could have found an excuse to talk to *him*, Romy acknowledged, but what could she have said?

I've never forgotten you.

Sometimes I think about your mouth, and it feels as if you've laid a warm hand on my back, making me clench and shiver.

Have you ever thought about me?

No, she definitely couldn't have asked *that*.

It was all so long ago now. Twelve years ago. Romy looked out of the window and sighed. She was thirty now, and a mother, and Lex was her boss, not her lover. You didn't worry about how you felt about your boss. You just did your job.

So that was what she would do.

Romy glanced doubtfully down at her daughter. It wasn't going to be easy to be coolly professional with Freya in tow, but she would manage it.

Somehow.

Phil already had the boot open and was starting to unload all Freya's stuff, while the pilot, spotting their arrival, set the engines whining impatiently. The message was clear: Alexander Gibson was waiting to go.

Cravenly, Romy wished she could stay in the car, but then she remembered the desperation in Tim's voice.

'*Please*, Romy,' he had begged. 'Sam needs me, but Lex has got to have someone from the team with him when he meets Grant, too. If we let him down on this one, I don't know what he'll do, but it won't be pleasant.'

No one else would do, Tim had said, and in the end Romy had given in. She owed Tim too much to let him down when he needed her most. So she scrambled awkwardly out of the car, Freya in one arm and her laptop in the other, and, putting her head down against the rain, she ran up the steps to the plane.

A flight attendant wearing a badge that read 'Nicola' was waiting to greet her at the cabin door, and, in the face of her perfectly groomed appearance, Romy found herself hesitating. It had been such a rush to get ready that she hadn't had time to wash her hair, put on any make-up, or do more than throw on some clothes, and now she was going to have to face Lex looking a complete mess.

Too bad, she told herself, lifting her chin. He was lucky she was here at all.

Taking a deep breath, she smiled in response to Nicola's greeting, hoisted Freya higher on her hip and ducked into the cabin.

The plane was narrow but luxuriously fitted-out. It had squashy leather seats, a plush carpet, glossy wooden trim everywhere. But Romy didn't notice any of it.

Lex sat, halfway down the cabin, a laptop open on the table in front of him, looking up over his glasses, and as their eyes met it seemed to Romy that everything stilled. Behind her, Phil and Nicola had paused, while the sounds of the airport faded abruptly, until the whine of the engines, the rumble and scream of planes taking off and landing, the crackle of the radio as the pilot checked in with the control tower, were all strangely muted and there was only the warm weight of Freya in her arms and the man whose pale grey eyes set her heart thudding painfully in her throat.

'Hello, Lex,' she managed, hoping that he would blame her dash up the steps for the breathless note in her voice.

'Romy.'

Lex didn't even see the baby at first. His first reaction was one of relief, so sharp it was almost painful. She wasn't as beautiful as he'd remembered. Oh, it was unmistakably Romy, with that tumble of dark hair and those huge dark eyes, but the enchanting, passionate girl he'd fallen so disastrously in love with had gone. The years had blurred the pure lines of her face and faded the once gorgeous bloom of youth and she was just a dishevelled young woman with a tired face and a baby in her arms.

Thank God, thought Lex, feeling the band around his heart ease very slightly.

There was a beat, and then his mind caught up with his eyes, in a double take so startled that it would have been comical if Lex had felt anything like laughing, which he didn't.

With a *what* in her arms? A *baby*?

Romy's baby. Another man's baby. The steel band contracted once more.

His brows snapped together. 'What,' he demanded, 'is that baby doing here?'

'This is Freya.' Romy put up her chin at his tone. Was that really all he had to say, after twelve years?

She was furious. With Lex, for daring to sit there, looking like that. Looking as if he had never kissed her, as if he had never made her senses snarl with the touch of his hand. As if he had never loved her.

With herself, for being so bitterly disappointed.

What had she expected, after all? That he would sweep her back into his arms? That the heat would still crackle between them, after twelve long years?

Fool.

'I explained to Tim that I would have to bring her with me,' she said in a voice quite as cold as Lex's. She could do remote and chilly just as well as he could. 'Didn't he tell you?'

'*What?*'

'Tim said he would clear it with Willie Grant's people.'

Lex wasn't listening. Behind Romy, he could see the driver unloading pushchairs and carry cots and God only knew what else into the cabin. 'What the hell is going on? You,' he snapped at Phil, who froze guiltily. 'Take all that stuff off right now!'

'Yes, sir.'

'Just a minute,' said Romy clearly, advancing down the cabin towards Lex. 'Freya needs all that.'

Lex snatched off his glasses. 'For God's sake, Romy, you're not seriously proposing to bring a *baby* along on a business trip?'

'I don't have a choice. I told Tim all this, and he assured me that it wouldn't be a problem.'

'No problem?' he echoed in disbelief. 'We're on the verge of negotiating a major deal with a difficult client and you don't think it's a problem to turn up with a baby in tow? We'll look totally unprofessional! It's out of the question,' he said with finality.

Romy was strongly tempted to turn on her heel and walk out, but if she did that, what would happen to Tim, and the deal the whole team had worked so hard on?

Drawing a breath, she struggled to keep her temper under control. 'I was under the impression that you wanted someone from Acquisitions to accompany you?'

'I do want you,' said Lex, and for one horrible moment the words seemed to jangle in the air, a bitter parody of the ones he had once murmured against her skin.

I love you. I want you. I need you.

He folded the glasses he wore when working at a computer and put them in the breast pocket of his shirt. 'I just don't want a baby.'

'Well, I'm sorry,' said Romy, 'but you can't have me without her. What do you want me to do, leave her on the tarmac?'

Lex scowled. 'Haven't you got…I don't know…childcare or something? What do you do when you're at work? Or is Acquisitions doubling as a nursery these days?'

Romy set her teeth at the sardonic note in his voice. 'She goes to the crèche at the office.'

'There's a crèche?'

'Yes, there's a crèche,' she said, holding onto her temper with difficulty.

'One of Phin's projects, I suppose.' Lex looked disapproving. His brother had reluctantly joined the company after their father's stroke, and Lex had put him in charge of staff development. It was meant to be a token position, but he was always coming across initiatives in unlikely places nowadays.

'I believe so,' said Romy in a cool voice. 'It's one of the reasons Gibson & Grieve is such a popular place to work.'

'Well, then, why can't the baby go there?'

'Because we're going to be away overnight, and the crèche closes at six. I don't know anyone else I can leave her with, especially not at this short notice. Tim only rang a couple of hours ago. I *explained* all this.'

Freya was getting heavy, and Romy shifted her to the other hip as she glared at Lex in frustration. Part of her was almost glad to find Lex so unreasonable. It made it easier to pretend that he was just a difficult boss.

Easier to forget how warm his hands had been, how sure his lips. How a rare smile would illuminate that austere face and warm the cool grey eyes.

'I don't think you quite realise how difficult it has been for me to get here this morning,' she went on crisply. 'I'm here because Tim seemed to think that it was important, but if you'd rather go on your own, that's fine by me.'

A muscle was working in Lex's cheek. 'It *is* important. I need someone who's up to speed on the details of the acquisition.'

'Then perhaps you would prefer to rearrange?' she suggested, and Lex made an irritable gesture.

'No, we're going today. I understand from Tim that Grant's not that keen on the deal, and it's taken long enough to get him to see me. If we start messing around and changing dates, it could jeopardise the whole deal and I don't want to do that. We've been working on this too long to throw it away now.'

Romy said nothing.

Lex glared at her. There was only one choice, and they both knew it.

'Oh, for God's sake, bring all that stuff back,' he snapped at Phil, who exchanged a look with Nicola and went back down the steps into the rain to collect everything that he'd just stashed back in the boot of the car. 'Tell the pilot we're ready to go as soon as you're clear. We've wasted enough time this morning.'

Annoyed, he smacked the lid of his computer down and directed another irritable look at Romy. 'You'd better sit down,' he said, pointing at the seat opposite him. '*And* the baby.'

'Freya,' said Romy, not moving.

'What?'

'Her name's Freya.'

Her chin was up, and the dark eyes looked directly back into his.

And Lex felt the world shift around him, just as it had done all those years ago. She was closer now, close enough for him to see the fine lines starring her eyes, and he struggled to hold onto his conviction that she was just tired and untidy and nothing special.

But his gaze kept catching on the lovely curve of her mouth, and when he looked back at her he had the horribly familiar sensation of falling into those eyes. Lex had never understood how so rich and dark a brown could be so luminous. He wasn't a fanciful man, but it had always seemed to him as if light glowed in their depths, warming and beckoning.

How could he have thought for a moment that she wasn't as beautiful as ever?

Twelve years ago, he had fallen into those eyes, heedless of the consequences. He had lowered his guard and made himself vulnerable, and there was no way he was going through that again.

Lex willed himself not to look away, but he had himself back under control. He could do this. All he had to do was think about the deal. That was all that mattered now, and the fact was that he needed Romy. Without Tim Banks, she was his connection to Willie Grant, and he wouldn't put it past her to take the wretched baby and walk off the plane. She always had been stubborn.

'Very well,' he said tightly. 'You *and Freya* had better sit down.'

'Thank you,' said Romy, and sat down opposite him, calmly buckling her seat belt and settling the baby—*Freya*—on her lap.

Lex's jaw worked as he regarded her with a kind of baffled resentment. She was mighty cool considering that he was Chief Executive and she was just a temporary employee, and a far from senior one at that.

This was all Phin's fault.

Twelve years. That was how long he had spent trying to forget Romy, and the moment he laid eyes on her again he knew he had been wasting his time. He'd known she was back in the country. He'd known she had a baby. His mother had heard it from Romy's mother and had sucked in her breath disapprovingly at the thought of her god-daughter as a single mother.

'Well, that'll bring Romy home,' she had said.

And it had.

He had even known Romy would be at Phin's wedding. He'd thought he had braced himself to meet her again, but when the organ had struck up and he had turned with Phin to watch Summer walking up the aisle, all he had seen was Romy, sitting several rows behind, and his heart had crumpled at the sight of her. Romy, with her dark, beautiful eyes and the mouth that had haunted his memory for so many years. Romy, who had loved another man and had a baby to show for it.

Lex had avoided her at the reception, and despised himself for it. He was Chief Executive of the fastest-growing supermarket chain in England and Wales. He didn't care about anything but the success of Gibson & Grieve. He had no trouble finding a woman if he wanted one. So he should have been able to greet Romy casually and show her that he realised her decision had been the right one.

Because of course it was. She had been far too young to marry. He was eight years older than her, much too serious to manage all that passion and spirit. He would have crushed her, or she would have crushed him, and left him anyway. The only sensible part of the whole affair was their pact to tell no one else.

So there should have been no problem about meeting her again. But every time he told himself he would go over and say hello there had been someone with her and she had been laughing and waving her arms around so that the collection of bangles she always wore chinked against each other. Or she had been lifting her hand to push the hair away from her neck and he had been gripped by the memory of how soft and silky it had felt twined around his fingers.

And with that memory had come a flood of others that he had failed to forget: the scent of her skin, the husky laugh, the curve of her shoulder and pulse that beat in the base of her throat. That stubborn tilt of her jaw. That smile, the way she had pulled him down to her and made the world go away.

And then Phin was there, clapping him on the shoulder, telling him, almost as an aside, that he had offered Romy a job in Acquisitions.

'What? *Why?*'

'Because she needs a job,' his brother told him. 'She's got a baby to support, and she's having trouble finding work. She's been working overseas and it's hard to get a job when you've got a CV that's quite as varied as hers.'

Lex managed to part his lips and form a sentence. 'She should have thought about that before she drifted around the world.'

'You put me in charge of staff development,' Phin reminded him unfairly. 'I think Gibson & Grieve needs people with Romy's kind of experience. She was telling me about a diving centre she's been running in Indonesia: she's got all sorts of skills that we can use.'

'Phin, are you sure this is a good idea?'

'Look, it's just a temporary job, replacing Tim Banks's assistant while she's on maternity leave. I think Romy will be good at it, and it'll give her the experience she needs to find a permanent job. It's a win-win situation.'

Lex hadn't been able to object any further, or Phin would have wondered why he was so reluctant to have Romy working for Gibson & Grieve. His brother might seem the most easy-going of men, but Lex was discovering that he was far more perceptive than he seemed.

'Fine,' he had said with shrug, as if he didn't care one way or the other. 'It's your call.'

But Phin wasn't the one who braced himself every day in case he saw her. Who looked up every time the door opened in case it was her. Who had to walk around with a fist squeezed around his heart, just knowing that she was near.

Everything had felt tight for six months now. His head, his eyes, his heart, his chest. Usually, work was a refuge, but not now, not when Romy could appear at any moment.

So he had seized on the chance of two days away in the

Highlands, finalising the deal that would garner Gibson & Grieve a foothold in Scotland at long last. It was something his father had long tried to set up, and Lex, who had spent his life trying to prove that he could run Gibson & Grieve even better than his father, was determined to seal this one and take the company in a new direction that was all his own.

Lex had planned it to be just him and Tim. No entourage, no fuss. Willie Grant, of Grant's Supersavers, was by all accounts a recluse and an eccentric. The last thing Lex wanted was to alienate him by arriving with a lot of unnecessary people. Tim had warned him that Willie was a straight talker, and he wanted to do this face to face. Lex was fine with that. He was a straight talker too.

But now Romy was sitting opposite him instead.

With her baby.

At the front of the cabin, Nicola was hurriedly stowing away the extraordinary amount of equipment Romy had seen fit to bring with her. The door had closed after the driver, who had escaped gratefully down the steps, and the pilot was already taxiing, anxious to make up for lost time.

Lex wrenched his mind back from the past and looked at his watch. Two and a half hours behind schedule, and they still had a fair drive after they got to Inverness. Willie Grant lived in a castle in the wilds of Sutherland, in the far north west of Scotland, and God only knew how long it would take to get there. Summer, his PA, would ring and explain the delay, but Lex hated being late.

He hated it when events were out of his control, like this morning. The way they always seemed to be whenever Romy was around.

His life was spent keeping a close guard on himself and his surroundings. Only once had he let it drop, in Paris twelve years ago, when he had lost his head and begged Romy to marry him. Lex had never made that mistake again.

The plane was turning at the end of the runway, and the engines revved until they were screaming with frustration. Then the pilot set them hurtling down the runway.

Lex resisted the temptation to close his eyes and grip the seat arms. He knew his fear was irrational, but he hated being dependent on a pilot. It wasn't the speed that bothered him, or even the thought of crashing. It was putting himself completely in someone else's control.

Romy loved take-off. He remembered how her eyes had shone as the seats pushed into their backs and the power and the speed lifted the plane into the air. Lex hadn't said anything, but she had taken his hand and held it all the way to Paris.

Did she remember?

Lex's face was set with the effort of keeping his gaze on the window, but it was as if his eyes had a will of their own. Like a compass needle being dragged to true north, they kept turning to Romy in spite of the stern message his brain was sending.

The baby, he saw, was looking as doubtful about the whole business as he felt. When the plane lifted off the tarmac and Lex's stomach dropped, she opened her mouth to wail, but Romy bounced her on her lap, distracting her from the pressure in her ears until she was gurgling with laughter.

'You're a born traveller,' Romy told her. 'Just like your old mum.'

She smiled at her daughter and Lex could see the crooked tooth that was so typical of the way Romy just missed being perfect. It was only a tiny kink, only just noticeable, but the faint quirkiness of it gave her face character. He had always thought it made her more beautiful.

Then her eyes met Lex's over the baby's head, and the smile faded.

She was remembering that flight to Paris, too. He could see it in her eyes. The memory was so vivid that they might as well have been back on that plane, side by side, shoulders touching, their hands entwined, her perfume filling his senses as she leaned into him, distracting him with her smile, until it had felt to Lex as if he had left his real self behind and was soaring up with the plane into a different reality where he was a man who didn't care about control or responsibility or being sensible, and could open himself to every pleasure that came his way.

And look where that had got him.

Obviously he might as well have spared himself the effort of looking unconcerned, though. Romy didn't quite roll her eyes at his clenched jaw, but she might as well have done.

'Why didn't you take the train?' she asked.

'It's too far,' said Lex shortly. He hated her thinking that he might be afraid. He wasn't *afraid*, and if he was, he would never admit it.

'It's going to take most of the day to get there as it is. I can't afford to waste all that time sitting on a train. There's too much else to do. I was hoping Grant would be prepared to come to London to discuss the deal.'

Romy shook her head. 'Willie never leaves Duncardie now,' she said. 'His wife died five years ago, and since then he's been a virtual recluse.'

'So Tim explained. He told me that if I wanted to persuade Willie Grant to agree to the sale, I would have to go there myself.'

'You must want it badly if you're prepared to fly,' said Romy with a faint smile.

'I do.' Lex's face was set in grim lines. 'My father never managed to get a foothold in Scotland, and it was his one big disappointment. If he hadn't had his stroke last year, he'd still be on this plane now, on his way to see Willie Grant. He would never have trusted the negotiations to me.'

'He must have trusted you,' Romy protested. 'You're the one who's carrying on his legacy.'

'Yes, that's what I've been doing,' he agreed, a trace of bitterness in his voice. 'And now I'm ready to move the company in new directions. It's not about my father any more.'

For years he had been trying to prove himself to his father, and now, at last, he had a chance to show him just what he could do with the company.

'This is my deal,' he said. 'The one I made, the one he never could.'

'It's not a competition,' said Romy, but he looked back at her, unsmiling.

'Yes,' he said. 'It is. And it's one I'm going to win. That's why I really needed Tim with me today. If this deal doesn't go through because of his *family crisis*…'

Romy leant forward at that and fixed him with a look. 'I know you won't take it out on Tim,' she said crisply. 'You're a lot of things, Lex, but you're never unfair, and that would be. Tim has to be with his son. His family has to come first. You know that.'

Lex did know that, but he didn't have to like it. 'I sometimes think it would be easier if we only employed people without families,' he grumbled.

'You wouldn't have a very large workforce in that case.'

'Without children, then. You can be sure that the moment an important deal comes up, the vital person has to go home because some child is ill or needs to be picked up from school or has to be taken to the dentist, and then everybody else has to run around rearranging things to cover for them, like you and Tim.'

'I don't mind,' said Romy, not entirely truthfully. 'I know Tim would do the same for me. It's part of working in a good team.'

Lex grunted. Phin was always going on about teams, but he liked to work on his own. 'That's all very well, but if we're going to make this work I need to know that you're as committed to the success of this deal as Tim is.'

She met his eyes squarely as she settled Freya more comfortably on her lap. 'I am,' she said. 'I owe Tim a lot, and I don't want to let him down. I owe Gibson & Grieve a lot, too. I know Phin took a risk giving me the job, and I want to prove that I'm worth it. I'll do whatever it takes.'

'Except leave your baby behind,' Lex commented sourly.

'Except that,' she agreed.

CHAPTER TWO

'ACTUALLY, I think Freya could work to our advantage,' Romy said, stroking her daughter's head so that the beaten silver bracelets chittered softly together.

The baby was a funny-looking little thing, Lex thought. She had very fine dark hair that stuck up in an absurd quiff, and round, astounded eyes as dark as her mother's.

'How do you work that out?' he asked, wishing Freya wouldn't stare at him like that. It was disconcerting having that uncompromising gaze fixed so directly on his face.

'Willie Grant is very family-orientated, in spite of the fact that he doesn't have any children of his own. Grant's Super-savers have always been targeted at the family market. It's a big thing with him. To be honest,' Romy said to Lex, 'you're likely to be more of a problem than Freya.'

'*Me?*'

'Willie lives in a very remote place, but he's not isolated. He reads the papers and uses the Internet, and you,' she said, pointing across the table, 'have a reputation.'

'Meaning what?' asked Lex dangerously, and Romy swallowed, remembering, rather too late, that he was her boss. But if they were to secure this deal that meant so much to him, he would have to understand Willie Grant's position.

'Meaning that you've got an image as a loner, unsentimental, a workaholic, none of which makes you seem exactly family friendly.'

Lex narrowed his pale grey gaze. 'So what are you saying, Romy?'

'Just that it would be a mistake to underestimate how strongly Willie feels about family,' she said. 'We had to work very hard to get him to agree to meet you at all. He thinks that you're more interested in profits than in families.'

'Of course I am,' he said with an abrasive look. 'I'm a businessman. Being interested in profits is what I do. My shareholders are more interested in profits too. That doesn't mean we don't offer a service to families. God, we've got children's parking spaces and special trolleys and even crèches in some of the bigger stores, I'm told—what more does Grant want?'

'He wants to feel that he's selling his company to one with the same ethos,' said Romy evenly. 'We've sold you to Willie on the grounds of your integrity. He'd rather you were a family man but that doesn't mean he doesn't respect your straightforwardness. On the other hand, if you make it obvious that you've got no time for policies that make it easy for your staff to work effectively *and* be effective family members, then I don't think Willie will want to work with you.

'We're not the only retail chain with an interest in Grant's Supersavers,' she told Lex, who scowled. 'He's already had the big four supermarkets up here sniffing around, but he likes Gibson & Grieve's reputation for quality, and he likes the fact that it still has a family connection with you and Phin. But if he doesn't like your attitude,' Romy warned, 'he'll sell to someone else. If you want this deal, Lex, you're going to have to keep on Willie's good side.'

Lex thought about what she had said as he looked out of the

window. The plane had burst through the thick cloud layer into dazzling light, but Lex's mind was less on the blueness of the sky up there than on Romy's crisp analysis of his position.

He was more impressed by her than he had expected, he acknowledged to himself. He remembered Romy as a lovely, eager girl, passionate about everything. When she'd talked, she had leant forward with her face alight and her hands moving, encompassing him in her warmth. Now, she was cool and capable, and, in spite of those exotic, distracting bracelets and the distinctly distracting baby, she seemed surprisingly businesslike. Lex suspected that Tim would never have dared talk to him so directly, but if Romy was right, then he had needed to hear it.

Because this was all about the deal, and nothing about feelings, right?

Right.

'All right.' He turned back to Romy with a nod of acknowledgement. 'If that's what I have to do to get him to sign, that's what I'll do.'

Romy's expression relaxed. 'It shouldn't be too hard. Just don't tell him you tried to throw Freya off the plane!' She tweaked Freya's nose as she grinned down at her, and the baby chuckled.

Still smiling, Romy glanced up to find Lex watching her, and their eyes snagged for one jarring moment before he looked away.

At the front of the plane, Nicola was making coffee. The smell wafted down the cabin, reminding Romy that she hadn't had time to do more than gulp at a mug of tea that morning.

She unbuckled her seat belt.

'Would you excuse me?' she said formally. 'I didn't even have time to brush my hair this morning, and I'd like to tidy myself up. I presume there's a bathroom of some kind?'

'At the back,' said Lex, then watched in consternation as Romy set Freya on the floor and gathered up her bag. 'Are you just going to leave her there?'

'She can't go anywhere.'

'Well, no, but…shouldn't she be strapped in, or something?'

'Strapped in to what? She's safer on the floor than on a seat she can fall off—unless you'd like to have her on your lap?'

Lex recoiled. 'No!'

'She'll be fine,' Romy soothed. 'I won't be long.'

Romy loved flying. She loved the way her body pressed back into the seat as the plane left the ground. She loved landing and walking across the tarmac with the aircraft fumes shimmering in the heat. She loved looking down onto a billowy carpet of clouds and knowing that she had left everyday life behind and was on her way to somewhere new and exciting.

The only thing she didn't love about flying was using the bathroom. She was used to queuing along the aisle, getting in the flight attendants' way, and manoeuvring awkwardly into narrow cubicles. Being on an executive jet was a whole new experience. Quite apart from the lack of queues, the bathroom here was almost as large as the one in her flat, and sumptuously decorated, with a mirror above a gleaming vanity unit.

Sadly, no amount of flattering lighting could disguise the fact that she looked awful. Romy regarded her reflection with dismay. Her hair was all over the place, there were dark circles under her eyes, and a stain on her blouse marked where Freya had gugged up her hurried breakfast that morning.

Romy rubbed at it with a damp towel, which only seemed to make it worse, so she abandoned that and washed her face instead. Brushing out her hair, she clipped it up in a careless twist and pulled out her make-up bag. By the time she had made up her eyes and put on some lipstick, she was feeling a lot better.

It was going to be OK, she assured her reflection as she brushed down her loose trousers and straightened her top. Now that they had got over the inevitable awkwardness of seeing each other again, everything should be fine.

Of course it was a little strange. Lex was remote, severe, the way he always seemed at work. Looking at him, sitting there in his immaculate suit and tie, you would never guess that he was a man capable of passion, but Romy knew.

Whenever she looked at his mouth, or his hands, she remembered that week in Paris. She remembered how sure his lips had been, how his touch had made her strum with excitement, how skilfully he had drawn her into a swirl of heat and pleasure. She had only been eighteen. How could she have known that there would never be anyone else who made her feel quite like that again?

The memory of that week curled voluptuously around the base of Romy's spine and made her shiver.

'Stop it,' she told herself out loud. 'Stop thinking about it.'

She had to put that week from her mind. It was over. Long over. There were more important things to think about. Freya was her priority now. Romy had been getting desperate before Phin offered her this job at Gibson & Grieve, and she couldn't afford to make a mess of it.

It was only maternity cover, and Jo, whom she was replacing, would be returning to work soon. At that point, Romy was going to need a good reference. If she could help Lex close this deal, it would be fantastic experience for her when it came to finding another job. A job she needed if she was to maintain her independence.

That was what she should be thinking about, not Lex's mouth and how it had once felt on hers.

Romy squared her shoulders. She could do this.

Meanwhile, Lex was left nervously eyeing the baby on the floor. Freya sat on her bottom for a while, looking around with wide-eyed interest, then to his alarm she crawled under the table.

Now what? He sat dead still, afraid to move his feet, but after a moment he bent his head very carefully to look under the table and see what she was doing.

Freya's expression was intent as she patted his left shoe, apparently pleased by its shininess. Then the small hands discovered the lace, and pulled at it experimentally. Delighted to find that it came apart if she tugged at it, she looked up to find Lex watching her under the table, and she offered him a gummy smile.

The smile had an odd effect on Lex, and he jerked upright once more and snapped his computer open. Where was Romy? He was terrified to move his feet in case he kicked the baby by mistake, but if he was stuck here he could at least try and get some work done. He would pretend everything was normal and that there was no baby undoing his shoelaces under the table.

'Where's Freya?' Romy asked when she came back at last.

For answer, Lex grimaced and pointed wordlessly under the table, and Romy peered beneath to see that her daughter had undone both his shoes, and was sucking one of the laces with a thoughtful expression.

'I thought it was an unexploded bomb at least!' she said as she scooped Freya up and straightened.

'I would have been just as nervous,' said Lex grouchily. 'You were gone ages. What have you been doing?'

'I didn't even have time to brush my hair this morning,'

Romy pointed out, settling back into her seat. 'I was still in bed when Tim rang. I had a real panic to get here, and I'm still worried I left something vital behind.'

'How could you have left anything behind? It looked as if you brought the entire contents of the house with you!'

She sighed. 'You should see what I left behind! It's not easy to travel light with a baby.'

'You've changed.'

It was a careless comment, but suddenly the air was fraught with memories. There had been a time when Romy would have packed everything she owned into a rucksack.

'Yes,' she said, trying to make her voice as firm and businesslike as possible. 'Yes, I have.' She eyed Lex under her lashes. 'And you?'

'Me?'

'Have you changed?'

He looked away. 'Of course. I'd hope we were both older and a lot wiser.'

Much too wise to run off to Paris for a wild affair, anyway. The unspoken thought hung in the silence that pooled between them until Nicola appeared to offer coffee and biscuits.

'Thank you.' Romy was grateful for the interruption, but even more for the sustenance. She hadn't had time for breakfast that morning.

Freya's eyes lit up when saw the biscuits and she set up a squawk that made Lex wince until Romy gave her a piece of shortbread to shut her up. This was promptly mangled into a soggy mess, watched in horror by Lex, and Romy rushed into speech in an effort to distract him.

'You never got married.' It was the first thing that came into her head, but as soon as the words came out of her mouth she wished she had stuck with the soggy biscuit.

Lex raised his brows.

'The last time we talked, you said you were going to marry Suzy Stevens,' Romy said with a shade of defiance.

Lex had almost forgotten Suzy. Romy's mother, Molly, had remarried about a year after that week in Paris. As her godson, he had had little choice but to go to the wedding. Romy, of course, had been there too. She had just started her first year at university. After Paris, she had got herself a job in some bar in Avignon. Lex had heard it from his mother, who had heard it from Molly. Romy had had a great time, he had heard.

He had been determined to show Romy that he was over her. Suzy was everything Romy wasn't. She was calm and cool, elegant where Romy was quirky, sophisticated where Romy was passionate. She was suitable in every way.

But she certainly hadn't been stupid. She had seen how Lex looked at Romy, and broken off the relationship when they got back to London that night.

'It didn't work out,' Lex said shortly.

No one had worked out.

'I'm sorry,' said Romy.

'I'm not. It was all for the best.'

Lex's pale grey eyes rested on Freya, still sucking happily on her shortbread. Her fingers were sticky, her face smeared and there were crumbs in her hair and dribbling down her chin.

'I don't want any family responsibilities,' he said. 'I've seen too many people—like Tim today—compromise their careers because of commitments at home. Children are a constant distraction, as far as I can make out. Even a wife expects attention. You can't just stay at work until the job is done. You've got to ring up and explain and apologise and make up for it by taking yet more time off… Relationships are too messy and demanding,' said Lex briskly. 'I long ago came round to your point of view and decided that marriage wasn't for me either.'

He looked at Romy. 'It's just as well you wouldn't marry me. It would have been a disaster for both of us.'

A disaster. Yes. Romy turned her bangles, counting them like beads on a rosary. She had eleven, in a mixture of styles, and she wore them all together, liking the fact that they were so different and that each came with its own special memory. Beaten silver. Beaded. Clean and contemporary. Ethnic.

One came from the *suq* in Muscat, another from Mexico. One was a gift from an ex-boyfriend, another she had bought for herself in Bali.

And *this* one… Romy's fingers lingered on the silver band. It was inlaid with gold and intricately carved. An antique.

This one Lex had bought for her at Les Puces, the famous flea market at the Porte de Clignancourt. They had spent the morning wandering around hand in hand, bedazzled by the passion that had caught them both unawares. Whenever Romy looked at the bracelet, she remembered how intensely aware of him she had been, as if every fibre of her being were attuned to the feel of his fingers around hers, to the hazy excitement of his male, solid body.

A disaster? Maybe. Probably.

She looked up from the bracelet to find Lex watching her, and their eyes met for a brief, jarring moment before she looked quickly away.

'I've never forgotten that week,' she said.

She wondered if Lex was going to tell her that he had, but instead he just said: 'It was a long time ago.'

Well, she couldn't argue with that. She nodded.

'We've both moved on since then,' he said.

Also true. Romy bit her lip. She wasn't quite sure why she

was persisting in this, but surely this was a conversation they needed to have?

'I've wanted to talk to you since I've been back, but there never seemed to be an opportunity. I'd thought perhaps at Phin's wedding, but…well, it didn't seem appropriate. And since then, it's been difficult. You're my boss. I didn't think I could just march into your office and demand to speak to you.'

'There's always the phone,' he pointed out unhelpfully. 'Or email.'

'I know. The truth is that I didn't have the nerve,' she said. 'I was really nervous about seeing you today. I know it's stupid, but it seems even more stupid to pretend that there had never been anything between us.'

Romy drew a breath, daunted by Lex's unresponsive expression. 'I just thought that if we could acknowledge it, we would be able to get it out of the way and then stick to business.'

'Fine, let's acknowledge it, then,' said Lex briskly. 'We had a mad week when we were young, but we both know that it would never have lasted longer than that week. Neither of us has any regrets about it. Nobody else knows about it. We've both moved on. What's the problem?'

'No problem, when you put it like that.' But Romy couldn't help feeling a little miffed. Lex was saying everything she had wanted to say, but there was no need for him to sound quite that matter-of-fact about it, was there?

'So now that we've agreed that, we can draw a line underneath the whole episode.'

'Precisely,' she said. 'From now on, our relationship can be purely professional.'

'In that case,' said Lex, opening his computer once more, 'let's go over the main points of the agreement we're offering Willie Grant.'

* * *

It was snowing when they landed in Inverness, dry, sleety flakes that spun in the air and did no more than dust the surface of the tarmac. Still, Romy was glad that Summer had arranged for them to hire a solid four wheel drive to take them the rest of the way.

She shivered as she carried Freya down the steps. She'd been living in the tropics for so long that a London winter was shock enough for her system, and she was unprepared for how much colder it would be up here in the north of Scotland. She wished she'd brought a warmer coat.

The vehicle was waiting as arranged just outside the terminal. It was black and substantial and equipped with all the latest technology.

Except a baby seat.

Lex was all ready to get in and drive away until Romy pointed out that Freya would have to travel in the seat, and that it would have to be installed properly.

'It doesn't take long. If you'll just hold her a minute, I'll do it.'

You would think she had asked him to hold a bucket of cold sick.

'I'll install the seat,' he said.

So Romy had to stand there in the cold, while he grew crosser and crosser as he tried to work out how to do it. She tried offering instructions, but Lex ignored her, cursing and muttering under his breath as he searched around for the belt, and then managed to clip it into the wrong buckle, so that he had to start all over again.

He was in a thoroughly bad mood by the time Romy was finally able to buckle Freya in and climb into the passenger seat beside Lex, and matters were not improved when Freya, who had woken as she was laid in the seat, started to grizzle fretfully when they had barely left Inverness.

'What's the matter *now*?' Lex demanded, glowering in the rear view mirror.

Romy looked over her shoulder at her unhappy daughter, then at her watch.

'She's hungry. I am too. Is there any chance we could stop for lunch?'

He sighed impatiently. 'We'll never get there at this rate,' he grumbled, but, according to the sat nav, it would be another two and a half hours before they got to Duncardie, and Lex wasn't sure he could stand the crying another two minutes, let alone two hours.

By the time he saw a hotel up ahead, he was only too happy to pull in. 'But for God's sake, let's be quick about it,' he said as they got out of the car.

To Lex, used to the most exclusive restaurants and the gleaming, high-tech efficiency of Gibson & Grieve's head office, it was something of a surprise to realise that hotels like this still existed. There was a swirly carpet patterned in rich reds and blues, stippled walls painted an unappealing beige and sturdy wooden tables, their legs chipped and worn by generations of feet. Sepia prints were interspersed with the occasional horse brass or jokey tea towel about the joys of golf, and the faint but unmistakable smell of battered fish hung in the air.

On the plus side, it was warm and quiet. Lights flashed on the jukebox in the corner, but it was mercifully silent, and the only other guests were an elderly couple enjoying lunch in the corner. It had a welcoming fire and a friendly landlady who was unfazed by a request for a high chair and was soon deep in discussion with Romy about what Freya would like for her lunch.

Having taken a cursory glance at the menu, Lex ordered a

steak and kidney pie and retired to a table by the fire while Romy bore a still-grizzling Freya off to change her nappy. Turning his back on the jolly décor on the wall beside him ("Why is a ship a she?"), Lex rang the office. He got twitchy if he was out of contact and it had been impossible to carry on a conversation on the car phone with Freya bawling in the background.

Not that it was much easier once Romy emerged from the Ladies. Seeing that he was talking to Summer, she carried Freya around the room, jiggling her up and down in her arms and showing her the pictures to distract her from her hunger. The trouble was, she was distracting Lex too. Every time she lifted a hand to point at a picture, her breasts lifted slightly, her back straightened and he seemed ever more unable to block out her shape from the edge of his vision.

It was as if all his senses were on high alert. Romy was wearing loose black trousers and a top in a peacock blue so vibrant that it lit up the entire room, and whenever she turned he was sure he could hear the whisper of the silky material sliding over her skin.

He was sure he could smell her perfume.

Romy was absorbed in her daughter, her face vivid as she chatted away, quite unaware of the fact that whenever she smiled Lex lost track of what Summer was saying.

'Sorry…run that past me again,' he had to ask, not for the first time.

There was a tiny pause. Lex could feel Summer's surprise bouncing up to a satellite and down again. He was famous for the fact that he was always focused and alert. Now Summer would tell Phin that he wasn't concentrating, and Phin would grin and come up with all sorts of ridiculous suggestions as to what might be distracting him.

None of which would be right.

Hunching an irritable shoulder, Lex turned in his chair so that he had his back to Romy.

'I was just wondering how you were getting on with the baby,' Summer said, her voice carefully incurious.

'Fine,' he said shortly. 'Did you warn Grant's people about that?'

'I did. There's absolutely no problem as far as they're concerned.'

'That's something,' he grunted.

The landlady appeared with their lunch at that point, and Romy came back to settle Freya into the high chair, where she started squealing with excitement at the sight of food and banging both her hands on the tray as she bounced up and down. Lex could only imagine how it sounded to Summer in her quiet, calm office as he rang off.

Romy tied a bib on Freya, no easy task when she wouldn't keep still. 'Everything OK at the office?' she asked, mindful of the need to stick to business.

'Yes. Summer has got everything under control.'

'I imagine Summer always does. She's terribly efficient, isn't she?'

'I wouldn't keep her as my PA if she wasn't.'

'Isn't it awkward having your sister-in-law as a PA?' Romy couldn't resist asking as she sat down opposite him and blew on Freya's plate to cool it.

'I'm just glad she wanted to keep on working,' said Lex. 'I don't know how long it'll last. No doubt it'll be a baby next,' he said morosely. 'Then I'll have to train yet another new PA. The wedding was disruptive enough.

'That was my fault for sending her to work for Phin in the first place,' he remembered, reaching for the mustard. 'She was supposed to stop him doing anything stupid, and look what happened! God knows what she sees in him. They couldn't be more different.'

Romy had been surprised when she had met Summer, too. Phin's wife was as crisp as he was laid-back and charming.

'It must be a case of opposites attract,' she said, then wished she hadn't. What else had it been between her and Lex? 'They seem very happy together, anyway,' she added quickly.

'Yes.'

Why couldn't *he* have fallen in love with Summer? Lex wondered. She was exactly what he needed. She was cool and capable, and hated mess and clutter as much as he did. God only knew how she coped with Phin's slapdash ways. She was very pretty, too, although in all honesty Lex had to admit that he hadn't noticed until Phin started stirring her up. The transformation had been quite remarkable.

At last Romy set Freya's plate on the tray of the high chair and picked up her own knife and fork, which meant that Lex could start too.

To his relief, Freya stopped squawking instantly and applied herself to her lunch as well. She was waving a spoon around but her preferred method of eating seemed to be to squash her fingers into the food and then stick them in her mouth. Lex averted his eyes. He had thought her biscuit eating technique was bad enough. This process was utterly revolting.

Every now and then Romy would load up a second spoon and try to hurry the process along by feeding her, but Freya only pressed her lips together and turned her face stubbornly away.

Romy sighed and laid down the spoon. 'She *will* insist on doing everything herself. I'm afraid it's a slow business. She won't be helped.'

'Like her mother,' said Lex without thinking and then cursed himself as she raised her brows.

'What do you mean?'

'Even as a very small child you refused to hold anyone's hand. You always wanted to do everything by yourself. I remember listening to my mother commiserating with yours about how independent you were.'

'I'd forgotten that.' Romy pushed the spoon hopefully in Freya's direction once more. 'I've always assumed I only realised how important it was to be independent after my father left, but maybe I was born that way.'

'Stubborn,' Lex agreed.

'You know, you're not exactly Mr Malleable,' she pointed out.

'I always did what my parents expected me to,' he said with a trace of bitterness. 'I had to be the sensible, responsible one, unlike you and Phin, who gaily went your own way. I used to envy how adventurous you both were,' he confessed, even as he marvelled at how easily he had strayed away from business. 'Neither of you ever seemed to be afraid of anything.'

'Dogs,' Romy reminded him. She had been badly bitten by a collie when she was five and had been very nervous of dogs ever since.

'All right, anything except dogs,' Lex conceded. 'And commitment, of course,' he added smoothly. 'Neither of you ever liked to be tied down to a plan either.'

'And yet there's Phin married,' said Romy, 'and here's me with a baby. It's funny the way life works out, isn't it?'

'Yes,' said Lex, thinking about the twists and turns that had brought them both to this shabby pub. 'Very funny.'

The elderly couple in the corner had finished their lunch, and stopped at the table on their way past.

'What a lovely baby!' The woman beamed and chucked Freya's cheek. 'Aren't you the bonny one?'

Intent on her lunch, Freya paid little attention, but Lex felt his jaw sag.

Lovely? In disbelief, he looked at the baby in question, who was happily rubbing mashed potato into her hair. One ear appeared to be encrusted with carrot and he didn't even want to think about what might be dribbling from her nose.

Romy avoided his eyes. 'Thank you,' she said with a smile.

'I'll bet she can twist you round her little finger, eh?' The man actually *nudged* Lex. 'Wait till she's older. She won't give you a moment's peace!'

'Make the most of it while she's small.' His wife nodded at Lex, who was too dumbfounded to do more than stare back at her. 'You've got a lovely wee family,' she told him. 'You're a lucky man!'

'Enjoy your lunch.' Her husband nodded farewell as he took her arm.

A gust of cold air swirled into the room as they opened the door, but the next moment it had swung to, and Lex and Romy were left alone in the dining room.

There was a moment of utter silence, and then Romy dissolved into helpless laughter. Diverted from her lunch, Freya stared at her mother, and started to chuckle as well, clearly puzzled by all the merriment, but perfectly happy to join in.

'What's so funny?' demanded Lex, looking from one to the other.

'Your expression,' Romy managed at last, wiping her eyes and drawing a shuddery breath. 'I wish you could have seen yourself! I've never seen anyone look so appalled at the thought of being associated with a *lovely wee family*!'

Her whole face was alight with humour. The dark eyes

were sparkling with laughter, and her expression was so vivid that Lex's heart tripped, and all at once he was back in that restaurant in Paris, drinking in the sight of her, dazzled by her warmth and her beauty.

He made himself look away. 'I've never been taken for a father before,' he said, his voice desert dry. 'I've always assumed it would be obvious that I wasn't.'

'It's an easy enough mistake to make,' said Romy. 'We must look like an ordinary family.'

CHAPTER THREE

'I SUPPOSE SO.' For some reason, the thought made Lex uneasy. He felt ridiculously thrown. He wanted to rush after the couple and ask them how they could possibly have thought that he was Freya's father. What did he need to do? Have *never in a million years* tattooed across his forehead?

Romy's smile still curved her mouth as she picked up her knife and fork once more. 'I don't think they were very impressed by your hands-off approach, though. I could see them watching you while I was trying to entertain Freya. They obviously thought you should have been helping me instead of making phone calls. I suspect that was why she thought she should remind you how lucky you are to have us.'

'Dear God.' Lex glanced at Freya, who had gone back to smearing lunch over her face, and shuddered. 'I'm glad to have amused you,' he added austerely when Romy started to giggle again.

'Oh, you have. It was worth the rush this morning just to see you!'

Freya was clearly a baby who enjoyed her food. There was a lot of gurgling and squealing and squeaking, with much smacking of lips together and banging of spoons. And the mess…indescribable! Lex decided, eyeing Freya askance as he put his knife and fork together.

'I just hope she's not going to be eating in front of Willie Grant!'

'Don't worry,' Romy soothed. 'I'll make sure he knows you're not responsible for her in any way.'

Lex pushed his plate aside. 'Who *is* responsible for her, Romy?'

'I am,' she said instantly.

It was none of his business, Lex knew, but he couldn't help asking. 'What about her father?'

The last amusement faded from Romy's face. 'I thought we were sticking to business?' she said, disliking the defensive note in her voice. She busied herself filling the spoon and offering it, without much hope, to Freya, who took it and wiped it on her nose.

He shrugged. 'I'm just interested in why you're having to do everything yourself.'

'Because I want to.'

Edgy now, Romy picked up her mat. It showed an unlikely hunting scene, with red-coated riders hallooing and urging their horses over a hedge, while the hounds bounded alongside. In spite of herself, Romy shrank a little at the sight of their lolling tongues and great paws. No one would think of putting spiders or snakes on a mat, would they? So why were dogs different? If she had noticed the dogs before, she wouldn't have enjoyed her pie nearly so much.

She twisted the mat around so that they faced Lex instead.

'Doesn't he get a say?'

'He doesn't know.' Romy balanced the mat between her hands, turned it so that it sat on the shorter edge. 'I haven't told him yet.'

'He doesn't *know*?' said Lex, incredulous.

'Look, it was just a fling,' she said, not looking at him. 'A holiday romance. I was running a dive centre in Sulawesi, Michael was travelling... He's an artist, very laid-back, very charming.'

Very everything Lex wasn't.

Round went the mat. 'We had a good time. Neither of us wanted any more than that. Michael was on the rebound. He'd been dumped by his girlfriend a couple of months earlier, and I...well, you know how I feel about commitment.'

Romy looked up then, and looked straight at Lex. The pale eyes were shuttered, his expression indecipherable.

'It wasn't just you, Lex,' she said, since they seemed to have abandoned the pretence of sticking to business. 'I don't want to marry anyone. I certainly didn't want to marry Michael. It was never a big deal for either of us. I liked him— he was great—but there was never any question of anything more than that.'

'So how did Freya happen?' asked Lex.

'The usual way,' said Romy with a touch of her old tartness. Then, when he just met her gaze, she bit her lip and went on. 'We took precautions of course, but...well, sometimes it happens. By the time I realised that I was pregnant, Michael had already left.

'He sent an email when he got home, just to say hello, but I knew that he wasn't interested in me beyond a fling. I had another message a couple of months later, telling me that he was back with his girlfriend, so an email from me saying that he was going to be a father would have been the last thing he wanted.'

Lex frowned. 'Wouldn't he want to know anyway?'

'I don't know...' Romy sighed. 'Sometimes I thought he would, and that it was wrong not to tell him, but then I thought of him being with his girlfriend, and I didn't want to spoil that for him. It's not as if he made any promises. Michael talked about Kate a lot when we were together, so I know how much he wanted to be with her. When he emailed, he sounded so happy—'

She broke off, flashing Lex a look. 'Would *you* have wanted to know?' she asked abruptly.

'Yes.'

'Just like that? No thought about how having a child would turn your life upside down?'

'I'd still want to know,' said Lex. 'If, after Paris…' He didn't finish the sentence, but she knew what he was thinking. 'I'd have wanted to know,' he said. 'I'd have thought I had the right to know.'

Romy eyed him in dismay. Of all the people she would have expected to understand, she had thought it would be Lex! Lex, who hated chaos and was clearly appalled by Freya.

'Maybe I was wrong,' she said, chewing her lip. 'It just seemed to me that learning that you're a father is such a big thing. Having a child…it changes everything. *Everything.* I imagined how I would feel if I was Kate, finding out that it wasn't just Michael any more, but Michael and a baby. It would have changed things for her too… Oh, I've been round and round about this so many times since I found out I was pregnant!'

Tiring of the mat, Romy let it drop to the table and started fiddling with a spoon instead, spinning it slowly between her finger and thumb. 'Should I tell Michael? Should I not? What if he didn't want anything to do with Freya? What would that do to her, to know that her father never wanted her? Would that be better or worse than not having a father at all?'

'That's not really the point,' said Lex severely. 'The point is that this Michael is partly responsible for her, and that means he should help support her.'

'I don't want help,' said Romy stubbornly. 'I don't need it.'

She caught the echo of her own words about Freya, and grimaced a little. 'I don't want to rely on anyone,' she tried to explain. 'It was my choice to have a child, my choice to bring her up on my own. Telling Michael wouldn't be about the money.'

She had begun to irritate herself with her fiddling and she made herself stop and put her hands in her lap. 'I expect he would want to support Freya if he knew,' she said. 'Michael's a decent man. He wouldn't run away from the responsibility.

'I'm the one that has done the running away,' she admitted. 'I didn't want to upset things between him and Kate, but the truth is that I used that as an excuse. I was afraid that if I told Michael he might want to be involved in Freya's life. He might want to see her, and she…she might love him.'

Romy's eyes rested on Freya, who was absently wiping a spoon in her hair and wearing a pensive expression. 'Children do love their fathers.'

Her voice was very sad, and Lex's expression changed. 'There's no reason to think that he would be like your father, Romy.'

'No, but what if he was? What if he disappointed her? What if he didn't love her the way she deserves to be loved?'

She had been such a daddy's girl. Her whole world had revolved around her father. She couldn't wait for him to come home at night and drove her mother mad, jiggling up and down with excitement. There was no joy to compare with that of seeing him appear, of running into his arms, of being swept up into a hug and swung round and round until she was giddy and giggling.

'Who's my best girl?' he would ask.

Romy would shriek, 'Me! Me!'

'And who do I love best in the world?'

'Me!'

Romy could still remember it, the blinding happiness, the utter, utter security of wrapping her skinny arms around his neck and knowing that her father was home and that nothing could go wrong when he was there.

And then one day he sat her down and told her that he would never be coming home again. That he was going to live with someone who was not her mother and have a new family. She was going to have a new brother or sister, he told her.

'But I still love you,' he said.

Romy didn't believe him. If he loved her, he wouldn't leave her. She was six, and she never felt quite safe again. Even now, the memory of that morning had the power to rip at her heart and bring back the black slap of disbelief. How could he have done that to her? How could he have left his best girl?

Twenty-four years ago, and it still made her feel sick with misery and incomprehension.

The thought that Freya might be hurt in the same way was unbearable. However hard it might be to struggle on her own, Romy knew it was better than letting herself rely on someone who might leave them both.

'It wasn't an easy decision, Lex,' she said slowly. 'I thought about it every day. I still think about it. I don't know if I did the right thing not telling Michael when I was first pregnant. It *felt* right, that's all I can say. It felt as if it would be better for Freya if it was just two of us.

'Recently though…I suppose it's partly seeing Tim and re-alising that there are great fathers out there, but I've been

thinking that I should tell Michael about Freya after all. Not
for the money, but because Freya needs a father as well as me.
And because Michael deserves to know that he has a daughter.

'But first I want to be sure I'm truly independent. This
deal with Grant's Supersavers is important to you, I know,'
she told Lex, 'but it's just as important to me. It's my
chance to really make my mark, something really impressive to put on my CV for when I have to look for my next
job. In the past, I've just drifted from country to country
and picked up work when I needed it, but it's different
now. I need a proper job, and I can't rely on anyone but
myself for that.'

'You're not exactly alone in the world,' Lex pointed out.

'No,' she acknowledged. 'Mum and Keith were great when
I came home to have Freya, but they've done enough. They're
too old to live with a baby. I moved out as soon as I could,
but I was getting desperate about finding anything when Phin
offered me this job at Gibson & Grieve.'

Romy looked across the table at Lex. 'I never thanked
you for that.'

'Thank Phin,' he said with a dismissive gesture. 'He
fixed it all.'

'You're Chief Executive. You could have said no.'

'I wouldn't have done that,' said Lex, but he avoided her
eyes, remembering how dismayed he had been when Phin had
told him what he had done. If he thought he could have per-
suaded his brother to change his mind, he would have done.

'Well, thank you anyway.'

'You can thank me by making sure this deal goes through,'
said Lex roughly, and Romy nodded.

'I'll do whatever I can to make it happen,' she said. 'For

both of us. And when it's done, and I've got the experience I need to get a permanent job, then I'll tell Michael that he has a daughter.'

The snow was little more than a light powder when they left the pub, but the further they drove, the heavier it got, until great, fat flakes were swirling around the car and splattering onto the windscreen.

The short winter afternoon was drawing in, too, and Romy began to feel as if they were trapped in one of the snow scenes she had loved to shake as a child, except in this one the snow didn't settle after a minute or two. It just kept on coming. Soon, Romy couldn't see the country they were driving through, but it felt dark and empty and wild, and it was miles since they had passed a vehicle going the other way.

'Do you think we should turn back?' she ventured at last.

'Turn back? What for?'

'The snow's very heavy. What if we get stuck?'

'We're not going to get stuck,' said Lex. 'We're certainly not turning round and going back on the off chance that we do. We're almost there. This meeting is too important to miss because of "what if".'

'We might break down,' said Romy, who had been checking her mobile. 'And I'm not getting a signal on my phone. How would we get help?'

Lex sucked in a breath. 'Romy, there is nothing wrong with the car,' he said, keeping his voice even with an effort. 'Anyway, I thought you were the one who wanted adventure? When did you turn into a worrier?'

'When I became a mother,' said Romy, glancing over her shoulder to where Freya was, thankfully, sound asleep. 'I used to pack up and go without a thought. It never occurred to me that anything could go wrong, but now…'

She sat back in the seat, turning the useless phone between her hands, her eyes fixed on the swirling snow but her mind on the day her life had changed for ever.

'I didn't know what terror was until Freya was born,' she said slowly after a moment. 'Until I held her in my arms and looked into her face, and realised that it was up to me to keep her safe and well and happy. What if I can't do it? What if I get it all wrong? I'm terrified that I'll be a bad mother.'

Where had *that* come from? Romy wondered, startled. She spent a lot of time assuring her mother and her friends that she was fine on her own, that she was managing perfectly well. She spent a lot of time telling herself that too.

And she *was* fine. She *was* managing. She just didn't tell anyone how hard it was. How scared she was.

Now, unaccountably, she had told Lex, of all people. The one person who would least understand.

'I worry about everything now,' she confessed. 'I worry about what will happen if Freya is sick or if she struggles at school. How will I pay for her university fees? What if she has a boyfriend who hurts her?'

Lex shot her a disbelieving look. 'It's a bit early to worry about that, isn't it?' he said. 'She's only a baby.'

'Thirteen months,' Romy told him, 'and growing every day. I know it's stupid, but I can't help myself. I'm afraid I won't be a good enough mother, that I won't be able to give her what she needs. I'm afraid I won't be able to support her by myself, and that I'll have to rely on other people, that her happiness will be in someone else's hands. I'm afraid her father will want to be part of her life and afraid that he won't. Oh, yes,' she said with a lopsided smile, 'I'm a real scaredy cat now!'

'Then you've changed more than I thought you had.'

'You should be glad. An irresponsible eighteen-year-old with itchy feet isn't much good to you.' Romy paused. 'She never was.'

'No,' Lex agreed, and his voice was tinder dry.

Romy blew out a long breath. 'I miss being that girl sometimes,' she said. 'I miss how fearless I was. I had such a good time. I can't believe I did all those things now, now that I'm scared and sensible and the kind of person who puts on a suit to go into work every day. It feels like remembering a different person altogether.'

'So if you hadn't got pregnant, would you still be drifting?'

'Probably. I'd been in Indonesia a couple of years. I was thinking of moving on. Thailand, maybe. Or Vietnam. Instead I'm a single mother living in the suburbs and struggling into work on the tube every day.'

Lex glanced at her, and then away. 'No regrets?'

Romy looked over her shoulder again. Freya's head was lolling to one side. Ridiculously long lashes fanned her cheeks and her lips were parted over a bubble of dribble. Her baby. Her daughter. Her best girl.

'No,' she said. 'No regrets.'

They drove on through the dark in silence. In spite of her earlier anxiety about the snow, deep down Romy wasn't really worried. There was something infinitely reassuring about Lex's coolly competent presence. He drove the way he did everything else, like a man utterly sure of himself. The only time he lost that sense of assurance was in the air, but now he was on the ground and firmly back in control.

Romy eyed him under her lashes. His hands were big and capable on the steering wheel, and the muted light from the dashboard threw the cool planes and austere angles of his face into relief.

That was the point she should have looked away, but her gaze came to rest on his mouth instead, and without warning the memory of how it felt against hers set something dangerous strumming deep inside her.

Alarmed, she forced her eyes away, but instead of doing something sensible like fixing on the satellite navigation screen, they skittered back to his hands, which only made the strumming worse as the memories she had kept repressed for so long clamoured for release.

Lex's hands. The feel of them was imprinted on her skin. He had long dextrous fingers that had sent heat flooding through her. They had been warm skimming over the curve of her hip, sliding over her thigh, gentle up her spine, hungry at her breast… He had played her body like an instrument, coaxing the wild, wondrous excitement with those possessive hands, that mouth, exploring her, loving her, unwrapping her, unlocking her as if she were some magical gift.

Desperately, Romy made herself stare out at the snow until the swirling flakes made her giddy. Or perhaps it was the memories doing that. Why had she let herself remember? She should have kept them firmly locked away, the way Lex had clearly done.

Now she was hot and prickly all over, and even the backs of her knees were tingling as if he had just kissed her there again.

He had been such an unexpected lover, so cool on the surface, so passionate below. Afterwards, Romy had realised that it shouldn't have been such a surprise. As a child, she had once seen Lex play the piano, had watched astounded as he drew the most incredible music from the keys.

Her mother had claimed that he was good enough to play

professionally. There had been a flaming row with his father when Gerald Gibson had dismissed Lex's talent.

'He can play the piano if he wants, but what's the point of him studying music?' he had demanded. 'Lex will be joining Gibson & Grieve. Economics makes much more sense.'

What Lex thought about the piano, Romy had never known. Only once more had she ever heard him play, in a dimly lit café in some Paris back street, which they had found quite by accident. They had sat late into the night, listening to the band.

Occasionally one of the musicians had drifted off for a drink, and someone from the audience would get up and play in their place. Lex had taken a turn at the piano at last, improvising with a guy on the saxophone, his body moving in time to the music, utterly absorbed, and Romy had listened, her throat aching with inexplicable tears. This was not the dutiful son, the boy who had joined the family firm and set out to please his father. This was her lover and a man she suspected Gerald Gibson didn't even know existed.

'Romy?'

Lex's voice startled Romy out of her thoughts and she jerked upright. 'What?'

'I wondered if you'd fallen asleep.'

'No. I was…thinking.'

'What about?'

For a moment, a very brief moment, Romy considered telling him the truth. She could turn to him in the darkness and confess that she had been thinking about him, about how he made music and how he made love and how he had made her feel.

But the thought had barely crossed her mind before she remembered how his face had closed on the plane. 'It was a long time ago,' he had said. 'We've both moved on.'

As they had. Lex was right. It was pointless to bring it all up again.

He wanted to draw a line under the whole episode and stick to business. And let's remember, Romy, she reminded herself, this is your boss, and you need this job. If he wants to stick to business, business it is.

'Nothing,' she said.

'Well, start thinking about how you're going to explain Freya's presence to Grant.' Lex tapped the sat nav. 'According to this, we're nearly there.'

Sure enough, a few minutes later they were bumping along a track and over a bridge, and then quite suddenly there were lights glimmering through the snow and the dark bulk of Duncardie was looming above them.

Concealing his relief at having arrived at last, Lex drove into a courtyard, and parked as close as he could to the massive front door.

'Only three and a half hours late,' he said grimly.

He switched off the engine, and there was a sudden, crushing silence, broken only by the sound of Freya burbling to herself in the back seat. She had woken half an hour before, and Romy had been on tenterhooks in case she started to cry again, but her daughter seemed perfectly content to play with her toes and chat away in her own incomprehensible language.

'OK,' said Lex. 'Now remember, the whole deal is riding on this meeting, so we've got to get it right.'

'Right,' said Romy.

'If we want Grant to take us seriously, we'll have to be professional, and that means making a good impression right from the start. We're going to have to work hard to make up for turning up late with the entire contents of a Mothercare catalogue.'

'Professional,' Romy agreed. 'Absolutely.'

The moment the wipers had stilled, the snow had started to build up on the windscreen, and already they could barely see through it.

Lex was calculating how quickly he could unload the car. 'You take Freya,' he told Romy. 'I'll bring the stuff.'

Romy thought doubtfully of everything she had brought with her. 'It'll take ages if you do it on your own. Why don't we do it together?'

'There's no point in two of us blundering around in the snow,' he said gruffly. 'Take Freya into the warm. Hopefully we'll have a chance to change and get rid of all this clobber before we meet Grant himself.'

'All right.' Romy drew a breath and looked at Lex. 'I'm ready.'

He nodded and reached for the door handle. 'Then let's go and get this deal.'

It wasn't far to the door, but it was bitterly cold and to Lex, labouring backwards and forwards in the dark through the snow, it felt as if he were trapped in an endless blizzard. Head down, he dumped stuff in the stone porch as quickly as he could before running back for the next load. At least someone was transferring it all inside, he saw, but he was very glad indeed to make the last trip, skidding and sliding over the snow.

Brushing the worst of the snow off himself in the porch, Lex shook out his sodden trousers with an irritable grimace. His feet were frozen, his hands numb, and melting snow was trickling down his neck, and he was cursing Willie Grant's refusal to go to London and meet in a warm, dry office, where all sensible deals were made.

But this was the deal he wanted, Lex reminded himself.

He bent to retrieve the last of Freya's luggage and stepped through the door.

He found himself in a vast, baronial hall, complete with antlers on the wall, some sad, glassy-eyed creatures stuffed and mounted long ago, and even the requisite suit of armour standing to attention at the foot of a magnificent staircase.

Lex didn't see any of them. He registered three things simultaneously. One, a small, portly man with a halo of white hair, holding Freya. Willie Grant himself, in fact, who turned to watch Lex's approach.

Two, the fact that he, Lex, far from presenting a crisply professional appearance, was dripping snow everywhere and had a bright yellow bag decorated with teddy bears wearing bow ties in one hand and a huge pack of nappies and a pushchair in the other.

And three, Romy, terrified and trying not to show it, standing rigidly beside Willie Grant while an Irish Wolfhound, easily the biggest dog Lex had ever seen, sniffed interestedly at Freya's feet.

Forgetting his humiliating appearance, Lex dropped the teddy bear bag and snapped his fingers. 'Come,' he said to the dog, who trotted obediently over to greet him.

'Sit.'

The great rump sank to the floor.

'Good dog,' said Lex, and rubbed the huge head that came up to his chest, while Romy sent him a speaking look of gratitude.

Willie Grant's expression was harder to decipher.

'That's Magnus,' he said. 'He doesn't usually go to strangers.'

'I like dogs,' said Lex, giving Magnus a final pat.

It was too late to hide the pushchair and nappies. He set

them down, tried to pretend that he wasn't dripping every-where, and stepped forward to offer his hand.

'Lex Gibson,' he introduced himself.

'Willie Grant.' Willie's grip was firm and he studied Lex with interest, not unmixed with surprise.

'I'm very sorry we're so late.'

'Oh, not to worry about that,' said Willie. 'Your secre-tary rang, so we got the message that you would be delayed and that you were bringing the wee lassie with you.' He beamed at Freya and tweaked her nose. 'She's a bonny one, isn't she?'

'Yes, I'm sorry about that—' Lex began, and then stopped short as Freya, clearly recognising him, broke into a gummy smile and reached out her arms towards him.

Instinctively, Lex took a step back, but Willie was watching Freya and didn't notice. 'Ah, I see who *you* want!' he chuckled. 'Old Willie's not good enough for you, is he?'

And before Lex could react, he had handed Freya over and turned to take Romy by the arm.

'Now come away in and have some tea in the library,' he said and bore her off up the magnificent stone staircase, leaving Lex, aghast, holding Freya at rigid arm's length.

It wasn't often that Lex was at a loss for words.

'Er...' was the best he could manage.

'Perhaps I should take Freya,' Romy said quickly, trying to hang back. 'Lex is rather wet.'

But Willie wasn't to be deflected. 'Oh, bring the wee one too, of course,' he tossed over his shoulder at Lex. 'You'll soon dry off by a good fire. Ewan's around here somewhere. He'll take your stuff to your room while Elspeth's bringing us some tea.'

That left Lex with little choice but to carry Freya gingerly after them, dangling between his hands. He was terrified that she was going to cry, but she just stared at him with those disconcertingly direct dark eyes.

The library was warm and cluttered, with heavy red velvet curtains closed against the night and a fire crackling behind a guard.

'We put that up as soon as we heard you were bringing the baby,' said Willie.

'I was afraid she'd be a nuisance,' Romy said, settling herself on the red leather sofa, and looking anxiously over her shoulder to see where Lex and Freya were.

To her dismay, the huge dog had followed them up the stairs and threw itself down on the rug in front of the fire with a great thud. Romy was convinced she could feel a tremor in the floor and wouldn't have been in the least surprised if the ornaments had come crashing off the mantelpiece at the impact.

She had been terrified in the hall when Magnus appeared. On one level, Romy knew it was stupid. Just because one dog had bitten her when she was a child didn't mean that every dog would bite. Perhaps it was knowing that they *could* that made her so nervous.

And this dog was a monster, the size of a small pony at least. When it had stuck its great muzzle towards her, she had frozen with terror. Unable to move, the breath clicking frantically in her throat, she had only been able to watch as it swung its head round to investigate Freya in Willie's arms. Her daughter's feet had been mere inches away from those huge teeth.

Willie didn't seem to have noticed anything amiss. He'd been laughing with Freya, as if unaware that a mere nudge from the beast beside him could send them both crashing to the ground where it could savage them.

She should snatch Freya back, Romy had thought frantically,

but that would mean pushing past the dog and panic had clogged her throat at the idea of touching it. What if it turned on her? What if its eyes went red and it went for her? What if—?

And then Lex had stepped into the hall, and the world had miraculously righted. He had taken in the situation at a glance. Romy had sagged with relief as he'd called the dog away. His effortless control of the animal had given her a queer thrill, she had to admit, even as she despised herself for feeling so safe with him. That smacked too much of neediness for one of Romy's independent turn of mind.

Still, there was no denying that Lex was a formidable figure, even dripping snow and burdened with ridiculous bags. He must have hated meeting Willie like that, Romy thought, remembering how much he had wanted to present a professional image.

It was all her fault for bringing so much stuff with her. Well, she would make it up to him, Romy vowed. She would do everything she could to make sure Willie agreed to sell to Lex.

Wondering where Lex and Freya had got to, Romy made herself focus on Willie, who was assuring her that Freya would be no trouble. 'I like to see the wee ones,' he told her. 'Moira and I dreamed of Duncardie full of children, but sadly it wasn't to be.'

'I'm sorry,' said Romy gently.

Willie looked sad, but squared his shoulders. 'At least we had each other,' he remembered. 'I never looked at another woman after I met Moira.'

'You must miss her very much.'

'I do. It's been five years now, and I still miss her every day. And every day I remember how lucky I was to have found her. It's a great thing to find a love like that,' he told Romy.

'It must be.'

Fleetingly, Romy found herself thinking about Lex, which was ridiculous, really, because although that week in Paris had been wonderful and intense, it hadn't been about love, not the way Willie meant. It had been passion, it had been desire, it had been sheer, unadulterated lust, but it couldn't have been *love*.

She hadn't wanted it to be love. Even at eighteen, she had known that love meant making compromises. It meant putting your heart and your happiness into someone else's hands, and Romy had done that once. She had loved her father absolutely, and she wasn't prepared to risk her heart again.

Never again.

CHAPTER FOUR

WILLIE was bustling around the tea tray when Lex appeared at last. He was walking very gingerly and holding Freya as if she were a grenade with a very wobbly pin. He must have come up those stairs very, very slowly.

Evidently forgetting his new family-friendly image, Lex handed Freya over with such an anguished grimace that Romy had to tuck in the corners of her mouth quite firmly to stop herself laughing. Fortunately, Willie was busy with the teapot and didn't notice.

'You must be frozen,' she said tactfully instead.

'Yes, indeed.' Willie looked up. 'Come and dry yourself by the fire, Lex. Just push Magnus out of the way.'

Romy thought it would take a bulldozer to move a dog that size, but Lex just clicked his tongue and pointed and Magnus heaved himself to one side with a sigh.

'I didn't have you down as a dog man,' said Willie, handing him a cup of tea.

Lex nodded his thanks. 'It's not the sort of thing that normally comes up in the business world.'

'I think it should. It helps to know who you're dealing with and so far, you've been something of an unknown entity. Oh, I know you're a canny enough businessman,' Willie went on as Lex opened his mouth to speak, 'but beyond that, there's not much information out there about what you're like as a person.'

'I don't like to mix my personal life with business,' said Lex stiffly.

'Fair enough,' Willie allowed, 'but I like to get to know a man before I decide whether we can do business or not.'

'I understand that.' There was a suspicion of clenched teeth in Lex's voice, and Romy could see a muscle jumping in his cheek.

She held her breath. Lex's temper, never the longest, would be on a very short fuse after the day he had had. He hated being out of control, and things had gone from bad to worse, with Tim unable to make it, a long delay until she turned up, and Romy didn't suppose he had been pleased to discover that he would be spending the following forty-eight hours with someone he had been comprehensively ignoring ever since she had started work. On top of all that, he'd been landed with a baby, forced to confront his fear of flying and had to drive through a blizzard. Small wonder if he was irritable now.

But in the end all he said was, 'That's why we're here.'

'Quite,' said Willie comfortably as he took a seat in a wing chair. His eyes, bright blue, rested speculatively on Lex's rigid face. 'I suggest we talk about the deal over dinner tonight. Enjoy your tea for now.'

Romy suspected the chance of Lex enjoying his tea was slight. Willie's personal approach to negotiations was not at all Lex's style. He was much happier in the boardroom, talking figures with hard-headed men in suits. Gibson & Grieve's Chief Executive had many strengths, but chatting sociably by a fire wasn't one of them.

At least here she could help. Romy might not be sufficiently ruthless when it came to negotiating, but she had advanced social skills.

'How old is the castle?' she asked, drawing Willie's attention away from Lex and setting out to charm him.

It wasn't difficult. Willie had been closely involved in setting up the negotiations. Unlike Lex, he liked to deal with the details himself and had been perfectly happy to talk to Romy, who was far from being the most senior member of the acquisitions team. They had already established a rapport on the phone and by email, and she had been touched by the warmth of his welcome. He had seemed genuinely delighted to meet Freya, too.

How Willie felt about Lex was less clear. Chatting away to Romy, he was studying him without appearing to do so, the shrewd blue eyes faintly puzzled.

Lex himself was starting to steam by the fire, and he stepped away, conceding the prime space on the rug to Magnus, who immediately reclaimed it.

Before he could choose a seat, Willie, in mid history, waved him to the sofa next to Romy. It would have been churlish to have opted for the other chair, so Lex had little choice but to sit down next to her, Freya wriggling between them.

Over the baby's head, his eyes met Romy's briefly. Hers were gleaming with laughter at his reluctance, or perhaps at the absurdity of the whole situation, and in spite of himself Lex, who had been feeling distinctly irritable, felt an answering smile tug at his mouth.

Though, God knew, there was little enough to smile about. His feet were so cold, he had lost all feeling in his toes, and his trousers were still clammy and uncomfortable. He had sensed Willie's reservation about him, too, and it didn't bode well for the negotiations.

Romy, though, was doing a fantastic job of charming the old devil. Lex contributed little to the conversation. He couldn't do small talk and, besides, how could he be expected to concentrate on lairds and battles and licences to crenellate when Freya was rolling around on the shiny leather, and beyond her Romy was leaning forward, listening to Willie. When her face was animated, when the firelight burnished the dark, silky hair and warmed the lovely curve of her mouth, of her throat.

Lex was still grappling with the fact that after twelve years of trying to forget her, she was actually there, warm and bright and as beautiful as ever, her vivid presence still with the power to send his senses tumbling around as if they were trapped in some invisible washing machine. The moment he managed to steady them by grasping onto a sensible fact, or remembering the deal and everything that rested upon it, Romy would smile or turn her head and off they would go again, looping and swirling until it was all he could do to string two words together.

It was most disconcerting, and the last thing Lex needed right then. He gripped his cup and saucer, holding them well out of Freya's reach, and wished, not for the first time, that Tim's son had chosen any day other than this to have his crisis.

Freya struggled towards him once more, preparing to clamber over him, and protested loudly when Romy scooped her away.

'Why don't you put her on the floor?' Willie asked.

'What about the dog?'

'Oh, Magnus won't mind.'

Lex could see that whether the dog minded or not was the least of Romy's concerns. 'I'll keep an eye on her,' he said gruffly.

Of course, the moment she was allowed down, Freya made a beeline for the dog, but Lex was there before her, catching her in one arm and making careful introductions between dog and baby. Freya squealed with excitement when Magnus sniffed her cautiously, and Lex showed her how to stroke the wiry head, but she soon lost interest and set off to explore the rest of the room while he sat in an armchair, relieved to have distanced himself from the heady sense of Romy's nearness, but nervous about the baby. Willie and Romy were so deep in conversation that it was obviously up to him to keep an eye on her, and it was a nerve-racking business.

For a start, Freya could crawl with alarming speed, and she was never still. One minute she was all over the dog, the next patting Willie's slippers. She tried to haul herself upright on an armchair, only to lose her balance and plump back down on her bottom. Undaunted, she tried again, and this time stayed upright long enough to take one or two wobbly steps while holding onto the cushion.

She would be walking soon, Lex guessed, and he was glad to think he wouldn't be responsible for her then. You wouldn't have a moment's peace. Look how quick she was on all fours. Now she was crawling back to the chair where Lex sat and tugging at his damp trousers to pull herself up against his knees. The creases in them would never be the same again. Lex tried to edge his legs out of her reach, but Freya's little fingers held tight, and, short of kicking her away from him, he was stuck and had to sit there while she treated him as another piece of furniture and manoeuvred unsteadily around him.

Meanwhile, Romy and Willie were getting on like fire in a match factory. Perhaps this visit wasn't going to be such a disaster after all. Watching Willie Grant laughing with Romy, Lex found it hard to believe he was going to turn round and refuse the deal. One wary eye on Freya, Lex let himself relax slightly and imagine the moment when he could announce to his father that the deal was secured, and that Gibson & Grieve had a foothold in Scotland at last.

And then?

Uneasily, Lex pushed the question aside. He had been planning this deal for a year now. Once this deal was done, there would be others, hopefully not involving a baby. Romy would find a new job. Life would go back to normal.

It would be fine.

Lex had lost track of the conversation between Willie and Romy entirely when Willie hoisted himself to his feet.

'You don't mind if we abandon you for a few minutes, do you, Lex? We won't be long.'

'Of course not.' Courteously Lex got to his feet, hoping he hadn't missed out on some vital conversation. Willie clearly wasn't expecting him to go with them, though, and Lex was delighted at the thought of a few minutes on his own. 'I'll be very happy to stay here and keep an eye on the fire.'

'Excellent.' Willie moved to the door. 'Magnus will keep you company. He doesn't like the stairs. Shall we go then, Romy? Oh, I don't think you'll want to take Freya, will you?' he added as Romy bent to pick up her daughter. 'It's chilly up there, and you might find the spiral stairs a bit tricky with her.'

'Oh.' Already by the door with Freya in her arms, Romy hesitated.

Willie flicked Freya's nose. 'You'd rather stay with your daddy, wouldn't you, precious?'

Daddy?

Lex opened his mouth, but Romy got in first. 'Er, Lex isn't actually Freya's father,' she said.

'Isn't he now?' Willie's brows shot up. He eyed Lex narrowly, and then gave a small approving nod, 'Well, that makes me think the better of you.'

Mystified, Lex looked at Romy, who could only lift her brows with a tiny shrug to show that she was as puzzled as he was.

'We won't be long, Lex.' Willie held the door open for Romy, who threw Lex an agonised glance. She could hardly insist on taking Freya with her against Willie's advice, he realised.

Heart sinking, Lex went over and she handed the baby over with a speaking glance. 'I won't be long,' she promised.

Freya watched the door close behind her mother and belatedly realised that she had been abandoned. Her eyes narrowed in outrage and she let out a bellow of outrage that startled Lex so much that he nearly dropped her.

'She'll be back as soon as she can,' he said with desperation, but Freya only opened her mouth to wail in earnest.

'Oh, God…oh, God…' Frantically, he jiggled her up and down, and for a moment he thought it would work. Freya definitely paused in mid-wail, and Lex could practically see her considering whether she was distracted enough to stop crying altogether, but she evidently decided that she wasn't ready to be consoled just yet because off she went again, at ear-splitting volume.

'Shh…. Shh…' Lex had a sudden vision of Romy walking Freya around the pub at lunchtime, so he set off around the room, jiggling the baby awkwardly as he went.

To his astonishment, this seemed to do the trick. Freya's screams subsided to snuffly sobs, and then stopped altogether.

Perhaps there wasn't so much to this baby business, after all? Obviously, the child just needed a firm hand.

Bored of circling the library, Lex stopped and put Freya on the carpet. She promptly started yelling again until he picked her up again, at which point the noise miraculously stopped.

A firm hand. Right.

Lex set off on another circuit of the library.

He was on his fifth when the door opened. He looked round, hoping it would be Romy, but instead it was Elspeth, the housekeeper, who had come to clear the tea tray.

'The wee one must be tired,' she said, noting the long lashes spiky with tears and the hectic flush in the baby's cheeks. And Lex's harassed expression. 'Would you like me to show you to your room?'

At least it would make a change from the library, thought Lex as he followed Elspeth up more stairs and along a labyrinth of corridors.

'I feel as if I should be leaving a trail of breadcrumbs,' he said, and Elspeth smiled as she opened a door at last.

'It's not as complicated as it seems the first time,' she promised as she left.

Lex was dismayed to see her go. He had considered asking her to look after Freya, but that would have meant admitting that he couldn't cope, and that wasn't something Lex could do. He wasn't the kind of person who admitted failure or asked for help.

It would have been different if Elspeth had *offered* to take Freya. Then he could have legitimately handed her over. But as it was, she simply smiled and assured him that she would make sure Romy knew where they were, and Lex was left to grit his teeth and get on with it.

He found himself in a magnificent guest room, dominated by a four-poster bed, and with swagged curtains at the windows. The cot, pushchair, high chair and assorted baby bags were neatly stacked in the corner, together with his own briefcase and overnight bag, which had clearly been put in here by mistake.

It was all boding very well for the deal, he thought. If Romy, as a very junior member of the negotiating team, had been allocated a room like this, Willie Grant must be doing more than considering their offer.

Feeling more confident, Lex tried putting Freya down again, but she was having none of it. She insisted on being picked up again, and amused herself for the next few minutes by pulling at his hair, batting his nose and trying to twist his lips with surprisingly strong little fingers.

'Ouch!' Lex began to get quite ruffled. Where was Romy? It felt as if he had been walking around with Freya for hours now, but when he looked at his watch he was astounded to see that barely thirty minutes had passed since Romy had handed him her daughter and left. Surely she had to be here soon?

Worse was to come.

Wincing as he pulled her fingers from his nose, Lex was alarmed to see that Freya's face had gone bright red and screwed up with effort.

'What's the—?'

He stopped as an unmistakable smell wafted up from her nappy.

'Oh, God. Oh, no…'

Dangled abruptly at arm's length, Freya started to cry again.

'No, no, don't cry…your mother will be here soon…just hold on…'

But Freya didn't want to hold on. She was miserable and uncomfortable and missing the reassuring solidity of his body. She cried and cried until Lex, who had been pretending to himself that he didn't know what needed to be done, was driven to investigating the bag he had seen Romy take to the Ladies with Freya in the pub, what seemed like a lifetime ago.

He did know what had to be done. He just didn't want to face it.

'Where are you, Romy?' he muttered.

The bag contained fresh nappies and a pack of something called baby wipes. Lex made a face, but took the bag and the baby into the bathroom and looked around for a towel. He had a nasty feeling things were going to get messy.

Cursing fluently under his breath, he spread the towel as best he could one-handed, and laid Freya, still screaming, on top of it.

'Please stop crying,' he begged her, wrenching at his tie in dismay at the task ahead of him.

In response, Freya redoubled her cries.

'OK, OK.' Lex dragged his hands through his hair and took a deep breath. 'You can do this,' he told himself.

He rolled up his sleeves and studied the fastenings on Freya's dungarees. So far, so good. Gingerly, he pulled them off her and then, averting his face, managed to unfasten the nappy.

'Ugh.'

Grimacing horribly, he tugged the dirty nappy free, holding it out as far away from him as humanly possible, and put it in a waste-paper basket. Then he braced himself for the next stage of the process.

'God, what am I doing?' Lex muttered as he pulled off some sheets of loo paper. 'I'm Chief Executive of Gibson & Grieve. I make deals and I make money. I negotiate. I direct. I don't wipe bottoms. How did I come to this?'

And then—at last!—came the sound of the door opening. 'Lex?' Romy called.

'In here.'

When Romy crossed to the bathroom door, she saw Lex crouched on the floor, a fistful of loo paper in his hand and Freya kicking and grizzling on a towel in front of him. Both of them looked up at Romy as she appeared in the doorway, with almost identical expressions of relief.

'Oh, thank God!' said Lex in heartfelt tones. 'Where have you *been*?'

'With Willie, then I went to the kitchen to find Freya some supper.'

Romy looked from her daughter to Lex. She had never seen him less than immaculate before, but now his hair was standing on end, his tie askew and his sleeves rolled up above his wrists.

He looked so harried that she wanted to laugh, but it seemed less than tactful when he had clearly been doing his best.

'She was crying,' Lex said defensively, as if she had demanded to know what he thought he was doing. 'I thought she needed her nappy changing but I'm not really sure what I'm doing...'

Romy could only guess what *that* admission had cost him. 'It was very brave of you to have a go at all,' she told him. 'Shall I take over now?'

'She's all yours.'

Lex couldn't get up quickly enough. He watched as Romy cleaned the baby and put on a clean nappy with the minimum of fuss.

'You make it look so simple,' he said almost resentfully, and she glanced up at him with a smile.

'Practice,' she said.

Freya was wreathed in smiles once more. Romy lifted her up and kissed her, and the tenderness in her expression closed a fist around Lex's heart and squeezed.

Turning abruptly on his heel, he went back into the bedroom, where a plate of bread and butter with some ham and a banana was sitting on a side table. Freya's supper, presumably. Lex dreaded to imagine what she would do with that banana.

Not his problem, he reminded himself. Thank God.

'I'll leave you to it,' he called back to Romy as he retrieved his bag and briefcase. 'What time are we expected
for dinner?'

Romy appeared in the doorway with Freya. 'Drinks at
seven thirty.'

'Fine. I'll have time for a shower and can change these
trousers.' Lex shook each leg in turn. Between Freya and the
snow, he didn't think they would ever be the same again. 'I
don't suppose you know which is my room?'

Romy settled Freya into the plastic chair that she had fixed
to the table. She handed her the plate of bread and ham and
turned to face Lex, drawing a breath.

'This one,' she said.

'All your stuff is in here,' said Lex. 'You might as well stay
here, and I'll take your room.'

'This *is* our room.'

Halfway to the door, Lex stopped. Frowned as he realised
what she was saying. 'You mean…?'

'I'm afraid so.' Faint colour touched Romy's cheeks. She
hadn't been looking forward to breaking this to Lex. 'There
seems to have been some kind of misunderstanding when
Summer rang up,' she said carefully. 'They thought that
because we were bringing a baby, we were all together.'

'Didn't you tell them that's not the case?'

She hesitated. 'Not yet.'

'Why on earth not?'

'I wasn't sure what to do.'

Edgily, Romy walked over to the window and pulled back
the curtain. Outside, the snow was still swirling in the
darkness while great, fat flakes piled up on the window sill.
If they weren't careful, they would be snowed in here, and
then what would happen?

Lex eyed her back in baffled frustration. 'What do you mean, you weren't sure? You could just tell the truth!'

'The thing is, Willie was so *pleased*.' Romy turned from the window, trying to make Lex understand what it had been like. 'He was supposed to be showing me some charter, but he really just wanted to talk about you, and how happy he was to discover you weren't at all like your reputation. There he was, expecting some soulless businessman, and you turn up with a baby and start bonding with his beastly dog…Willie was absolutely delighted to discover that you were a family man after all!'

'But I'm not Freya's father,' Lex objected, pacing back from the door. 'We told him that.'

'I know, but that only makes it better from his point of view. Apparently his mother was a single mother who struggled without any support from her family or his father or anyone, and helping single mothers is a big issue with him.'

Romy fiddled with her bracelets. 'He just assumed that you and I were…' Somehow she just couldn't bring herself to say 'lovers'. It was too close to the truth. And too far.

'Together,' she said in the end. 'So the fact that you're prepared to be in a relationship with me and be a hands-on father figure to Freya…well, that clinched it for Willie.'

Hands-on? Lex raked a hand through his hair. This was getting worse and worse!

'Why didn't you put him right straight away?'

'Because *you* told me you wanted this deal signed at all costs!' said Romy defensively. 'This is important, you said.'

'Good God, Romy, you can't have thought I meant you to lie to the man!'

'I didn't *lie*. I just…didn't tell him he'd got it all wrong. I could barely get a word in edgeways as it was.'

Romy was starting to get cross. 'Willie was going on and on about how pleased he was to discover that you weren't at all like your reputation, and how much happier he felt knowing that Grant's was going to be part of a chain run by a man with the right priorities. At what point was I supposed to interrupt and say that actually you weren't like that at all, and that actually you didn't want anything to do with me at all and that you'd rather stick pins in your eyes than deal with a baby?'

'There must have been something you could do!' Lex took another turn around the room, watched round-eyed by Freya, who was intrigued by his agitation. 'Eat your supper!' he said to her irritably as he went past, and obligingly she stuffed another finger of bread in her mouth.

'Leave Freya out of it!' snapped Romy, moving to stand protectively over her daughter.

Picking up the banana, she began to peel it as she made herself calm down. There was no point in getting into an argument with Lex. She didn't for a moment think he would sack her out of spite, but, when all was said and done, he was still her boss.

'Look,' she said after a moment, 'I know it seems awkward, and I'm sorry, but I just didn't know what to do. It seemed so important to Willie.'

She sliced up the banana and put it on Freya's plate, while Lex continued to prowl around the room. 'I got the sense that he'd almost decided that he didn't want to sell to you, but, between Freya and the dog, you've changed his mind. He told me in the tower that he's really keen for the deal to go ahead as soon as possible now.'

Lex sucked in his breath at the news. This was the moment he had been waiting for. He wanted to punch the air and shout *'Yes!'* but it didn't seem appropriate now that everything was muddled with this misunderstanding about his relationship with Romy.

He paced some more. He wanted this deal—oh, how he wanted it!—but did he really want it under false pretences?

Romy was watching him warily. 'I was afraid that if I told Willie the truth, he would be so disappointed that he'd change his mind back again,' she said.

'I wasn't just thinking about you,' she added as Lex pinched the bridge of his nose between finger and thumb. 'I was thinking about all the work Tim and the rest of the team have put in on this deal. We all want it as much as you do. So rather than throw up my hands in horror when I realised what Willie was thinking, I thought I should talk to you first. You're the boss,' she said. 'I think you should decide whether you tell him the truth or not.'

Lex had ended up at the window. He stood, exactly where Romy had done, looking broodingly out at the snow that spiralled silently past, catching the light from the room in a brief blur of white before drifting down into the darkness. His hands were thrust into his trouser pockets, his shoulders stiff with exasperation.

'God, what a mess!' he said with a short, humourless laugh.

Romy said nothing. It seemed to her that there was little more that she *could* say now. It was up to Lex.

Freya, quite oblivious to the tension in the room, was stuffing banana into her mouth. Romy sat down next to her and turned her bracelets while her eyes rested on the back of Lex's head. How was it that it could still look so familiar after all this time?

Unaware of her gaze, Lex tried to roll the tension from his shoulders and she sucked in a breath at the stab of memory. He was such a guarded man, such a cool and careful man, and he held himself so tautly that it was easy to forget that beneath the suit, beneath the tie and the immaculate shirt, was a man of bone and muscle, of firm flesh and sinew, a man hard and smooth and strong.

Romy remembered running her hands over those shoulders, feeling the flex of responsive muscles beneath her touch. His back was broad and solid and warm, his skin sleek and underlaid with steel.

She couldn't see his face, but she knew that it would be set in harsh lines, and that a nerve would be jumping in his jaw. She could go to him, put her arms around him from behind, and lay her cheek against his back. She could hold onto his hardness and his strength, and offer in return the comfort of her warmth and her softness. She could tell him that she would be there for him, whatever happened.

She could, but she wouldn't.

It was just a fantasy. A stupid fantasy, Romy knew. A *dangerous* fantasy.

The trouble with Lex was that he made her feel things she didn't want to feel. Something about him bypassed all her rational processes and tugged at a chord deep inside her. Romy didn't want it to be love. Love, she knew, laid you open. It made you vulnerable, made you blind. It was a trap that could spring shut at any moment, and she had no intention of blundering into it. She couldn't afford to get tangled up in loving anyone, least of all a man who had made it plain that he had no interest in Freya.

I do want you, he had said. *I just don't want a baby.*

And that wasn't a problem, because she didn't want *him*, Romy reminded herself.

So, no fantasies. No remembering, no thinking about how he had felt or the clean, male smell of his skin. She was here on business, and she had better not forget it.

The silence lengthened, broken only by Freya loudly enjoying the banana. Bath time next, Romy thought, and was about to get to her feet when Lex spoke at last.

'I went to see my father last week,' he said suddenly, without looking round.

Thrown by the apparent change of subject, Romy hesitated. 'How is he?' she asked at last.

'A stroke is a terrible thing.' Lex kept his eyes on the snow. 'He's trapped in a useless body, but his mind is as sharp as ever. He was such a powerful man, always in control, and now all he can do is lie there. He can't bear the humiliation of it.'

'He must be glad to see you,' Romy said, not entirely sure where this was going.

'Must he? I think he hates the fact that I can walk into the room on my own. He hates the fact that I can walk out. He hates the fact that I run Gibson & Grieve now. I don't know which of us dreads my visits more,' said Lex bleakly.

'But still you go.'

'My mother says he wants to know what's going on at Gibson & Grieve now he's not there any more. She says it's all that keeps him going. It's certainly all we've got to talk about.'

Lex's mouth turned down at the corners. 'You know what's the worst thing about those visits? It's that every time I hope that he'll think the company is doing all right. You'd think I'd know by now that he's never going to say, "Well done",' he added, unable to keep the bitterness from his voice. 'I could tell him we'd quadrupled our profits, and he'd still say it wasn't good enough!'

'Is that why you feel you have to prove something with this deal?'

'Damn right it is.' Lex turned to face her at last. 'When I told him about taking over Grant's, my father said that Grant wouldn't sell. He said he'd approached him before, and they couldn't make it work, so I wouldn't be able to pull it off either. Talking is a big effort for him nowadays, and his speech is slurred, but he made sure I got that message. It won't work, he said.'

Lex's jaw was clenched. 'I'm going to go back and tell him that Grant *will* sell, that it *will* work. I want him to know that he was wrong, and that Gibson & Grieve is bigger and better without him.'

CHAPTER FIVE

ROMY bit her lip. 'Lex, he's very ill. Making him admit that he was wrong won't make you feel any better.'

'It's not about *feeling*,' said Lex angrily. 'It's about doing what's best for the company. And signing this deal with Grant is the best thing for Gibson & Grieve.'

'So…?' Romy's dark eyes were wary.

'So let's not disillusion him.' Lex made up his mind so abruptly that he couldn't believe that he had been hesitating. Surely it had been obvious?

He pulled the curtain back across the window and came to join Romy and Freya at the table.

'You've told me it makes a difference to Willie if we're together or not, and if that's the case I'm not prepared to risk him changing his mind. If we start bleating on about separate rooms and not really being a couple, it'll just be embarrassing for everybody.'

'That's what I thought,' said Romy.

'What does it matter if Willie thinks we're a couple?' Lex, talking himself into the whole idea, made the mistake of looking at Freya, who smiled at him through a mouthful of banana. He averted his eyes quickly. 'It'll only be for a night. How hard can that be?'

'As long as he doesn't ask too many personal questions.' Romy thought she should inject a note of caution, but Lex was committed now.

'We're going to talk business tonight,' he said. 'If Willie is really concerned about getting the best deal for Grant's Supersavers, he'll have more important questions to ask.'

How hard could it be? Lex had asked, and at the time it had seemed all quite straightforward. The deal was within his grasp. He and Romy would have dinner with Willie Grant. They would discuss the arrangements and come to a gentleman's agreement, and the deal would be done. The next day, he and Romy would return to London. Romy would go back to Acquisitions, Freya would go to the crèche that he had had no idea existed, and he could tell his father that he had succeeded where he never could.

Simple.

Only he hadn't counted on the intimacy of sharing a room with Romy. Lex flipped open his computer to check the markets, while Romy had a bath with Freya, but it was impossible to concentrate with the squeals and splashes and laughter coming out of the bathroom. Romy's vividly coloured outfit hung on the wardrobe door, and her perfume lingered distractingly in the air, coiling around his mind and making the Dow Jones Index dance in front of his eyes.

Worse was to come. The door opened, and Romy came out, carrying Freya. 'I found this behind the door,' she said, gesturing down at the towelling robe. 'I hope no one will mind if I use it.'

'I'm sure they won't.' Lex's voice came out as a humiliating rasp, and he cleared his throat and scowled at the screen. Much good it did him. There might as well have been a photo of Romy there instead, her skin glowing, her hair damp to her shoulders, her face alight with joy in her daughter....

Romy threw a towel on the floor and laid Freya on it. 'There's not much room in the bathroom,' she explained over her shoulder, 'so I thought it would be easier to dry her out here. It's all yours.'

Of course, what he should have done was get up straight away and have a shower, but instead Lex sat on at the computer, pretending to himself that he was working, forcing his eyes back to the screen whenever they drifted over to where Romy was kissing Freya's toes and blowing raspberries on her tummy while Freya shrieked with delighted laughter and clutched at her mother's hair.

Lex knew exactly how silky it would feel in Freya's fingers. He knew how it felt tickling his skin, and memory hit him like a blow to his diaphragm: the hitch in his chest at Romy's pliant warmth in his arms, her soft laughter in his ear, her kisses drifting down his throat, down, down, down... All at once he lost track of his breathing. It got all muddled up with the twist of his guts and the vice around his chest and he had to force his lungs back to order.

Inflate, deflate. In, out. In, out. Slow, steady.

No problem. There was no need to panic. There was plenty of oxygen.

Lex switched off the computer. There was little point in sitting there staring at nothing.

'I'll go and have a shower then.' Even to his own ears his voice sounded unfamiliar.

Romy looked up briefly. 'Good idea. I'm going to take Freya down to the kitchen and warm some milk for her.'

She wasn't bothered by the intimacy of the situation at all,

Lex realised, chagrined. She was too absorbed in her baby to think about him.

To remember Paris.

To wonder about that four poster bed or where he would sleep.

Frankly, it was a relief when Romy and Freya had gone. Lex showered and shaved and reminded himself what they were doing there. This was business. The deal was what mattered, and it was almost within his grasp. This was not the time to get distracted by silky hair or bare feet or joyous laughter.

By the time Romy came back with a sleepy Freya, Lex had himself back under control. He was buttoning a dark blue shirt when she knocked lightly and opened the door.

'Don't worry, I'm decent,' he said with a sardonic look. 'Although I'm not sure there'd be much point in being shy even if I wasn't. It's not as if we haven't seen each other's bodies before.'

That was better, Lex told himself. He sounded indifferent, as if he hadn't even *noticed* that she had been naked beneath that towelling robe earlier. As if it would never occur to him to think about touching her, tasting her.

Romy had set the cot up in a corner. She laid Freya down and switched off the lamps nearby, glad of the excuse to dim the light and hide the colour staining her cheeks.

'That was a long time ago,' she reminded him uncomfortably. 'We're different people now.'

She just wished she *felt* different. It had been bad enough when Lex was sitting there at his computer, but now he was tucking his shirt into his trousers, doing up his cuffs, slinging a tie around his neck, as if they were a real couple getting ready to go out for the evening.

But if they were a real couple, she could go over to Lex

and slide her arms around his waist. She could kiss his newly shaved jaw and run her fingers through his damp hair.

She could tug the shirt out of his trousers once more and slide her hands over his bare chest.

Make him smile, feel his arms close around her.

Whisper that there was time before they had to leave. Time to hold each other. Time to touch. Time to make love.

Romy swallowed hard. There was no time now. That time was past.

'I'd better change.'

Wincing at the huskiness in her voice, she took her outfit into the bathroom. She saw immediately that Lex had tidied up. The bath mat had been hung up, the towels neatly folded and drying on the rail. The top was back on the shampoo and the toothbrushes were standing to attention in a glass.

Romy sighed. She would have tidied the bathroom herself if he had left it. Growing up, she had often heard Phin mock Lex for his nit-picking ways, and the chief executive's insistence on precision and neatness was something of a joke in the office, but it didn't seem quite so funny now. It just underlined the fact that a man with Lex's obsessive need for order would never be able to cope with the chaos of living with children.

And why would that be a problem? Romy asked her reflection.

It wouldn't, because Lex would never have to live with a child. He would never want to. Tonight was the closest he would get to family life, and Romy was quite sure it would be enough for him.

And that wasn't a problem for her, either.

Was it?

* * *

Freya was asleep. Romy left one of the bedside lamps on and closed the door softly behind her. 'Let's go,' she said.

They made their way back to the library together. 'This place is enormous,' said Lex as they turned the corner to find themselves in yet another picture-lined corridor. 'Why does Willie stay here on his own?'

'Duncardie reminds him of his wife. She loved it here, apparently, so don't go telling him he'd be better off back in the city.'

'I'm not completely insensitive,' Lex said huffily.

He was hummingly aware of Romy next to him. She had emerged from the bathroom wearing silk trousers and a camisole, with some kind of loose silk jacket. Lex wasn't very good on fashion, but the colours and the print made him think of heat and spices and coconut palms swaying in the breeze.

He could hear the faint swish of the slippery fabric as she walked, could picture it slithering over her skin, and he swallowed painfully. Her hair was piled up in a way that managed to look elegant and messy at the same time, and, with her bracelets and dangly earrings, she came across as vivid, interesting, and all too touchable. Next to her, Lex knew, he seemed stiff and conventional in his suit.

Willie was waiting for them in the library. He was standing in front of the fire, Magnus at his feet, and in an expansive mood. 'We'll talk details over dinner,' he said when he had welcomed them in and complimented Romy on her outfit, 'but I'm happy to agree in principle to a merger of Grant's Supersavers with Gibson & Grieve.'

'Oh, that's wonderful news!' Getting into her role, Romy smiled and hugged Lex, whose arm went round her quite instinctively.

She was warm and soft and slender, and his hand rested on

the curve of her hip. He breathed in the scent of her hair and felt silk slip a little under his palm, a sharp, erotic shock that made his heart clench.

Head reeling, incapable of saying anything, Lex gave himself up to the pleasure of holding her for the first time in twelve years, until Romy widened her eyes meaningfully at him. 'Isn't it, darling?' she prompted him as she disengaged herself.

'Wonderful,' he managed.

It was barely more than a croak, but Willie wouldn't notice. He was too busy being kissed by Romy. It was Willie's turn to have that smooth cheek against his own, to feel that vibrant warmth pressed against him. To be enveloped in her glow.

Lex wanted to kill him.

Now Willie was returning Romy's hug. Patting her shoulder. Smiling at her. Good God, why didn't he stick a tongue down her throat and be done with it? Lex thought savagely, just as Willie looked over Romy's shoulder. The expression on Lex's face made the shaggy white brows lift in surprise, and then amused understanding.

'I think we should celebrate, don't you?' he said as he let Romy go.

The deal of his career, and Lex had never felt less like celebrating. What was the matter with him? he thought, appalled at his own behaviour. This was the moment he had been waiting for, the deal within his grasp at last, and all he could do was think about how smooth and warm Romy's skin would be beneath that silk top.

He rearranged his face into a stiff smile. 'Excellent.'

'I've got something really special to mark the occasion.' Willie beamed at them both.

'Champagne?'

'Oh, much more special than that,' he promised, turning

away to a tray behind him. Reverently, he poured what looked like rich liquid gold into plain crystal tumblers.

Romy buried her nose in the glass when he handed one to her. 'Whisky,' she said, surprised, and Willie tutted as he passed a glass to Lex.

'This is no ordinary whisky. This is a fifty year old single malt. A thousand pounds a bottle,' he added just as Romy took her first sip.

'*What?*'

She choked, coughing and spluttering while Lex patted her on the back. Well, what else could he do? Lex asked himself. He was supposed to be a concerned lover. Of course he would pat her on the back. It wasn't just an excuse to touch her.

He was just playing his part. He wasn't thinking about how little fabric there was between his hand and her skin or how easy it would be to let the jacket slither off her shoulders. He wasn't thinking about how inviting the nape of her neck looked. How easy it would be to press his lips to it. To pull the clips from her hair and let it tumble down.

Without his being aware of it, his patting had turned into a slow rub. Romy, her eyes still watering, moved unobtrusively out of his reach.

'Thanks,' she managed, and Lex's hand fell to his side where it hung, feeling hot and heavy and uncomfortable. Not sure what to do with it now, Lex stroked Magnus's head instead.

'Better?' Willie smiled and lifted his glass when she nodded. 'In that case…*Slainthe!*'

'*Slainthe!*' echoed Lex and took a sip.

'Well?' Willie eyed him expectantly. 'What do you think?'

'Unforgettable.'

It was true. Lex was gripped by a strange sense of unreality, shot through with an intense immediacy, as if he had shifted into a parallel universe where all his senses were on high alert. He was would never forget anything about this evening: the castle in the snow, the great dog beside him, the taste of this extraordinary whisky on his tongue.

The deal of his life.

And Romy, in the firelight.

Pleased with his response, Willie waved them to the leather sofa where they had sat before. 'Sit down and tell me all about yourselves,' he invited. Or perhaps it was a command.

So much for him not asking personal questions. Romy couldn't resist a glance at Lex, who ran a finger around his collar and didn't quite meet her eye.

'What would you like to know?' he asked Willie stiffly after a moment.

'Call me a nosy old man, but I like to know who I'm doing business with,' said Willie, settling himself comfortably into his chair. 'I'm interested in how somebody with your reputation turns out be so different when you meet him face to face. I was expecting a soulless businessman, and I get a man capable of building a relationship with a beautiful woman, her baby and even my dog!'

His bright blue eyes fixed on Lex's face. 'Why do you keep Romy here a secret? I was so proud of Moira, I used to show her off whenever I could, so that everyone could see what a lucky man I was.'

Romy saw Lex's jaw clench with frustrated irritation and she slid over the sofa and put her hand on his taut thigh before he could snap back that it was none of Willie's business. Willie might have said that the deal would go ahead, but it wasn't signed yet.

'That's not Lex's fault,' she said quickly. 'I'm the one who wants to keep things a secret for now. It still feels very…new.'

That was true enough, Romy thought. By her reckoning they had been a 'couple' for all of two hours.

'Lex is technically my boss,' she went on. 'I didn't want my colleagues to think that I'd got the job because of him. I want to prove myself first.'

Willie chuckled. 'So all this time we've been talking about the deal, you've known more about Lex than anyone?'

Also probably true. Faint colour tinged Romy's cheeks.

'We don't normally work together,' she said. 'It's just that Tim couldn't come, and I couldn't leave Freya…so we all came together.'

'And I'm glad you did,' said Willie. 'I'm surprised to hear that this is a new thing. I got the impression that you've known each other a long time somehow.'

'We have.' To Romy's relief, Lex managed to unlock his jaw, and she took her hand from his thigh before it started feeling too comfortable there. 'Our mothers have been friends since they were at school,' he said. 'I've known Romy since she was born.'

That went down very well with Willie. 'Ah…childhood sweethearts? Just like Moira and I.'

'I wouldn't say that exactly, would you, Lex?' Romy decided it was better to stick to the truth as far as possible, or they would get hopelessly muddled. 'Lex was older,' she confided to Willie. 'The truth is, he was hardly aware I existed before I was eighteen!'

'Of course I knew you existed,' said Lex with a touch of irritation, and he yanked at his tie as if it felt too tight. He looked cross and more than a little ruffled, Romy thought. Not at all like a man who was madly in love with her.

Funny, that.

She plastered on an adoring smile and leaned into his shoulder. Winsome wasn't a look she did well, but it looked as if she was going to have to do the work for both of them.

'It's not as if it was love at first sight, though,' she pointed out.

'It felt like it.'

Much to Romy's surprise, Lex appeared to have come to the same conclusion, or at least to have realised that he wasn't giving a very good impression of a man who had found the love of his life.

'I hadn't seen Romy for three or four years.' He turned to tell Willie the story. 'You know what it's like when you first leave home. I'd lost track of family occasions once I was at university. I remembered a gangly, unruly girl of fourteen or so, but then I called in to see my parents one weekend and Romy was there, and suddenly she was all grown up.'

And then before Romy realised quite what he was doing, he had taken her hand. His fingers closed around hers, warm and strong, and her heart began to bump against her ribs. She remembered that day so well.

'I just stood and stared,' Lex said, looking into Romy's eyes, and it was almost as if he had forgotten Willie entirely. 'Until then, I thought falling in love was just an expression,' he said, his voice very deep. 'But falling was just how it felt.'

He could still remember that moment, the lurch of his heart, the tumbling sensation as if he had slipped over the side of a cliff, the terror and exhilaration of falling, falling, out of control.

The pain of crashing into reality.

Lex took a gulp of his whisky. It burned down his throat, steadied him. Maybe thousand-pound bottles of whisky would have helped twelve years ago. Belatedly realising that he was still holding Romy's hand, he let it go.

'Eighteen?' Willie was evidently doing some calculations in his head. 'You've been together a long time, then.'

Romy glanced at Lex, and then away. 'No. That time, the first time, we just had a week. We ran off to Paris together. It was very romantic. We had the most…' She made a helpless gesture, unable to describe to Willie what that week had been like. 'It was like stumbling into a different world, but we both knew then it couldn't last.'

'I thought it could,' Lex contradicted her. 'I asked her to marry me,' he told Willie, 'and she said no.'

'I was only eighteen!' Romy cried. 'I was much too young to think about getting married. You agreed that it would have been crazy—'

She stopped, realising that Lex had agreed that morning. He hadn't thought it was a crazy idea in Paris. But this wasn't something they should be discussing in front of Willie. They were supposed to be in love, not two people still wrangling about the past.

She pinned on a smile. 'Anyway, the upshot was that we went our separate ways,' she told Willie. 'I stayed in France for that year, and then I came home to go to university, but when I graduated I still had itchy feet. I spent the next few years working my way around the world. I ended up in Indonesia.'

Sensing Lex growing restless, Romy decided to speed the story up a bit. 'That's where I got pregnant. I came home to have the baby, but I didn't see Lex again until his brother's wedding last summer.'

No need to tell Willie that Lex hadn't come near her all day.

'Meanwhile, I'd been at Gibson & Grieve, doing what I'd always done,' said Lex. 'Then last summer, Phin got married, and Romy was there…'

'And you fell in love with her all over again?'

Lex drew a breath, then let it out slowly. 'Yes,' he said. When he looked at Romy, her eyes were dark and wary. 'Yes,' he said again. 'I'd never forgotten her—how could I? I think I'd spent all those years just waiting for her to come home. I'd try going out with other women, but none of them made me feel the way Romy did. I was Phin's best man. I remember standing by his side, and turning to watch the bride, and seeing Romy sitting a few pews behind.'

Willie seemed to be enjoying the story. 'And that was that?'

'That was that,' agreed Lex.

There was a pause. Romy couldn't believe how convincing he sounded. Beside him on the sofa, she studied him under her lashes. He was so lean and solid and restrained in his suit. What must it be costing him to come out with all this rubbish about being in love with her still? Only that morning, on the plane, he had reminded her that any feelings he'd once had were long dead.

We've both moved on, he had said.

He was a much better actor than she had expected him to be. Romy was sure he must be hating the need to pretend, to talk about *feelings*, but then, he had an incentive. He would do whatever it took to get Willie's agreement.

'Well, you've done a good job of keeping all this a secret,' Willie was saying admiringly. 'I've been trying to find out everything I can about you and there's been no hint of it. I don't mind telling you, it made all the difference to me that you were happy to get involved with a baby as well as Romy,' he said to Lex. 'That told me that you're a man I can trust with Grant's Supersavers, that you're a man who understands what's really important in life.'

'I do,' said Lex. He smiled at Romy, who did her best to

conceal her amazement at how whole-heartedly he was
entering into the pretence, and took her hand once more. 'I
thought I'd never find her again, and now that I have, I'm not
going to let her go again. Freya's part of the package.'

Romy's eyes widened as he lifted her hand and kissed her
knuckles. 'I've waited a long time for Romy to agree to marry
me, and now she has. Between that and a deal to secure
Grant's Supersavers, I've got everything I ever wanted.'

Willie was delighted. 'That deserves another toast!'

He hauled himself out of his chair to find the malt, thus
missing the look Romy was giving Lex, who looked blandly
back at her. She tried to tug her hand away, but he kept a firm
hold of it as Willie splashed more of the precious whisky into
their glasses.

'Congratulations,' said Willie, lifting his glass towards
them both. 'Here's to love lost and found!'

'Here's to love,' Lex and Romy agreed, smiling hard, but
not meeting each other's eyes.

'What on earth did you say that for?' Romy demanded as the
bedroom door closed behind them at the end of that mem-
orable evening.

'Say what?' said Lex, tugging his tie loose.

'You know what! About getting married!'

Romy would have liked to have shouted, but Freya was
asleep in the corner, so she was restricted to a furious whisper,
which didn't improve her temper.

Lex just shrugged and pulled the tie from his neck, undoing
the top button of his shirt with a sigh of relief. 'If we're going
to pretend, we might as well do it properly. And you've got
to admit, it did the trick. Willie was delighted.'

'He was delighted before. You didn't need to complicate

it with marriage.' Romy sat on the edge of the bed and kicked off her shoes bad-temperedly.

'People of that generation feel more comfortable with marriage. How else could I convince him that I was going to do right by you and Freya?'

'Everyone knows that I'm never going to get married,' she said, unable to explain just how uneasy the very idea made her.

'People change.'

'Not me!'

'No,' Lex agreed with a sardonic look, 'I know not you. Fortunately, Willie doesn't have any idea how stubborn you are.'

'It's not about stubbornness,' said Romy.

'Isn't it?'

'No. It's about being realistic, not stubborn.'

Lex shook his head. 'No, it's not. It's about being afraid. You're afraid of marriage because you think it might end up badly like your parents' marriage did, and you'll be hurt again. Fair enough. I understand that. But I don't quite see what the problem is here. We're not getting married. It's just a pretence.'

'I know.' Romy sighed, and twisted her bracelets fretfully. 'I know you're right. I just wish Willie wasn't quite so thrilled. I don't like lying to him.'

'It's a bit late to worry about that now,' said Lex, exasperated. 'This was all your idea in the first place!' His voice had risen, until Romy pointed at Freya's cot and laid a finger over her lips. 'And you were the one who started on the "darlings",' he added more quietly.

'I thought it would make us look more convincing,' she said. 'Little did I know that, once you got going, you would turn in an Oscar-winning performance! You nearly had *me* convinced!'

'Look, what's the problem?' Lex had started on his buttons now. 'We've done it. Willie's agreed to the sale.'

As promised, they had discussed it over an excellent dinner, and come to what Willie called a 'gentleman's agreement'. The lawyers would draw up a detailed contract. He and Willie would sign it and the deal would be done.

'We've done exactly what we set out to do,' he reminded Romy. 'We can go home tomorrow, and no one else will ever know that you once pretended for five seconds that you would consider the possibility of marriage.'

Romy wished he would stop unbuttoning his shirt. It was distracting her. Averting her eyes, she began to pull off her bangles one by one.

'What if Willie finds out that we're not really engaged?'

'You said yourself he never leaves Duncardie now,' Lex pointed out. 'And we've already told him why we're keeping it a secret for now.'

'I suppose so.'

Romy wasn't sure why the whole question had made her so twitchy. It was something to do with sitting next to Lex all evening. With the feel of his fingers warm around hers, his palm strong and steady on her back, his thigh beneath her hand.

She had been desperately aware of him. Ever since she had walked into the bathroom and seen him looking harassed at the prospect of changing Freya's nappy there had been a persistent thumping low in her belly. A jittery, fluttery, frantic feeling just beneath her skin that was part nervousness, part excitement.

How was it possible to be furious with someone and still want to wrap yourself round him? To kiss your way along his jaw and press against the lovely lean hardness of his body?

At least the argument about the stupid marriage thing had got them over the awkwardness of being alone. Having divested herself of bracelets and earrings, Romy stomped into the bathroom to get undressed. Lex might be happy to start stripping off in front of her, but she didn't have his cool.

She didn't possess a nightdress. She hadn't been expecting to share a room, so all she had with her was an old sarong. Romy eyed it dubiously as she wrapped it tightly under her arms. It was hardly the most seductive of garments, but she couldn't help wishing it were a little more substantial.

If she had had time to think about her packing, she might have considered that a castle in the Highlands in the middle of winter might not be the most appropriate place for a sarong, and then she would have been prepared with a sensible winceyette nightie that would have kept her warm and, more importantly under the current circumstances, covered. Not that Lex had shown any sign of preparing to pounce, but, still, it was unnerving to contemplate the prospect of sharing a bed with nothing but a skimpy strip of material for modesty.

Well, it would just have to do.

When Romy went back into the bedroom, holding her clothes protectively in front of her, Lex was peering in the wardrobe. He had stripped off his shirt, but still wore his trousers, to her relief. The sight of his broad, bare, smooth back was enough to dry her mouth and set her heart thudding against her ribs as it was. God only knew what state she'd be in if he'd taken off any more clothes!

'What are you doing?'

'Looking for an extra blanket,' he said without turning round. 'I'll sleep on the floor.'

'Lex, it's snowing outside! You'll freeze to death, even on the carpet.' Romy dumped her clothes on top of her overnight case and checked that Freya was still sound asleep. Having been stomach-twistingly anxious about the prospect of sleeping with him, she was now perversely determined to prove to Lex that it didn't bother her at all.

'It's an absolutely huge bed—and it's not as if we've never shared a bed before, is it?'

'No,' he said, turning to face her, 'but as you said before, that was twelve years ago and we're different people now.'

'We're twelve years older and twelve years more grown up,' said Romy firmly, hoping to convince herself as much as Lex. 'We've got over all that.' She saw Lex's brows rise and flushed. 'You know what I mean. And even if we hadn't, how could I possibly sleep knowing that you were on the floor? There's room for ten in there,' she said, gesturing at the bed.

An exaggeration, perhaps, but it was certainly a very large bed. They would easily be able to avoid rolling into each other.

She hoped.

CHAPTER SIX

PULLING back the heavy cover, Romy climbed up into the bed and made a big show of making herself comfortable. 'It's up to you, of course,' she said, 'but if you're worried about me making a fuss about sharing a bed, then don't. I really don't see why it needs to be a big deal.'

'Well, if you're sure…'

Lex splashed water over his face and brushed his teeth. He knew Romy was right. It was only sensible. The floor would be uncomfortable, not to mention cold, and there was no convenient sofa.

She clearly wasn't bothered at the prospect, so he could hardly say that it bothered *him*. Romy might think that there was room for ten in the bed, but Lex was pretty sure that it wouldn't feel like that when he was lying beside her. It wouldn't take much to roll over and find himself next to her, and then what would happen? How would he be able to stop himself reaching for her?

No big deal, she thought.

Hah.

But there was nothing for it.

He didn't even have any pyjamas with him. Normally he slept in the buff and he hadn't expected tonight to be any different. He would definitely have to keep boxers on, Lex realised. It was going to be difficult enough without adding naked bodies into the equation, and he didn't care what Romy said about being twelve years older. Some things didn't change that much.

Remembering how cool Romy had been about the whole business, Lex took his time folding his trousers and hanging them up before he crossed over to bed. To his relief Romy had snuggled down under the cover so that only her nose and eyes were showing. That was good. It meant he couldn't see her bare shoulders, or her bare arms, or her bare legs.

But he knew they were there. Oh, yes.

The dark eyes watched with a certain wariness as he pulled back the cover on his side of the bed, switched off the light and lay down.

They weren't touching at all, but Lex was aware of her with every fibre of his being. His right side was tingling with her nearness. It would take so little to touch her.

Big enough for ten people? Lex didn't think so.

He stared up at the canopy through the dark. He should be jubilant. The deal was done. Willie Grant had agreed to sell and Gibson & Grieve would have the foothold in Scotland they had wanted for so long. He could go back to his father and show him what he had been able to do. He had everything he'd wanted.

But all he could think about was Romy, lying beside him in the darkness. He'd been aware of her all evening, and it had been a struggle to concentrate on the conversation when his mind kept swooping between memories and noticing the pure line of her throat, how her hair gleamed in the candlelight. Her face had been bright as she leaned across the table to talk to Willie, and her earrings had swung whenever she threw back her head and laughed.

Lex's throat had been so tight it was an effort to talk.

Twelve years, he had been trying to forget.

Her hair, dark and silky. The way it had swung forward as she leant over him, how soft it had felt twined around his fingers. Breathing in the scent of it as he lay with his face pressed into it, how it had made him think of long summer evenings.

Her eyes, those luminous eyes, so dark and rich and warm that brown was laughably inadequate to describe their colour. Looking into them was like falling into a different world, where nothing mattered but the feel of her, the taste of her, the need that squeezed his heart and left him dizzy and breathless.

Her mouth, too wide, too sweet. The way she turned her head and smiled sometimes.

The quicksilver feel of her, warm and vibrant and elusive. The harder he'd held onto her, the faster she'd slipped away.

The swell of his heart, the feel of it beating, when she lay quietly in his arms.

The aching emptiness when she had gone.

And now she was lying only inches away. It was a wide bed, as she had said, but it wouldn't take much to slide across the gap between them. If he rolled over, if she did, they could meet.

But Romy wasn't moving. Lex was fairly sure that she wasn't sleeping either. She was too still, her breathing too shallow.

She wasn't going to roll over, and neither was he. It was the last thing he should do, Lex knew. It had taken him a long time to gather up the wild emotions that had been flailing around inside him, but at last he had managed to press them together into a tight lump that had been settled, cold and hard, in the pit of his belly ever since. He couldn't risk dislodging it and letting all that feeling loose again.

Besides, Romy had made it very clear that she wasn't interested in resuming a relationship—look at the fuss she had made about even pretending to be engaged!—and, even if she had been, he didn't have room in his life for a lover, let alone a baby. It was too late for that now.

Twelve years too late.

There was a muffled quality to the atmosphere when Romy woke the next morning, a strangeness about the light that was filtering through the heavy curtains on her right.

At first, puzzled by the musty fabric above her, she wondered if she was still dreaming, but a moment later memories from the day before came skidding and sliding in a rush through her mind.

Freya, sucking Lex's shoelace.

The long drive through the snow.

Willie Grant's monstrous dog.

Lex's hand on her spine.

Lex. The sag of the bed as he climbed in beside her. Knowing that he was there, near enough for her to simply reach over and…

Romy jerked upright, realising belatedly that she was alone in the four-poster. From the cot in the corner came a cooing. Freya, it seemed, was also awake, but where was Lex?

The thought had barely crossed her mind before the door was shouldered open and Lex came in carrying two mugs. He was looking positively relaxed in his suit trousers with a shirt open at the collar and the sleeves rolled above his wrists, but he still managed to exude a forcefulness that seemed to suck some of the oxygen out of the room, and Romy found herself sucking in a breath.

'Good morning,' she said, feeling ridiculously shy.

'Good morning.' Lex offered her one of the mugs. 'There

doesn't seem to be anyone around, so I helped myself to some tea. I thought you might like some.'

'Thank you.' Romy pulled herself further up the pillows and took a sip of the tea. It was black and sweet, just as she liked it. She lifted her eyes to Lex. 'You remember how I take my tea!'

His gaze slid away from hers. 'I've got a good memory.'

Romy wished her own memory weren't quite so good. It might have made it easier to lie next to him all night.

But now it was morning, and Freya was singing happily to herself. Romy threw off the cover, only just remembering to secure her sarong in time, and went over to the cot.

'Hello, my gorgeous girl. How are you this morning?'

It was impossible to feel awkward or cross or anything but joyful when Freya smiled like that. Romy picked her up and cuddled her, loving her warm, sweet smell and compact body, and Freya bumped her head into her mother's neck and grabbed fistfuls of her hair as she babbled with pleasure.

Lex looked away from their glowing faces. 'How did you sleep?' he asked after a moment.

'Fine,' said Romy, and then wondered why she was lying. 'Actually, if I hadn't just woken up, I could have sworn I didn't sleep a wink,' she confessed.

She had been too conscious of Lex, of the lean, muscled length of his body on the other side of the bed.

After so long, it had been hard to believe that he was actually there, close enough to touch, but utterly untouchable. How many times over those years had she found herself remembering that week? Remembering the feel of his body, how solid and safe he had felt, remembering how sure his hands had been, how warm his mouth, marvelling at the passion he kept bottled up beneath the austere surface.

'I didn't sleep much either,' Lex admitted.

'Looks like we'll both have to catch up tonight,' said Romy lightly.

'I've got a nasty feeling we'll be spending another night here.' He pulled back the curtains. 'It's stopped snowing, but I doubt we'll be going anywhere today.'

She looked at him in dismay. 'We're snowed in?'

'I'm afraid so.'

Carrying Freya, Romy went to join him by the window, and caught her breath at the scene.

Outside, it was a monochrome world. Bare black trees, rimed in white. A black loch. Over everything else, a blanket of white that blurred the features of the landscape, so that it all looked oddly blank and two dimensional. Above that, a sky washed of colour, except for the faintest hint of pink staining the horizon. It was going to be a beautiful day.

But not for travelling. There were no roads visible, not even a track.

'Ah,' said Romy.

'Quite.' Lex's voice was as crisp as the snow piled high on the window sill.

Romy took Freya over to the bed and let her clamber around on the pillows while she drank her tea. 'What shall we do?'

'There's not much we *can* do. It looks as if we're stuck.' He looked at his watch. 'Summer should be in the office soon. I'll ring her in a few minutes. She'll have to reschedule tomorrow's appointments, and she can let Acquisitions know why you're not in.'

'And meanwhile, we'll have to be engaged another day?' said Romy, who thought there were more important issues to be dealt with than Lex's meetings.

'Yes,' said Lex after a beat. 'One more day. Do you think you can manage that?'

She looked back at him over the rim of her mug, her eyes dark and cautious. 'I'll have to, won't I?'

Lex fully intended to spend the day working as normal. He had the technology. Between his iPhone and his laptop, there was plenty he could do. But breakfast turned into an extended affair, with Romy chatting easily to Willie while Freya ate porridge with her fingers, and then, when Freya had a nap, Romy was determined to go outside and enjoy the snow.

'There's masses of old boots and coats in the utility room,' said Willie when Lex pointed out that she had nothing suitable to wear. 'Help yourself.'

Lex thought he might slope off to a quiet room and get on with some work then, but Romy was unimpressed. 'You're supposed to be madly in love with me,' she said when he suggested it. 'What's Willie going to think if you let me wander off into the snow on my own while you huddle over your laptop?'

Which was how Lex came to be wearing a pair of old wellies and a faded oilskin jacket over a jumper he'd borrowed from Willie, who'd raised his brows when Lex had appeared at breakfast in a suit and tie.

Romy had never seen him in anything so shabby before, and she laughed that deep, husky laugh of hers at his expression. She was swathed in a similar jacket that had to be about six sizes too big for her, and the boots were nearly as big. A woolly hat was pulled down over her ears and a scarlet scarf wrapped jauntily around her throat. Her eyes were dark and bright. She looked, Lex thought, rather like a robin.

'I don't know what you think we're going to do out there,' he said grouchily as he pulled on a pair of gloves. 'The snow's far too deep to walk anywhere.'

'It'll be fun,' said Romy, opening the door to a glittering world. 'Just look how beautiful it is!'

Lex had been right about the snow making walking difficult. It came almost up to Romy's knees, but she refused to give up and insisted on trudging down to the lochside.

It was so cold that her teeth ached with every breath, but she was conscious of exhilaration bubbling along her veins. The light was dazzling. Every twig, every leaf bending under the weight of a pristine mound of snow, seemed to jump out at her, and when they turned to look back at Duncardie it rose out of the snow like something out of a fairy tale, with its battlements and turrets and the backdrop of the mountains.

'It looks like a stage set, doesn't it?' said Romy. 'You could almost believe a princess was sleeping in one of those towers. Perhaps we've stumbled into a magical kingdom without realising it!' She sniffed happily at the crystalline air. 'There's something unreal about today.'

'That would certainly explain why we're freezing our butts off out here when we could be warm and dry inside,' said Lex, slapping the arms of his waxed jacket for warmth.

'Come on, Lex, you've got to admit it's beautiful.' Romy turned and headed along the edge of the loch. It was hard going. She had to lift her feet high and stamp down through the snow, and she was soon puffing, but at least the exercise kept her warm.

'It looked beautiful from inside,' Lex grumbled, but he fell into step beside her.

'Look, there's Willie,' Romy said, spotting the portly figure watching them from one of the windows. She waved, and Willie waved back.

'I notice *he's* staying tucked up nice and warm. He's got more sense. Probably there shaking his head at crazy Sassenachs. '

Romy rolled her eyes and pushed him. 'Oh, stop being such a crosspatch! I know you hate being unlashed from the office, but it'll do you good to get outside like this. You're getting some exercise, breathing in all this clean air…'

'Getting frostbite,' Lex put in.

'Can you put a hand on your heart and tell me that no part of you finds this exciting?'

Lex stopped and, surprised, she stopped too. She was smiling. Her skin glowed, and her eyes were brilliant. The light was so crisp that he could see her in heart-stopping detail—the few strands of hair escaping from beneath the hat, her brows, the crooked front tooth—and he felt something shift and crumple inside him.

He hoped it wasn't his heart.

He opened his mouth to answer. Afterwards, Lex often wondered what he would have said, and if it would have been the truth, but before he could decide Romy caught sight of something behind him and terror rinsed the smile from her face. Sucking in a sharp breath, she stumbled towards him, grabbed him by the waist and buried her head in his chest.

Instinctively, Lex closed his arms around her, and looked over his shoulder. Magnus, the Irish wolfhound, was bounding towards them, snapping at the snow with his great jaws. His muzzle was encrusted with white and as he got close he barked with exuberance and shook joyously, spraying snow everywhere.

Romy made a tiny sound deep in her throat and burrowed closer, as if she were trying to get inside his jacket.

'He's playing,' said Lex calmly. 'He won't hurt you.' Then, to the dog, 'Magnus, *sit*!'

Surprised at the sudden command, Magnus skidded to a halt and sat, tongue lolling.

'Let him sniff your hand.'

In response, Romy held tighter, but Lex was stronger and had already taken her hand in its glove and was stretching it towards the dog, who sniffed curiously.

'Now stroke his head.'

'I can't,' muttered Romy, shrinking as far from the dog as she could get without letting go of Lex.

'You can.' Lex moved her hand to the wiry head. Heart pounding, Romy let her glove rest there for a second before she whipped it back.

Lex clicked his tongue. 'That's not a stroke. Do it again.'

'He'll bite me.'

'Romy, look into his eyes.'

Romy was stuck. She didn't dare let go of Lex and walk away past the dog, but if she stayed where she was she would have to touch the dog again.

Resentfully, she turned her head against Lex's chest and made herself look into the dog's eyes. They weren't a rabid red, as she had imagined, but a warm, liquid brown and their expression, she realised once she had got past the dog's monstrous size and those fearsome teeth, was calm and alert and not in the least aggressive.

Very, very cautiously, Romy let go of Lex and laid her hand on the dog's head once more. Her heart jerked as Magnus butted his nose upwards, and she would have snatched her hand away if she hadn't been afraid that Lex would think her a coward or, worse, make her stroke him again.

'See?' said Lex. 'He likes that.'

And Magnus didn't bite her hand off. He just sat there, watching her with intelligent brown eyes as she patted him. Romy let out a shaky breath. She was stroking a dog! She felt quite giddy with it.

'Well done,' said Lex, and added to the dog, 'Good dog. Go on, off you go now.'

With that, Magnus took off, scattering snow as he went.

Romy laughed unsteadily. 'I can't believe it! I stroked that huge dog!' She watched him running in wide, exuberant circles, a faint, puzzled frown between her brows. 'I feel…liberated,' she realised after a moment.

'That's because you confronted your fear,' said Lex. 'It's a hard thing to do.'

'I bet *you've* never had to do it.'

Romy set off again through the snow. She was remembering how she had clutched at him and wincing inwardly. For someone so determined to look after herself, it had only taken the sight of a big dog for her to throw herself into Lex's arms, acting entirely on instinct. And the worst thing was how *safe* she had felt there. It wasn't a comfortable thought.

'I can't imagine you ever being afraid of anything,' she said.

There was a tiny pause. When she glanced at Lex, she found him watching her, but as their eyes met he looked away. 'You'd be surprised,' he said.

'What are *you* afraid of?' she asked, her expression rife with disbelief, but he shook his head.

'I'm too scared to tell you.'

Romy laughed. She was suddenly very happy. She wasn't sure if it was the snow, creaking and squeaking beneath their boots, the sunshine or the purity of the air.

Or the man beside her.

When she glanced at him under her lashes, his austere profile was etched in startling detail against the sky. She could see the texture of his skin, every hair in the dark brows, the touch of grey at his temples that made her feel oddly wistful. He had a big nose that suited his strong face, and something about the line of his jaw made Romy ache with longing and memory.

She could remember how it felt to trail her lips along that jaw. She remembered the smell of him, the taste of him, the roughness of his skin where a faint stubble pricked.

She wanted to do it again. Lex was so big, so solid. She wanted to throw her arms about him and hold onto all that hardness and all that strength, not because she was scared of the dog, but because she could.

Which was pathetic, she knew. And wrong. Because she didn't need anyone else to be strong. She could be strong on her own. She had to be.

Anyway, it wasn't his strength that appealed, Romy told herself as that sudden wash of happiness was sucked away like a wave and something darker and more primitive crashed through her in its place.

Lust, plain and simple. She wanted to run her hands over him and press her mouth to his throat. She wanted to push her fingers through his thick hair and lick his skin. To taste him, touch him, kiss his lashes, his mouth, his *mouth*, and, oh, God, in spite of the cold, Romy could feel heat flooding her, burning in her cheeks and pooling deep inside her.

Desperate to distract herself, she bent and grabbed a handful of snow. Packing it into a ball, she threw it at Lex, who was stamping along beside her, absorbed in his own thoughts. The snowball glanced off his arm, and he turned, startled to see Romy eyeing him with a mixture of guilt and wariness as she stooped to try again.

Something flared in Lex's pale eyes. 'Right, you asked for it!' he said, scooping up his own snowball. His aim was much better than Romy's and, although she turned quickly away, it hit her right on her hat.

Her attempt missed him completely, of course, but she was already backing away, laughing as she tried to collect more ammunition. Lex's next snowball caught her on the shoulder and she fell back For the next few minutes, they hurled snow at each other like a couple of kids, until Romy stumbled in the deep snow. She would have fallen if Lex hadn't grabbed her arm and held her up with one hand. In his other, he held a huge snowball that he lifted, ready to stuff it down her neck.

'No, no, please!' Romy was laughing and shrieking at the same time. She was covered in snow by then, but the thought of it down her neck... Ugh! She couldn't remember the last time she'd had so much fun.

'Do you give in?'

'I give in ! I give in! You win!'

'All right, then.' Lex let the snowball fall, but he didn't let go of her arm. They had both been laughing, but all at once their smiles faded and their eyes locked with an almost audible click as the glittering landscape shrank to a bubble where there were just the two of them, staring at each other.

'Do you think Willie is still watching?' he asked softly.

'I...don't know,' said Romy with difficulty.

'If we were really engaged, I'd probably kiss you now, wouldn't I?'

'You might.' Romy's throat was so tight, it came out as an embarrassing squeak.

'And would you kiss me back? If we were really engaged?'

'Probably,' she managed.

Lex brought his gloved hands up to cup her face, and Romy trembled with a terrible anticipation.

'Then let's show Willie just how in love we are,' he said, and bent his mouth to hers.

His lips were warm, so warm in contrast to the stinging cold of the air, and so sure. They sent Romy plummeting through twelve long years, and she clutched at Lex's jacket, gripped by a dizzying mixture of excitement and fear and utter peace. Her senses whirled as she swung wildly between extremes, between heat and cold, between then and now. Between stillness and rush. Between the sense of coming home and the sense of standing on the edge of a dizzying drop.

When Lex pulled her closer and deepened the kiss, Romy wrapped her arms around him and kissed him back harder, breathless at the rightness of it. It felt so good to taste him again, to hold him again. Every cell in her body was sighing— no, was singing—'At last! At *last*!' The sunlight glinting on the snow was inside her, sparkling and flickering and shimmering along her veins in a glittery rush.

They broke for breath, kissed again before they could realise just what they were doing. Or that was how it felt to Romy, who had abandoned any attempt to think and was desperate to hold onto this moment, pressed against Lex's hard body, kissing him, being kissed, and the dazzling light all around them.

And then, out of nowhere, there was a huge bump, like a ship knocking into them, and they both lurched to one side.

'What the—?'

Magnus, bored, was looking for attention, and was rubbing his great rump against Lex, who drew a long and not entirely steady breath and let Romy go.

'I think maybe I needed that, Magnus,' he said.

Romy swallowed. She felt jarred, as if she had been on a spinning roundabout that had suddenly stopped, and it was all she could do not to throw herself back into Lex's arms.

But that would be a very, very bad idea, she remembered. Because they weren't in Paris now. They were in Scotland,

and it was twelve years later and very cold, and they were just pretending. It had just been a kiss for show, in case Willie was watching.

Hadn't it?

She moistened her lips. 'We'd better go in,' she said, barely registering the dog gambolling beside them. 'Freya might be awake.'

'Yes,' said Lex, 'perhaps we better had.'

What chance had he had of working after that? Lex switched off the light and climbed into bed beside Romy. It had been madness to kiss her out there in the snow, but he hadn't been able to stop himself. She had been so close, so perfect, and it had felt so right. The feel of her, the taste of her had set tremors going in his heart. He could almost hear it cracking.

It had been his own fault. He should have stayed inside and worked, the way he had intended to do. But when they came back to the house, and Romy went off to find Freya, instead of sitting down at his computer and emailing Summer, Lex had wandered around, eventually finding himself in a room that was empty of all but a few chairs and a piano.

And not just any piano. A Bösendorfer, no less. Lex had a grand in his penthouse apartment, but it wasn't as big as this one. To Lex, it seemed to exert a pull that drew him across the room, to run his hand over its gleaming mahogany top and then lift the lid to press a key, then another and another. Without quite knowing how it had happened, Lex found himself sitting on the stool and letting his fingers run over the keys and then he was playing.

He played out the tumult of feeling inside him that had gripped him ever since Romy had ducked her head and stepped into the cabin. He played out the memory of her touch, the way she made him feel, and then, so gradually he hardly noticed that he was doing it, he started to play the strange feeling of liberation that morning, that sense of being dropped into a different world, isolated by the snow, where all the usual rules were suspended.

And after a while, the tune changed again, to echo old Scottish folk songs that he had once learnt, and to play out the glittering morning and the air and the hills and the water, and Romy, laughing in the snow.

Lex played on, absorbed in the music, unaware of anyone else until a movement from doorway made him look up. Willie was there, listening, and the grief in his eyes made Lex's fingers still.

'I'm sorry,' he said. 'I should have asked if I could use the piano.'

Willie waved the apology aside. 'I'm glad you did. I haven't heard it since Moira died, but I can't bring myself to get rid it.'

He asked if Lex would play again that evening, and Lex was glad to. He didn't normally like performing for an audience, but playing was better than sitting next to Romy and feeling his hands itch with the need to touch her. Better than having to pretend to her that he didn't want her, while pretending to Willie that he did.

He found some music in the piano stool, and played the most battered scores, which he guessed would have been Moira Grant's favourites. Romy sat next to Willie and held his hand while the tears rolled down his face.

'Thank you,' he said simply when Lex had finished. 'I'm glad you came. I'm glad my store's going to be run by a man who can play like that.'

The thaw had set in already. By lunchtime, the glittering morning had vanished beneath the cloud cover, and the temperature had risen with remarkable speed. Tomorrow, it was clear, they would be able to leave. Lex lay in the dark and listened to the steady drip, drip, drip of melting snow outside the window.

Get through tonight, he told himself. That's all you have to do.

Beside him, Romy was concentrating on breathing very quietly. The curtains hanging round the bed smelt musty, but the sheets were clean and faintly scented. The mattress was comfortable. It was dark. She had hardly slept the night before and now she was very tired.

There was no reason why she shouldn't be able to sleep.

Except the memory of that kiss that had been thrumming beneath her skin all day. And then Lex's playing had stirred up emotions Romy had rather left buried. She hadn't been able to take her eyes off his hands while he was playing, hadn't been able to stop remembering those long, dextrous fingers smoothing and stroking, exploring her, unlocking her.

Stop thinking about it, she told herself. Get through tonight. That's all you have to do.

CHAPTER SEVEN

AFRAID to move in case she disturbed Lex, Romy stared into the darkness and told herself to be sensible while the silence lengthened, stretched, and at last grew so painful that she couldn't bear it any more.

'Lex?' she asked quietly, just in case he was asleep after all.

There was a tiny pause, and then he let out a breath. 'Yes?'

'You're not asleep?'

'No.'

'Neither am I.'

'I gathered that.' Lex sounded resigned. Or amused. Or exasperated. Or maybe all three.

Romy sighed and rolled onto her side to face him through the darkness. 'I can't sleep. I keep thinking about that kiss this morning.'

'That was a mistake,' he said after a moment.

'Was it?'

She could just make out his profile. He wasn't looking at her. He was looking up at the ceiling. 'I've spent twelve years trying to forget Paris,' he said. 'Trying to forget *you*. One kiss, and I might as well not have bothered.'

He sounded bitter, and Romy bit her lip.

'I think about that time too,' she said quietly. 'I think the reason I can't forget it is because we never ended it properly. You just…left. We never talked about it, never had a chance to say goodbye.'

'What was the point of talking?' asked Lex. 'You didn't want to be with me. You wanted to make a life on your own, and you were right. There was no point in me staying. It was over.'

'It didn't feel over,' said Romy. 'It didn't feel over this morning when we kissed.'

There was a silence, loud with memories. Then Lex turned and lay on his side so that they faced each other at last. 'Do you remember what you said out there in the snow? You said that I wasn't afraid of anything.'

'I remember,' she said softly.

'I'm afraid of how I felt about you. I'm afraid of feeling that way again.' The words came out stiffly, forced through tight lips as if against his will. 'I don't want to fall in love with you again, Romy,' he said.

Romy drew a breath, heart cracking at the suppressed pain in his voice. 'I don't want to fall in love with you either,' she told him. 'I don't want to need you. I don't want to need anybody.' She swallowed. 'I'm not suggesting we try again. It didn't work twelve years ago, and it's not going to work now. We both know that.'

She could feel Lex's eyes on her face through the darkness, sense the tautness of his body. 'What *are* you suggesting?' he asked.

'That we have one more night,' said Romy. 'One last time together and, this time, we'll end it properly. Tomorrow, we'll say goodbye and draw a line under everything we've had together. We can get on with our lives without wondering how it would have been.'

Hardly able to believe how calm she sounded when her

pulse was booming and thumping, she edged towards the middle of the bed. 'We could think of it as closure.'

Lex shifted over the mattress and laid his palm against her cheek in the darkness, feeling her quiver at his touch. 'Closure,' he repeated, as if trying out the word.

He liked the idea. One last night. No more wondering, no more regretting. Just accepting at long last that it was over.

'It's just been such a strange day,' said Romy, lifting her hand to his wrist, unable to stop herself touching him in return. 'I've felt unreal all day, as if I've stepped into a different world.'

'I know what you mean.' They were very close now. Lex let his fingers slide under her hair, curl around the soft nape of her neck, and her hand was drifting up to his shoulder. 'As if the normal rules don't apply today.'

'Exactly,' she said unevenly.

'Tomorrow, we're going back to the real world.' Already he was unwinding her sarong, his hand warm and sure, curving now around her breast, dipping into her waist, over her hip and then slipping possessively to the base of her spine to pull her closer. 'Tomorrow, we go back to normal.'

'I know.'

Romy's senses were reeling. She had a vague sense that they should be talking this through properly, but how could she talk when he was smoothing possessively down her thigh to the back of her knee and up again, gentling up her spine, making her gasp with the warmth of his hand? When he was rolling her onto her back, when she was pulling him over her? When he was pressing his mouth to the curve of her neck so that she sucked in a breath and arched beneath him.

'It's just tonight,' she managed, barely aware of what she was saying, loving his warm, sleek weight on her, loving the feel of his back beneath her hands, the flex of response when she trailed her fingers up his flank. It felt so right to touch him again that her heart squeezed and she could hardly breathe with it.

'Just tonight,' Lex murmured agreement against her throat.

Beneath his hands, beneath the wicked pleasure of his lips, Romy felt all thought evaporate. There was only Lex and the heat and the rush and the wild joy, so she didn't even hear when he said it again. 'Tomorrow, it'll be over.'

The car was packed. Freya, strapped firmly in, was kicking her heels petulantly against the car seat, her face screwed up in sullen protest. When Willie waved through the window, she refused to smile back at him.

The crispness of the day before had vanished under thick grey cloud. There was still snow, but it was slumped and saggy now. Great clumps kept slipping off the branches in a shower of white.

Romy kissed Willie affectionately as she said goodbye, and even managed a brief pat for Magnus.

Lex shook Willie's hand. 'Thank you,' he said. 'Thank you for everything. It's been a pleasure doing business with you.'

'Likewise,' said Willie, wringing his hand in return. 'I'm glad to know my stores will be in good hands.'

'We'll let the lawyers draw up the contract, then, when we're both happy with it, we'll arrange a formal signing.' Lex was all business this morning. 'I presume that you would like that to take place here?'

'Well, I've been thinking about that,' said Willie, 'and I've decided that I should come to London.'

'To London?' Lex repeated, not quite succeeding in keeping the consternation from his voice. 'I wouldn't ask you to do that, Willie. I'm very happy to come back here, honestly.'

'No, I'd like to,' Willie said. He looked from Romy to Lex,

who were carefully not looking at each other. 'Seeing you two together, hearing you play piano... I'm not sure how to explain, but you've made me realise that it's time to start living again,' he told them.

'Ever since Moira died, I've been hiding away here, but she wouldn't have wanted that. She used to like to go to London. We always stayed at Claridges.' He nodded firmly, mind made up. 'I'll stay there. I'll sign the contract. I'll see you both again, and Freya, I hope. It'll be good for me.'

There was a pause. Afraid that Willie would hear the dismay in it, Romy rushed to fill the silence. 'Well...that's great, Willie. You must come to dinner. I don't think Claridges is quite ready for Freya yet.'

Willie beamed. 'That would be very nice.'

Lex was left with little choice. 'We'll look forward to it,' he said.

There was silence in the car as they bumped carefully down the track. Willie was lost to sight and they were turning onto the single track road before Romy spoke.

'Now what?' she asked.

'Now we go back to London.'

'You know what I mean. Willie's coming to London. He's going to expect to see us together.'

'He is,' Lex agreed grimly. 'Especially now you've invited him to dinner.'

'I had to! It would have looked really odd if neither of us said anything, when we've been staying with him and drinking all his whisky.'

'I suppose so.' Lex's mouth was pulled down at the corners, his brows drawn together in an irritable line. 'But now we're going to have to stay a couple until this bloody contract is signed, and who knows how long it will be before

we can do that. Once the lawyers get their hands on it, it could
be months!'

'Months?' Romy was dismayed.

'Weeks, anyway.'

'Whatever happened to "tomorrow it'll be over"?' She sighed.

It was the first time either of them had referred to the night
before. When Romy stirred that morning, Lex had already
showered and shaved. His face was set, his eyes shuttered, and
she could see that it was over, just as they had agreed.

Romy told herself that she was glad that he was sticking
to their agreement. Closure, wasn't that what she had called
it? Easy to say before his mouth was hot and wicked against
her, before the heat and the wildness drove them into a different place where there was nothing but touching and feeling
and the heart-stopping joy of *now*.

If Lex had woken her with a kiss, if he had touched her at
all and suggested that they made love one more time… Romy
wanted to think that she would have been strong enough and
sensible enough to resist, but she wasn't sure.

'It *is* over,' said Lex, without taking his eyes from the road.
'Last night was about us. This is about business. We've started
on a pretence and now we're going to have to keep it going.
It would have been fine if Willie had stayed at Duncardie like
he was supposed to, but too many people in London will be
able to tell him we're nothing to do with each other.'

'We told him we were keeping it a secret,' Romy pointed out.

'No relationship is that secret. Even Willie is going to
wonder why no one at all has any inkling that we've even met,
let alone are engaged. I'm not prepared to take that risk,' said
Lex. 'If Willie even suspects that we've been pretending, it
would be even worse than if we'd told him the truth about my
lack of family man credentials in the first place.'

'Oh, dear,' Romy sighed again. 'I wish now I'd been straight with him right at the start.'

'It's too late for wishing,' Lex said. 'We're stuck with this pretence now, and we'll have to see it through to the bitter end. It's not as if I'm a monster. I may not be prepared to share my life with a kid, but that doesn't mean I send little boys up chimneys. Gibson & Grieve have plenty of family-friendly policies, as you pointed out. It's a good deal for Grant's Supersavers as well as for us.'

Part of Romy marvelled that they were able to talk so dispassionately about the situation. It was bizarre to be having such a practical conversation when last night… But there was no point in thinking about last night, she caught herself up quickly. Much better to be talking about how they were going to handle the pretence than to sit here in silence, her body still thrumming, remembering, and reminding herself of all the reasons why it was sensible that they never made love again.

I don't want to fall in love with you again, Lex had said. Until then, Romy hadn't appreciated just how much she had hurt him. She couldn't do that to him again.

And she couldn't hurt herself. The need to protect herself was too deeply engrained for Romy to be able to contemplate loving Lex the way he deserved to be loved. To risk *needing* him. She would be too exposed when it ended, as end it would.

How could it last when they were so different, when they wanted such different things? Lex couldn't have made it clearer. He wasn't prepared to share his life with a child.

Romy glanced over her shoulder at Freya, who had fallen asleep before they got to the road. The sight of her daughter steadied her. Even if Lex changed his mind, even if she were brave enough to take the risk for herself, she still wouldn't do it. If Freya spent too much time with Lex, she would learn to love him. That was what children did. And then, when he left, when he couldn't bear the mess and the noise any longer, her heart would break. Romy knew what it felt like to be abandoned. She wouldn't let that happen to her daughter.

She turned back to face the front, and glanced at Lex. 'OK, we're stuck with it,' she said briskly. *This is about business*, he had said. Business it would be. 'What do you suggest?'

'I think you—and Freya—should move into my flat.'

'I'm not sure that's a good idea,' said Romy.

'Why not?'

'People at work will realise. Someone's bound to see us.'

'That's the whole point,' he said irritably. 'We want them to realise. Then when Willie turns up, nobody is going to act surprised if we're together. And you and Freya are there when he comes to this dinner you've invited him to.'

Romy stuck out her bottom lip. 'But that's weeks away! Why can't I stay in my flat, and just come and cook dinner that night?'

'Because nobody is going to believe that we're a real couple if you're flogging back to your flat. When are we supposed to have this mad, passionate affair if you're spending two hours every day on the Northern Line?'

'Nobody needs to know where I'm going,' she said stubbornly, and Lex threw her a disbelieving glance.

'Want a bet?'

Romy folded her arms crossly. She could see it made sense, but living with Lex for weeks on end, trying not to think about touching him, trying not to remember… How was she going to bear it?

'Are you sure you've thought this through?' she said. 'You think there's a lot of Freya's stuff in the back, but that's what we needed for a night away. Imagine what we'll need if we're staying for weeks.'

'I'm not expecting to enjoy the experience,' said Lex, 'but if it means the deal with Grant's Supersavers goes through, then I'll put up with it.'

'And what about me?'

'What do you mean?'

'What do I get out of it?'

'You get a fantastic reference, and the experience of working on a successful project,' said Lex. 'That's worth a lot when you're looking for a good job.'

Romy knew that it was true. She badly needed both. She had had a lovely time drifting around the world, but she was ill equipped when it came to supporting her daughter. Phin's offer of a temporary job with Gibson & Grieve had been a godsend, but finding a well-paid permanent job would be more of a challenge.

And even if she hadn't needed something impressive on her CV, there was Tim and the rest of the acquisitions team to think about. They had made her welcome, taught her all they knew. They needed the deal with Grant's Supersavers to go through, too. She couldn't let them down either.

'All right,' she said, turning her bracelets as she tried to think it through. 'Freya and I move in with you. We let people think we're living together. Fine. How long before our mothers get wind of it?'

'Oh, God,' said Lex. He hadn't thought about his mother. Or Romy's mother. The mothers together. 'Oh, God,' he said again.

'We can't tell them the truth.'

He actually blanched. 'God, no!'

'So that means they're going to have to believe that we're in love,' Romy went on remorselessly.

'Oh, no...' He could see exactly where she was going with this.

'And *that* will mean that there'll be hell to pay when it turns out that we're not getting married after all.'

Lex gripped the steering wheel, his knuckles white as he imagined the scene in appalling detail. 'We'll just have to say that it didn't work out,' he said. 'We'll say it was a mutual decision.'

'I could say that I wanted to take Freya to be near her father,' Romy offered. 'I've been thinking that's what I should do anyway.'

There was a tiny pause. 'That would work,' Lex agreed tonelessly.

'But your mother will be furious with me.'

'I'll tell her I don't care,' he said. 'I'll say that I couldn't cope with living with a baby. She'll believe that.'

It was Romy's turn to pause. 'There you are then.'

Lex shot her a swift penetrating look, then fixed his eyes on the road once more. Neither of them said anything about the night before.

'Problem solved,' he said.

'Where would you like to sleep?'

It had been a long day. The drive to Inverness, the flight back to London, and then, deciding to get all the upheaval over with in one fell swoop, the limousine that picked them up from the airport had detoured via Romy's flat so that she could pack up everything she would need for the next few weeks.

Now they stood in Lex's penthouse flat, surrounded by a sea of bags and toys and bumper packs of nappies. Freya's things looked even more incongruous here than they had done at Duncardie. Holding Freya in her arms, Romy looked around her, impressed and chilled in equal measure.

The living area was a huge open space with a whole wall

of glass looking out over the Thames. There was a grand piano in one corner, a sleek leather sofa, a black-granite-topped table with striking chairs. No clutter, no mess, no softness or colour. Hard edges wherever she looked. It was hard to imagine anywhere less suitable for a crawling baby.

'What's the choice?' she asked.

'There are two spare rooms,' said Lex. 'So you can sleep with Freya, sleep on your own.' He hesitated. 'Or sleep with me.'

Romy stilled. 'I thought it was over.'

'It was. It is.' He moved restlessly. 'It should be.'

All the way home he had been wrestling with memories of the night before. Closure? Hah! How could there be closure when Romy was sitting beside him, when the feel of her, the taste of her, was imprinted on his body and on his mind?

'I just thought…if we're going to be living together…' He dragged his fingers through his hair, not really knowing what he was trying to say. At least, he knew what, but not how to say it. 'It was good, wasn't it?'

'Yes.' Romy set Freya on the floor, where she immediately set about unpacking toys from one of the bags, throwing them all over Lex's pristine carpet. 'It was too good,' she said.

Hugging her arms together, she stepped over the bags and wandered over to the huge window. 'It would be so easy to spend the next few weeks together, Lex. It would be good again—it would be wonderful, probably—but how would we stop then?'

'Maybe we wouldn't want to.'

'Look at all this stuff!' Romy swung round and gestured at the sea of bags and baby gear. 'We've only been here five minutes and already your flat looks like a bomb has hit it. How are you going to cope with this level of mess for weeks on end?'

Her eyes rested on her daughter, who had discovered a

much-loved floppy rabbit and was sucking its already battered ear. 'Freya isn't always as happy as this,' she told Lex. 'Sometimes she wakes in the nights, and the screaming will sound like a drill in your head. There'll be dirty nappies and sticky fingers all over your furniture... You'll hate it!'

She tried to smile. 'Remember how you said you would tell your mother that you couldn't cope with living with a baby? I don't think you'll have any difficulty sounding convincing about that.'

'Perhaps you're right.' Lex rubbed a hand over his face in a gesture of weary resignation. 'I know you're right, in fact.'

'We may be different, but we're the same in one way,' said Romy. 'We're both afraid of getting too involved. Me because I'm afraid of being hurt, and you because you're afraid of the mess that comes along with any kind of relationship. You could say that we're made for each other,' she added with a crooked smile.

'Neither of us is prepared to commit to a relationship that we're not sure will last, but, apart from that, what have we got in common?' Romy went on, still hugging her arms together as she paced restlessly around the immaculate room.

'This apartment is so you, Lex. It's cool and it's calm and it's perfectly ordered. I can see why you like it like this, but it's no place for Freya, and if it's no place for her, it's no place for me. So we'll be leaving as soon as Willie has signed that contract. And the more nights we have like last one, the harder it will be to say goodbye.'

She was terribly afraid of falling in love with him. She was afraid of needing him. Surely Lex could see that?

'You're right,' said Lex again. He straightened his shoulders. 'It would be a big mistake. Madness. What was I thinking?'

He looked across the room into Romy's dark eyes and

knew exactly what he had been thinking. He had been thinking about the satiny warmth of her skin. About the heat and the piercing sweetness and the aching sense of peace when he lay with his face buried in her throat.

He hadn't been thinking about reality. He hadn't been thinking about business.

Fool.

'I'm sorry,' he said to Romy. 'Really sorry. Forget I suggested it. Let's make it easy on ourselves, and stick to business from now on.'

Over the years, Romy had slept in bus stations and on beaches. She had spent nights cold and muddy and soaking wet, huddled under rocks on a hillside, or swiping at mosquitoes in the rainforest. Every single one of those long, uncomfortable nights had been easier than the ones she spent in Lex's apartment, trying to sleep in the room next to his and thinking about how close he was.

Thinking about how easy it would be to slip into bed beside him, and whisper that she had changed her mind, that nothing could be harder than never touching him again.

But Romy only had to think about Freya to remember that of course there could be something harder. There could be seeing her daughter hurt and lost, looking for someone who wasn't there, just as she had once looked for her father after he had left.

It was the strangest month of Romy's life. During the day, she went to the office, just as she had done before, and collected Freya from the crèche at half past five. But instead of squeezing onto the tube with all the other commuters to get back to the poky rented flat that was all she had been able to afford, she put Freya in the pushchair and walked back to Lex's luxury apartment.

They decided not to make an announcement about their

supposed relationship, but wait for speculation and gossip to start circulating around the office. Romy assumed this would happen very quickly, but it took a surprisingly long time for her colleagues to suspect that anything might have occurred between her and Lex on the trip to Scotland.

This might have had something to do with the fact that Lex ignored her completely at the office. Romy returned to a heroine's welcome the day after their return. Her fellow members of the acquisitions team were full of admiration.

'How brave of you to spend all that time with Lex Gibson,' was the typical reaction. 'I'd have been terrified!' And then, leaning closer, 'What was he like?'

Romy thought about Lex in the snow, grinning as he held the snowball over her. She thought about him struggling to change Freya's nappy, his hair on end and his tie askew. She thought about the way his hand had skimmed lovingly over her hip, his slow smile as he drew her to him again, and her throat closed.

'He was fine.'

'I hear he's coming to the meeting this morning. He must be pleased with us. He *never* leaves his office!'

There was much shuffling and straightening of ties when Lex appeared at the departmental meeting. He had a formidable presence, Romy thought, trying to see him through her colleagues' eyes. He wasn't particularly tall or particularly handsome, but he had an air of cool authority that meant he dominated a room just by walking into it.

To the others, their chief executive must look austere and remote. His manner was brusque, and with that severe expression, the inflexible mouth, and those unnervingly pale eyes, it was easy to see how he had gained a reputation as an unfeeling tyrant. Lex might be respected, even admired, by his staff, but he wasn't liked. He lacked his brother Phin's easy charm.

But when Romy's eyes rested on his stern mouth, her heart crumbled. When she watched his hands, a flood of warmth dissolved her bones. She shifted uneasily in her chair, convinced that everyone must be able to see her glowing, *humming* with awareness of him, but no one was looking at her. Their attention was focused on Lex, who outlined the discussions at Duncardie and congratulated Tim and the team on their hard work setting up the deal.

'Perhaps we should make a special mention of Romy?' said Tim, who had thanked Romy effusively earlier. 'I'm certainly very grateful to her for stepping in at the last moment.'

Then, of course, they *did* all look at her. There were some smiles and even winks from those in no danger of being seen by Lex.

'Indeed.' Lex's eyes rested indifferently on Romy's burning face. 'She was very helpful.'

Helpful! Romy's lips tightened with annoyance. Couldn't he have found something a little less chilly to say? What was wrong with, I couldn't have done it without her, for instance? Nobody was ever going to guess they were having an affair if he carried on like that!

It was clear that the others thought he could have been more effusive, too. There was a slightly awkward pause.

'Well…well done, everybody!' Tim brought the meeting to a close. 'I think a team outing is called for.' He raised a hand to quell the stir of anticipation before it got out of hand. 'Keep next Friday free and we'll celebrate in style.'

Lex got to his feet. 'Good work,' he said to everyone and that cool gaze didn't even pause on Romy as it swept impersonally round the room. 'Enjoy yourselves next Friday. You've deserved it.'

Correctly interpreting this to mean that, (a) he wasn't

planning on spoiling their fun by turning up, and, (b) the celebratory bash would be covered by the company, everyone relaxed and a buzz of conversation and laughter broke out the moment Lex had left the room.

Romy forced herself to join in, but it was an effort. Reluctant as she was to admit it, she was miffed. Lex shouldn't have been able to look at her with that expression of utter indifference, not when she had been sitting there positively throbbing with awareness!

She was still feeling cross that evening when Lex came home. She had just finished bathing Freya and the sound of the door opening made her heart jerk, which did nothing to improve her temper.

Well, she wasn't going to rush out and welcome him home, Romy decided. If he thought she was going to have his pipe and slippers ready for him, he had another think coming! Trying to ignore the knotting of her entrails, she finished tidying the bathroom before she picked up Freya and made her way out to the open plan living area.

Lex was in the kitchen at the black granite worktop that divided the cooking from the living area. Romy had cooked Freya macaroni cheese for her supper earlier, and the counter behind him was still cluttered with open packets of butter and flour, with milk and cheese and apple cores. Wisely, Lex had turned his back on the mess and was reading his post, but he looked up when Romy appeared.

'Oh. Hello,' she said, deliberately cool.

Unfortunately, Freya was sending out a very different message by beaming at him in a way that disconcerted Lex quite as much as it annoyed Romy.

Freya had only just learnt to flirt, and had spent most of the flight home the day before practising on him. There had been a lot of smiling and peeping glances under her lashes. Quite why her daughter had picked Lex as a favourite, Romy wasn't sure. He certainly did nothing to encourage her. It was clear, in fact, that all the attention made him uneasy, but Freya was undeterred by his lack of response.

Now here she was, looking delighted to see that he was home, while he just stood there looking dour! Quickly, Romy put her on the floor with all her toys, where she was soon diverted.

CHAPTER EIGHT

'HELLO,' said Lex, dropping the credit-card statement he'd been studying onto the worktop. There was no mistaking the coolness in Romy's voice, and he eyed her warily. 'How did you get on today?'

'Well, I spent most of it accepting commiserations about having to spend three whole days with you,' said Romy. She moved past him to start clearing up the debris from Freya's supper. 'Having seen the way you barely recognised me in that meeting, they all think you ignored me the whole time. If you want word to get round that we're a couple, you're going to have to try harder than that!'

Lex wrenched at his tie to loosen it. 'I thought we'd decided not to make an announcement?'

'Yes, because we want people to guess and start gossiping. They're never going to guess if you look through me and have trouble remembering my name! You had the perfect opportunity to hint that you think I'm special, but no! *"She was very helpful,"*' Romy mimicked his austere tones as she scraped the last few pieces of pasta from Freya's bowl and let the bin close with a rattle. 'Was that really the best you could do?'

'What did you want me to do? Throw you across the table and ravish you in front of all your colleagues?'

'A smile would have done it.' Romy began closing packets and putting everything away. 'That would have been so unusual they'd all have twigged straight away that there was something going on. As it was, none of them have a clue!'

'Well, I'm sorry,' said Lex stiffly, 'but it felt awkward.'

'You can say that again. I'm now the person who can spend three days with her boss without him realising that I even exist!'

Lex rolled his shoulders uncomfortably. 'I suppose I was thrown,' he admitted. 'I knew you'd be there, of course, but it was…odd…seeing you in a work context.'

A little mollified, Romy wrung out a cloth and wiped down the counter. 'I'd say you'd have to try harder next time, but we're not likely to have another meeting together, are we? We managed to work in the same office for six months without even seeing each other. I wonder if we should go in together for a few days? Someone is bound to notice that.'

Lex was usually at the office by seven o'clock, but the next morning found him walking into the gleaming reception area with Romy almost two hours later. Normally, he would stride straight to the lifts, with a brief nod of acknowledgement to whoever was on Reception. There weren't many other people around at that time and that was the way Lex liked it.

Now he felt extraordinarily self-conscious. Although no one actually stopped and pointed, he could tell that his arrival with Romy—and a pushchair!—had indeed been noted and would provide food for much comment and speculation by the coffee machines that morning.

'Well,' said Romy awkwardly. 'I'd…er…I'd better take Freya to the crèche.' Burningly aware of the covert stares in her direction—why on earth had she suggested this?—she mustered a smile. 'See you later.'

'Do you think I should kiss you?' Lex muttered and her heart promptly performed a back flip that threw out her breathing completely.

'*Kiss* me?'

'We're making an exhibition of ourselves just by standing here,' he said, still talking out of the corner of his mouth. 'We might as well really give them all something to talk about. You were the one keen to get the message across that I know you exist. I mean, that's what couples do, isn't it?' he added when she hesitated. 'Kiss each other goodbye?'

Romy swallowed. 'Usually just a peck on the lips.'

'I wasn't thinking of sweeping you into my arms!'

Her colour deepened at the sardonic note in his voice. 'Of course not.' She cleared her throat. 'OK, then.'

Lex put a hand at the small of her back to draw her closer and she lifted her face. It was ridiculous. They had kissed before. This would just be a brief brush of the lips.

But still her pulse was booming so loudly that the hubbub in Reception faded to nothing in comparison, and when he pressed his mouth to hers her hand rose instinctively to clutch at the sleeve of his jacket. The polished marble floor still seemed to drop away beneath her feet, and she was still intensely aware of the firmness and warmth of his lips, of the steely strength of his arm.

And when Lex lifted his head, she still felt hot and dizzy.

Lex's expression was impenetrable as he let her go. 'See you tonight,' he said coolly and walked off to the lifts, leaving Romy to make her way to the crèche with burning cheeks.

'Did that kiss this morning do the trick?' Lex asked that night as he pulled off his tie.

Romy had hoped to have the kitchen tidy before he got

home, but she was still washing up. At least it gave her a good excuse to stand with her back to him so that, after a quick greeting over her shoulder, he couldn't read her expression.

Ever since she had brought Freya home earlier, she had been practising how she would be when Lex appeared. Her lips had been tingling from that one brief kiss all day, and she was annoyed with herself for letting it affect her so much. Not that she had any intention of letting Lex guess that. She could do cool, too.

'It certainly did,' she said, proud of her casual tone. 'It must have taken all of two seconds for the news that you had kissed me in Reception to reach Acquisitions. Then, of course, I had to spend all day fending off questions and explaining why I hadn't told them about you.'

'What did you say?'

'The truth.'

'What?'

'Oh, not about the pretence.' Romy rinsed Freya's plate under the tap. 'Just that we'd known each other a long time ago, and got together again on the trip to Scotland.' She glanced at him over her shoulder again. 'I don't suppose anyone dared ask *you* about it?'

'No, but Summer smiled at me in a very knowing way.' Lex was regarding the chaos in the living area with dismay. 'Thank God Phin is out of contact in Africa. Summer's extraordinarily discreet, but she's bound to tell him, and then it'll only be a matter of time before my mother knows, and then *your* mother will know, and then there'll be no end to it.' He sighed and dragged a hand through his hair.

'We'll tell them we wanted to keep it a secret,' said Romy.

'So secret that I kissed you in the middle of Reception in front of half the staff?'

'Well, it's done now.' Romy dried her hands on a tea towel and turned. 'We went through all of this,' she reminded him.

'I know.'

Restless, Lex hunched his shoulders. He had been like this all day, ever since that damned kiss. No one had *said* anything, but he could tell that speculation was rife and that behind the bland expressions they were all wondering what on earth had happened to turn their tough chief executive into the kind of sap who kissed his girlfriend in front of his entire staff.

Lex cringed inwardly at the memory. What had he been thinking? He had humiliated himself in public, and for what? The chance to kiss Romy one more time.

Pathetic.

Surely he had had enough rejection. He had suggested they make the most of the time they had together, and Romy had said no. How many times did she have to tell him that they had no future together? How many times did he have to tell *himself*?

And still he only had to touch her, and reason evaporated. Romy would never know what an effort it had been to keep that kiss brief. It had been all Lex could do not to pull her down onto the floor, and to hell with their audience.

That would have given them all something to talk about!

Lex sighed. Continuing the pretence had seemed to make sense, but if they weren't careful it would spiral out of control. The very thought of losing control made him shudder, but what could he do? They couldn't stop now.

And it would be worth it when Willie Grant finally signed that contract, Lex reminded himself as he picked his way across the floor.

Freya, newly bathed and with a quiff of dark hair sticking up, was sitting in the middle of a sea of toys. She offered him a toothless smile but didn't clamour to be held the way she had the day before.

Well, good.

Just as well, thought Lex. He had no intention of picking her up.

So why did it feel like yet another rejection?

Splashing water on his face in his bathroom, Lex pulled himself together. The deal, that was all that mattered. Once it was done, Romy and Freya would leave, and his life could go back to normal. Until then, he would just have to put up with the humiliation and the mess and this feeling that everything was on the point of slipping out of control.

Romy was still clearing the kitchen when he went out. For the first time in his life, Lex had found it hard to concentrate at the office, and he had brought a report home to read, but the chances of concentration here were even slimmer until Freya had gone to bed, he realised.

His space invaded on every front, Lex took refuge at the piano. Alone in the evenings he would sit and play to unwind from work. Perhaps it would help now.

He played a few chords softly, letting his fingers warm up and go where they would, but he had barely started before there was a tugging at his trouser leg as Freya desperately hauled herself upright, loudly demanding to be lifted up to the source of the magical sounds.

'Freya!' Realising too late what was happening, Romy hurried over to take her away. 'Leave Lex alone! I'm sorry,' she added to Lex as Freya wailed in protest.

'Oh, let her come up if she's so insistent,' he said brusquely. 'Here—' He held out his arms, and after a moment's hesitation Romy put Freya in them.

Freya's tears cleared magically as Lex settled her on his

lap and let her lean forward to crash her little hands onto the piano keys.

Wincing at the noise, Romy perched on the arm of a sofa and watched as Lex let Freya bash away for a minute or so before he took her hands very gently and helped her to press the keys properly. Freya's expression was transfigured as she heard the notes sing out from beneath her fingers, and Romy felt her throat tighten at his patience with her daughter.

Naturally, Freya's attention span was limited, and she was soon back to 'playing' on her own. 'I hope she's not damaging your piano,' Romy said, raising her voice over the crashing chords.

'She's all right,' said Lex. 'It's a good thing to let her get used to just sitting at a piano if she likes it. Maybe she's going to be musical.'

Romy opened her mouth to suggest that he could teach Freya to play properly when she was a bit older, but shut it again almost immediately. What was she thinking? By the time Freya was old enough to learn the piano, they would be long gone.

'She wouldn't get it from me,' she said instead.

'Perhaps her father is musical,' Lex said evenly.

'Perhaps. I must ask him.' Romy shifted on the arm of the sofa. 'If I remember, I'll ask him this weekend.'

Lex looked up sharply. 'This weekend?'

'Yes, I...I emailed Michael this morning.'

She shouldn't feel awkward about it, Romy knew. It was past time for her to let Michael know that he was a father. She had been putting it off because it felt as if she would somehow lose some of her independence if he decided he wanted to be part of Freya's life.

Whichever way she looked at it, a relationship between Freya and her father would be a tie. Never again would Romy be able to move on the moment it suited her. There would always be someone else to take into account. Of course, she had to take Freya into account now, but it wasn't the same.

What if Michael wanted to see Freya regularly? What if he wanted a say in where she lived or where she went to school? Romy knew that she ought to be glad if it turned out that he wanted to be involved in his daughter's life, but she hated the idea of anyone limiting her freedom in any way. She knew it wasn't logical or justifiable or fair, but the prospect of involving anyone else in the life she had built with Freya smacked too much of commitment for Romy.

And yet, today she had emailed him. It didn't make Romy feel any better to realise that she had only done it because she had been so thrown by that kiss this morning.

It was stupid. It hadn't meant anything, but she hadn't been able to get it out of her mind all day. This was just what Romy had been afraid of. She didn't want her pulse to jump every time Lex walked into a room. She didn't want to be waiting for him, looking for him, unable to settle unless he was there. Next thing she knew, she would be hopelessly in love with him. She would be needing a man who had been very straight about not wanting anything to do with a baby.

Romy knew how that would end. So she had done what she always did when she felt herself getting too close to anyone. She made her plans to move on.

'I asked if we could meet,' she told Lex. 'He replied straight away.'

Lex's head was bent over Freya's as he guided her hands on the piano keys. 'Did you tell him about Freya?'

'Not yet. I thought it would be better to tell him face to face. I've got a friend who lives in Taunton, which isn't far from

Michael. I'm going to stay with her tomorrow, and she's going to look after Freya while I go and see him on Sunday morning. It might be too much of a shock if I turned up with her.' Romy had a nasty feeling that she was babbling, and made herself stop.

'He must be keen if he's meeting you at such short notice,' said Lex after a moment. 'You've arranged it all very quickly.'

'Well, I've waited long enough. I thought I might get too nervous if I had to think about what to say to him for too long.' Romy fiddled with her bracelets. 'Besides, I thought it might be nice for you to have the flat to yourself for the weekend.'

'Thanks for the thought, but I won't be here myself. I was going to say the same to you.'

'Oh?' Her fingers stilled. 'Where are you going?'

'To visit my parents, who I sincerely hope won't have heard any rumours about our supposed relationship just yet.' Lex's smile gleamed briefly, but without much humour. 'I'll be able to tell my father about the deal with Willie Grant. It looks as if both of us will be passing on surprising news this weekend, doesn't it?'

Lex drove back to London early on Sunday afternoon. A chance for some time to himself, he had decided. Some quiet. Some order. To catch up on some work. To walk across his living room without tripping over a squeaky toy and to admire his spectacular view without Freya squealing and shouting in the background.

But when he let himself into the flat, it didn't feel quiet. It felt empty.

Romy and Freya had only been in residence two days. What was it going to be like when they left after a month?

By then he would be desperate for some peace, Lex told himself. He would be sick of tripping over the pushchair every time he came through the door. He could take those rounded rubber clips off the corners of the coffee table, and the plastic covers off his state-of-the art steel sockets. The waxed tablecloth with its pattern of brightly coloured dots would be gone, and he would be able to see his stylish dining table again.

There would be no little clothes drying on airers. No baby food in the fridge. No toys scattered on the floor or plastic ducks in the bath.

No Freya.

No Romy.

Lex could smell her perfume in the air. She was such a vivid presence that her absence was a shout in the silence. He could picture her exactly, barefoot, swinging Freya into the air, dark eyes aglow.

Was he going to have to endure another twelve years of memories? Twelve years of remembering the nape of her neck, the back of her knee, the scent of her hair. And this time it would be worse, Lex knew. Now he knew there was more to Romy than that wild, passionate girl she had been at eighteen. She was intelligent and capable and charming. She was warm. She was practical. She was tender.

And she was so damned stubborn.

Romy would never change her mind. If she said she would leave, she would leave. He had better get used to it.

Alarmed at the maudlin train of his thoughts, Lex pulled himself together sharply. Why was he feeling so glum? He had what he wanted. What he *needed*. He had the Grant's Supersaver deal in his pocket. He had control of Gibson & Grieve. Control of his life. No one asking anything of him that he couldn't give.

What more did he want?

Refusing to let himself even *think* about an answer to that, Lex sat at the piano and started to play, but he wasn't able to lose himself in the music the way he usually could, and when he heard the sound of the front door his hands paused above the keys and, in spite of everything he'd had to say to himself, his heart missed a beat as Romy appeared in the doorway.

Her dark hair was spangled with rain and she pushed it behind her ears with a stilted smile. 'I thought I heard the piano.'

'Where's Freya?' The constriction in Lex's chest made it hard to speak.

'Asleep in the hall.' Romy glanced over her shoulder. 'I've left her in the pushchair.'

There was a pause.

'I wasn't expecting you back yet,' he said at last.

'I didn't think *you'd* be back until later.'

'I decided to come home early.'

Romy moved into the room, hugging her arms together. 'Wasn't it a good weekend?'

'It was fine.' He shrugged. 'The usual.'

'How was your father?'

Lex made a face. 'Not so good. He seemed…tired.'

'Did you tell him about the deal?'

'Yes.'

'What did he say?'

'Nothing. He just looked away.'

Romy found herself clenching her fists on her sleeves. She knew Gerald Gibson was ill, but would it have been so hard for him to congratulate Lex, to somehow make it clear that he was proud of him?

'I'm sorry,' she said.

Lex pressed down a key with his forefinger, then another. 'I thought I would feel good about telling him,' he said abruptly. 'I thought I'd have proved something, but I just looked at him and realised that he didn't care. He's dying.'

'Oh, Lex.' Without thinking, Romy put her hands on his shoulders, and just for a moment Lex let himself lean back against her. Then he remembered that she was leaving and straightened.

'What about you? How did it go with Freya's father?'

'Fine.' Romy let her hands fall and moved away to the window, too restless to sit down. 'It was fine,' she said again. 'Michael was a bit stunned at first, understandably, but once he'd got used to the idea and met Freya he was quite chuffed. He said he'd like to get involved in her life.'

Lex raised his brows at her lack of enthusiasm.

'That's good news, isn't it? Most single mothers would welcome some support from the father.'

'I know.' With a sigh, Romy threw herself down on the sofa. 'I'm going to take Freya down again in a couple of weeks.'

'To stay with him?' Jealousy sharpened his voice, but she didn't seem to notice.

'No. Michael's back with his fiancée and they're getting married next year. Obviously he wants her to meet Freya, so I'll stay with Jenny again, and we'll have what I imagine will be quite an awkward get-together. But Michael seems to think Kate—that's his fiancée—will be OK about it once she meets me and sees I'm no threat.'

'And then what?' asked Lex harshly.

'What do you mean?'

'What happens once you've established a cosy relationship with this Michael and his oh-so-understanding fiancée?'

'I come back here and we see out this farce we've started,' said Romy. 'Jo should be back from maternity leave soon, and then I'll have to decide. I might move to Somerset. It's a lovely area, and it would be cheaper than London. And if Michael does want to see Freya regularly, that would work quite well.'

'Oh, I can see that would be the perfect set-up for you,' said Lex, bitterness threading his voice. 'Then you'd have everything you wanted, wouldn't you, Romy? Freya's father there for when you need him, but he's nicely tied up with his fiancée so there's no danger he'll try and get too close to you. No danger that you'll lose your precious independence!'

'You'll have everything *you* want too,' Romy pointed out, caught unawares by the animosity that was suddenly crackling in the air. 'You'll have your precious deal and your nice, quiet life. What's the problem?'

'No problem.' Lex pushed back the piano stool and got abruptly to his feet. He was going out. He didn't know where. Just out. 'No problem at all.'

'Aren't you going out tonight?'

Lex was thrown when he let himself into his apartment the following Friday to find that Romy was sitting on the sofa with Freya, reading a story—or, rather, counting caterpillars while Freya smacked the pages. He had been coming home later and later that week, to avoid spending too much time with Romy, but that night he had expected her to be at the acquisition team's celebration dinner.

'I'm not going,' said Romy, looking up from the caterpillars. 'It's too difficult with Freya.'

Lex hung up his jacket and went back into the living room, frowning as he unbuttoned his cuffs and rolled up his sleeves. 'You should be there,' he said. 'You were an important part of the team, and if it hadn't been for you they might not have had anything to celebrate.'

Now he said it!

'It doesn't matter.' Romy managed a careless shrug, hoping to conceal her disappointment. She really liked everyone in the team, and it promised to be a fun evening. They had all been dismayed when she said that she wouldn't be able to make it.

'I can't leave Freya,' she said. 'If I'd been at home, I could have asked my neighbour's daughter to babysit, but I don't know anyone I could trust around here.'

'You know me,' said Lex, and she stared at him, the book forgotten in her hands.

'I can't ask you to babysit!'

'Don't you trust me?'

'Of *course* I trust you, but... I couldn't ask you to do that.'

'I don't see why not,' Lex said. He sat down on the sofa opposite her and there was a squeak. Leaning to one side, he pulled out a much-chewed teddy bear.

Freya gave a cry of recognition and held out her hands for it.

'We've been looking for him,' said Romy as Lex leant over and handed the teddy back to Freya, who immediately stuffed its arm in her mouth.

'I'm just going to be here working,' he went on. 'As long as you put her to bed before you go, we'll be fine.'

'She doesn't usually wake up,' Romy agreed, weakening. It had been a long time since she'd been able to go out on her own, and she could already feel a lightening of her mood at the prospect. 'Are you sure you wouldn't mind?'

'If I minded, I wouldn't have offered,' said Lex brusquely.

So Romy got to go to the celebration dinner after all. Barely had the door closed behind her than Freya woke up. Lex tried to settle her in her cot, but nothing would console her, and in the end he succumbed and lifted her out. He had seen Romy walking her around, rubbing her back and humming soothingly, so he tried that, and it seemed to work.

Until he tried putting Freya back in her cot. She screamed and screamed and only stopped when Lex picked her up again and set off round the apartment once more.

Romy rang from the restaurant. 'Is everything all right?' she asked anxiously.

Lex was holding Freya in one arm, and the phone in his other hand. He craned his neck to peer at the baby, who was snuggled into his collar. Ridiculously long lashes, still damp with tears, lay across her flushed cheeks. She seemed to be all right. If he admitted that she'd been crying, Romy would come home and miss the dinner after all. There was no point in both of them listening to Freya cry.

'Everything's fine,' he said.

Lex didn't even get to open his briefcase that night. Freya categorically refused to go back into her cot and he spent the entire evening walking her round and round the flat. He hummed and he sang and he rocked her gently, and at last, worn out, he stretched out on the sofa and let Freya sprawl on his chest, where she promptly dropped into a deep slumber.

When Romy came back, she found them both sound asleep. Held securely by Lex's large hand, Freya lay flopped across his body, rising and falling with his chest.

Romy stood looking down at them, and her throat felt very tight. In sleep, Lex's stern features relaxed, and he looked younger and infinitely more approachable than when those piercingly pale eyes were open and he had himself under rigid control. The normally hard mouth was slightly ajar, and a soft whistling sound came out with every breath.

I don't want to fall in love with you, he had said. *I just don't want a baby.*

And yet he had looked after Freya all night, just so that Romy could go out and enjoy herself. Very lightly, she touched his hair.

Was she doing the right thing in running away from any thought of commitment? Romy wondered. It would be so easy to slip into a relationship. If she had said yes when Lex suggested that they continue to sleep together, she would have saved herself all the itchy, prickly, churning frustration of not being able to touch him. She would have been able to take it for granted that Lex would look after Freya when she went out. Romy had clung to her independence for so long, it was second nature to her now, but, still, there were times when even she could see how appealing it would be to have someone else to share the responsibility, someone else you could rely on utterly.

The trouble was, she could also see how painful it would be when that someone decided they didn't want to be with you any more. Romy's thoughts went round and round in familiar circles. She and Lex might be sexually compatible, but a relationship needed more than great sex. It needed more than Romy could give. It needed trust.

At one level, she trusted Lex completely. He would never betray her with another woman. He wasn't like her father, who had revelled in his double life. Lex had an almost old-fashioned sense of integrity. He might be short on the social skills in which his brother excelled but he was completely trustworthy in that sense.

No, Romy wasn't afraid he would leave her for another woman. What she feared was his inability to compromise. He would hate the mess and unpredictability of family life. He would hate not being able to control life with a baby, with a child, even with a woman.

And if he couldn't compromise, they couldn't live together, and they would split up. Romy wouldn't—*couldn't*—face being abandoned again. She couldn't trust that it wouldn't all go wrong and end in exactly the pain and mess that she was so determined Freya shouldn't suffer. She couldn't bear Freya to feel what she had felt when her father left.

No, better to keep her distance, Romy decided, and carry on as they were, but it was difficult to stay distant with Lex when they were living together. They walked into the office together in the morning, but after that first time he never again kissed her in Reception. Once there, they went their separate ways. Lex was far too senior for Romy to have any professional dealings with him. Rather to her surprise, her colleagues seemed to have accepted the idea of her being in a relationship with their chief executive.

'He's a behind-closed-doors kind of guy,' Romy had said to explain why Lex ignored her in the office. She wasn't sure whether the others believed her or not, but if they were baffled they kept any speculation to themselves.

It was surprising, too, how quickly she and Freya had adjusted to a completely new routine. Romy collected Freya from the crèche when it closed at five thirty and took her home. No, *not* home, she corrected herself and rewound her thoughts. She took Freya *back to Lex's flat*, gave her supper and a bath, and by then Lex was usually home.

Freya loved to sit on his lap at the piano while Romy tidied up the worst of the mess. Lex was stiff with her at first, but Freya was irresistible when she put her mind to it. Romy wondered if Lex realised how much he had changed. She liked to listen to him talking to Freya. He made no concessions to the fact that she was a baby, but talked to her as if she were an adult.

'That's F sharp,' he would say, pressing a key. 'And this one here is E. Now listen to this chord… And then if I do *this*, see what happens…'

Conversation wasn't a problem when Freya was around, but there was always a pool of silence once she was in bed. Occasionally Lex had some function to go to, but, if not, Romy usually prepared a meal for them to share.

'You don't need to cook for me,' Lex had protested, but Romy didn't like the prepared meals he was happy to cook straight from the freezer.

'I'm cooking for Freya anyway,' she said. 'Besides, I enjoy it.'

It was true, and it gave her something to do in the evenings. Something that wasn't remembering how sure, how warm, his hands had been. That wasn't reliving that night at Duncardie. Something that wasn't wishing that she had said yes instead of no, so that she could stand behind him and massage the tension from his neck and shoulders. If she could do that, she could press her mouth to his throat, trail kisses along his jaw until he turned his head to meet her lips with his own, let him pull her down onto his lap…

No, cooking was a much safer option.

CHAPTER NINE

AFTERWARDS she would pretend to read while Lex worked, but what Romy liked best was when he sat at the piano and forgot that she was there at all. During the day, he held himself rigid and guarded, shutting out the rest of the world, but at a piano his whole body seemed to relax and he swayed instinctively with the music while his fingers drew magic from the keys.

Her book would fall unheeded into her lap, and she would tip her head back and close her eyes. Romy had never had much of a feeling for music before, but when Lex played it felt as if he were strumming a chord deep inside her, and an intense *feeling* swelled in her chest and closed her throat.

'You should play professionally,' she said to him one night when he paused.

'I don't want to,' said Lex. 'And I don't have time. In case you haven't noticed, I've got a company to run.'

On the sofa, Romy tipped her head right back on the cushions until she could see him behind her. 'You could let Phin run the company.'

'Phin?' He gave a bark of laughter. 'Phin would give away all our assets and spend all our profits on staff development!' He was only half joking. 'Gibson & Grieve would never recover!'

'He's not as irresponsible as you think he is,' said Romy,

leaping to the defence of her old friend. She and Phin had been close long before she had thought of Lex as anything more than Phin's intimidating older brother. 'Everyone I know thinks very highly of him.'

'Of course they do. Everyone likes Phin.' Resentment he hadn't even known he felt splintered Lex's voice. 'He's one of the most successful people I know. He goes his own sweet way, and because he makes people laugh, he gets away with it.

'Our father wanted him to join Gibson & Grieve when he left university, but you didn't catch Phin knuckling down and doing what he was supposed to do. Oh, no, Phin was off, drifting around the world, doing exactly what he wanted to do! He never cared about responsibility or the family or putting something back into the company that had paid for everything he had.'

Romy twisted right round so that she could look at him over the back of the sofa. 'Is that what you've been doing all these years?'

'Someone had to.' Lex closed the piano lid. 'I was the eldest. I suppose it was inevitable that I was expected to be the sensible one. Phin just clapped me on the shoulder, told me not to let it get me down, and took off.' His mouth twisted in a humourless smile at the memory. 'My parents were beside themselves, but Phin didn't care.'

'He came back when your father had a stroke.'

'Yes, he did. He's the golden boy now that he's married Summer and settled down. Talk about the prodigal son!'

'You sound like you resent him,' said Romy carefully.

'I do, don't I?' Lex got to his feet and prowled over to the long, glass wall. He could see the lights along the Embankment and the dull gleam of the river.

'I think I envy him more than resent him,' he said at length.

'Everything seems to come easily to Phin. He's never cared half as much about our father's opinion as I do, but he's got his approval by doing exactly what he wanted.'

He turned back to face Romy. 'And I'll admit, he hasn't been quite such a disaster as a director as I feared he would be. Mind you, I think that's mostly down to Summer. Marrying her was the most sensible thing Phin ever did. But he hasn't got the dedication to run Gibson & Grieve, even if he wanted to.'

'There must be other directors who could take over as Chief Executive,' Romy pointed out. 'It's not as if you need the money.'

'It's not about money,' he said curtly.

'Then what *is* it about?'

Lex hunched a shoulder, wishing Romy would stop asking awkward questions. 'It's about my career. It's what I do. What I've always done. What I *am*. If you think I've spent my life wishing I could have been a musician instead of going into the family firm, forget it. Music is just…an escape.'

Romy looked up at him with her great dark eyes. 'Escape from what?' she asked softly.

Lex didn't answer immediately. He went back to the piano, laid his hand on the smooth mahogany. Even silent, he could feeling the piano's power strumming through the wood, calling to something inside him.

'We all make choices,' he said finally. 'I made mine, and I don't regret it. Do you regret any of the choices you've made?'

Romy thought about hot wind soughing through palm trees. About desert skies and coral reefs and drinking beer at a roadside *warung* while the tropical rain thundered down. And then she thought about Freya and the friends she had made at Gibson & Grieve and this crazy pretence she and Lex were engaged in. She had chosen them all.

'No,' she said in low voice. 'The only choices I regret are the ones that were made for me. I wasn't allowed to choose whether my father stayed or not, and nor was my mother. We just had to live with the consequences of a choice *he* had made.'

She looked at Lex, still smoothing his hand absently over the piano. 'I learnt from that,' she said. 'I learnt to never give anyone else the power to make a choice for me, and I never will.'

Freya was crying again. Lex squinted at the digital display on the clock by his bed. Three seventeen.

She had been restless the night before as well. Teething, Romy had said. This was the fifth time he had heard Romy get up tonight, and Lex couldn't stand it any more. Pulling on a pair of trousers, he went to see if he could help.

Romy was walking Freya around the living room, just as he had done the night she had gone out to celebrate with the acquisitions team. She was barefoot, and wearing a paisley-patterned silk dressing gown that she had bought from a charity shop. The merest glimpse of it was usually enough to make Lex's body tighten with anticipation, imagining the slippery silk against her skin, but tonight it was a mark of how exhausted Romy looked that his first thought was not what it would be like to pull at the belt and let the dressing gown slither from her shoulders, but to wonder how best he could help her.

He rubbed a tired hand over his face. 'Is there anything I can do?'

Romy felt as if there were lead weights attached to her eyelids. The effort of putting one foot in front of another was like wading through treacle. And yet it seemed there were enough hormones still alert enough to stir at the sight of Lex's lean, muscled body. His hair was rumpled, his jaw prickled with stubble, and the pale eyes shadowed with concern. She must look even worse than she felt, Romy realised. And that was saying something.

'I'm sorry—' she started but Lex interrupted her.

'Don't be sorry,' he said. 'Just tell me how I can help.' He moved closer, craning his neck to try and see Freya's face. 'What's the matter? Are you sure she's not sickening for anything?'

'No, she's just miserable with this tooth coming through. And I'm just miserable because I've got to go to Windsor for a meeting tomorrow with Tim,' she added wryly. 'Although I'm not sure how much use I'll be. I'll be lucky if I can string two words together.'

A frown touched Lex's eyes. 'In that case, why don't you let me take her while you try and get some sleep?'

Romy's body was craving sleep. The need to lie down and close her eyes was so strong that, instead of insisting that she could manage on her own as she would normally have done, she said only, 'But what about you?'

'I haven't got anything urgent on tomorrow—or today, I should say.' Lex jerked his head in the direction of her room. 'Go on, go back to bed. You won't be any good to Gibson & Grieve otherwise,' he said gruffly. 'If I can't manage, I'll wake you, I promise.'

To Romy's surprise, Freya allowed herself to be handed over to Lex without a murmur. She subsided, sniffling, into his bare shoulder, and for one appalling moment Romy actually found herself thinking, *Lucky Freya*. She must be more tired than she thought she was.

She managed four hours' sleep and felt almost human when she woke. Freya was quieter than normal, but she

seemed better, so in the end Romy decided to leave her in the
crèche and headed off to Windsor with Tim. They were due
back by four. Freya ought to be OK until then, she tried to
reassure herself.

'But ring me if there's a problem,' she told the girls in the
crèche, who promised they would. They were used to
anxious mothers.

Up in the chief executive's office, Lex was also feeling the
results of a broken night. His eyes were gritty and there
seemed to be a tight band snapped around his skull. He was
distracted all morning.

'What?' he snapped at Summer when he caught her
watching him narrowly.

'I was just wondering if you were feeling all right,' said
Summer, who wasn't in the least frightened of him. 'You're
not yourself today.'

'I'm fine,' he said shortly. 'I didn't get much sleep last
night, that's all.'

When she had gone back to her office, Lex took off his
glasses and sat rubbing the bridge of his nose. He was
thinking about Freya. She had barely slept all night. Romy
seemed sure teething was the problem, but what if it was
something else? What if she needed a doctor? The crèche presumably had lots of children to deal with. Would anyone
notice if she wasn't well?

He glanced at his watch. Romy would still be in Windsor.

On an impulse, he leant forward and buzzed Summer.
'Where's this crèche we provide?'

'On the mezzanine.' Summer didn't even seem surprised
by the question.

'I'm just going to have a look,' Lex said on his way out,
and then wondered why he was making excuses to his PA.

He would just go and check that Freya was all right, he decided. And then perhaps he could get on with some work.

The crèche manager, flustered by the unannounced arrival of the chief executive, showed him round. The room was full of small children and babies, and the noise was indescribable. Amongst all the tiny tables and chairs, Lex felt like a clumsy giant who had stumbled into a world on quite a different scale. He picked his way carefully across the room, terrified of treading on something.

Freya was being comforted by one of the staff in a quiet corner and looking very woebegone. She had clearly been grizzling but offered a wobbly smile when she saw Lex and held out her arms to him. The girl exchanged looks with the manager as the chief executive took the baby and let her clutch his hair.

'She doesn't seem very happy,' he said severely.

'We've just rung her mother to say that Freya's a little poorly today. She's on her way back.'

Lex frowned. 'It might take her some time to get back from Windsor.'

'Yes, she said it would be a while, but we'll keep Freya here. She'll be fine,' the manager reassured him.

'As long as she's all right.' Lex tried to hand Freya back then, but she wailed in protest and clung to him until the manager prised her off him.

Feeling like a traitor, Lex headed for the door. Freya's heartbroken screams followed him until he couldn't stand it any more. Stopping abruptly, he pulled out his mobile phone and rang Romy.

'How long will it take you to get back?' he asked.

'I'm waiting for a train now. I'll get a taxi when I get to Paddington, but I'll still be about an hour, I think.' Romy's voice was riddled with guilt. 'I shouldn't have left her.'

'The manager says that she's fine, but it's pretty noisy in there,' said Lex. 'Shall I take her to my office? It'll be quieter there.'

Romy was silent. He could almost hear her instinct not to rely on anyone else warring with her concern for her daughter. In the end, Freya won, as Lex had known she would. Romy spoke to the manager on his mobile, and the moment Lex took her back Freya's screams subsided. They faded to shuddery little gasps as he waited for the lift.

There were three other people already in the lift when the doors opened. After a startled glance at Lex and his unusual burden, they all kept their eyes studiously on the floor numbers as they lit up one by one, but Lex was sure that behind his back they were exchanging looks. In a matter of minutes, the word would have spread around the building that the chief executive had been spotted in a lift with a baby in one arm , a bright yellow bag sporting teddy bears over the other, and a pushchair in his spare hand.

If Summer was surprised to see Lex reappear with a baby, she gave no sign of it. Coming round her desk, she tickled Freya's nose, and Freya managed a very little smile for her, but refused to be handed over or put down. Lex ended up dictating as he paced around the office while Summer wisely kept her inevitable reflections to herself.

Eventually, Freya dropped off, worn out. Lex wished he could do the same. He tilted the pushchair back as far as it would go and was laying her carefully in it when the phone rang.

'That was Romy.' Summer put the phone down. 'Apparently there's some delay on the line. She doesn't know when she'll be able to get here now. She sounded frantic, but I told her not to worry, that Freya was fine and sleeping.'

'Yes, it's all right for some, isn't it?' Lex straightened

the blanket over Freya, caught Summer's eye and stood hastily. 'Well, perhaps now we can get on with some work,' he said brusquely.

Summer smiled. 'Perhaps,' she agreed. 'You haven't forgotten you've got a meeting at four-thirty, have you?'

Lex slapped a hand to his forehead. 'God, yes! I had forgotten.'

What was happening to him? He *never* forgot meetings. He knew Summer was thinking exactly the same thing.

'Let's just hope she stays asleep,' he said, looking down at Freya dubiously.

He might have spared his breath. She woke up, bang on time, a minute before the meeting was due to start, all smiles and apparently miraculously cured. She was ready for some attention, she indicated, and had no intention of being left out of the action. When Lex left her with Summer to join the directors waiting in his office, Freya's bellows of outrage could be heard clearly through the wall.

Lex put his head back round the door. 'Can't you keep her quiet?' he demanded irritably.

'No,' said Summer, not mincing her words. 'She doesn't want to be with me. She wants to be with you.'

So Lex had to conduct the meeting with Freya tweaking his nose or tugging at his ear lobes. It was hard to look intimidating with a baby on your lap.

That was what was left of his reputation shot to pieces, thought Lex in resignation.

It was almost half past five before Romy got there, looking hot and frazzled. 'Oh, thank God!' she said as she swept up a smiling Freya and kissed her. 'I've been so worried. How has she been?'

'Absolutely fine,' said Summer. 'In fact, I'm thinking of

taking her on as an assistant. She had all those men in suits terrified. They were in and out of that meeting in double quick time!' She slid an amused glance in Lex's direction. 'And she can run rings around our chief executive!'

'I thought she wasn't well,' Lex said defensively.

'It was quite a revelation. I'd no idea you were so good with babies.' Summer's eyes twinkled. 'I can't wait to tell Phin!'

'God, I'll never hear the end of it once Phin knows,' Lex grumbled as he walked Romy and Freya to the lift.

The afternoon might have been designed to prove that work and children didn't mix. Between lack of sleep and having to drop everything the moment a child was ill, it was impossible to get any work done. He was just glad he didn't have to deal with crises like this one on a regular basis.

'I'm sorry Freya threw out your afternoon, but I'm so grateful,' said Romy. 'I don't know what I'd have done without you.'

He hunched a shoulder. 'I dare say she'd have been all right in the crèche.'

'Yes, but she was much happier with you.'

Romy pushed Freya back to the apartment, feeling deeply uneasy. Yes, she was grateful that Lex had been able to help, but it was disturbing to realise just how comfortable Freya was with him. He wasn't supposed to be important to her. That was exactly what Romy hadn't wanted to happen.

She was going to have to do something about it, and soon.

'Is there any news of the contract?' she asked Lex that night as she wiped down Freya's high chair.

'There is.' Lex had almost forgotten about it in all the anxiety about Freya. 'Everything's going ahead much quicker than we thought. Summer has been in touch with Willie's assistant, and they're trying to arrange the formal signing at the end of next week.'

'Next week!' Romy was horrified at the way her heart leapt in dismay. She was supposed to be looking forward to ending this awkward situation and moving on. Hadn't she decided that things needed to change soon? It was just that she hadn't counted on them changing quite that soon.

She summoned a smile. 'Well, that's great news.'

'Yes,' said Lex, then, thinking that sounded a bit bald, 'Yes, it is.'

Romy stashed the chair in the corner and began to pull the waxed cloth off the table. 'I'll be able to make some plans now.'

'What sort of plans?'

'About the future. I had time to think while I was stuck on that train today, and I've realised I can't go on like this.' She concentrated on folding the cloth neatly. Lex hated it when she just scrumpled it up and tossed it on the floor beside the high chair. 'Tim offered me a permanent job today,' she told Lex, who stilled. 'But I've decided not to take it.'

When she glanced at Lex, she saw that his brows were drawn together. 'Why not?'

'Because it's too difficult being in London. Luckily you were there to take Freya today, but what if she was unwell another time and I couldn't get to her in time?'

'I could always help,' Lex offered stiffly, but Romy shook her head.

'I couldn't ask you to do that again. You're Chief Executive, and I know how busy you are. You've got more important things to do.' She drew a breath. 'No, I've decided I'm going to move to Somerset. If I live near Michael, at least he'd be able to help if necessary.'

She and Freya had met Kate, Michael's fiancée, the

previous weekend. She had seemed very nice, and if she resented the fact that Michael had been suddenly thrust into fatherhood, she didn't show it.

'Jenny's down there, too,' Romy went on. 'She said she'd be happy for me to stay until I find a job and a place of my own.'

It made sense, Lex told himself as he lay in bed and tried to ignore the weight pressing on his chest. And not just for Romy. Once she and Freya had gone, life would go back to normal.

He was sick of the edginess that churned continually in the pit of his stomach. He was tired of the way his lungs tightened whenever he caught sight of Romy in the morning, looking sleepy and rumpled and gorgeous. He had had enough of the painful grip on his heart, and the way it squeezed every time she smiled. It was a ridiculous way for a grown man to feel.

He was glad Willie Grant was coming soon, so they could end this absurd charade. He had already ruined his reputation because of it, Lex reminded himself sourly. The whole company would be talking about him carrying a baby in the lift, and if he hadn't wanted to make it seem as if he cared he would have asked the directors at the meeting to keep quiet about the fact that he had conducted an entire meeting while Freya tugged at his lips and bumped her head against his.

What had he been thinking? It was as if he had taken leave of his senses since Romy had reappeared.

Well, that would end soon. She would leave, and take Freya with her. Let her set up house near her artist, if that was what she wanted. Lex imagined Michael dropping by to see his daughter every day. Freya would have him wound round her little finger in no time. Michael would be the one she held out her arms for. The one she flirted with and played with and wanted when she was teething.

Lex's jaw set. And that was as it should be. Michael was

her father. He would be able to make her happy in a way he, Lex, never could. How could he be a father? He knew nothing about relaxing or laughing or playing. The thought of being responsible for anyone else's happiness made him recoil. He wouldn't know where to begin, and he didn't want to.

No, better that Romy took Freya away as soon as possible. It was all for the best.

'That was a fine meal,' said Willie, leaning back in his chair and patting his stomach appreciatively. 'If only all business dinners were as good. You're a grand cook, Romy. And, Lex, you're a very lucky man!'

Lex's smile was brief. 'I know,' he said. He didn't look at Romy.

Willie's visit was going exactly as planned. Willie himself was in high good humour, as well he might be, Lex reflected. He had been delighted to come to the apartment and Freya had been on her best behaviour with him before she went to bed. Romy had remembered that Willie's favourite food was lamb, and she'd roasted a leg with a herby crust. Lex had handed over a staggering amount of money for a bottle of Willie's favourite whisky.

Rarely had a major business deal taken place in such a cordial atmosphere. There was no question of Willie changing his mind now. Everything was perfect.

So why was Lex's stomach knotted with unease? Why was there this uncomfortable feeling between his shoulders?

Realising that the smile had dropped from his face, Lex put it back and forced his attention back to Willie, who was telling Romy about his marriage.

'Moira and I were together forty-seven years. She was a wonderful woman. Not everyone gets as lucky as you and I ,

Lex,' he added with a twinkling look. 'You're clearly a man who was prepared to do whatever it took to hang onto a good woman when you found her.'

And that was when Lex realised that he couldn't go through with it.

'Willie,' he said. 'There's something I have to tell you.'

'Oh?' Willie's smile faded and he put down his glass. 'That sounds serious.'

'It is.' Lex swallowed. 'I've brought you here under false pretences.'

Romy drew a startled breath and he held up a hand to stop her protest, keeping his eyes steadily on Willie.

'Romy and I aren't a couple, Willie, and we don't normally live together. This is nothing to do with Romy,' he added. 'When we realised that you thought we were a couple, it seemed important to you, and I saw a chance to persuade you to sign.'

'Actually, it was my idea,' Romy tried to put in, but Lex overrode her.

'It was my responsibility,' he said firmly. 'I told Romy I'd do anything to make this deal, but I should have drawn the line at lying.'

After the first moment of surprise, Willie's eyes had narrowed, but he said nothing, just watched Lex, who found himself trying to loosen his tie that all at once felt too tight.

'I'm sorry,' he said. 'I should have confessed all this before, and given you the chance to change your mind about the deal. You still can, of course.'

There was dead silence round the table. Willie looked from Lex to Romy and then back to Lex.

'Why are you telling me this now?' he asked at last.

Lex, who had braced himself for anger or disgust or disappointment, was thrown by the mildness of Willie's tone.

'I think the deal will be a good one for both our companies,' he said carefully after a moment. 'It's one I've wanted for a long time, and I thought I would do anything to make it happen, but…'

He stopped, tried to gather his thoughts. 'Before, you were just the owner of a chain of stores. I had respect for your business acumen, but I didn't know you. Now I do, and I've realised that your opinion matters to me.' Lex sounded almost surprised. 'Now I respect you as a person, and going ahead with this deal while effectively lying to you isn't respecting you. I don't want to do it.'

'I see,' said Willie thoughtfully. 'So you're telling me you don't love Romy?'

Lex hesitated. 'I'm telling you we're not a couple.'

Willie turned to Romy. 'And you don't love Lex?' he asked, sounding genuinely interested, and she bit her lip.

'I'm so sorry, Willie. We've just been pretending all this while.'

'Well.' Willie sat back in his chair, shaking his head in disbelief. 'You're not a real couple?'

'No.'

'Why not?'

There was a short silence. 'I'm sorry?' said Lex.

'Why *aren't* you a couple?' Willie said, all reasonableness. 'It seems to me that you're good together, and I notice you both avoided a direct answer when I asked about love.'

Romy glanced at Lex. 'Love isn't the problem,' she said in a low voice.

'Then what is?'

She couldn't tell Willie how her father had swept her up into his arms and called her his best girl, and abandoned her the next day. How could she explain how hard it was to trust when the man you loved most in the world, the man you trusted above all others, let you down? How could she tell him about Lex, who strove for his father's approval and kept his world under tight control?

'It's...complicated,' she said.

'What's complicated about loving each other?'

'I think Romy's trying to explain that we're incompatible,' Lex tried. This was the most bizarre business conversation he had ever had, but he supposed it was his fault for raising the matter in the first place.

Willie raised a sceptical brow. 'Is that right? I seem to remember seeing you two walking in the snow at Duncardie and you looked pretty compatible then.'

The colour rose in Romy's cheeks and Lex set his teeth. 'We just...want different things.'

'Haven't either of you heard of compromise? A fine pair of cowards you both are!'

Willie shook his head and pushed back his chair. 'I can't say I'm not disappointed,' he said, 'but it's not the first disappointment of my life and I dare say it won't be the last. Ah, well.' He hoisted himself upright. 'That was still a delicious dinner, Romy, so thank you for that—and for an interesting evening all round.'

Lex and Romy exchanged a glance, and Lex got to his feet. A limousine would be waiting below to take Willie back to his hotel. 'I'll see you to the car.'

'I didn't have you down for a fool, Alexander Gibson,' said Willie in the lift down to the basement garage, 'but I've changed my mind!'

'I can only apologise again,' Lex said stiffly. 'I wanted to make the deal so much, I let it override my judgement. I accept that it was a mistake.'

'Well, I've made some mistakes in my own time,' Willie allowed. 'I've tried to learn from them, and I hope you will too. What you learn, of course, is up to you.' He clapped Lex on the shoulder as they stepped out of the lift to see the limousine waiting. 'I'll see you tomorrow.'

'You mean you'll still sign?' Lex hardly dared believe that it would be all right.

'Oh, yes. You're right about it being a good thing for both companies.' His shrewd blue eyes rested on Lex's face. 'It's a funny thing,' he said, 'how you can feel disappointed in someone and yet proud of them at the same time. I've been watching what you've done for Gibson & Grieve, laddie. You've moved into a whole new league, and you've got yourself a fine reputation. If you hadn't, I would never have agreed to sell, no matter how married you were.

'And knowing how much this deal matters to you means I can appreciate what it took for you to tell me the truth,' he said. 'It was the right thing to do, and I'm glad you did it. So I'm proud of you, and I'll be happy to sign that contract tomorrow.'

He smiled at Lex as they shook hands. 'But that doesn't mean I don't still think you're a fool when it comes to Romy!'

Romy was clearing the table when Lex let himself back into the flat. She looked up, her hands full of plates, but put them back on the table when she saw his face.

'So, no more pretending,' she said.

'No.' Lex dropped his keys onto the side table.

'Why did you tell him, Lex?'

'I had to.'

Loosening his tie, he went over to the window and stood looking down at the river. The lights along the Embankment were blurry in the drizzle, and he thought about Willie, driving back alone to his hotel.

He turned to look at Romy, who was wiping her hands on a tea towel and watching him with dark, wary eyes.

'He's going to sign anyway.'

Romy's shoulders slumped with relief. 'I thought he'd be furious that we'd been lying to him.'

'He told me I was a fool,' said Lex. 'But he also understood what I've been trying to do with Gibson & Grieve. He said he was proud of me.' Ashamed of the strain in his voice, he looked back at the view. 'Do you know how long I've waited for my own father to say that?'

Dropping the tea towel over the back of a chair, Romy went over to stand beside him. 'Just because he hasn't said it, doesn't mean he doesn't think it, Lex. If Willie can appreciate what you've done for Gibson & Grieve, then your father must be able to as well. It's just more difficult for him to accept that he wasn't indispensable, and that the company is moving on without him. You know that,' she said gently.

'Yes, I know that.' Lex's expression was bleak. For a while they stood side by side, looking out across the lights of London. Then he let out a long breath, letting the old frustration go.

He glanced at Romy, then away again. 'What did you mean when you told Willie that love wasn't the problem?'

'It isn't,' she said. 'The problem is that love doesn't last. The problem is that it isn't enough.'

'Willie thinks it is. It lasted forty-seven years for him and Moira.'

'They were lucky,' said Romy. 'We might not be.' She turned restlessly, rubbing her arms. 'It's all very well for Willie to say compromise, but how would that actually work? Do you *really* want to give up your tidy flat and your nice, ordered life?'

'We could compromise in other ways,' Lex suggested.

'How? A flat like this isn't suitable for a toddler.' She gestured around her. 'How long before I get fed up with all the sharp angles and slippy floors? Before I start resenting the fact that there's no garden or other children nearby? Before I think that if I have to manoeuvre that pushchair into the lift one more time I'm going to scream?

'And how long before you're gritting your teeth about the mess? Until you're exasperated by the chaos and the noise and disgusted by the dirty nappies and Freya's runny nose?'

Romy shook her head. 'Compromise is hard, Lex. And I can't take the risk that you'll be able to do it. If it was just me, then perhaps. But I've got Freya to think about too. When you've got a child, you have to put practicalities before passion. I have to think about Freya and what she needs. She'd be better off in the country, where I can afford to give her a better life.

'It would be so easy to stay here with you,' she said. 'To think, oh, well, let's give it a go, but you said it yourself: we're different, and we want different things. I don't see how it could work, and if we try and it doesn't work it'll hurt all of us.'

Lex was watching her pace fretfully to and fro, her arms hugged together.

'So you're saying that you love me, but you don't love me enough to be sure it would work out?'

Romy lifted her chin. 'Do you love me enough to put up with all the mess and uncertainty that comes from living with a child?'

Fatally, Lex hesitated, and she smiled sadly. 'I didn't think so.'

'I think it might be worth a try,' he insisted, but she shook her head.

'I can't take that risk, Lex. I don't dare.'

She drew a breath, let it out shakily. 'Freya and I will go back to my flat tomorrow,' she said. 'Jo's back next week, so the maternity cover finishes then. I'm going to move down to Somerset straight away.'

'And what do we tell all those people who are now convinced that we're having a raging affair?'

'Tell them it didn't work out,' said Romy. 'For once, we won't have to pretend.'

CHAPTER TEN

'I THINK that's everything.' Lex set down the high chair and the changing mat. The hallway of Romy's tiny flat was crammed with bags and baby equipment.

It had been a long day. They had both gone to the signing ceremony, and had smiled and smiled for the inevitable photographs. Then they had said goodbye to Willie Grant, who told them to get in touch when they'd come to their senses. And after that there had been nothing to do but to collect up all Romy's stuff from the flat, and Lex had driven them home.

Except it didn't feel like home any more. The flat was cold and poky and dreary and Romy's throat was so tight she could hardly speak. Any moment now, she was going to have to say goodbye to Lex, and she didn't know how she was going to bear it.

He looked all wrong in this shabby flat.

Freya was sitting on the floor of the living room, puzzled by suddenly finding herself somewhere new. She looked around doubtfully as if not at all sure what she was doing there. Romy knew how she felt.

'Will I see you before you go?' Lex asked at last, and she drew a breath to steady herself.

'I think it's probably easier if we don't.'

His eyes shuttered. 'Perhaps you're right.'

The silence was excruciating.

'Well.' Romy lifted her hands and let them drop. 'I…er…I should probably give Freya her tea.'

'Yes. I'll go.'

Lex squatted down next to Freya and smoothed down the absurd quiff of hair. She looked up at him with those round, astounded eyes, her face dissolving into a smile, and the cold stone where Lex's heart had once been splintered into shards. 'Be good,' he said, and straightened before his voice could crack.

Romy was waiting by the door. Her dark eyes were shimmering with unshed tears.

'I don't know how to say goodbye,' she confessed.

'Then don't,' said Lex. He put his hands on her arms and wondered if this was the last time he would see her for another twelve years. 'I love you,' he said. 'I've always loved you.'

'And I love you.' Romy was desperately blinking back the tears, but it was a losing battle. 'I do,' she insisted as if he hadn't believed her. 'I just wish…'

She wished it were enough, but it wasn't.

'I know,' said Lex, and, because there wasn't any other way to say goodbye, he smoothed his hands up over her shoulders and up her throat to cradle her jaw. 'I just wish too,' he said, and kissed her.

Romy leant into him, slipping her arms around his waist to hold him close, and they kissed, a fierce, desperate kiss that said everything words couldn't.

This will be the last time, Romy thought, even as her senses spun. The last time I touch him. The last time he kisses me. The last time I feel as if I'm exactly where I'm meant to be.

Even as she tried to hold onto the sensation, Lex was giving her one last, longing kiss and dropping his hands. He stepped back and reached for the door. Opened it.

Romy was standing exactly where he had left her, her mouth pressed in a straight line to stop it shaking, and her eyes dark and dazed.

Unable to resist one last touch, Lex wiped a tear from her cheek with his thumb. 'Goodbye, Romy,' he said gently, and then he was gone.

The phone was ringing as Romy manoeuvred the pushchair into the narrow cottage hall and shut the door behind her. Keys still clenched between her teeth, she ran into the kitchen to grab the cordless phone, only just remembering to spit out the keys in time.

'Hello?' she said breathlessly.

'Romy? It's Mum. I'm afraid I've got some sad news.'

Gerald Gibson was dead. 'Another stroke,' Molly told Romy. 'A merciful release in some ways, but of course Faith is devastated. He wasn't an easy man, but she adored him and she feels so alone now. She's got Lex and Phin, I know, but it's not the same. She and Gerald loved each other so much, I often thought those boys missed out.'

The funeral was to be the following Friday. 'You should be there for Faith,' her mother said. 'She's your godmother. And Phin was always a good friend to you, wasn't he?'

And Lex, Romy wanted to cry. Lex mattered most of all.

She had been in Somerset for seven weeks, and everything had fallen into place as if it were meant to be. She had found a little cottage in the same village as Jenny. It was a bit like living in a doll's house, with tiny rooms and a handkerchief garden, but it was enough for Freya. If Romy sometimes felt as if she couldn't breathe, and thought longingly of Lex's spacious apartment, well, that was a price of independence and she was happy to pay it.

Michael lived nearby, but not too close, and he and Kate had taken Freya for the afternoon a few times now. She hadn't spent the night with them yet, but Romy had no doubt that would come. Michael was making the effort to get to know his daughter, and that could only be a good thing. He had offered Romy financial support, but she had suggested that he invest the money for Freya instead. A relationship between Freya and her father was one thing. Accepting money was quite another. Money would be a tie. Romy wasn't ready for that.

She had found a job. Only part-time for now, but it was a start. People in the village were friendly. They could live cheaply. She ought to be happy, Romy reminded herself. She had everything she needed.

Except Lex.

Time and again, Romy assured herself that she had made the right decision. She and Freya couldn't have stayed in the apartment. They would have driven Lex mad. Much better to have made the break now, before either of them had a chance to be hurt.

It didn't feel better though. There was a dull ache inside her, all the time, like a weight pressing on her heart, and misery clogged her throat so that speaking was an effort and even swallowing hurt.

In spite of the claustrophobically cluttered rooms in the cottage, it felt as if something was missing, and it took Romy a little time to accept that she was constantly looking round, hoping to see Lex. She wanted to see him peering over the top of his reading glasses or tugging at the knot of his tie. She wanted to see the stern mouth relaxing into a smile as he picked up Freya, or holding the tiny hands between his large ones as he helped her to play the piano.

Always in the past Romy had been able to move on without a backward glance, but this time it was different. She missed London more than she thought she would. She had always liked wild, exotic places, but now she missed the buzz of work and the banter with her colleagues. She missed standing at Lex's window and looking down at the great city spread out below.

She missed Lex most of all.

Freya missed him, too, Romy was sure. She couldn't say so, but she was lacklustre and fretful. Romy knew exactly how she felt. For the first time in her life, she was lonely. Oh, Freya was there, and she could always pop round to see Jenny, but it wasn't the same as living with Lex. There was no one to tell when Freya learnt another word, no one to laugh when she put her pants on her head. No one to say hello to in the morning. No one to make her heart leap at the sound of the key in the door.

She wanted to tell him when Freya took her first step. She'd told her mother, she'd told Jenny, she'd even told Michael, but the person she really wanted to tell was Lex. She even picked up the phone and got as far as dialling his mobile before she cut the connection.

What was the point of calling him?

She would hear his voice and he would hear hers, but wouldn't that just make it worse? And after Lex had said, 'Great news,' or whatever you said when a baby took their first step, what then? What would there be left to talk about? She and Lex couldn't be friends—they were too close for that— but they couldn't be lovers either. She should leave him to get on with his life, and get on with her own.

But now the father Lex had tried so hard to please was

dead, and Romy wished desperately that she could have been there for him when he needed her.

Except Lex hadn't wanted her there, she reminded herself. If he had, he would have phoned and told her himself, instead of letting her hear it from her mother. Perhaps, like her, he had decided that in the end it would just make it harder. So Romy didn't ring him either, but wrote a short note that said everything that was proper about his father and nothing at all about what she really wanted to say.

That Friday she left Freya with Michael, and made her way to Gloucestershire. The funeral was to be held in the village where Lex's parents had lived for forty years. A car was beyond Romy's budget, so it was a complicated journey involving buses, trains and taxis, and she only just made it to the church in time for the service.

Her mother, so long a friend to Faith Gibson, was sitting behind the family. Romy slipped into the end of the pew, exchanging a glance of apology for her lateness with her mother.

In front of her, Faith sat between her two sons. Summer was there, too, sitting next to Phin. They were a family, and yet Lex looked alone. He was staring straight ahead. Something about the rigid set of his shoulders, the careful way he held his head, twisted Romy's heart. He was suffering, and there was nothing she could do to help.

The organ struck up, and the priest was moving to address the congregation. Romy saw Lex brace himself, and without giving herself time to think she got up and slid into the pew in front. He shouldn't have to be on his own, not today.

She caught Lex unawares. The vicar had already begun the service, so there was no chance to talk, but Romy saw the startled look in his eyes change to a fierce gladness, and when she took his hand his fingers closed around hers hard. He didn't say anything and he didn't look at her again, but he held her hand tightly all through the service, only letting her go when he got up to give the eulogy.

After the service, Romy stepped back, still without a word, and let Lex take his mother to the graveside, while her own mother eyed her speculatively.

'Is there something I should know?' she asked after the burial was over and they were walking slowly to the Gibsons' house behind the family. It was an inappropriately beautiful day, and the village was so small no one had thought to get in a car to drive the short distance from the church to the house.

Romy flushed under her mother's scrutiny. She had acted on impulse, and she was glad that she had, but to her mother it must have looked odd the way she had pushed into the family pew.

'I didn't want Lex to be on his own.'

Incredibly, neither her mother nor Faith Gibson seemed to have heard anything about the time she and Freya had spent with Lex. Summer had certainly known that they were living together, which meant that Phin must have known too, but evidently he hadn't passed the news on around the family. Romy wondered whether this was tact on his part, or if Lex had asked him not to say anything.

As far as Romy's mother knew, Lex was no more than a family friend to Romy. Someone you bumped into at weddings and funerals like this. She knew nothing about that crazy week in Paris all those years ago. She had no idea that Lex knew Freya or that he made her daughter's heart turn over just by walking into the room.

But Romy had had enough pretending, she realised. 'I'm in love with Lex,' she told her mother abruptly, and it was a huge relief just to say the words.

Molly's eyes rounded and for a moment she looked exactly like Freya. 'With *Lex*? But how…? When…?' She shook her head to clear it. 'Why didn't you tell me?' And then, unable to help herself, 'Does Faith know?'

'I don't think so.'

'But, darling, this is wonderful news!' In deference to the other mourners, Molly kept her voice down, but she couldn't resist giving Romy a hug. 'Why the big secret? And why move to Somerset? I thought you wanted to get back together with Freya's father!'

'No.' Romy's steps slowed. She was remembering all the reasons why going to Somerset had seemed such a good idea. Was *still* a sensible idea. 'I just wanted to get away from Lex. I don't want to love him, Mum. You know what Lex is like. We're too different. Anyway,' she said, 'we agreed it wouldn't work.'

'Ah.' Her mother's gaze rested thoughtfully on Romy's face. 'Does Lex love you?'

'I think he loves me, yes.' Romy sighed. 'That isn't the problem,' she said, just as she had to Willie Grant. 'What if love isn't enough? What if it doesn't last? You and Dad loved each other, and look what happened to you!'

'Oh, Romy,' said her mother a little helplessly. 'Yes, I loved your father, but it wasn't all perfect. It takes two to make a marriage, and two to let a relationship break down. I know how much it hurt you when he left, but I'm not sure it would have been better for you if he'd stayed. Would you really have wanted to have grown up in a home where the adults resent each other, knowing that you were the only reason they stayed together? I don't think so.'

Romy stopped at that and stared at her mother. 'Are you saying you think it was a good thing that he left us?'

'No, never that. Not knowing what it did to you. But it

wasn't actually the end of the world, was it?' Molly took her daughter's arm and made her keep walking. 'I was very unhappy for a time, but then I met Keith, and I'm happier being married to him than I ever was with your father. I don't have any regrets about marrying Tony, though. We had you, didn't we? How could either of us regret that? And now I can remember the good times.'

She smiled at her daughter. 'There are no guarantees when it comes to love, Romy. Maybe it won't work out with Lex, but maybe it will, and if you never take the risk, you'll never know how happy you could be.'

Lex's jaw felt rigid but he kept a smile in place as he went to greet his godmother. He had always been fond of Molly, who had luminous dark eyes just like her daughter's, but he had been avoiding her, just as he had been avoiding thinking about Romy, who stood now by her mother's side.

He had been feeling so alone in the church, and then suddenly Romy had been there. The feel of her hand in his had been so comforting that Lex had almost convinced himself that he had made it up. His mother had been too bound up in her own grief to notice anything, and Romy had slipped away when they followed the coffin out to the grave-side. It was almost as if she had never been there at all.

But he had seen her as soon as she came into the house with Molly, and he had spent the afternoon torn between joy at her presence and despair that he was going to have to get used to her not being there all over again. He hadn't talked to her. He didn't know what he would say. The only thing he could think of to say was, 'Come back, I miss you,' but what was the point? Romy had made her choice, and he had to live with it. Better not to say anything at all.

So Lex moved through the afternoon like an automaton, talking to guests, agreeing that they would all miss his father, not letting himself think. Especially not letting himself notice Romy, slender and vibrant in the dark suit she had used to wear to work. Today she had substituted a dark purple top for her usual brightly coloured blouses, but she still looked more vivid than anyone else in the room.

She was a flame, constantly catching at the edge of his vision. It didn't matter that she was only talking quietly to other guests. She spoke to his mother, to Phin and Summer. She did nothing to draw attention to herself at all, but Lex was intensely aware of her all the same. She might as well have been the only other person in the room.

Now Lex kissed Molly's cheek, and let himself look properly at Romy at last. She looked gravely back at him, her eyes dark and warm, and as his gaze met hers there was such a rightness to it, as if everything were suddenly falling into place, that Lex was sure that everyone in the room must surely hear the click of connection.

His jaw was clenched so tightly he could feel the tendons standing out in his neck. 'Thank you for coming,' he said.

There, he hadn't seized her in his arms. He hadn't humiliated himself by begging her to come home. It wasn't much of a victory, but Lex felt as if he had negotiated a long and arduous obstacle course.

'Faith looks all in,' said Molly, apparently not noticing the way her daughter and Lex were staring desperately at each other.

With difficulty, he dragged his eyes from Romy's. 'Yes. Yes, she is. Phin and Summer are going to take her home with them.'

'And you?'

'I'm going back to London too.'

'On your own?'

'Yes,' said Lex, unable to keep the bleakness from his voice. 'On my own.'

There was a pause. 'I think I'll go and say goodbye to Faith,' said Molly.

Lex was left alone with Romy. The moment he had longed for. The moment he had dreaded.

Romy drew a breath. 'Can I come with you?' she said.

'Where?'

'To London.'

The dark eyes were drawing him in. Lex could feel himself slipping. Any moment now and he would be falling again, tumbling wildly out of control once more. He made himself look away.

'I think I need to be on my own,' he said.

Romy put her hand on his arm. 'No, you need someone with you,' she told him gently.

'Romy, I can't...' Lex broke off, groped for control. 'I can't say goodbye again.'

'We're not going to say goodbye.'

Mutely, he shook his head, and Romy shattered what was left of his defences by stepping closer so that his senses reeled with her nearness, with the warmth of her hand, the piercing familiarity of her fragrance.

'Lex, you buried your father today,' she said. 'I know you've been strong for your mother, but you need to grieve for yourself. Now let me be strong for you. Let me drive you. You don't have to do everything on your own.'

The longing to be with her, to put off the moment when he had to watch her leave, was too much. Strong? He had never been strong where she was concerned. Lex did his best to resist the temptation, but then handed over his car keys. It felt deeply symbolic. He wanted to say, 'Be careful, that's my heart I'm giving you there.'

He didn't, of course, but Romy smiled reassuringly at him anyway. 'Don't worry,' she said. 'I'm a careful driver.'

Lex was used to being driven. He often sat in the back of limousines, but this was different. He was sitting in the passenger seat of his own car, and Romy was at the wheel, and he was very aware of having ceded control. It felt dangerous. And it felt like letting go.

Letting go of responsibility.

Letting go of the pretence that he could be happy without Romy.

Letting the jumble of feelings overwhelm him. Guilt and grief and resentment for his father. Love and loneliness and joy and despair and desire and everything else that Romy made him feel, everything he had been trying not to feel for so long.

Tears were unmanly. Gerald Gibson had taught his son that long ago, and Lex hadn't cried since he was a very small boy. He didn't cry now, but inside he could feel himself crumbling. He stared straight ahead, his face set like stone, his mouth pressed into a rigid line, and his throat too tight to speak.

To his intense relief, Romy didn't try to make conversation. She just drove him back to the apartment, unlocked the door with the key he handed over without a word, and poured him a great slug of the whisky he had bought for Willie Grant a lifetime ago, all without a word.

Lex sat on the sofa, head bent, the glass clasped between his knees. He swirled the whisky, letting the warm, peaty smell of it calm him before he drank, and its mellowness settled steadyingly in his stomach.

Romy sat quietly beside him, her hand on his back infinitely comforting.

'He never said well done.' The words burst out of him without warning. 'Not once. But do you know what he did? He left me a controlling share in Gibson & Grieve. I had to listen to some lawyer tell me that my father thought I'd done well. That I'd shown I was worthy. He said he was confident that he was leaving the company in capable hands,' said Lex bitterly.

Romy's throat ached for him. 'He was proud of you.'

'It's too late for him to tell me *now*! Why couldn't he…?' He broke off, too angry and frustrated to speak.

'Why couldn't he tell you?' she finished for him. 'Perhaps he was afraid to, Lex. Perhaps, deep down, he was afraid that if he gave you the approval you craved, you wouldn't need him any more.'

She rubbed his back, very gently. 'I think you and I need to forgive our fathers,' she said. 'I certainly need to forgive mine. I loved him so much, but I wanted him to be somebody he couldn't be. I didn't understand that he was just a man, wrestling with his own fears.'

Lex said nothing, but she knew he was listening. 'And your father,' she went on, 'he didn't know how to be a man who could admit weakness. I think he didn't know how to tell you how important you were to him, but that doesn't mean he didn't love you. He just couldn't say it. But he did the best he could, and maybe my father did the best he could, too.'

Lex took a slug of whisky, felt it burn down his throat. 'I thought you would never forgive your father.'

'I thought so, too. It was only when I talked to my mother today, and she made me think. And watching you bury your father, I was imagining how I would feel if it was my father who had died.' Romy swallowed. 'He's the only father I've got. Perhaps I should just accept him for what he is.'

'He hurt you.' Lex looked up at her, pale eyes fierce. 'He left you.'

'He left my mother, not me,' said Romy. 'I think the truth is that *I* left *him* when I refused to see him. I thought that he had chosen his other child over me, but now I think that he chose happiness over duty. Perhaps I need to learn from that. Perhaps we both do.'

'Learn? Learn what?'

'We could learn to be happy,' she said.

'Happy?' Lex stared into his glass and thought of the long, lonely weeks since she'd been gone. The wasteland he had trudged through every day. He thought of the years he had spent trying to forget her, the years he would have to spend forgetting her all over again. '*Happy?* Hah!'

'I thought I could make myself happy,' said Romy as if he hadn't spoken. 'I was afraid to rely on anyone else for happiness. I thought all I needed was to be able to provide for Freya and keep her from being hurt, and I can do that now, but I'm not happy.' She took her hand from his back. 'I can't be happy without you, Lex.'

He did look up at that, his eyes narrowed in sudden attention.

'I don't know if this is the time for it,' she said, 'but there's something I want to ask you.'

'What is it?'

'Will you marry me?'

Lex straightened abruptly, sloshing whisky. '*What?*'

Romy's heart was knocking against her ribs but she made herself look levelly back at him. 'Will you marry me?' she said again. 'I'll understand if you say no,' she said, when he just stared at her. 'I probably deserve it. I had a chance to marry you and I turned it down. We could have had the last twelve years together, but I was too afraid that it would all go wrong.'

Lex put his glass on the table, very carefully, and turned to look at Romy. She was twisting the bangles around her wrist, her eyes huge and dark. 'What's changed? Why aren't you afraid now?'

'I *am* afraid,' she said. 'But I'm more afraid of spending the rest of my life regretting that I was too much of a coward to take a chance at happiness. I'm afraid of spending the rest of my life missing you, the way I've missed you the last few weeks. I'm afraid of never really being happy again without you.'

'Romy…'

'I'm afraid that it might not work,' she said again, 'but I want to take the risk, if you will.'

Lex was looking stunned and Romy took her bottom lip between her teeth, all at once regretting the words that had come tumbling out of her. 'I'm sorry,' she said remorsefully. 'I shouldn't be talking like this, not today. Today should be about your father, not about me. Oh, Lex, I'm sorry,' she said again. 'What was I thinking?'

'Perhaps,' Lex said slowly, 'you were thinking that this is exactly the day we should be talking like this. Perhaps it takes death to make us realise how we want to live.'

Might it be all right after all? Romy took a breath and let it out very carefully. 'I don't want to live without ever seeing my father again,' she said. 'But most of all, I don't want to live without you, Lex.'

'Romy,' he said again, laying a hand against her cheek. 'Romy, what if I can't make you happy? You're so…*alive*. You need warmth and laughter and love.'

'You love me, don't you?'

He half smiled. 'Yes, I love you. I've never stopped loving you,' he said, unable to stop his fingers slipping under her hair to the nape of her neck. 'Loving you isn't the problem. You were the one who said that. But love wasn't enough before. We're still different people. I'd like to think I can change to be more like you, but what if I can only be like my father?'

'You're not your father,' said Romy, ' and you're not my father either. You're you, and I love you the way you are. You don't have to change. You just have to be brave enough to love me and believe that I love you too, just as I need to be brave enough to trust that you won't leave me and Freya. Love *isn't* enough,' she said. 'We need courage, too, just like Willie said.'

Lex's hand was warm at the nape of her neck. 'Then we'll be brave together,' he said and drew her towards him.

It was a gentle kiss at first, like a first kiss, as if he couldn't quite believe that she was *there*, that she was real. Then it was tender and it was sweet, and the world shifted and righted itself at last.

They kissed and kissed in a torrent of relief, sinking down into the soft cushions until the sweetness grew hard and hungry, but when they broke for breath the world was still right. This, *this*, was right. Romy was lying tucked into him, her arms round him, her face pressed into his throat. Lex could feel her lovely mouth curved into a smile against his skin and the tight band that had been clamped around his chest for so long unlocked and loosened.

He tried breathing in and out experimentally, and the ease of it made his head reel. Wrapping his arms around Romy, he held her close.

'Romy, are you sure?'

'I'm sure,' she said, tilting her head back to kiss his jaw. 'Are you?'

'What about all those practicalities that were such a problem before?'

She wriggled up so that she could look at him properly. 'I

suppose we could always take Willie's advice and compromise. Maybe you could learn to live in a less than perfectly ordered flat, and maybe I could learn to tidy up more. I don't think it would be easy, but we could both try.'

'This flat isn't suitable for Freya anyway,' said Lex. 'Why don't we buy a house in Somerset?'

'Somerset's not very convenient for the office,' she pointed out.

'Then we'll have a house in London as well.'

'But you like this flat! It's perfect for you.'

'It wasn't perfect when you left. I hated it without you,' he said. 'I missed you both so much. Every night I'd sit here with the phone in my hand and think about calling you and begging you to come back.'

Romy pulled away slightly, wondering what she would have done if he had called. 'But you never rang?'

'I thought you'd say no. I thought you wanted Freya to get to know her father, and I thought that was the right thing to do. Michael's her father, not me.' Lex hesitated. 'You said it, Romy. You said your father was the only one you'd ever have.'

'But that was me,' she said. 'There was no one else for me. Being a parent is about more than biology,' she told him. 'I hope Michael will always be part of her life, and if he is Freya is going to be lucky. She'll have two fathers, and I hope she'll love you both, but you're the one who's going to teach her to play the piano and comfort her at night when she's teething…oh, and change her nappies, of course!'

Lex laughed at that. 'When you said I had to be brave, I didn't think you meant *that* brave!'

'Losing your nerve?' she asked, smiling, and he pulled her against him for a hard kiss.

'No, I don't mind what I do, as long as I'm with you. I'll even change nappies!'

'Now I know you love me,' said Romy, kissing him back.

'Always,' said Lex.

Pushing herself up so that she could lean over him, Romy rested her hand over his heart. 'You haven't given me an answer yet,' she reminded him. 'I asked you to marry me. Will you?' Stupidly, she could hear a hint of anxiety in her voice.

Lex didn't answer immediately. 'Are you sure you want to be married, Romy?' he asked seriously. 'I know the idea of commitment isn't easy for you. We can be together without marriage if that's more comfortable for you.'

'But that wouldn't be brave,' said Romy. 'I don't want to keep my options open or to know that I move on if I need to. Lex. I want to spend the rest of my life loving you and trusting you and knowing that every day you'll come home and love me back. Marriage is a promise. I want to make that promise in front of everybody, and I want to keep it, with you.'

Lex picked up the hand that covered his heart and kissed her palm before he drew her down to him once more. 'Then since you ask so nicely,' he said, 'yes, I will.'

* * * * *

ADOPTED: FAMILY
IN A MILLION

BY
BARBARA McMAHON

Barbara McMahon was born and raised in the South USA, but settled in California after spending a year flying around the world for an international airline. After settling down to raise a family and work for a computer firm, she began writing when her children started school. Now, feeling fortunate in being able to realise a long-held dream of quitting her 'day job' and writing full-time, she and her husband have moved to the Sierra Nevada mountains of California, where she finds her desire to write is stronger than ever. With the beauty of the mountains visible from her windows, and the pace of life slower than the hectic San Francisco Bay Area where they previously resided, she finds more time than ever to think up stories and characters and share them with others through writing. Barbara loves to hear from readers. You can reach her at PO Box 977, Pioneer, CA 95666-0977, USA. Readers can also contact Barbara at her website: www.barbaramcmahon.com.

To my dear friend Carolyn Samuels.

Here's to fun in the sun
and happy memories of days gone by.

PROLOGUE

November

"I HAVE a son." Zack said the words aloud. The reality wasn't there. The pain was. He tried to focus on the revelation in the letter and ignore the injuries that had landed him in the hospital with months of healing and physical therapy ahead before he was fit again. Shifting slightly, he reread the letter.

The letter was dated three months ago. Why had it taken so long to reach him? Being on a remote building site in the middle of a Middle Eastern desert probably had a lot to do with it.

Did it matter? What if it had arrived shortly after it had been posted, he would have still been in shock. Would it have changed anything? Would he have been on the phone asking questions instead of being in the vicinity of that land mine?

"I have a son and his name is Daniel," he repeated softly.

"Did you say something?" A nurse poked her head into the room. "Everything okay? Need more painkiller?"

"I'm okay," he said, impatient with the interruption. He wanted to read the letter again. Try to understand.

He couldn't take it in. Alesia Blair had been his steady girl-friend the last time he had been Stateside on leave. They'd had a great few months together, until he had accepted another overseas assignment. There had been no great love between them, but he had enjoyed taking her places where others had admired her beauty. To think of her as dead was hard. She'd relished life.

But she'd never contacted him after he had left. Not even to tell him about their son.

He was grateful to her sister, Brittany, however, for letting him know, however delinquent the notice. She explained she had been against her sister's decision to keep quiet about the baby. A child should know his father. She'd wrestled with the situation after Alesia's death and finally decided to write to him, telling him what she knew. He'd railed against fate for Alesia's silence. How could she not have told him five years ago she was carrying his child?

At least he had the opportunity and means to locate the boy, his only living relative. That thought was amazing. He'd accepted years ago that he'd probably spend his life alone. He had friends, but no one close. His formative years had been in a series of foster homes. Moving from place to place had taught him not to form attachments. Nothing lasted beyond the next move. His job did nothing to change that as an adult. He was a nomad, no home, no family.

Zack had no idea when he had left the United States almost five years ago that Alesia had been pregnant. They had used precautions. She had never contacted him. At first he thought she might. But his job assignment had been for two years. Alesia had been a fun-loving, party girl. Two years waiting for a man was not her style. Yet the pregnancy would have changed all that.

She should have told him. Why hadn't she?

Her sister's letter also informed him of Alesia's death. For that he was truly sorry. She had been pretty and vivacious and fun. Which was probably the reason she'd given their son up for adoption. A baby would have definitely cramped her style.

But I could have taken him. The thought came out of nowhere. Zack didn't know the first thing about children. He was thirty-four years old and had never seriously thought about getting married or having a family.

His job was not exactly conducive to a happy family— gone two years at a time to inhospitable locales where they fought to bring modern roads and bridges and dams to countries that had progressed little from the beginning of time.

Lying back on the pillows, he tried to imagine his son. The boy would be four now. Zack couldn't remember back to when he had been four. He had already been placed in his first foster home by that age. There had been other children there, but his memories were hazy. What was a four-year-old like?

That led to wondering what the family who had adopted his son was like. Did they think his father had abandoned him? Did they know Zack had not even known of his son's existence until he'd received this letter a few hours ago?

He had an overwhelming urge to find his son. See him. Make sure he was happy and well cared for. Even in the foster care system, bad things happened to children. Did adopted families have regular visits from Social Services to make sure the child was being properly looked after? Was Daniel happy and secure in the family that was raising him?

Zack was scheduled to be sent back to the States next week—if he continued to improve. The surgeries had drained him of all energy. He was fighting to recover. But it would be several months before he could return to work. Just maybe he'd have time to find his son to make sure he was all right. To see what he and Alesia had produced.

Did Daniel have dark hair like his, or was it lighter like Alesia's blond hair? Was he fearful or brave? Adoptions were usually confidential. Did he really have any hope in the world of finding the child he'd fathered?

He picked up the paper and pen the nurse had provided. The least he could do was thank Brittany for letting him know. It had been the right thing to do. And just maybe, it had given him even more reason for getting fit again as soon as possible. He had a son to find.

April

"Here's the final report." Ben Abercrombie slid the folder across the desk. "I know it took longer than originally anticipated, but you know adoption records are hard to access. Here's what I found out. Your son was adopted by T. J. and Susan Johnson of New York City. I've located Mrs. Johnson, the husband has since died. Killed by a drunk driver two years ago."

Zack Morgan reached out for the folder and flipped it open. The first thing he saw was a picture of a small child. It was not a close up, but he could tell the boy had dark hair. He looked so little. Was he small for his age? Zack had no idea how big four-year-olds should be.

Ben frowned as he glanced at the paperwork. "So how did you want this handled? Just show up one day and ask to meet your son?"

Zack shook his head. "Despite what you may think, I have some feelings for the child and the situation. The last thing I would do is give any reason to rock his security." He thought briefly of the different families he'd lived with. He never knew how long he'd stay. He couldn't imagine deliberately causing that kind of panic and uncertainty to anyone, much less a little boy.

"I just want to know he's okay. That he's loved and the family life he has is good."

The detective leaned back in his chair, steepling his hands. "Mother appears to be doing the best she can. It was a comedown from the lifestyle they enjoyed when the husband was alive. He was an attorney and made a good income. Since his death, they've moved to a less affluent neighborhood. She's gone back to work. Still, from what I could see, the mother takes good care of the child and he seems happy enough. Quiet, not as boisterous as other little kids I've seen. But, hey, everyone has a different personality."

"But he's got a good mother, right?" Zack couldn't remember his own mother. The best foster mom had been Allie Zumwalt. He hoped Daniel had a mother as sweet as Allie.

Ben nodded. "Doing the best she can."

"What do you mean by that?" Zack asked quickly.

"She has to work, leaves the child with an older woman in their building. The apartment building is old, a bit run-down. The neighborhood's not the best place to be after dark."

"Should they move?"

"Takes money to live where they did before. New York's not a cheap city."

The one thing Zack had was money. He spent little, had amassed a small fortune working overseas with the extra hardship pay. Judicial investments had the money growing steadily. The detective had delivered, and the cost had been nothing Zack wouldn't have paid three times over or more to find out about his son.

He looked at the photograph again. Would he recognize the child if he tripped over him in a crowd somewhere? Shouldn't there be some kind of tie between biological parents and children? Some sort of instant connection? To Zack, there was nothing but wonder that he could have fathered this little boy.

Railing silently against Alesia once again, he closed the folder and stood. "Thank you," he said, offering his hand.

"I'll be here if you want anything else," the detective said.

Zack carried the folder out with him. He was staying in a

small hotel near Central Park while he finished recuperating. He could walk without the limp as long as he didn't overdo it. His shoulder was still stiff. Maybe he needed to get back to work to loosen those muscles. But he was on medical leave and still doing his physical therapy routine each day.

When he reached his room, he settled down to read every word in the report the detective had compiled. Even if he never got to meet him, Zack knew he'd left a legacy to the future. Thinking about it, he could do more. On Monday, he'd make an appointment with an attorney to leave his estate to his son. They may never meet, but someday Daniel would know his father had cared about him.

CHAPTER ONE

SUSAN JOHNSON was frantic. She could scarcely think as she rushed down the crowded New York sidewalk, dodging pedestrians, searching for her son. How could one small boy disappear so quickly. Why wasn't someone looking for his mother? When she found him, she'd never let him out of her sight again!

Of course that was impossible, but she was so scared she couldn't think straight. Where was Danny?

"Please, God, let me find my baby," she prayed as she searched the crowded sidewalk in front of her.

"Do you think he'd try to cross the street alone?" the teacher's aide next to her asked, already puffing slightly from the fast pace Susan set.

"No. I don't know. If he thought he saw his father across the street he might, though I'm always careful to make sure we stop and look both ways even when the light is green. But he's only four." And always after tall dark haired men thinking they were his daddy. Ever since Tom had died, Danny had been searching. Children his age didn't understand death, she'd been told.

How could the preschool have let him get away? The play yard was fenced and the front gate should have either been latched so a little child couldn't open it, or monitored by an adult. Had the teacher turned her back? For how long? Where was Danny?

Were they going in the wrong direction? Had he turned right when exiting the preschool? Or left? She'd opted for left because it was in the direction of their apartment. Familiar territory to a little boy. But what if he'd gone the other way? If he'd darted out to follow some stranger, he wouldn't have cared for direction—only his goal to find his father. She could be increasing the distance between them, not closing it. Panic closed her throat. Fear seized her heart. Her precious son was out on the streets of New York and could get into who knew what kind of trouble.

Susan stopped and looked ahead, then behind her. Indecision. Seconds were ticking by. Where was her child? Fear increased. New York was a dangerous city. And her son was adorable. What if someone snatched him up? What if she never saw him again?

She moaned softly at the thought.

Her child was missing. Was there anything worse for a parent to face?

"What?" the aide asked.

"I'm thinking he could have gone the other way. Tell me again how long ago it was until you noticed he was missing?" Susan had been given all that information when she had arrived at the preschool. But she'd scarcely listened, dashing out to try to find her son.

"Less than five minutes before you showed up. Mrs. Savalack was busy with the little boy who had a bloody nose. She didn't know Danny would leave before you arrived. She went the other direction as soon as one of the other teachers came to watch her children. She'll find him if he went that way."

"Maybe," Susan said, her eyes searching. She didn't see a child anywhere.

Glancing around, she noticed a man walking slowly along the street. He looked out of place in the midday crowd—ambling along when everyone else was walking briskly, with places to go. Tall, with dark hair and a deep tan, he looked competent and reliable. His casual attire blended in with the men and women on the sidewalk at the lunch hour, but were of higher quality than the cheaper clothing more common in this neighborhood. What a stupid thing to notice, she thought as she approached him.

"Excuse me. Have you seen a little boy? He's four and should not be out on his own. We don't know if he came this way, but we need to find him!"

He shook his head. "I haven't seen any kids. Wouldn't they be in school at this time of day?"

"He's in a preschool and wandered away." Susan bit her lip, her heart pounded, fear increasing with every heartbeat. "Maybe I'm going the wrong way."

"Which way is that?" he asked, glancing at the aide and then scanning the sidewalk behind him.

"No one saw him leave, so we didn't know if he came this way or went the other way. The preschool is back there." She pointed to a small building at the end of the block. "I just hope he didn't try to cross the street." The traffic was lighter than midtown, but still heavy. A small boy might be overlooked by a motorist in a hurry—until it was too late.

"Someone would have stopped a small boy from dashing into danger," the man said. He glanced at the aide. "Is someone looking in the other direction?"

"Yes, the teacher." She glanced back up the street. "I don't see her, so I guess she hasn't found Danny."

"Danny?" the man asked, his voice odd.

Susan looked at him, her eyes holding appeal. "My son, Danny. He's missing. I've got to find him. Oh Lord, I can't lose him, too!"

"I'll help look. Name's Zack Morgan. Where did you lose him?"

"I didn't lose him. He left his preschool without an adult. I can't believe he's run off like this. New York is so dangerous for a little child if someone isn't right there with him every minute."

"I'm sure he'll be fine, Mrs. Johnson," the aide said, her worried expression belying her words.

"We'll find him," Zack said.

"Unless someone's taken him," Susan said, voicing her worst fear. What if someone had kidnapped her son? She swayed with horror at the thought. Zack reached out and took her arm gently, seeming to give her strength.

"No one's taken him in this direction. I've been on this street for several blocks. No little boy. And I'm sure no one would let him cross the street by himself, so let's try the other direction." His reasonable tone calmed her.

"Okay." For a split second she felt as if the burden had lifted slightly and been placed on the broad shoulders of the stranger who held her arm.

She swallowed and turned, wanting to race the wind to find her son. He was so precious to her. He could not have been taken. He was just searching for Tom.

Less than five minutes later they saw Mrs. Savalack heading toward them, Danny's hand firmly held in hers.

Susan burst into tears and raced to her son. "Danny, you scared me to death." She swooped him up in her arms, hugging him tightly, her heart still pounding. "Don't ever run off like that again."

He struggled a bit with Susan's tight hold, and she set him on his feet, taking his hand firmly in hers. "You know you are not to leave the school until I get there."

"I thought I saw Daddy." He looked sad. "But it wasn't him."

Susan reached out and brought Danny's face round to face hers. "Your daddy died. He's gone to heaven. You will not find him on this earth. Honey, he loved you, but he's gone."

"No! I want my daddy!" Danny stuck his lower lip out and glared at his mother.

The stranger stooped down until he was Danny's level.

"Hi," he said.

Danny looked at him warily, pout still in evidence.

"You should mind your mother," Zack said gently. "She was scared you'd get hurt or lost." He reached out and brushed Danny's dark hair off his forehead.

"I thought I saw my daddy," Danny repeated.

Susan wiped the tears from her cheeks and tried to smile at Zack. "He's got this fixation in his head that my husband is just gone out. Every time he sees a man who looks the slightest bit like Tom, he's running after him. He hasn't done this in a long while and I'd hoped he'd stopped by now. Thanks for your help. I'm Susan Johnson. This is my son, Danny. I appreciate your concern."

Zack rose and nodded. "You two take care now."

He turned and walked away, when every cell in his body screamed to stay. He'd actually touched his son. Met his adopted mother. Been scared for a few moments that Susan Johnson's fear would turn into reality.

It had been a quirky idea to wander by the preschool the detective had listed in his report. Zack had had no idea whether the playground could be seen from the street. Or if he'd recognize his son among a few dozen playing children. Fate had stepped in and he had actually spoken to his son.

He had thought that seeing Daniel from a distance would suffice. Now that he'd actually met him, he wanted to know even more about him. He was adorable. His eyes were brown and his hair a darker brown. He seemed small, but so did the other children Zack glimpsed in the playground. Daniel obviously missed his father. The report said Tom Johnson had died two years ago, which meant Danny had been grieving for two years. A long time for a child. Wasn't he happy with his mother?

Wanting to think about the encounter, Zack walked a few more blocks until he found a coffee house. Ordering a hot drink, he sat at a table near the window and gazed outside, his thoughts back with the boy he'd just met. And his mother.

There had been no photo of Susan in the report. She looked younger than he expected. And tired. She was thin like Alesia had been. But where Alesia had always worn trendy, stylish clothing, Susan's looked plain and serviceable. Her hair had been pulled back and she wore a minimum of makeup. The appeal in her eyes when she asked if he'd seen her son had touched him. He could tell she loved the boy.

For some reason, Zack felt a need to do something for her as well. It couldn't be easy raising a child alone. She had no relatives close by. According to the detective, her parents lived in Florida. Her mother worked in a travel agency and her father was in frail health. The warmer climate was a necessity for his well-being in winter months.

Her dead husband had been the only child of an older couple. His mother had moved west to be with her sister when her husband had died before Tom and Susan were married. She now resided in an assisted care home in California.

There had been little insurance money; the man had been younger than Zack was now when he had died. They must have thought they had their entire future together. Neither had known two years after adopting Danny that Tom Johnson would be dead.

Would they still have gone through with the adoption?

Zack felt funny knowing so much about Susan Johnson and

her family history. She didn't know him at all except as a stranger stopping to help for a few minutes. Yet he wanted to know about her, to assure himself his son was getting the best of everything. And with the dearth of money in her life, was that possible?

Maybe he could set up a blind trust to make sure they had enough money. Would Susan accept? The character sketch the detective had done indicated she probably would not. She seemed big on independence. She hadn't applied for any aid. She'd quickly moved from the apartment she and her husband shared in Manhattan to one more affordable in Brooklyn. Even returned to work when she'd obviously planned to stay home with Danny if the first two years of his life were any indication.

He sipped his coffee and wondered what he could do. Maybe the best thing would be to leave mother and son alone. Danny looked healthy. His clothes had been neat and clean. He obviously missed his father, but he was well cared for.

For a moment Zack wondered what it would be like to be a father to a child. He'd have to change his job, quit the nomadic life he'd enjoyed the last decade and put down roots. Get a job that would allow him to be home evenings, attend school events.

Would he grow bored? Long for faraway lands?

Slowly Zack smiled. Danny was a cute kid. His dark hair probably came from him. And his brown eyes. Did he look at all like Alesia? With soft baby cheeks, it was hard to tell. He wished he had some baby pictures of himself. Maybe he could see a resemblance to himself at that age.

He finished his coffee and rose. He'd walk by their apartment and then return to his hotel. It would be enough to know where they lived. Then he had to think about what he wanted to do for the rest of his medical leave. Walking had been strongly recommended, as had light exercise in addition to the P.T. he was doing. He had an entire schedule for the next couple of months tacked to the mirror in the bathroom. By then he should be ready to return to the Middle East and work.

He needed to decide on what to do about the future, but there was no rush. He had time.

Danny jumped up and down, his face shining with excitement. "Let's go, Mommy. Let's go!"

"In a minute, sweetie. I need to get some bottled water and a snack for us. You know you always get hungry at the park." Susan smiled at her son as she headed to the kitchen to gather what she needed. Yesterday's scare had faded to the background, but hadn't totally disappeared. She sometimes didn't know if she was going to make it as a single mother. Danny was a handful. Somehow she had to get him over chasing after strangers thinking they were Tom.

Yesterday's trauma had been a strain but everything was fine—for now. Danny loved going to the park. Actually he loved going anywhere—to the store, preschool, visiting Mrs. Jordan, her neighbor who watched Danny when Susan had to work.

Susan put some dried fruit and two water bottles in the small backpack, checked to make sure the sunscreen was there and the wet-wipes. Picking up her dark glasses, she was ready. This spring had proved balmy and warm for New York City. She took advantage of the nearby park every chance she got. The grassy area gave plenty of running room for Danny and the playground section provided slides and swings and other equipment that he loved. It was a great way for him to burn off some of that energy he had.

Their apartment was tiny. It was all she could afford with her salary and the expense of preschool and Edith's pay. The neighborhood wasn't the best, but it was the best she could afford and be close enough to work that she didn't spend hours commuting. She'd rather spend the time with Danny.

Passing through the crowded living room she glanced at Tom's picture out of habit. She still missed him with an ache that never seemed to go away despite the two years that had passed since his death. They'd taken Danny for walks together before he died, but Danny had been in the stroller then. Wouldn't Tom have loved watching Danny at the park playing with the other children—running around, yelling in sheer joy?

"Okay, I'm ready." She smiled at her son, her heart swelling with love. He was such a darling boy. She wished Tom had lived to see Danny grow up. He'd been as excited as she when Danny had come into their lives. They'd made such plans for the future—family vacations, maybe buying a house one day with a yard so Danny could have a dog. Tom had wanted him to attend NYU. Sighing softly for what was not to be, she helped her son put his jacket on. It was up to her to make sure Tom's dreams came true.

"Yay!" Danny ran to the front door and waited impatiently while his mother unlocked it and opened it. He was off like a shot to the elevator. "I can push the button," Danny said proudly and pressed the down arrow.

Susan locked her door and hurried to follow her son. She wouldn't put it past him to jump into the elevator without her in his excitement to get to the park.

Danny raced out of the elevator when it reached the lobby.

"Danny, wait!" She hurried after him and took his hand before he reached the large glass door that led outside.

Danny did not move slowly. She laughed as they raced the light at the corner. In only moments they reached the grassy expanse. Releasing Danny's hand, she followed as he headed directly to the playground area. Several children she recognized were already running around, swinging, sliding down the slides and having a great time. Danny joined in with no hesitation.

Susan glanced around at the benches, looking for an empty seat. She spotted the man she'd met briefly yesterday, Zack Morgan. Did he live in the neighborhood? She didn't remember seeing him before. And he was someone she would have remembered. Slowly she walked over. He looked up when she drew near and nodded in greeting.

"Good morning," he said.

His voice was amazing, deep and husky. She remembered how tall he was. Even sitting, he gave the impression of strength and size. His hair was almost black. A dark tan gave him a healthy look, while faint lines around his eyes proved he squinted in bright sunshine. Spring had been nice, but not that nice. Was he a skier? That would explain the tan so early in the season. He was broad in the shoulders, muscular without appearing to be a bodybuilder. He looked totally out of place in the park. She glanced back at Danny. Seeing the man had her thinking of wide-open spaces and endless vistas. A man used to doing, not sitting. Why was he in the park today? Did he live nearby? Had he been a regular she'd overlooked before meeting him?

For an instant she had the insane urge to make sure her hair was tidy and she still wore lipstick.

She looked back and smiled politely. After a second's hesitation, she sat beside him.

"I'm sorry I didn't thank you properly yesterday," she said.

"I didn't find your child. The teacher did."

"Just being willing to help was a good thing. I appreciate it. And the fact that you looked. Many people would have been too busy."

"I'm glad he was safe," Zack said, glancing over at the children. The folded newspaper at his side indicated he'd been there for some time. Did he have a child playing with the others?

"I'm Susan Johnson." She reached out to shake his hand. His palm was hard, calloused. His grip was firm without being too hard. The tingling sensation that ran up her arm surprised her and she pulled back quickly, more aware of the man than she ought to have been.

"We met yesterday. You were a bit flustered, though. No lasting aftereffects after your scare?"

"Just a constant worry of that child of mine making me gray way before my time," she replied, sitting back and relaxing, her gaze on Danny. She was not taking the chance he'd run after some other man today.

After a few moments of silence, she glanced at Zack and was surprised to find him watching the children play. Somehow he didn't seem like a man who spent a lot of time with children.

He noted her look and returned her gaze. "I haven't seen kids play like this in a long time. I've been on assignment overseas for the last five years."

"Are you in the military?" she asked, curious.

"No, construction. We've been building bridges and dams and housing projects in the Middle East. When I had leave, I toured Europe. I'm on leave right now—enforced unfortunately. Got too close to a land mine."

"Oh my gosh," she said. "I'm sorry. Are you all right?"

"Things will work out. I'm back on my feet and everything is functioning. But it'll take a little while until I'm one hundred percent again. I've been gone overseas so long, I feel like a stranger in my own country."

"You'll get used to things quickly, I bet. Are you from New York?"

"No. Originally from Chicago. But I haven't lived there in

fifteen years. I'm thinking of subletting an apartment close to
the hospital where I'm getting physical therapy until I decide
where to settle."

"You picked a great place to recuperate. I love New York. I'm
from here originally and can't imagine living anywhere else."

"Hard place to raise a kid, though, isn't it? Don't you wish
for a backyard where he could play safely by himself? Maybe
get a dog? A safer neighborhood?" Zack asked.

Susan took a breath, startled that he captured the ideal Tom
had often voiced. Was it a universal male thing? Her defenses
rose when he mentioned a safer neighborhood. It was something she thought about a lot. The few blocks surrounding
their apartment were not the best in the city, but it was the best
she could afford. It wasn't too much of a problem while Danny
was still little. She worried about when he got older. What if
he fell in with the wrong crowd. Even a gang. She would like
a better home, but her talents were limited and she earned
more where she was than a teacher would. Which was the only
other thing she had trained for. But she wasn't sharing that
with a stranger, no matter how much he interested her.

"He's too young to take proper care of a dog. Maybe when
he's older. Pets are allowed in our building, you know." There
would be no house with a yard for them.

"Oh," Zack said.

"The preschool he goes to two mornings a week is close,
as is shopping. And I don't have the upkeep of a yard."

"Do you work nearby?" he asked.

"At the UN. I'm a translator. German."

And lucky to get such a well-paying job after her husband's
death. They'd planned on her staying home with the baby, not
having a day care provider be with their child all day.
Unfortunately things didn't turn out that way.

"And your husband?"

She took a deep breath. The shock of loss still startled her. "He died a couple of years ago. He was an attorney." Susan sought Danny. He laughed as he slid down the slide, chased by two friends. She smiled at his happiness. So often he lapsed into sulks with his father gone. He and Tom had enjoyed a special bond by the time Danny turned two.

"Sorry to hear about your loss. Cute kid you have."

"I'm so grateful for Danny. He kept me going when Tom died."

Susan watched her son. She didn't want him to forget Tom, so she had photographs all around the apartment. She told him stories about Tom as a boy. And about how they had met and got married. She wanted Tom to be a part of his life even though Danny's memories would fade over time. She wondered even now if he had any real memories, or just the stories she told about his daddy, and the pictures he saw every day.

Sometimes Susan couldn't remember a detail or two. She'd panic and search in her mind. She never wanted to forget anything about the man she'd loved so much.

"Do you have a child here?" Susan asked, looking at all the children. There had to be twenty, of all ages from toddlers with their mothers nearby to children aged seven or eight.

"No. I just wanted a place to sit in the sun and read the paper. It was only after I was here a while that children started arriving. The playground is quite a draw, isn't it?"

"Closest playground in this area. With all the apartments around here, you know there're lots of kids," she explained. "We come as often as we can. It's a great way for Danny to play with friends and get fresh air and sunshine. Probably not so appealing to people who want to also enjoy the fresh air but not have the noise."

Zack shrugged. "It suits me. I like to watch them. I know very little about children. I live in a world of men in a harsh environment. No grass where I've been the last eighteen months. This is like an oasis."

"Where have you been?"

"In a small country in the Arabian desert. We were building a dam across a river. The lake behind it will give irrigation to hundreds of acres for agricultural purposes."

"Did someone protest?"

"No." He looked puzzled.

"You said you are recovering from a land mine explosion," Susan said.

"Oh, that. I was temporarily assigned to another site our company is handling, closer to the war zone. That's where the mine was."

"Anyone else hurt?"

He shook his head. "One man killed, but no one else injured."

"That's awful."

"It's amazing how life can change in an instant," he said. "Or end as quickly."

She nodded. "That's what happened to me. One minute my husband was alive and on his way home from work, the next dead when a drunk driver ran a red light and killed him. No warning. No time for goodbyes."

He glanced at her but she watched Danny. The aching grief was never far away. "That must have been tough. Especially with a child."

She nodded. "But we're getting by," she said—to convince Zack or herself?

Zack had taken a chance that Susan Johnson would bring Danny to the park this morning. The weather forecast had been for a warm day and he hoped she was in the habit of letting her son play outside. He'd read the entire newspaper and about given up when he'd seen them cross the street.

Patience was not a virtue he considered he had. But it had paid off today.

And luck, as well, when she joined him on the bench. There were other empty spots she could have chosen. He was glad she sat beside him.

The more she spoke, the more he wanted to know about her. There was sadness in her eyes. She still grieved her husband. But when she looked at Danny, she seemed to light up inside.

How would it feel to have someone look at him that way? He hoped his mother had at least one time, but he would never know. He'd never met a woman who loved him. He wasn't sure it was possible. There had to be something wrong with someone who had been abandoned by his parents, shuffled around in foster care and unable to make a lasting commitment.

Zack frowned. That wasn't true. He had made a commitment to work and stuck by it despite the real hardships and uncomfortable—even dangerous—living conditions.

But relationships were different.

He hadn't even warranted a note from Alesia telling him about his son.

He shifted slightly, trying to ease the ache in his back. He was stiffening up. He needed to walk again. But he hated to leave. He might never get another opportunity like this to speak with the woman who was now mother to his child.

There was so much to find out.

"Are you staying nearby?" Susan asked.

He nodded. "In a small hotel." Nearby was relative. The hotel was certainly closer than his work site. It required a subway ride and a walk of several blocks, but he wasn't going to tell her that if he didn't need to.

"I wish I knew of someone subletting an apartment or something," she said. "It has to be costly to stay in a hotel, no matter how modest."

Zack decided not to tell her the company was picking up the expenses. All medical costs as well. Then what she said registered. She would suggest a place for him to sublet? Close enough he might see Susan and Danny again? He hadn't thought about getting to know them. He'd only wanted to make sure his son was healthy and happy.

He had at least two more months, maybe longer, before the doctor would certify him for work. He could spend some of it here—with the woman beside him and his son.

"I appreciate the thought," he said.

She frowned. "I'll ask around. There has to be something, though sublets get snapped up fast. Housing is so expensive here."

"Why not move to a more affordable place?"

"This is the closest apartment to the UN I could afford. I don't want to spend any more time away from Danny than I have to, which moving out farther would entail."

He hadn't thought about that. There was a lot more involved to family life than he'd originally considered. Maybe he should look for a sublet closer to the UN, in a nicer neighborhood, and then give it to Susan when he left.

"I guess you won't be here long enough for a sublet," she mused.

"Another two or three months. If someone was traveling or something, I could house-sit. But not for longer than that."

"I'll let you know if I hear anything," she said. "How can I reach you?"

Zack started to say just look for me here every day, but thought better of it. He reached into his pocket for his wallet, withdrawing one of his business cards. He stared at it. He couldn't remember the phone number of the hotel and if he told her the name she'd know it wasn't that close.

He looked at her. "I don't remember the hotel number. Tell

you what, I'll get a cell phone later today and if you're here tomorrow, give that number to you." He held out his card to her. "In the meantime, this is information about the company I work for. In emergencies, they can always contact employees. They know where we are."

"Okay." She smiled and then took the card. The company was a well-known construction firm that built large-scale buildings, dams and roads worldwide.

For a moment Susan wanted to give her number to this stranger. She'd run into him briefly yesterday and then again today. She didn't know him from Adam, but he had helped her yesterday. He didn't know where she lived, so couldn't be following her. If he were staying around here, this park was a nice place to sit in the sunshine.

He interested her in a way a man hadn't in a long time.

She felt suddenly alive around him.

Blinking, she looked away. For some reason he seemed more confident and secure than the men she usually saw on a daily basis—without being overbearing or arrogant.

She checked on Danny again and then looked around at the other benches occupied with parents and others visiting the park. She always kept watch to make sure Danny was safe. Today she'd forgotten to pay attention to Danny every second. He was fine, but it was unlike her to forget him even for a second.

Being with Zack stirred her senses and made her more curious than warranted. And had her offering to help where no help was asked for. Maybe he liked living in a hotel. Why had she opened her mouth and made such an impulsive offer? It was unlike her. Or at least the her she'd been the last couple of years.

Susan waved to Danny when he yelled to her. He ran over, eyeing Zack suspiciously.

"Come and have a drink of water. You've been running around so much," she said, drawing a bottle of water from her tote.

"Who is that?" Danny asked, staring at Zack.

"The man who helped me look for you yesterday, remember? Zack Morgan," Susan said.

Danny drank his water and then smiled. "Hi," he said.

"Hi yourself," Zack replied. He studied the child for a moment then smiled. "You like the slides I can tell."

"Yes. I can climb up all by myself and then go down. Watch." Danny thrust the water back at Susan and ran back to the slide, waiting his turn to mount the stairs and slide down. He looked at Zack with pride.

Zack made a thumbs-up sign.

"He's so proud of his accomplishments," Susan said. "I keep hoping he'll adjust to his father's death. He keeps looking for Tom whenever we go out."

"Tough break for both of you," Zack said.

Susan nodded. "And scary if he runs off like yesterday."

Zack stretched slowly and then rose. "I have to get moving. I'm stiffening up," he said. He reached for the paper and looked at Susan. "Want this or shall I toss it?"

"I'll take it if you're finished with it. Are you okay?"

"I will be, just need to keep moving. Nice to talk to you."

"We'll come tomorrow, you can give me your phone number and I'll let you know if I hear of a sublet." She watched as he walked away. She could tell he was in pain. She hadn't noticed a limp yesterday, but he definitely was favoring his left leg as he slowly walked on the path through the park. Once he reached the sidewalk, it wasn't long before he was lost from view.

Susan studied his card. Zackary Morgan, engineer. He was as different from Tom as any man she knew. His hand had been callused and hard. He was tanned and rugged. He lived in foreign countries and did work only a very few could handle. Yet their paths had crossed and Susan was glad for it.

She may have been a tad pushy about offering to find him a place, but she wanted to do something for him. He'd offered her help yesterday. Now it was her turn.

Was that all? To repay his offer? She refused to dwell on why, but she hoped she had not seen the last of Zackary Morgan.

CHAPTER TWO

SUNDAY it rained. Susan was disappointed. There would be no going to the park that day. After breakfast, she stood at the window for a little while, watching the water trace down the pane. It was not a quick shower that would end soon. She had wanted to take Danny out.

And maybe run into Zack.

Sighing softly, she turned and went to gather the laundry. It was a chore she never relished. The dark basement that housed the two washing machines for their building gave her the creeps. She wished it could be painted and more light added. At least she didn't have to go to a public laundry and wait. So far no one had taken her clothes when she had left them in the apartment laundry.

It was early afternoon when the phone rang. Susan answered quickly. Danny was sleeping and she didn't want him to waken.

"Hi, darling," her mother greeted her.

"Hi, Mom."

"Your father's napping, so I thought I'd call." Her mother usually called once every week or so from Florida. Susan missed her parents and relished their chats on the phone.

"Danny's sleeping, too," Susan said, settling down on the sofa.

"How are things?" her mother asked.

"Okay. Danny scared me to death on Friday." Quickly Susan gave her mother a recap. "I don't know what to do with his chasing after men thinking they are Tom."

"He'll grow out of it sooner or later," her mom said.

"But in the meantime, I could die of fright if he disappears again. Or he could seriously get lost or abducted."

"What he needs is a father figure. That's what he's missing. I wished we lived closer. Your father loves the time he spends with Danny."

The image of Zack Morgan rose. She frowned. Why had he sprung to mind when her mother spoke of a father figure? He was the last person who would be interested in children. He said he hadn't been around them. His job would not be good for any kind of family life.

But she could fantasize. That he'd ask her out. That he'd like to spend time with Danny. The bubble burst. The only dates she'd had in the last two years had not ended well. She resigned herself to her single status—at least for another ten years or so.

"I worry about you two living in that neighborhood," her mother was saying.

"We've been through this, Mom. It's the best I can do."

"You could move down here. It's less expensive."

"And do what?"

"Teach."

"I love my job. It's exciting and keeps me up on all the world events."

"But you are so far away and we miss seeing Danny."

Susan refrained from reminding her mother they had moved away three years ago, not her. Florida offered a better climate for her father. She missed them, even more after Tom had died. But she did not want to move there herself. She'd miss New York too much. Besides, she was managing fine.

"I'll send more pictures," she offered.

"It's not the same. I'll call back later and talk with Danny," her mother said.

"He'd like that, Mom."

They chatted a few more minutes. Susan hung up and leaned back on the sofa. It was still raining. She might have chanced the park had it been warmer. Just to walk over in case Zack had walked there for exercise. She could tell he had been in pain yesterday sitting on the bench. She wished she knew more about his injuries and if he would completely recover. She hoped so. He looked too virile and active to be satisfied with a desk job when he could be out building mammoth structures.

The rainy weather continued until Friday and by Saturday morning, Susan was anxious to get to the park. She'd asked around about a place to sublet and a woman at work knew of one.

That was the only reason she wanted to see Zack, she told herself. To tell him about the apartment before it was taken.

Danny was delighted to be heading to the park after so many days inside. He had tried Edith Jordan's patience by Thursday and she'd been glad for preschool on Friday.

When they reached the park, Danny dashed to the playground. Susan looked at each bench. No sign of Zack.

Only when she felt the sweep of disappointment did she realize how much she had hoped to see him again.

She sat on the bench they'd shared last week and watched Danny play. The usual group of children were here. She waved at a couple of mothers she knew but didn't walk over to talk with them. Maybe Zack would still show up.

It was getting close to lunchtime. She hoped Danny wouldn't put up a fuss to return home. She had some chores to do and wanted to call one of her friends and discuss dinner

one night next week. Laura had a son a year older than Danny.
The two boys loved to play together.

She glanced around as a sixth sense kicked in. Zack was
crossing the grass, a white bag held in one hand. His gaze
was focused on her as he cut the distance swiftly. No sign of
a limp today.

"Hi," he said when he was close.

"Hi." Susan felt fluttery inside. She had hoped to see him,
but now that he was here, she felt positively shy. That was so
not like her.

He lifted the bag a couple of inches. "I took a chance and
brought coffee. If you don't want any, that's okay. I even
brought some apple juice for Danny."

"I'd love a cup of coffee. I've only had one so far today
and sitting here in the sun was making me sleepy."

He nodded and sat beside her. In seconds she was sipping
the heavenly brew.

"I brought cream in case," he said, rummaging around
in the bag.

"No, I like it black."

"Me, too." He lifted a bottle of apple juice and a straw,
setting them on the bench between them.

Susan was touched he'd thought to bring something for
Danny.

"Thank you." She caught Danny's attention and waved
him over. He ran all the way.

"Hi," Zack said.

"Hi. Did you come to watch me play?" he asked.

Zack smiled and nodded. "I sure did."

"Zack brought you some apple juice," Susan said, opening
the bottle and removing the wrapper from the straw.

"I love apple juice!" Danny exclaimed. He drank almost
half the bottle and then stopped, gasping for breath.

"You don't need to drink it all in one go," his mother commented wryly. "What do you say?"

"Thank you for my apple juice," he said to Zack. Then he turned and ran back to the swings.

"Does he ever get tired?" Zack asked.

"Oh, yeah. After lunch he'll sleep for about two hours. Then be raring to go until bedtime. I'm glad you came today. I have a lead on a sublet, if you're still interested."

"I am. I spent the better part of this week looking."

Susan reached into the backpack and pulled out the note with the information about the small apartment not too far from a subway stop. She handed it to Zack. She wished it had been closer to this neighborhood. It would take some effort to come to the park from that place.

He read the information she'd jotted down then reached into his pocket and pulled out his wallet. He extracted another business card, then put her note in its place. Taking a pen, he wrote a phone number and handed her the card.

"I also bought a cell phone this week. Here's my number. Just in case."

"In case of what?" she asked, taking the card.

He shrugged. "You find another place available, or just want to talk."

She wondered if he was lonely. Though she couldn't imagine any woman would resist long if he showed some interest.

Including her.

"Thanks." She hesitated a moment. "I can give you our number if you like."

Zack nodded and in a moment had her number on the same paper as the sublet information.

"What did you do all week?" she asked.

"Worked on the physical therapy on my shoulder and hip. Hurts like crazy. They didn't tell me that when I started. Just some discomfort they said. Ha, I'd like to see them try it." He rotated his shoulder and grimaced. "Then I called about vacancies. Everything was taken by the time I called."

"You aren't trying to get back in shape in a week, are you?"

"Hey, no pain, no gain. Besides, I've been working on this since last November. "

"You need to follow instructions exactly for maximum recovery," she murmured.

"You a nurse?" He glanced at her. His dark eyes held amusement.

She grinned. It was fun to banter with him. "Better, I'm a mom. I know things. Didn't your mother tell you not to argue back?"

His look became pensive and he looked across the playground to where Danny and his friends were climbing the bars. "I don't remember my mother," he said.

"Oh." Susan was stricken. She couldn't have known he had lost his mother early. "I'm sorry," she said. She couldn't imagine her mother not being a part of her life, even though she lived in Florida.

He shrugged. "Things happen."

She longed to ask some questions, but didn't want to pry. If he wanted her to know more, he'd tell her.

Seeking a safe topic, she remembered the sublet. "My friend said the apartment will be sublet fully furnished. They want less than six months. They're taking a long tour of Europe, but not so long to tie up the place for a year. I thought it might work out."

"The way places get rented around here, I'll call this afternoon."

Susan sipped her coffee, feeling happier than she had in a long time. The day was beautiful, a cloudless blue sky, just enough breeze to keep the temperature from climbing uncomfortably high. She was watching her son have a great time. And sitting beside one of the most gorgeous men on the planet. She even caught a glimpse of some other mothers staring, and then talking among themselves. She resisted the urge to glance at Zack. Did he feel awkward being the only male around? No, wait, there were two fathers with their children playing Frisbee on the grass. But Zack wasn't with a child.

He took the last drink from his coffee and put the cup in the bag.

"I thought about seeing the sights, showing myself New York so to speak. Would you and your son like to go to the zoo with me tomorrow? I've seen nothing but sand and more sand in the last few years. It occurs to me that kind of outing would be more fun with a child along who would really be captivated by the animals."

Susan drew in a breath, surprised at the strong inclination to accept on the spot. She'd love to spend more time with him. Yet—she wasn't sure she was ready to date. She'd tried it twice and hated both outings. Was this a date? She didn't know the man, but they would be in a public place. How dangerous could going to the zoo be? Danny loved the zoo. They'd gone twice last summer.

"Let me check my calendar when I get home," she said, stalling. She wanted to think this through before making a decision. "It is fun to visit the exhibits with a little boy who's fascinated by everything. He's a bundle of energy and won't settle for a sedate pace."

"I checked—the zoo opens at nine, so I thought an early start to see as much as we can. I warn you, I may not have the stamina to last all day."

"Sounds like fun. I'll let you know. Thanks for inviting us to join you. Danny loves animals."

Zack nodded. He had asked. It was up to her. His gaze was

drawn again to his son. The wonder was hard to accept. When Danny's laughter rang out, Zack wanted to scoop him up and hug him. He could watch this child for hours, fascinated to know he and Alesia had produced such a darling boy.

Anger simmered at his former lover for keeping this miracle from him. He would have dropped everything to return to the States if she'd only told him. Now he'd missed the opportunity to be a part of his life.

When Danny got in line for the large, curved slide, he was hidden from view for a few moments. Zack glanced back to Susan. She was not what he expected. Instead of being a nebulous figure, she was a pretty woman with soft looking honey-gold hair and grave gray eyes. She wasn't tall, reaching only to his shoulder. She kept her eyes on Danny, watching out for him, ready to spring to the rescue if needed.

She obviously loved him. That was one lucky little boy. Zack wondered how his own life might have been different if his parents had lived. If they had expressed the love he could see shining so clearly in Susan's expression.

Looking back at the little boy, Zack watched every move, every expression that crossed his son's face. Soon Zack would be healed and returning to the Middle East—or another project in a foreign land. For a few weeks he might get the chance to know Danny. He wished for him a better childhood than he had experienced.

"How long is your leave?" Susan asked.

"I have at least two more months." Two months to regain his strength and range of motion in his shoulder. He would do all the exercises the PT insisted upon. And walk the entire island of Manhattan every day if it meant full recovery. He didn't know what he'd do if he couldn't pass the company physical. Look for a new kind of work, he supposed.

"Wow, I love it when I get two weeks off in a row," Susan said.

"Yeah, vacation is far different from medical leave. When I had time off before, I'd visit different European countries."

"We'll be lucky to get to Europe once before Danny leaves home," she said wistfully.

"Who watches Danny when you're at work?" he asked. "I assume you work normal business hours." Careful, he warned himself. You shouldn't know anything about her. She needs to tell you herself or you'll give away the fact a detective investigated her.

"It's nine-to-five most of the time. Sometimes if something big is going on, I'll be on call for weekends or late night sessions. I do get three weeks vacation, but depending on what's going on in the world, I might not get it all at once," Susan said.

"Does Danny go to a child care center?" Zack racked his brain for what limited knowledge he had about children. Some of the men who rotated into the field for the chance to make extra money had families. He'd listened to their tales of woe regarding children and child care while their wives worked. Most of the time he'd wandered away, seeking time alone. He hadn't related before.

"There is a lovely retired schoolteacher who lives in our building and watches him for me. It works out perfectly. She needs a bit of extra money to supplement her retirement pay. Danny gets to stay in our apartment with his own toys and books. She takes him for walks here in nice weather. I was so lucky to connect with her."

"Is it hard to get good child care?" Zack asked. There was so much he didn't know about this family. His foster mothers had all stayed at home to be there for the children. How did a single working parent manage?

"The hard part is leaving him for so many hours. I wish I could work nights and be home with him during the day. He's growing so fast. Edith gives me a report each day—how he liked preschool, when he napped, what he had for lunch, if any little friends from the neighborhood came to play. Things like that. It makes me feel more a part of his daily activities. But I miss the actual being there."

Zack nodded. He hadn't planned to get involved with Danny and his adoptive mother. But now that the opening had been made, Zack was intrigued with the mother of his child. He liked being with her. Would she consider expanding her circle of friends to let him in? He'd made the first step by inviting them to the zoo. He hoped Susan would accept. If not, he'd take one day at a time. He'd already attained more than he ever expected regarding his son.

Susan softly closed the door to Danny's room. He was already asleep. Amazing how he could go from full speed to instant sleep. She felt tired enough to fall in bed herself, but still had some cleaning to do and another load of laundry. She'd dust and vacuum the living room to give Danny a chance to wake up if he were going to. Then she'd quickly run the last basket of clothes to the laundry area. Danny would stay asleep all night and she'd only be gone a few moments. She normally took him with her, but this weekend would prove to be different. If she were going to spend the day at the zoo tomorrow, she needed to get a load done tonight. When he'd been younger, she had never left Danny alone, even to dash down to the laundry room. Now she felt better about leaving him for a few minutes. She carried a baby monitor that would alert her if he awoke before she returned. It wasn't ideal, but working single parents made do.

As she tidied the living room, she thought about Zack Morgan. How involved did she want to get with the man? He was only in New York to recover from injuries. Once he was fit again, he'd return to the Middle East and she'd likely never see him again.

It wasn't as if she were planning a long-term friendship. But he was at loose ends and she had not been so intrigued with a man since her husband. What harm could it do to go to the zoo? Danny would love it.

And she'd love to spend the day with Zack.

Guess that meant she'd decided to accept the invitation to the zoo. Danny would be thrilled when she told him. And it would be more fun for her to see it with another adult. Not that she didn't delight in her child. But sometimes she just wanted adult conversation.

When she returned from the laundry room, she'd call Zack and let him know they'd be happy to join him. Glancing at Tom's picture, she almost apologized. "It's not a date," she explained. "Just an outing with Danny. He seems nice." She wasn't telling her husband how she'd felt a surprising attraction to Zack. She wasn't interested in remarrying. How could she when Tom had been the love of her life? They had made such grand plans—all dust now that he was gone. She couldn't risk that kind of heartache again. Love made a person hostage to all the bad things that could happen.

"He's just a new acquaintance." Was she trying to convince herself or Tom?

"Maybe he'll become a friend. But he's only here for a short time. Once his convalescence is up, he'll move on and I'll probably never see him again." The thought disappointed her.

As Susan was inserting her key into the lock upon her return from the laundry room, she heard the phone ringing. She rushed to answer it hoping it hadn't wakened Danny.

"Susan? This is Zack."

"Hi." She suddenly felt as shy as a schoolgirl when a boy called. "I was going to call you later." She took a breath.

"Danny and I would love to go to the zoo with you. We can be ready before nine if you want to get an early start."

"Sounds good. I'll swing by your apartment about eight-thirty if that suits. Thought we'd take a cab rather than the subway. I could have rented a car for my stay, but the traffic is too much to deal with. And I'm not sure I could find parking anywhere."

She laughed. "That's one of the reasons I don't have one." Susan felt oddly nervous about the outing. It wasn't a date. She was merely going to the zoo with a new friend. And Danny would love it.

"Is Danny asleep?" Zack asked.

"Yes. We have a schedule. He does better with set times for things. So we're up every morning before seven. He eats lunch at noon and we usually eat dinner at the same time every evening. Then it's bath and bed by eight. Kids like routine."

She'd admit to a rampant curiosity about the man. If she was planning to spend the day with him tomorrow, she could devote a bit of time tonight to get to know him better.

"So, tell me about working in the Middle East. What happened with the land mine?" Susan said, settling in on the sofa.

Zack began telling her about the land mine accident that had killed one construction worker and injured him. It had only been the heavy earthmover that had shielded the other workers from harm.

Glossing over his time in the hospital, he soon turned the topic to heavy construction projects outside of the U.S. He told her about the heat and dryness of the desert. How for the most part the people were grateful for the improvements made—especially when dams afforded water to heretofore barren land.

A buzzer sounded. Susan jumped. "My clothes are ready for the dryer," she explained. "I'll need to put them in." She hated to end the conversation. But if she waited too much longer, she'd have to stay up later than normal waiting for the clothes to dry. With a full day planned for Sunday, she wanted to get a good night's rest.

"How long does it take to do that? I can call back."

"Great. Give me ten minutes."

Zack hung up. The last forty minutes with Susan on the phone had been unexpectedly nice. His friends were still on the job site. He knew no else in New York except the private detective he'd hired. She was easy to talk with, but he wished he'd learned more about Susan. She'd kept the conversation clearly on him, which made sense. She wanted to know more about him if she was seeing him in the morning.

He liked that. When he called her back, though, he'd make sure to ask her questions. He considered the possible complications of getting to know them while he was in the States. Would he develop a bond with his son? Or just know him these few weeks, and keep the knowledge of his paternity a secret? He wasn't sure how things would play out. But for the time being, he was content just to get to know Susan and Danny.

Ten minutes later he called again. She answered at the first ring. He pictured her rushing back to be there when he phoned. It was a nice feeling—and he wouldn't ask for confirmation. He wanted to hold on to those feelings.

"So tell me a bit about you—I dominated the conversation before," he said.

"That's because your life is more exciting. I fight the crowds to go to work. Come home and spend time with my child until he goes to bed. Stay up as long as I can keep awake then go to bed myself."

Zack tried to think like a man who knew nothing about this woman, instead of knowing most of the facts of her life, thanks to the detective. "What do you do on weekends?"

"In nice weather I always take him to the park. It's our only grassy area. During the winter, we often visit museums so he can run around without getting cold. Sometimes in the summer we take a ride to the beach. Must sound pretty boring to a man who vacations in Europe."

"It depends on whom I'm doing it with. One appealing part of your lifestyle is the stability you have. I'm a nomad."

"By choice."

"Maybe."

"So by that do you mean you might be interested in settling down at some point?"

"I hadn't considered it. First I was going to make my mark on the world."

Zack didn't go into how he'd wanted to leave something behind to mark his being alive. He had no family so he built structures that would endure for decades and beyond. Now things had changed. Whether he ever let Susan and Danny know who he was, *he knew*. He had a son.

"It would be a change. But at some point surely you want a family?" she said.

"And if I die and they had to go into foster care? Too risky."

"Whoa, where did that come from?" she asked.

"It happened to my parents. I was raised in the foster care system in Chicago."

"Oh." Susan was taken aback. She remembered he said he didn't remember his mother. For some reason she'd thought his father was still alive.

"Hey, it's not a recent thing. I never knew either of my parents. I'm still in touch with one foster family," he said.

"That must have been tough." Susan wondered what Danny would do if something happened to her. She knew her mother would step in, but with her father in frail health, it would mean total turmoil for a long time. She couldn't bear the thought of not being there to see her son grow up.

"But what if you didn't die? What if you lived to be an old man and then had no children, no grandchildren? Wouldn't that be worse?" she asked.

Zack tried to envision himself old, with lots of little children racing around yelling and laughing while he sat on some nebulous porch and watched. They would play in a big yard with old trees shading the grass. He would have his wife of many years beside him.

For a moment Zack wondered if he was losing it. The image popped and he was back in the small hotel room.

"I'll keep that under consideration," he said. "I called about the apartment sublet. It's still available and I'm going over on Monday to look at it," he said. "It's not close to your place."

"No, but a much better section of town. If they were subletting for longer, I might be tempted. But they want a short-term tenant. It sounds nice."

"I'll let you know if it works out."

They talked for another half hour. Susan finally said she had to get her laundry now that it was dry and gave Zack her address for the morning. He said good-night. After replacing the phone, he gazed out into the dark night. He'd see her again in a few hours. How did he feel about that?

Susan hadn't opened up to someone like Zack in years. She felt awkward now that the evening's companionable conversation had been broken. Riding down the small elevator, she wondered if she was being wise in going out with Zack. What if she grew attached—or worse, what if Danny did. He still searched for his father everywhere. She didn't want him doing the same for Zack if the man became part of their lives for the weeks he was recovering and then left. Little children didn't understand.

She and Tom had known from the first they were meant for

each other. To think about another man felt odd. But she'd done it! She'd accepted a date for Sunday. She and Danny would spend several hours with Zack. Her heart gave an unexpected skip. It was just for the day. Neither she nor Danny would grow too attached in such a short time.

When Zack rang the bell the next morning, Danny ran to the door. His mother had told him about the visit to the zoo at breakfast and he was raring to go. Flinging open the door he beamed up at Zack. Susan entered the living room in time to see her son open the door without even asking who was there. She was trying to instill some common sense in him, but he was too excited today to pay attention.

"Hey, there, Danny," Zack said, stooping down to smile at the small boy at his level. "Ready to go?"

"Yes!" Danny flung himself at Zack, his arms going around his neck. "The zoo is my bestest place. I love the elephants!"

Susan smiled at the stunned look on Zack's face. He hadn't planned on her exuberant son. "Danny, you're probably strangling Zack. Let go."

"No!" Tentatively Zack's arms came around the child and he hugged him gently. "He's okay, just excited, I think."

"You've nailed that. We're about ready." She put another bottle of water in the backpack and zipped it shut. By the time she donned her jacket and put Danny's on him, Zack had straightened to his full height and reached for the backpack.

"What do you have in here, bricks?" he asked, hefting it.

"No, just essentials." She raised her hand and began counting on her fingers. "Water, sunscreen, wet towelettes, snacks, cuddle blanket, dark glasses, wallet—"

"Cuddle blanket?" Zack asked, dumbfounded.

She grinned. "Danny still is comforted by a certain blanket when he gets tired or cranky. Usually he keeps it on his bed, but we take it with us on longer trips just in case. He likes to put it against his cheek and rub against it. I call it his cuddle blanket. Hopefully we'll leave the zoo before he starts getting tired. He can get really cranky."

"I expect I'll get tired long before he does," Zack said, slinging the backpack over one shoulder.

"I can carry it," Susan said. She remembered his brief recount of the land mine. She didn't expect him to carry her things.

"I'm okay with it. I didn't realize you had to tote so much on an outing," he said.

"This is nothing. When Danny was smaller, we had blankets and bottles and changes of clothes in addition to everything else. You can't imagine how much a small baby needs to travel."

Zack shook his head. "I'm learning every second."

"Danny, what did I tell you about this trip?"

He scrunched up his face for a moment then beamed at his mother. "Hold your hand in mine!"

"Good memory," she said and they exchanged a high-five.

As they walked down to the elevator, she said softly to Zack. "Of course I tell him that every time we leave the house. He ought to remember. But watch and see if I don't have to remind him at least a half dozen times."

"He seems to be a happy kid," Zack said.

"I hope so. I'm doing my best. It's hard being a single parent. My husband and I had always planned that I would stay at home when we had children. His death makes that impossible."

"Didn't he leave any insurance? Sorry, that's none of my business."

"That's okay. Tom left some, but I want that for fallback purposes, or for college. Do you know how expensive college is these days?"

Once at the street level, Susan insisted Danny hold her hand. They caught a cab and sat in the back, Danny in the middle.

"Are we at the zoo yet?" Danny asked at the first traffic light.

"No, it'll take a little longer to get there," Susan said. "We'll tell you when we arrive."

"Do you have zoos at your home?" Danny asked Zack.

"No. I haven't been to the zoo since I was a little boy like you."

"I'm glad we can go today."

Susan smiled at Zack. He looked bemused. She'd have to remember he wasn't used to being around kids and keep Danny from pestering him as he could do sometimes.

"My daddy goes to the zoo. Maybe he will be there today," Danny said, bouncing on the seat.

"No, Danny. Daddy's gone to heaven. He won't be at the zoo."

"I want my Daddy!" he said, kicking the back of the seat in front of him.

"You miss him so much, sweetie. I do, too. But he won't be at the zoo," she said softly. She glanced at Zack. "We'll really have to make sure he doesn't take off after some guy with light brown hair."

Zack nodded, realizing more and more each day how much he had missed. He hated the fact his son ached for another man. How could Alesia have kept this child from him? It hurt to think she'd given him away rather than tell Zack he was a father. He would have been home before the baby was born, and loved him from the first moment.

He'd accomplished his initial goal—discovered that his son was happy and healthy. Somewhere the goal had changed. Now he wanted to get to know the woman who was raising his son. See if he could help out in some way without being intrusive in their lives.

The cab arrived at the zoo. It had been years since Zack had been. One of his foster families had lived near the zoo in Chicago and they'd gone each summer the three years he'd lived with them. He had often wondered what the zoo looked like in winter, especially for African veldt animals in the snow of Chicago. Today the Bronx Zoo was warm and green. Families with children running were everywhere.

Susan stepped a bit closer to Zack and held Danny's hand. "I didn't expect such a crowd," she said. "It's only April."

"I didn't know what to expect. But after the rain, it's beautiful weather. I'm glad we came early. What do you want to see first?"

"Monkeys." She gave Danny's hand a swing. "I know he's descended from them."

The morning passed swiftly. Zack watched as Danny hung on every word his mother read about the animals. The child delighted in the Children's Zoo, exploring all the exhibits, and feeding the pygmy goats by hand.

"I'll pass," Zack said when Danny offered him a turn after a goat licked the boy's palm.

Susan laughed. "Definitely a wet wipes time. Before we eat, he needs to get his hands washed properly." She pulled out a wet towelette and wiped off Danny's hands. She offered one to Zack and took one herself. "No telling what we've touched so far," she said with a laugh. "Thanks for inviting us—we're having fun."

By the time they found a table at one of the eating concessions, Susan was feeling more comfortable around Zack. He kept the conversation going without filling every moment of silence. Sometimes he just seemed to enjoy being in the day, looking around at the exhibits, studying the people. Probably a result of a near miss with the land mine. Had he always been like this, or had that event changed him in some ways? Curious, she watched him as they ate, wishing she knew more about him, but afraid to ask too much. She didn't want to give the wrong impression.

It was after one when they started lunch and by two o'clock, Danny was showing definite signs of flagging.

"I think we need to head for home," Susan said when Danny asked to be picked up for the third time. "You don't have to come with us. It'll be out of your way, I'm sure. Thanks for a great day. We've both enjoyed it."

"Actually I was thinking of returning myself. Here, let me carry him," Zack said, reaching out to take Danny. The boy weighed so little, but for Susan it would have been a greater burden.

The minute Danny put his arm around Zack's neck and lay his head against his shoulder, Zack wondered if he could ever let this child go again.

"Thanks. He's getting heavier by the day. I love him dearly, but he's almost too big to carry anymore." She looked a bit sad at the thought.

Zack wanted to erase the sadness from her eyes, but he didn't know how. He wanted her to be happy, have that love for her son be the only emotion he could detect.

"All kids grow up," he said inadequately.

"I know, but I didn't realize they'd grow so fast."

Zack carried Danny to the taxi, which he insisted they share. By the time they reached Susan's apartment building, the boy had fallen asleep and Zack carried him to his bed.

"Thanks so much," Susan said again as she pulled off Danny's shoes and covered him with a light blanket. "He'll remember this day for a long time."

"I will, too," Zack said, with a look at his son. And then he turned to leave the room. "Maybe you'll take pity on me another weekend and spend some time with me."

"We'll see," Susan said brightly. She had enjoyed the day more than she'd expected she would. But she was wary of getting too friendly. Yet he had done nothing toward pushing them closer. He was just a new acquaintance who hadn't met many people yet. He hadn't even offered a specific activity— just a nebulous spend time together.

She wasn't ready to date, she decided. When she was, she wanted to meet men who lived nearby, with steady jobs that didn't include the danger of a mine exploding.

After Zack left, Susan kept busy in the hopes of keeping her disturbing thoughts at bay. Once she had caught up on chores and checked to make sure Danny was still asleep, Susan picked up a magazine and glanced through it, but her thoughts returned to Zack.

Somehow she needed to make it clear to him she wasn't looking for a new man in her life. She glanced at the closest picture of Tom. She had gotten used to being alone, though she still missed him like crazy. They should have had decades together. More children. She hated the thought of Danny being an only child. Yet she couldn't imagine getting married again.

Unless it was to someone like Zack, the thought crept in. He could almost make her forget Tom.

She frowned. Zack was nothing like Tom. She didn't want to even go there. He said he'd only be around for a few weeks, then he'd probably be off to some exotic country for another few years. The nomadic life might suit him, but it wouldn't suit her or a family.

Just then she heard Danny. She jumped up, magazine forgotten.

Monday morning Susan received a phone call at work from Edith Jordan. It was so rare, she was instantly concerned.

"Just a quick confirmation, my dear," Edith said. "We came to the park and Danny went to talk to a young man at a nearby bench. He said Zack took him to the zoo yesterday."

"Zack Morgan. And yes, he took us both to the zoo. Is there a problem?"

"Not at all, I just wanted to make sure he was a friend."

"Is Danny bothering him? I think Danny's taken a fancy to him." She took a deep breath and tried to think about it rationally. It would do no harm as long as her son didn't become too attached. She wouldn't want Danny to be upset when Zack left.

"Mr. Morgan doesn't seem to mind. I'll go and introduce myself and let him know he's free to tell Danny to stop if he gets too demanding," she said.

"Sounds like a plan. Make sure Danny knows just because Zack treated us to the zoo, it does not commit him to spending more time with him."

Susan hung up a moment later and shook her head. She knew Zack took long walks as part of his recuperating process. And sitting in the sunshine in a quiet park was probably just what he needed. For a moment she was envious. She wished she could sit in the park on such a nice day and enjoy the sunshine.

And spend time with Zack.

By Wednesday, Susan had managed to push thoughts of Zack to the back of her mind. Danny had been full of conversation on Monday evening about Zack and how high he'd pushed him on the swing and how he played catch with a ball. Checking with Edith, Susan had discovered Zack had stayed at the park the entire time Danny had been there that day. But he had not been there on Tuesday or Wednesday. Probably afraid Danny would enlist him as a playmate again, she thought.

After tucking Danny in bed, Susan debated going to bed early herself. It had been a stressful three days at work and she still had two days to go to the weekend. Maybe a long hot soak in the tub and then an early night would be the perfect ending to a not-so-perfect day.

Just then, the phone rang.

It was Zack. Susan was suddenly swept away with anticipation at the sound of his voice. Leaning back on the sofa, she smiled. "I heard about your big day on Monday," she said.

"At the park with Danny?"

"Right. I hope he wasn't a pest."

"Not at all. But it was humbling—he wore me out," Zack said in his husky voice.

Susan closed her eyes to better concentrate on that timbre.

"It took you two days to recover?" she teased. "Danny said you've been conspicuously absent from the park since then."

"Checking up on me?" The low murmur of his voice made her think of dark rooms, intimate settings, just the two of them together. She reached over and dimmed the lamp. Settling back in the cushions again she smiled at their silly talk. It had been a long time since she'd flirted with anyone.

"Hardly, but perhaps I should warn you, if you make an appearance in Danny's vicinity, I'm bound to hear about it, if not from Danny then from Edith."

"At least you know your baby-sitter is conscientious."

"Did she introduce herself?" Susan asked.

"And gave me the third degree. She knows more about me than my employer, I think. She's not a stand-in for your parents, by any chance?"

"Not at all. They've only met once."

"Both your parents are living?" he asked.

"Yes. In Florida. My dad isn't doing so well. But they love it there. Typical New Yorkers, flocking south for better weather."

"You have no yearning to join them? Florida beats New York winters."

"I'm not ready for that scene yet. There's too much to do in the city. Besides, I love skating at Rockefeller Center in winter. Seeing everything dusted in snow. Bet you didn't do much skating in the Middle East."

"Not where I worked, but I took winter vacations in Switzerland. Didn't do much skating, but the skiing's terrific."

"I guess you got to see a lot of Europe whenever you took leave," she said wistfully. One of the trips she and Tom had planned had been to see London, Paris and Rome. If she saved enough, maybe she and Danny could make that trip.

"I've spent more time in European cities than I ever expected to before I took the job. Now I've seen enough. It's time to explore my own country, once I'm up to par again."

"Danny wasn't too much for you, was he?"

"No. I had to fly down to D.C. to confer with some of my colleagues at the company. And to discuss the possibility of working in the States."

"And?"

"There's time yet to seriously consider the future. In the meantime, I'm going to enjoy my R&R and explore New York. As a native, maybe you could act as tour guide. What should I see first?"

There was so much to see. Her heart skipped a beat when she imagined herself showing Zack all her favorite places.

"Come by the U.N. one day and I'll give you a tour," she offered before she had really thought about it. Immediately she wished she could snatch back the words. Holding her breath, maybe he'd refuse. What was she doing inviting him to the place she worked?

"Wouldn't you be working?"

"I can always take a break." She did want him to come, see where she spent most of her day. No, she didn't.

She didn't know what she wanted.

"How about next Tuesday? Can we time the tour so we end

at lunch? You can show me one of your favorite places and I'll treat," he asked.

"Sure. Come around ten. Depending on what's going on, I'll give you the deluxe tour." Susan's heart tripped faster. She was going to see Zack again. Just the two of them. Was she ready for this? Quickly she sought Tom's image in a photo— like a talisman. Zack was just a new acquaintance; she was simply being friendly. That's all there was to it. But even as she silently explained to Tom, she knew she was lying. This excitement at the thought of seeing Zack was more than being friendly.

"I'd like that," he said.

His deep voice sounded sexy, intimate. Susan shivered, suddenly reacting to the phone call in a very different manner. She usually spent her evenings alone. Now she had a connection with another adult. One who disturbed her senses in many ways and had her wondering more about him than she should be doing. This man made her feel more like a woman than she had in a long time. She had not died with her husband. Her emotions had been so concentrated in grief over the last two years, she had almost forgotten what other emotions felt like. This giddy anticipation set her nerves tingling.

"You didn't tell me what happened with the sublet," she said.

"After saying I could see it Monday, they sublet it on Sunday. I'm still at the hotel," Zack said.

"I'm sorry. I thought that was so promising."

"Sublets go fast, I was told. The company is paying the room, I'll just stay here for the time being."

"If I hear of something else, I'll let you know. It has to be easier in a home than a hotel."

"Not much difference to me. This beats the tent I have been living in for the last seven months. Hot and cold running water. Good food. Nice bed."

"You lived in a tent? You didn't mention that before." Susan was intrigued.

"It was only the last assignment." He began telling her of palatial housing, subpar housing and everything in between that they made do with when on assignment.

Susan remembered flat hunting with Tom. They'd had such fun picking out locations, arguing about floor plans, always with a future eye on a baby. The flat they had shared had been perfect. She was glad they'd had those years together. Glancing around, Susan knew Tom would have hated this place. It was small, dark and not at all what they'd chosen.

Which drew her up short. She was on her own now. She did the best she could and that was that. She was not going to sink into a pity party—especially when she had an intriguing man on the phone.

Zack was talking again. "After our outing on Sunday I was hoping I could convince you and Danny to join me for dinner Friday night. I saw a pizza place close by you that has games for little kids. Does Danny like pizza?"

"I think little boys are born liking pizza. I know the restaurant you mean." She had rarely gone inside, but had ordered home delivery from the place several times.

"When do you get home from work?" Zack asked.

"Usually around five forty-five. Give me a few minutes to change. We can be ready to go around six-fifteen if that works." It was only pizza. Not a date. Men didn't take little kids on dates. The three of them would have a nice time together and it would be one less lonely night for both adults.

She'd see him the day after tomorrow. Susan didn't know whether to be delighted, or nervous. For once, looking at Tom's photograph didn't help.

CHAPTER THREE

ZACK hung up questioning if he was making a mistake continuing to see Susan. She was so unlike the women he'd dated over the last dozen years it made him wonder why she fascinated him. He was curious to know if she was a sleepyhead in the mornings or if she bound out of bed raring to face the day. Did she prefer coffee or tea? The one time he'd brought coffee, she'd drank it black. Did she like long walks? He was growing addicted to them. They made him feel better, even when he was tired afterward and needed to rest.

What were her routines? Her favorite activities? Did she like action movies? He and the men on the job sites loved fast-paced action films. He himself also enjoyed mysteries. Did Susan?

He frowned. He was getting too involved. Alesia had been the epitome of party girl—always out for a good time. The kind of woman he had liked to date. She had known the score—no commitment, no ties. His job over the last decade had not been suitable for any kind of long-term relationships.

But Susan was totally different. She was a forever kind of woman. And a devoted mother. Despite the difference, he liked her. Leaning against the pillows he gazed out the window at the minuscule view he had. Lights gleamed in the night. New York never slept. Rising, he went to stand by the window. He was too high up to hear more than a low hum of sound from the street. The lights glittered from towers and apartments and, far below, from cars zipping along.

He wondered what Susan was doing right now. He liked watching her expressions, she didn't seem to hide a thing. When she laughed, her whole face lit up. But, more often than not, he'd caught her looking sad.

She didn't deserve it. She and her husband should have had fifty or more years together. They'd adopted Danny in good faith. There were no guarantees on a happy ending in life, but he wished that for her. And Danny.

He walked to the small wet bar to get something to drink. The evening loomed long and lonely. He missed being on the job site where there was always work to be done or places to see. Guys to hang out with in the small bars that sprang up at all sites.

But even if he were back, he wasn't sure that would suit him now. The land mine had changed his perspective on what was important. Or was it learning he had a son? He popped open the can and drank. Some of each, probably.

Now that he'd met Susan and Danny, heard the love in her voice, Zack knew his son was better off than he would have been with Alesia. She had definitely not been the maternal type. If Alesia had told him before she had given birth, he would have come home to take his child. But would it have worked out for the baby? A single guy working in foreign locales? How would he have managed?

He knew Susan was a good mother. He could see Danny was doing fine. Another visit or two and then Zack would pull back. No sense getting too caught up in their lives. It would make it harder to leave when the time came.

* * *

Thursday evening when Susan returned home, Edith Jordan had started supper for her. Danny ran to meet her, waving an envelope.

"You got a note from my teacher," he said, jumping up and down.

Edith smiled as she gathered her things. "I think he believes that is good news."

"Are notes from teachers ever good news?" Susan asked as she slipped her finger beneath the flap and tore the envelope open.

"Not when I was teaching," Edith said. "Good night, Danny. See you tomorrow."

"'Kay," he replied, his eyes full of excitement as he watched his mother pull out the sheet of paper.

Edith remained by the door, her curiosity evident.

"They need repairs to some of the school rooms and to the playground equipment," Susan said as she quickly read the letter. "They are asking all parents to lend a hand. Apparently the school needs to come up to code on various things in order to keep going. If not, the city could shut them down."

"What kind of help do they want?" Edith asked.

"Either monetary donation or actually physical participation. Gee, what should I do, give them the extra seventeen dollars from my last paycheck, or go hammer nails, which I've never done, and thus probably could cost them more than any pittance I can give them."

"I'm sure there are other things you can do. You could paint. Or clean up trash. Do they have a list of things needed?"

"It says each room has a list of tasks and goods needed. Could you check for me when you take Danny in tomorrow?"

"Sure. Are major renovations planned?"

"It says the full scope is listed in the classrooms. Maybe I should go in late and take him myself to see what is needed."

"I'll see if they'll give me a copy of what they have. I think they should have sent all that information to the parents."

"Me, too, but they didn't."

Susan bid Edith good-night and went to change into casual attire. Soon she and Danny were sharing dinner. She delighted in hearing about his day. He knew some of the plans at the school because he talked about his classroom getting their bathroom fixed.

"I didn't know it was broken," she said.

"We have to use the bathroom in Mrs. O'Donald's room. So we have to tell our teacher early when we have to go potty," he said earnestly.

Susan nodded, thoughtful. She knew the building that the preschool operated from was old, but she'd never paid much attention to its state. If Edith couldn't get a list of tasks needed, she'd call herself Friday afternoon.

How she would manage another expense remained to be seen. She didn't want to take Danny out of preschool if she could help it. It provided his only interaction with other children except for when he played at the park. But her money only went so far.

Zack leaned against the wall in the hallway outside of Susan's flat Friday evening. Glancing at his watch, the second hand swept around another time. Zack had three more minutes until six-fifteen. He'd already been waiting for more than eight minutes. Once six o'clock had arrived, he'd been hard-pressed to contain his impatience. They were all going out to dinner together and he was very much looking forward to the experience.

It was close enough. He rang the doorbell.

A moment later he heard Susan calling for Danny to wait.

But the little boy was too exuberant. He flung open the door and beamed up at Zack.

"Hi!" Danny said. "We're going to eat pizza."

"I know," Zack said, smiling down at the child. He wanted to lift him up and hug him tightly. But caution was his watchword. He had to take this one step at a time.

Susan came hurrying into the entryway. "Danny! I told you not to open the door until I got here."

"It's Zack," Danny said, as if he'd known beforehand.

"You didn't know that. It could have been anyone."

"It's Zack."

She shook her head and grinned at Zack. "I don't want to scare him with tales about ax murderers, but good grief, he can't throw open the door every time someone knocks."

"Danny, next time, ask who is there before opening the door, okay, sport?" Zack said, stepping inside.

"'Kay," the little boy said running back to his room. "I'll get my sweatshirt."

Zack closed the door and looked at Susan. She wore slim slacks and a pretty green shirt. A sweater was slung over her shoulders. She looked a bit tired, but almost—happy to see him? A man could hope.

"I'm a bit early," he said.

"We're almost ready. Come in and sit down, I'll be right back." She fled down the hall after Danny. Zack stood where he was, listening to the murmur of voices, watching as Danny ran back toward him a moment later. Love filled him for this small child he scarcely knew. Had things been different, Danny would be running toward him calling Daddy.

In less than two minutes they were in the elevator and on their way to dinner.

"This is such a nice treat," Susan said as they stepped into the early April evening. The shadows filled the canyons of the streets. The air was cooler than it had been. He watched as she took a deep breath and seemed to relax before his eyes.

"Tough week?" he asked, glancing from her to Danny. His son had taken his mother's hand and then reached for his. He looked up at Zack.

"Swing me," he said.

"What?"

"Oh, Danny, not now. Zack isn't up to that."

"What?" he asked again.

"Danny likes to swing between two adults who are holding his hands. But it's the last thing you need with a shoulder injury."

"I don't think swinging a little boy is going to put me back in hospital."

"Is one side stronger than another?" she asked.

He shrugged. It felt odd to have someone concerned about him. He'd been making his way alone for a long time.

"So what do I do?" he asked.

"Hold on tight and on three we'll swing him forward and then back. One time, that's all."

Danny shrieked with laughter with his swing. "Again!" he said.

"No, Danny. That's it." Susan was firm.

Danny shot her a frown, then spied several pigeons ahead of them. "Can I catch the birds?"

Susan laughed. "No, we are on our way to dinner. What would you do with them while we ate pizza?"

Zack looked at her. "He could catch them?"

"Of course not. Didn't you ever chase pigeons when you were a kid? He thinks he can catch them and I don't want to rain on his parade. Childhood is a fragile time. One to be cherished and to keep dreams alive as long as we can. We're a long time adults."

Zack wondered if she'd had dreams shattered before their time. Then he remembered her husband. She'd lost him a couple of years ago, decades before she should have. He didn't like thinking about it. He couldn't picture Susan married. Now that he knew her, he would always remember her as she was tonight.

She was young, pretty, personable. She'd most likely find another man to love. He wondered who had been the one unable to make babies? Susan or her husband. Perhaps another man would give her all the children she would want. Zack shook his head as if dislodging the image of her in the arms of another man. He watched the way she interacted with Danny. She'd be great with two or three more kids running around.

The pizza parlor was crowded. Families and teenagers on dates filled the space. There was a children's section at the back, with one lone table still empty.

"I'll grab that table," Susan said, nodding and urging Danny onward. They'd discussed what kind of pizzas they liked on the walk.

Zack ordered, getting a pitcher of cola and made it back to the table Susan had claimed. He glanced around. Danny was playing on one of the tot toys in the fake castle.

"He'll be entertained until the pizza arrives," Susan said, smiling at him when he set the pitcher down.

Slipping into the bench opposite her, he nodded. "I didn't realize how noisy it would be."

"Not a place for quiet discussions, that's for sure," she almost shouted. "But I like it. Lots of energy and fun. Did you go out for pizza a lot as a child?" she asked.

He shook his head. "Not until I was a teenager and bought my own. Many foster parents don't have lots of money. They spend more on the children than the state pays. Most of them do it for love. Which means money is generally tight."

"My mother is from an Italian family. She made pizza for us. I still think my mom makes the best pizza around. Next time she's up, I'll have her make you one. She loves to cook."

Zack nodded, wondering how soon that might be. That opened an entirely new line of thought. He hadn't thought about grandparents in a long time. Not knowing his own parents, of course he had not known any grandparents. Alesia had been estranged from her own parents, but surely that breach would have been healed with a grandchild? In the meantime, he was glad his son had grandparents from Susan.

Despite the noise and commotion constantly churning around them, Zack enjoyed the evening. He couldn't say he and Susan had a meaningful conversation—it was too noisy for that. Danny dashed back when the pizza was delivered to eat a few bites, then he was off again to play. The conversation was sporadic, Susan always keeping a careful watch on Danny.

"Does he know all those kids?" Zack asked, keeping an eye on the group of preschoolers enjoying the castle and tot toys.

"I don't recognize any of them. But kids that age love to play with others. They haven't started being shy or holding back. Having a child is a great way to meet others when moving into a new neighborhood."

"Tell me about the world's situation these days. No threats at the UN?" he asked. Much as he was enchanted with his son, he wanted to get to know Susan better, too. He'd never met anyone before whom he considered connected to. She'd forever be the woman who started his son on the road to maturity whatever the future held. But she was special in her own way. He wanted to learn everything he could, to bring out in the future and remember.

He liked watching her, the ways in which she gestured with her hands, the seriousness when she leaned forward to make a point, or the way her laughter rang out when she was amused. And though he knew she was talking to him, she continued to keep a careful eye on Danny. If he were injured or in trouble she'd be there in an instant.

Nothing untoward happened. Danny had fun, and surprisingly, so did Zack. The pitcher had long been empty and the pizza only a memory when he reluctantly suggested they start for home.

"Oh, I didn't realize how late it is. Danny usually goes to bed around eight. It's almost nine. I've had such fun," she said, almost in disbelief.

"That was the point, to have fun," Zack said, glad he hadn't been the only one enjoying himself.

"Then it worked! Help me corral my son?"

Danny resisted leaving, but Susan was firm. The walk back to the apartment wasn't as fun as the outbound one had been, due to a cranky child.

"Will he let me carry him?" Zack asked after a block.

"I guess he will. I can manage, though," Susan said.

"No! Zack carry me," Danny said when his mother reached for him.

"No problem," Zack said, swinging him up into his arms and holding him against his chest.

The heart was a funny thing. Zack didn't think it could get any larger, but it felt as if it were swelling with love for this child he was only just getting to know. Like must recognize like and he knew he would love Danny forever.

Susan tucked her hand in the crook of his elbow and they walked in silence for another block. It felt right, Zack thought. Like families he used to watch when he was a child. Longing for that special connection that joined father, mother and children, he felt the yearning again. Would he ever be part of such a family?

For a moment the thought of making Susan and Danny his

family flashed into mind. He'd have his son and a loving mother for that son. There'd be family gatherings at holidays and birthdays. He'd belong as he never had before. And his son would be secure all his life in love from his father and the only mother he'd ever known.

It was a perfect solution.

Zack caught his breath. It would work. He could make it work. He already liked being with Susan. He thought she enjoyed being with him. Of course it was too early to discuss marriage. But with a special courtship, could they both come to want the same thing? Marriage?

He couldn't believe he even had such an idea. He'd never expected to marry. His work took him all over the world. And not to locations where he'd want a family. Maybe it was because he'd almost died in that land mine explosion that he had such an idea. Was it a pie-in-the-sky idea, or one with serious merit?

A woman wanted more than just a father for her fatherless son. She wanted to be wanted for herself.

Zack glanced down at Susan. She was pretty in ways that would last—not for her the flashy makeup and fleeting fashion statements his former girlfriend had embraced. She was nothing like Alesia. She would bring security to a marriage he doubted Alesia would ever have managed had she consented to marry him for their child's sake.

Susan glanced up and smiled. "Is he getting heavy?"

"Not at all. I've enjoyed tonight." More than he had expected.

"Me, too." She squeezed his arm slightly and looked away, a slight smile on her lips.

When they reached Susan's apartment, she invited him in.

"I'll put Danny to bed and we can have some coffee, if you like," she said, as she worked the key in the lock.

"Sounds great. I'd hate the evening to end so soon," he said. "I can help put him to bed."

"You don't need to."

"Want Zack," Danny mumbled, snuggling closer to the man who held him.

Susan laughed. "Okay, then. You have to get right into pjs and brush your teeth. No dawdling tonight, it's late."

"'Kay," he said.

Zack carried Danny into his bedroom and sat on the edge of the bed. Susan handed him a set of pajamas and Zack set Danny on his feet and helped him take off the sweatshirt and T-shirt he wore. It wasn't easy getting Danny to put on his pajama top; the child wanted to flop against him, already half asleep.

Finally he was ready and Zack followed the two of them to the bathroom to watch Danny brush his teeth. Leaning against the doorjamb, he enjoyed the routine Susan and Danny had with his son standing on the closed toilet lid and first brushing his teeth by himself, then with Susan helping.

"All done!" he sang out when Susan had him rinse his mouth.

He jumped from the toilet, straight for Zack. Only his quick reflexes had him catch his son before the boy landed on the floor.

"Danny, don't do that. It's dangerous," Susan scolded.

"Zack catched me," he said, beaming.

Zack vowed to always be there to catch his son if humanly possible.

"He's fearless," she said, shaking her head. "A little caution wouldn't hurt."

"Within reason," Zack said.

"You don't think I baby him too much, do you?" she asked uncertainly.

"Not that I can see. He's learning independence, and that's what parents want, right?" Zack asked, carrying Danny back to bed. He laid him down and covered him.

"Read me a story," Danny said, his eyes already drooping.

"Please," Susan added.

"Please."

Zack looked at the book Susan handed him. "If you read, I'll start the coffee."

Zack had never read a book to a child. He opened the first page noting there were only two sentences on most pages. It wouldn't take long to get through the book.

Even so, before he was halfway to the end, Danny fell asleep.

Zack leaned over and kissed his cheek. "Sleep well, little man." For several minutes, he just sat and gazed at this miracle—his son. His cheeks had healthy color, his eyelashes skimmed the top of the pudgy cheeks. His chest rose and fell, scarcely moving the sheet and light blanket. Time seemed to stand still.

Finally Zack rose and turned off the light. Did Susan close the door or leave it open? There was so much he still didn't know about his own son. He left it open and headed for the living room.

"Your timing is good—coffee's ready. I have some cookies, too, but nothing fancy for dessert," she said, bringing the coffee in on a tray. Macaroons were piled on a decorative plate. Napkins and mugs crowded in.

She had switched on two lamps in the room, and opened the curtains to let in the night lights from the city. It was cozy. A far cry from the rented places he'd lived in over the last decade. Most were only a place to get mail and eat and sleep. No photographs crowded tables, no paintings hung on the walls. No toys dotted the floor.

Susan had made a home for herself and Danny even in this small, old apartment. Something Zack envied.

If they married, he'd be included in her home. It was an odd feeling.

Glancing at the photographs of her husband, he wondered if he had a chance getting her to let go of the past and move ahead.

Whoa—he was getting way ahead of himself. He wasn't certain he was cut out for marriage. The first thing he'd have to change would be his job. He couldn't marry and expect a wife to live alone for two years at a time while he went off to build a bridge.

He'd never thought about settling down, making a family, buying a home.

Yet, why not? He'd wanted permanence when he'd been a child. He could make his own permanent arrangement. Buy a house with lots of yard space. Get a dog. Have cookouts in the backyard. Get to know his neighbors. Put down roots.

Would Susan want to leave the city? She said she loved it, but would she also be open to the idea of living in a house with a yard? It was something he'd yearned for when younger. If he stayed in the States, he could afford to buy the perfect house—suitable for a child and pets.

Susan watched as Zack's gaze roamed around her living room. She glanced around, trying to see it through his eyes. It reflected her personality and idea of home more than her late husband's. It was a comedown from the apartment she and Tom had shared, but she liked it. Did Zack like it? Or was it too feminine for him? He lived a rugged lifestyle—far different from what she liked.

"Do you miss being back at the job site? Will you go back to the same place?" she asked.

He leaned back against her sofa cushions and looked at her, his eyes narrowed in thought. "I do miss it. It's great work. I enjoy being part of the construction team bringing modern conveniences to a desperate place. But I think I'm ready for a change. I want to set down roots and find a niche here that will bring me as much satisfaction. Maybe not right away, but I no longer see myself as a nomad for the rest of my days."

"And you once thought you would be all your life?" she asked.

He shrugged. "It's what I know. I had four foster homes growing up. By the time I was in high school, I knew not to become attached—there was always the possibility of being yanked to yet another one. This kind of life followed suit. The upside is the travel to countries I'd never have visited if I weren't doing this kind of work."

"So what changed?"

"Almost getting killed. Life is suddenly more precious than I expected. Things can change in a heartbeat. You and your husband had hopes for the future, he died. I don't plan to live in fear the rest of my life, but I don't plan to take it for granted, either."

She nodded, surprised to realize the crushing ache she used to feel when reminded of Tom's untimely death didn't threaten her tonight. She studied Zack for a moment. He looked tired, but virile and intriguing. She didn't usually relate to people as easily as she had him. Or invite them into her home. But it seemed right with Zack. Was it because he was recuperating from serious injuries and she felt compassion for all he'd been through?

No, she didn't feel a bit sorry for the man. The truth was he fascinated her. He lived abroad and worked at a job most men never even dreamed about. He'd faced danger and survived. On a purely physical level, he attracted her. His eyes were dreamy. His lips drew her attention again and again. Despite the recovery mode he was in, he was muscular and strong and made her feel special.

She blinked and looked away, seeking a picture of Tom. For once the connection she normally felt was missing. It was merely a colored photograph of a man she'd once known, loved and now mourned. Tom was gone.

Susan was not dead. And while they'd never discussed what the other should do if one died young, she knew Tom would have wanted her to explore all facets of life. To move on and find happiness elsewhere if she could. He had loved life, loved her and loved Danny. He would want the very best for them even if he couldn't provide it.

Did that mean getting to know someone else? Someone so different? Someone who made her feel like she was on the edge of something wonderful and thrilling—yet scary. She wasn't ready for that. She'd had a great marriage with Tom. It would be highly unlikely she'd find another man who could give her the same thing.

"Are you okay?" he asked.

She looked at him. "Yes, why?"

"Your expression looked almost scared."

"Sorry, I was thinking of something else." She glanced almost apologetically at Tom's picture then smiled at Zack. "Do have a cookie, or aren't macaroons ones you like?"

"I like them. I'm still full from pizza. That was fun tonight. I think Danny preferred the toys to the food, though."

"Yes, he loves to explore new things."

Zack reached out to place his cup on the coffee table and in doing so, knocked off an opened letter. He reached for it, glancing at it briefly.

"What's this?" he asked, putting it back on the table. "Danny's school needs repairs?"

"It's an old building, as is everything around this neighborhood. Last winter one of the storms found a weak spot in the roof and it leaked like crazy. The building inspectors came to check for mold. In doing the inspection, they found other items not up to current code. And the playground equipment is a bit antiquated. That letter is a call to parents for help."

"So what are you going to do?" he asked.

"I don't know yet. I'm not very handy. I don't think I've done more than hammer a nail into the wall to hang pictures. I did paint the kitchen. Guess I'll do what they assign me and hope for the best."

"Need more help?"

"You?"

"I'm at a loose end and going a bit crazy with inactivity. I'm not ready to return to work full-time. I need a doctor's release for the company first. But I could manage a bit of repair work."

"I can't ask you to do that."

"You're not asking, I'm volunteering."

She studied him for a moment. "I think that would be amazing. I doubt any of the parents have the kind of knowledge and experience you have. But it's strictly volunteer."

Zack smiled. "I know that, Susan. I'd be happy to help."

"Wow. Great. I'll let them know Tuesday when Danny goes again. There's a planning meeting on Wednesday evening and the projects begin Saturday. Are you sure?"

Zack nodded.

"Thank you. Do you remember where the preschool is?"

"Just a few blocks from here."

"Yes. I was going to walk over after dinner on Wednesday. If you want to come here for dinner first, we can go together."

"Sounds like a plan. Will Danny be coming?"

"No, Edith is going to watch him. I really appreciate this, Zack. It'll really help the school."

"No problem. As I said, I could use the activity." He rose. "I think I should be heading out. It's getting late."

Susan nodded and put down her cup. Standing, she led the way to the door. "Thanks again for taking us to dinner. I know Danny loved it."

"Thanks for going with me," he said. He leaned over and brushed his lips against hers.

Susan caught her breath. For a moment Zack's eyes met hers, then he leaned in again, reaching for her this time, pulling her into his embrace. When his lips met hers, she closed her eyes and kissed him back.

She didn't know Zack well, but the attraction she'd been fighting surged to the front. His mouth moved against hers, his arms held her securely. She leaned in, wanting more. Thrilled at the sensations that swept through her, she opened her lips to return his kiss. When he deepened the embrace, she felt herself spinning through space tingling with desire.

Before she could begin to think coherently, he pulled back a little and then brushed her damp lips with his thumb. Looking into his dark eyes, she could see wonder, desire and something else in them. She had a million questions, felt a dozen different emotions. But knew she wanted more from this man. He ignited her senses, filled her with a delight she hadn't experienced in a long time.

"I really enjoyed tonight," she said. She wanted to say more, but felt suddenly uncertain. Was he kissing her because he hadn't been with a woman in a long time? She couldn't bear it if that were the case. Susan hoped he had meant more by it. She wanted to know more about Zack. Was she being susceptible to the first man she'd been attracted to since Tom's death, or was there truly something special about Zack himself?

He dropped his hands and stepped to the door. Opening it, he turned and looked at her. Susan felt her heart skip a beat at the look in those dark eyes.

"Want to go on a picnic with me to Central Park tomorrow?"

"Danny?"

"Always included," he said.

"We'd love to." How had she lucked out in finding a man who would include her son whenever he saw her?

CHAPTER FOUR

SUSAN called her mother for their weekly chat early on Saturday morning. As usual, she asked after her father first.

"He's going strong and I plan to keep him that way for a long time!" Amelia Molina said. "How is that precious boy of ours?"

"Danny's doing fine. He still loves preschool and now that the weather allows him to get to the park more often, he's in heaven. He loves the spiral slide best."

"Are you going to the park today?" her mother asked.

"Actually we're going on a picnic to Central Park," Susan said. She realized she hadn't told her parents about meeting Zack. There was not much to say.

"With that friend of yours who has a child?" her mother asked.

"Actually it's with someone I met recently. He's on leave right now and trying to see as much of New York as he can."

"He?" Her mother almost pounced on the word.

"Zack Morgan." She hadn't told her parents about Zack's role when Danny had run after a stranger thinking it was Tom. Now it seemed too late. "Someone I met because of preschool." That was the truth, just not all of it.

"An older man?" her mother asked.

"Not so old—just a few years older than I am." Susan

hadn't considered how old Zack was. "He's been working in the Middle East the last few years."

"Ah."

"What does that mean?"

"I didn't realize you had started dating again. It's a good thing, honey."

"Mom, we're not dating. We've hardly spent any time together and Danny is always with us. I don't consider that dating."

"He likes Danny?"

"Zack seems to like him very much." Susan remembered how he'd carried Danny home from pizza and tucked him into bed. "And I'd say Danny likes him a lot. He insisted Zack read him his book last night at bedtime." Now that she thought about it, Danny had not looked at every man in the pizza place to see if he were Tom. Maybe meeting Zack had been a good thing.

"This Zack was there last night?"

"Mom, we went to pizza. He walked us home, read Danny a book and that's all. Don't go making more of this than warranted." She didn't see any reason to tell her mother about that kiss. The kiss that had kept her awake half the night, and dreaming X-rated dreams the other half.

"I want you to be happy, honey. We all miss Tom. It's dreadful his dying so young. But you need not be a widow all your life. If you find happiness with another man, Tom would never have stood in your way. Clinging to the past won't bring him back, honey."

"I know." She looked at the closest picture. Tom was smiling into the camera. For a moment she felt the happiness in that day. He had loved life. He would want her to embrace it as well. But it was hard. She missed him so much. She didn't know how to move on.

Could she with Zack?

Too early to tell. Though she had been thinking about him a lot. And about the feelings she was coming to expect when around him—excitement, anticipation, desire.

"So your father and I should come up to meet Zack," her mother said.

"No, you should not. If anything develops, I'll let you know. For the moment, he's just a lonely guy who wants some companionship when he goes sightseeing. We went to the zoo last week."

"Sounds to me like it's more than being acquaintances, but I'll wait for you to tell me if we need to come up. Is Danny around? I'd love to talk with him. Poppa wants to talk to him as well. Then your father will want to talk to you."

Susan called Danny and stayed nearby listening to his side of the conversation. At one point she almost interrupted. To hear Danny talk, Zack was the center of his world. She hoped her parents weren't getting the wrong idea. Or getting their hopes up. She knew her mother felt a woman was incomplete without a man. Not that she couldn't do whatever she wanted, but she loved being married and thought that should be the goal of every woman on the planet.

Susan wasn't sure she would ever go down that road again. She and Tom had shared something special. Could she ever find that a second time? What if she married and found she continued to miss Tom. Or compared a new husband to Tom. Or worse fell in love and lost him again.

"Okay." Danny turned and handed her the phone. "Poppa wants to talk to you."

"Hi, Dad."

"How's my best girl?"

"Mom must not be nearby," Susan said.

He laughed. "She's right here, but knows you are my best

girl. Danny talked of nothing but this Zack. What do you know about the man?"

Susan spent a couple of minutes filling in her father with what limited information she had on Zack. Then she changed the subject and asked after her dad's bingo nights.

When the conversation ended, Susan couldn't say she was sorry. She needed to be careful about what she said in the next phone call with her parents. She didn't want them projecting their own desires for her future on to Danny.

As she got Danny ready for their picnic, she wondered if she should be so quick to accept all Zack's invitations. She'd been happy they included Danny. Her little boy still missed his father, even two years later. She ached for him and knew he was too young to fully understand his daddy was never coming home.

But he was not too young to bond with another male. She wasn't changing one heartache for another, was she?

When Zack arrived and knocked, Danny ran to the door. "Who is it?" he yelled, then quickly opened the door.

"Hi, Zack," he said, smiling up at the man.

"You didn't give me time to answer," Zack said, reaching out to tousle the little boy's hair. "Next time let me tell you who is at the door before you open it, okay?"

"'Kay," Danny said. "Mommy, Zack's here."

"So I see," Susan said, coming into the tiny hall. She felt breathless with anticipation. For one crazy moment she wished he'd reach out and kiss her senseless. But not in front of Danny. And maybe never again. She needed to keep her head straight.

The day was lovely. A slight breeze blew from the west, keeping the temperatures down, but the sunshine more than made up for it. Danny had only been to Central Park a few times. When they arrived and he saw the vast expanse of lawn, he was awed.

"Most green I've seen in years," Zack said, surveying the same expanse.

"I bet it's really brown in the desert," Susan said. She was prepared to enjoy the day and not remember their kiss. And she refused to wish for more.

Or she tried to. As the morning wore on, she found herself looking at Zack's mouth more and more, remembering the tingling awareness that had swept through her when he had fastened his lips against hers. Darn it, she did want another kiss. Just to see if the first had been a fluke.

And if it hadn't? She didn't know what she'd do. She hardly knew him. They had so little in common. He worked thousands of miles away. How could she expect some kind of long-term relationship? Yet he was the most exciting man she knew. There was so much to discover, and enjoy in the process.

They saw the Alice in Wonderland sculpture and rode the carousel several times to Danny's delight. Susan laughed more than she had in months. Zack had a way of making the day special and fun. Danny was enchanted to have the man stoop down and talk to him on his level. More than once he leaned against Zack's shoulder when he explained something to the boy. And he had stopped looking at other men trying to find Tom.

Shortly after noon Zack pointed to a sheltered spot and asked if they'd like to have the picnic there.

Susan nodded as Danny ran ahead and then turned to wait for them.

Zack had toted a large canvas bag around all morning and now he began to unpack it

"I bought fried chicken, crusty bread and chocolate milk," he said, taking first a blanket from the bag then a small, soft sided cooler.

"Something we'll all like," she said, touched he'd gone to such trouble.

Lunch proved to be fun. They were still within range of the carousel music so when conversation ebbed and flowed, the music filled the silence.

When they finished, Zack leaned back and closed his eyes. "The sun feels good. Warm, not blazing like the heat of Arabia."

"Time for everyone to rest," Susan said, grabbing Danny when he jumped up and was ready to run.

"I'm not tired," he protested.

"Well I am and so is Zack."

"Lie down here by me, Danny, and we'll look at the clouds," Zack invited.

Susan glanced up. There were only a couple of small puffy white clouds in the sky. Danny lay down right beside Zack.

"Now we look at the clouds and see what pictures we can see," Zack said.

"Where are pictures?" Danny asked, looking around.

Zack glanced over at Susan. "Aren't you joining us?" he asked.

She scooted down until she lay beside her son. Smiling she studied one cloud, pointing it to Danny. "I see a rabbit," she said.

Soon Danny caught on and the three of them found the most outlandish pictures in the few drifting clouds. Before long Danny fell asleep and when Susan glanced over, Zack looked as if he had as well. She felt such a feeling of well-being. It was fun to shed responsibilities for a few hours and just enjoy herself. She closed her eyes and let the sun warm her.

She awoke with a start a short time later. Danny was still asleep, but Zack sat on the edge of the blanket, his gaze a million miles away.

"Sorry, I didn't mean to fall asleep," she said, sitting up.

"I dozed a bit myself." He turned to look at her. "Danny's not going to get sunburned, is he?"

"I put on sunscreen this morning, but let's rig up some shade." She moved the canvas bag so it was beside her son, then took off her sweater to make a lean-to shade for him.

"You won't get cold?" Zack asked.

"I'm warm now. If it gets cooler, I'll wake him up. But for now the nap is good for him. Keeps him from being cranky."

"How do you manage all you do with a rambunctious four-year-old?" Zack asked.

"I didn't have to work when he was younger. Edith has been a lifesaver since Tom died. It would be so much harder if I didn't have her to help me."

"It would be better if he had a parent at home all day."

"That was our plan. Only Tom got killed and so I had to go to plan B. Or maybe it was plan C, because we never even considered one of us dying before Danny grew up. I had planned to stay home at least until he started school. I miss so much. He changes every day. Edith takes pictures for me and my parents. I mail a bunch out every few weeks so they'll keep connected. But it's not the same."

Zack nodded.

"I guess you don't have any photographs of you as a child," she said thoughtfully.

"Actually I do have one album in storage. The foster parents took pictures at birthdays and Christmas. And I have my senior high school yearbook. The past doesn't mean so much to me—it's the future I look forward to."

She could understand the past didn't hold special memories for Zack. It was too sad that children had to grow up that way. "I should have brought a camera today, but I don't have any film. I need to pick some up."

"I took pictures of different bases, not many but enough so I can remember them down through the years," Zack said slowly. "Before and after shots, and some as the work progressed."

They seemed a poor substitute for family photos.

"Do you have access to them? I'd love to see them sometime," she said. It would give her more information, help understand him better perhaps.

"So one night we'll share photo albums. I'm glad you came with me today."

"I've enjoyed myself." Once again Susan's glance dropped to Zack's mouth. She quickly looked away.

Zack felt her look like a physical touch. She'd done that several times today; looked at his mouth and then quickly looked away. Was she remembering their kiss? He'd thought of it ever since last night. He was coming to really like this mother to his son.

He had also enjoyed today. Danny seemed to feel comfortable around him. He expected more resistance. Would it take long to win his complete confidence and trust? Could he at some point in the future reveal who he really was?

The longer Zack was around the boy, the more he wanted to be. This was his son, his own flesh and blood. So many things he'd wished for as a child he could give to this boy. He never wanted anything bad to happen to him. What if Susan was killed unexpectedly like her husband? Who would take care of Danny? Had she made provisions? Or was she hoping she never needed another plan B?

He hoped she never did.

Zack watched his son nap. He was so trusting and loving and full of life. Had Zack once been like that? Before circumstances had taught him to be wary of bonds that could be shredded in a heartbeat when he was reassigned a different family. He'd sometime imagined his parents had lived and been searching for him. And one day found him.

He wondered if Danny had been told he was adopted? If not, would Susan tell him when he was older? What kind of questions would he have about his birth parents? Zack never wanted him to think his father had let him down. Family ties were important.

He was happy Danny had been adopted by the Johnsons. Susan was a great mom, just like he would have liked as a boy. Danny was lucky despite the heartache of the only father he knew dying.

"I'm thirsty," Danny said.

"You're awake," Susan said, moving her sweater. "There's another bottle of water."

Zack watched as Danny drank almost half the contents and then jumped up. "Where are we going now?" he asked.

"I thought we'd take a carriage ride later," Zack said.

"Let's go!" Danny said, excited.

"Wait until we pack up," Susan said.

Danny began running.

Zack rose, ready to give chase if needed. "Danny," he called. The little boy stopped and turned.

Zack crooked his finger. When Danny slowly walked back, he said, "We have to pack up as your mother said. You're growing up now, you need to take responsibility for some chores you can handle."

Danny's eyes got big. "I have respons'bility?"

"Yes. Right now, you can take the trash to that can over there. Then come right back." Zack handed him a small bunch of napkins and foil.

Susan watched, bemused, as Danny carefully held the trash in both hands and took it to the trash can. Smiling, he ran back.

"Good job," Zack said. He glanced at Susan who was studying him.

"Did I overstep a boundary?" he asked.

"Not at all. I think I'm keeping him a baby too long. But he's growing fast and while I love each stage, I really cherished the baby time."

"I think I can understand that, but a child needs to push boundaries. That's how they grow and learn."

"So you know about kids?" she teased gently.

"Only from growing up around them," he said gravely. "I had a lot of different families to compare, and to see what worked and what didn't." At least that part of his childhood had been beneficial—helping him formulate his own code of behavior, and the desires he had for a family of his own. He'd almost forgotten the days he'd sat on a lonely park swing, dreaming of how things would be when he had a family. Work over the last decade had demanded all his focus.

Now that he was in an enforced resting period, he had time to think. And plan for a future that possibly included his son in some way. And Susan. He glanced at her, taking a good long look. Her hair was slightly disheveled by the nap and the breeze. Her cheeks were glowing and her eyes sparkled. He felt a tug on his heart. She was open and fresh and sexy as any woman he knew. If it weren't for Danny, and they weren't in the middle of Central Park, he'd draw her into his arms again and kiss her. Last night had been chancy; now all he could think about was kissing Susan again.

"I welcome all suggestions," she said as they began walking in the lush grass. "Parenting does not come with a handbook. Being a solo parent isn't easy. No one to bounce ideas off of, or discuss serious situations."

"Your parents don't help?" He tried to focus. Forget kissing her anytime soon. But sooner or later they'd be alone.

"To a degree. But I don't want them to feel they have to put their lives on hold while I struggle with mine. Their living so far away doesn't make matters easier. And Tom's mother is in bad health, lives in an assisted-care facility in California. His dad died before we were married. So Edith is really a huge help. A member of our family, so to speak. Anyway, enough about me. What do you want to do next?"

Spend more time with you, was the immediate involuntary thought. Zack glanced down at Susan as she called to Danny to come back to walk with them. He felt a small spurt of contentment. She was having a good time because he'd invited her on this picnic. Did he have the capacity to give her a good time always?

"I brought a ball. Would Danny like to play catch?" Zack asked.

She laughed. "He'd love it. But don't expect any coordination yet. If you lob it gently right to him, he'll catch it one time out of three. He's pretty good at throwing," Susan said. "Danny! Want to play catch?"

"Yes!" He ran back to them, his eyes shining. "Did you bring a ball?"

"I did," Zack said, reaching into the bag and pulling out a small, soft ball.

"Thank you!" Danny said, hugging Zack's leg.

The three of them played catch for as long as Danny was interested. Then Zack gave him the ball and sat on the grass to watch as Danny threw it high in the air and tried to catch it. His lack of success didn't seem to dim his enjoyment.

Susan sat beside Zack. "You seem to know exactly how to entertain a little boy. Remarkable since you haven't had much to do with children lately."

"I was a boy once."

"Did your foster parents play ball?"

He shrugged. "The Zumwalts did. George Zumwalt was big on bonding, on giving the children they watched lots of experiences and fun times."

"What happened to him?"

"He died unexpectedly of a heart attack when he was only forty-three," Zack said. He remembered the pain of that loss. His wife had not been able to continue in the foster care program and Zack and the two other foster children had been split up and sent to new homes.

"I'm sorry."

"Yeah, I was, too."

Susan looked at Danny. "As time goes on, Danny will remember less and less about his father. I wonder even now how much he remembers and how much he knows from the stories I tell. I guess I'm one of the lucky ones—both my parents are still living."

"You are. One day you'll marry again and that man will be a role model for your son. He will have parents and Danny would have even more grandparents," he said.

Susan shrugged. "I don't know. I loved Tom so much. I still can't believe he's gone." She rubbed her chest. "The ache just doesn't seem to go away."

"There are other reasons to marry. To form a family. For companionship."

"I know. But somehow without love, I just don't think it would work. It's hard enough to be tied in a marriage when bad things happen. Disappointments. Frustrations. If there's no bond of love, how would two people survive all that life throws at them?"

Zack leaned closer, reaching out to catch her hand in his and threading his fingers through hers.

"By working together through whatever hardship comes. Even if deep love doesn't come, there could be affection and respect and liking. Would that be enough?"

Susan stared into his eyes. Zack could see the hesitation.

He leaned back and squeezed her hand gently, letting her go. He was pushing too fast.

"I'm a fine one to talk. I've never married."

Susan gazed at her hand, clinching it into a fist.

Zack couldn't expect Susan to give him all the love her first husband had. But he would always be a devoted husband and always love Danny. That should count for something. Could she see it that way?

They walked to where the carriages queued up. Zack paid as Susan lifted Danny into the white carriage and then climbed up after him. Danny was excited with the prospect and asked if he could ride the horse.

"No. The horse's job is to pull the carriage. You can watch the driver and maybe one day you'll want to drive a carriage," Susan said as Zack joined them on the bench seat.

Slowly the horse started off. Danny bounced on the seat with excitement.

Zack stretched his arm on the back of the seat, his hand just inches away from her shoulders. Susan tried to relax and enjoy the ride, but her senses were revved up and attuned to Zack's every move. It had been a long time since she'd felt this way around a man. Not since Tom.

They left for home after the carriage ride. Danny wanted Zack to come in and play with him.

"Not today, sport. Zack's spent enough time with us. He has to do things on his own," she said, with a quick smile at Zack. It wasn't Zack who needed time alone, it was her. Her heart had kicked up a notch when he'd taken her hand this afternoon. She'd wanted to recapture his when they walked to the taxi stand in the Park, but had been too uncertain of how he'd take it.

She never wanted him to think she was some lonely widow looking for a man any place she could find him. Was her mother right? Did a woman need a man? She hoped not, for her sake.

"Thanks again for the picnic. I can't remember the last one I went on," she said to Zack in the elevator as it rose to her floor.

"Thank you for coming. A picnic for one just wouldn't have been the same."

"I guess not." She stepped off when the elevator reached her floor and the doors opened. Not Danny.

"I could come to your house and play," he told Zack, gazing up at the tall man.

"Danny, no more today. Come along." For a moment Susan was tempted to say the same thing. Only the play she had in mind wouldn't be for children, but two adults.

Shocked at her thoughts, she reached for Danny and urged him from the elevator. She knew people couldn't read minds, but she had to clamp down on her emotions before Zack picked up an inkling of what she was feeling.

She marched to her front door, resolutely refusing to turn to watch as Zack was enclosed behind the doors of the elevator and whisked away.

"Get a grip," she said softly as she fumbled with the key in the lock.

"What?" Danny asked.

"Nothing. Let's wash our hands and have some juice, then you can play in your room for a while."

Zack's talk of marriage had been sad. Wasn't he looking for love? She thought he was expecting too little. She and Tom had had a wonderful marriage. They'd loved the same activities, same movies. They'd never ran out of things to talk about. Especially after a long day at the office when he came home and wanted to know every detail of Danny's day. That first year they had Danny had been especially amazing. She longed for that close tie again. Maybe her mother was right: she did need another husband.

But her expectations for a mate seemed higher than Zack's. Maybe because she came from a loving family and he had none. Or maybe because of a myriad of other reasons. Whatever—was she softening in her no-more-marriage view? Was it time to let go?

It was too hard. She wanted to cling to all they'd had for as long as she could. Her marriage to Tom had been the best time of her life, and she hated to know it was gone. If she could just talk to him once more, spend an afternoon together. She had not properly cherished their time together, had taken it for granted and in an instant it had vanished. Could she ever move on, trust in the future enough to take a chance with another man? She didn't think she could live through the heartache of losing a husband again.

Yet, did she want to live a lonely life from now until she was old and gray? That would mean possibly passing up a happy future simply to cling to the past. That sounded equally unacceptable. She didn't like feeling so confused.

It was just too hard.

CHAPTER FIVE

Sunday it rained.

Susan was grumpy because of lack of sleep. She had tossed and turned all night, thinking about Zack. She wouldn't settle for a companion role, but could see the appeal to a man who might not know much about love. Just to have someone to make a family with would be important to him.

Once she had fallen asleep, she'd dreamed about Zack. She couldn't escape the man!

Danny was fussy. He wanted to go to the park, but Susan had said no. Summer rain could be fun to walk through, but it was still early spring and cold outside.

By ten o'clock, Danny had tired of playing in his room, didn't want to watch a DVD and yelled at Susan that he wanted Zack to play with.

She put him on time-out for five minutes for yelling at her, but felt sorry for the little guy. She wouldn't mind Zack stopping by to visit herself.

In desperation, Susan bundled him up and they went to the market. The closest one didn't have all the things she wanted, but she bought two full bags of groceries, including chocolate chips. She and Danny could bake cookies when they got home. It beat having him drive her crazy.

"Hello, Susan, dear," Edith said, coming around the end of the aisle and seeing the Johnsons.

"Edith, how are you?" Susan looked sharply at her neighbor and baby-sitter. The older woman looked pale.

"Not feeling so well. I'm sure I'll bounce back and be right as rain tomorrow. Oh, dear," she said with a slight grimace. "Rain today isn't so right."

"I wish you'd told me you needed something from the store—it would have saved you coming out in this nasty weather," Susan said. "Can I help you home with your things?"

"I bought plenty of soup. Just in case. If I'm not better in the morning, you may need to make other arrangements for Danny. I don't want him to get sick."

"Don't worry about that. You concentrate on getting well. Let me help."

Susan carried the bag with Edith's soup cans, plus her own items. Danny was subdued around her and Susan hoped he was being attentive to her situation and not coming down with something himself.

"Thank you, dear," Edith said when they reached her apartment. "I'll just put the food away and then lie down."

"No, you go lie down now. I'll put things away, and make you some of this soup. When did you eat last?"

"I couldn't eat anything earlier. A small cup of soup does sound nice about now," the older woman said, taking off her raincoat and laying it across the back of her sofa.

Susan knew she was sick. Edith was fastidious about caring for her things. Normally she'd never put a wet raincoat over her sofa.

Susan hung it up to dry in the kitchen and quickly put away the few items Edith had purchased. She then prepared a cup of soup for her and carried it into her bedroom.

"Here you go," she said. Edith had already changed into a nightgown and was beneath her covers.

"Thank you. I shall be fine in short order," the older woman said. She still looked pale.

"Maybe not. Even if you are, you won't want to watch Danny tomorrow. I'll see if I can find another sitter, or stay home with him myself."

The fact her child-care provider didn't argue showed Susan how sick she truly was.

"Do you need anything else?" Susan asked, resisting the urge to feel her forehead to see if she had a fever.

"I'll be fine."

"Well, I'll check back later."

"Thank you, Susan, you run along now." Her lids were already dropping. Susan waited long enough for her to finish the soup and took the cup.

"You were a good boy, Danny," she said when she entered the kitchen and found her son gazing out the rain drenched window. She was proud of how well he could behave when the chips were down.

"Is Edith going to die?" he asked, looking worried.

"No, honey, not for a long, long time. She's just a little sick. Come on, we'll head for home and make our cookies. We'll come back down in a little while to check on her, okay?"

"'Kay," he said, climbing down from the chair and looking closely at Susan.

"You won't get sick, will you, Mommy?"

"I won't. At least I hope neither one of us does. Come on, tiptoe so we don't disturb Edith."

A couple of hours later several batches of cookies cooled on wire racks on her counter. Susan and Danny surveyed them proudly.

"I helped," Danny said.

"Yes, you did. You were a good helper."

"Can we give some to Zack? I bet he doesn't have chocolate chip cookies at his house," Danny said.

"That would be a good idea." And a good excuse to see him, just for a moment. She had his phone number. Would he like them to come and bring him cookies? Probably taking a child to a hotel room wasn't the wisest move. Maybe he was tired enough of his hotel he'd relish the walk over.

Glancing out the window, she saw the rain had stopped. For how long, she wasn't sure. It was still gray and overcast.

"And we can give some cookies to Edith," he added.

"I'm not sure she'll be up to cookies, but we'll take her some just in case," Susan said.

They carefully packed two plates with cookies. Heading out to check on Edith, Susan gave the plate to Danny to carry. He solemnly walked to the elevator and waited for her to press the button.

Edith had grown worse. Admonishing Danny to sit on the sofa and not touch anything, Susan prepared Edith some more soup and brought her a warm washcloth to freshen up. The woman had a high fever and Susan made sure she had aspirin before giving her the soup.

"Shall I call a doctor?"

"No. Don't get near me, Susan. You need to stay well for Danny. I'll ride this out and be better before you know it. Go on now. I thank you for stopping by."

"When you finish the soup," Susan said. "We'll be quiet in the living room. But I want to make sure you're holding it down before we leave."

"I'll be fine," the older woman said, but she sat up against the pillows Susan plumped up for her and began to sip the soup.

It was more than a half hour later when Susan and Danny left. Edith had fallen asleep again. Susan knew the older woman had no one else, so vowed she'd check in on her each day at least once or twice.

When she returned to her apartment, she gave way to impulse and called Zack.

"Morgan," he answered. Her heart began pounding at the sound of his voice.

"Hi. Miserable day, isn't it?"

"I like it. I walked to a coffee shop this morning in the rain. When you live in a desert most of the time, rain is a treat."

"It's cold and damp and dreary," she countered.

"But rain keeps that grass in Central Park green. And washes the air. It is clean and crisp outside."

"So, want to take another walk in that crisp, clean air?" she asked.

"To?"

"My place. Danny and I baked chocolate chip cookies this morning. I wish it was nice enough to take him to the park. That would burn off some of his energy. Be prepared, if you come over, you'll have to participate in entertaining a rambunctious kid." She was talking too fast, as if she didn't leave an opening for him, he couldn't refuse.

She hoped he'd want to come over. She wanted to see him.

"Sounds like a plan. I love chocolate chip cookies. I don't think I've had homemade ones since I was a kid. I can be there in a half hour."

"We'll be here." She hung up feeling breathless with anticipation. He was coming over. Granted, Danny would be a perfect chaperone. But she didn't care; she'd get to see Zack again. And then it was only a couple of days until he came to see where she worked. And then there was the school meeting on Wednesday evening.

She could use the time until Zack arrived to line up a babysitter for a couple of days.

It was midafternoon by the time Zack arrived.

"We made cookies!" Danny announced, beaming up at him.

"So you did. Chocolate chip, my favorite."

"Come on," Danny said, racing for the kitchen.

Susan laughed, bubbling with happiness. She was glad he'd come over.

"Let me take your jacket then follow the enthusiastic kid for cookies."

Zack reached over and brushed his lips against hers. His were cool. The kiss was too brief, but still caused Susan to catch her breath. Her gaze dropped to his jacket. When he took it off, she hung it up, feeling the warmth from his body.

"Here you go," Danny said, coming out of the kitchen holding a plate of cookies. It tipped dangerously.

"Hey, thanks, buddy." Zack moved swiftly to get the plate from the little boy before all the cookies landed on the floor.

"These look great. You made them?" he asked Danny.

The child smiled widely and nodded his head. "Mommy said I could help."

"Good for mommy. How are they?" Zack took one and bit into it. "Delicious!" he declared turning to look at Susan.

Susan walked past him, catching a hint of his scent—aftershave and Zack. It kicked up her pulse rate. She was glad she'd brushed her hair, put on fresh lipstick and made sure all traces of flour were gone from her dark sweater.

"Danny loves to make cookies so any rainy day, that's often a project," she said, feeling suddenly shy and as awkward as a schoolgirl. "Want some milk or coffee to go with that?"

"Do you have hot chocolate?"

"Yes. That would be good for all of us on such a day," she said, heading for the kitchen. Making the hot chocolate would give her something to do until her nerves calmed down.

Zack followed her and put the plate of cookies on the counter.

Danny rushed in and looked around. "Aren't you going to eat the cookies?" he asked.

"I had one. I'll have another when your mom has the hot chocolate ready."

"I like marshmallows in mine," Danny said. In a moment, bored, he left.

Zack leaned against the doorjamb and watched as Susan prepared their hot drinks.

"If I didn't have to act like an adult," Zack began, "I'd gobble up all those cookies. But I had better be a good example to an impressionable kid."

She laughed. "Good idea. How was your walk over?"

"Cold. I think the temperature dropped twenty degrees. But it felt good."

"I'm ready for summer. It was cold all winter long. I think this is ready. Want to call Danny for me?"

"I'll go get him," Zack said.

Zack returned a moment later, carrying a laughing Danny. "Found him."

"We'll sit at the table. It's less chancy for him spilling things," she said, pointing to the small round table with three chairs that served as her dining area. Sometimes Edith shared a meal with them, so Susan had three chairs. This would be the first guest she'd had in the apartment except for Edith.

"We went to see Edith," Danny said. "She's sick."

"Did you take her cookies?"

"Yes! We make the bestest cookies," Danny said.

"She has the flu...not too interested in cookies," Susan added.

Zack looked at Susan. "Will she be able to watch this young man in the morning?"

"No. She didn't look so good when we saw her earlier. I've been calling around to find someone."

"Any luck?"

"Two of my backup women already have plans. The third is also sick. Apparently the flu is going around."

"Don't you get sick," Zack said.

"Exactly what Danny said," she replied. "I'll do my best not to. But Edith has been such a help to me, I need to return the favor and help her out when she's sick. She doesn't have anyone else. I thought I'd go down before supper to make sure she doesn't need anything more today."

"Why don't you leave Danny here when you check on her? No sense exposing him to germs if you don't have to."

"Thanks," she said, "He's been there, but stayed in the living room. I feel really badly for her—having no one to take care of her when she's sick."

"Who takes care of you when you're sick?" he asked, taking another cookie.

"No one. She'd help, I'm sure. Fortunately, I'm rarely sick."

"I want to get down. I'm finished," Danny said.

"I should find a way to burn off some of that energy," she said, helping Danny to the floor, pushing his empty cup away from the edge of the table.

"If it weren't so late, we could take him to a museum or someplace indoors and let him run around."

"But it is late and it's started raining again. I wish it would rain at night and leave the daylight for kids to play outside."

"Does this mean the preschool is leaking again?" he asked, turning to look out the window.

"I hope not. The roof was repaired. It's the water damage from the previous leak that needs fixing."

They finished their chocolate and then moved into the living room. Susan asked him to stay for dinner and Zack quickly accepted. He explained he'd never turn down a home-cooked meal.

They talked in between playing with Danny and finally settling in to watch a Disney movie.

When Susan went in to prepare dinner, Zack stayed in the main part of the apartment to entertain Danny.

She dashed down just before eating to check on Edith. Satisfied the older woman was holding her own, she returned and dished up dinner for the three of them.

Sitting at the table she was reminded of meals with Tom. Danny had been too little to eat his meals at the table; he'd still been in a high chair. Looking up once she was startled to see Zack's dark hair and eyes when she expected to see Tom's light brown.

By the time dinner was over, Danny was growing sleepy.

"What did you do to my son?" she asked when he yawned again at the table.

"We had races. I remember one foster mother having all the kids race around the yard to wear us out. He loved it."

"You ran around with him?"

"No, I timed him with my watch. And he got faster and faster, didn't you, Dano?" Zack said.

"Yes, I can run fast as a superhero," he said. "Want to see?" Without waiting for Susan's answer, he got off the chair and raced down the hall. A moment later she could hear his footsteps as he ran back.

"Very good. And what a great idea, as long as he doesn't drive the downstairs neighbors crazy."

Zack and Danny helped clear the table and then Zack stayed in the kitchen with Susan while she quickly did the dishes. It was cozy, the rain on the window, the companionship of the two of them while she washed and set the dishes in the drainer.

She glanced over at Zack. He was watching her as if he'd never seen a woman washing dishes before.

"What?" she asked.

"Soaking in the atmosphere," he said slowly.

"Dishwashing?"

"Different from the desert. And from having a real kitchen. The room where I'm staying doesn't have much except a small refrigerator. I order in when not invited for a home-cooked meal."

"Every night?"

"And lunch, too. Breakfast I usually catch at the local coffeehouse."

"What do you do when on the job site? Surely they don't have restaurants on every corner over there," she asked.

"We usually have a mess tent. No point in fifty men each cooking for themselves if the company can have a cook to prepare meals for everyone. Keeps morale high and men focused on the work they were hired for."

"So that's kind of home-cooked," she said, wiping down the counters and turning to face him. He looked tired. She forgot sometimes he was still recovering from being hit by a land mine. Had Danny worn him out?

"Don't confuse mess food with home-cooked. Yours is the best."

Delighting in his compliment, she smiled. "You're easy to please," she said. She draped the dishrag over the sink edge and wiped her hands on the towel. Hanging it on the rack, she turned. Zack was just inches away.

"I meant it, Susan," he said, his voice low and sexy.

He reached out to put his hands on her shoulders, pulling her closer. His mouth covered hers and Susan let out a soft sigh as the magic of his kiss took over.

She kissed him back, wanting a closer contact. Stepping closer, she put her arms around his neck and was delighted to have him encircle her with his arms and pull her in for full body contact.

It was the most exciting kiss she'd ever had. Every cell in her body tingled with anticipation. Her mouth grew greedy, moving against his, relishing every press of lips, every sweep of his tongue. His hands splayed on her back, pressing her into him. She could feel the weight of them, wondering what they'd feel like on her bare skin.

Time had no meaning as the kiss continued. Susan could have stayed in Zack's arms forever.

He moved from her mouth to kiss her cheek, along her jawline, down her throat.

Susan flung her head back, eyes still closed as she relished every tantalizing touch of his mouth against her skin. When he kissed the rapid pulse point at the base of the throat, she clung, shivering in pleasure.

"Mommy, why is Zack biting your neck?" Danny asked.

The moment shattered. Susan pulled back so fast she almost lost her balance. Zack's hand on her arm steadied her.

"I wasn't biting your mother, I was kissing her," Zack said.

Susan couldn't utter a sound. How could she have forgotten her son? What was she doing kissing a man she hardly knew? This was so wrong.

"Why?" Danny asked.

"I like her. When people like each other, sometimes they kiss each other," Zack said, stooping down to be at Danny's eye level.

"Know how your mommy kisses you good-night when you go to bed?"

Danny nodded.

"That's because she loves you and wants to kiss you to sleep at night."

Danny looked at Susan, a frown on his face. "But she doesn't kiss me so long."

"Ah, that's a special kind of kiss between a man and a woman. When you are all grown up, you'll understand."

"You need to take a quick bath, get in jammies and get to bed," Susan said. She reached out for Danny's hand, afraid to look at Zack. No telling what he thought of her wanton display. She wasn't sure what to make of it herself.

"Want help?" he asked.

"No," she said quickly. Taking a quick breath she tried to smile. "We'll just be a few minutes." She wished he'd offer to leave, but he merely nodded and slid his hands into the side pockets of his slacks.

"I'll wait, then."

"Want to give me a bath?" Danny asked hopefully.

"Not tonight," Susan responded before Zack could. She needed a few moments away from him!

Twenty minutes later, Danny was in pajamas and ran to the living room to bid Zack good-night.

"Mommy's going to read my story tonight. Maybe you can another night," he said gravely.

"I look forward to it," Zack said, reaching down to give him a quick hug.

Susan had her emotions under control by the time she returned to the living room a short time later.

"Danny asleep?" Zack asked, rising as she entered.

"Yes." She smiled and paused for a moment, then deliberately sat on the sofa. Zack sat beside her.

"I've been thinking," he began.

She almost held her breath. Had he been thinking the same thing she had been? That there was something special between them? She wasn't sure if she wanted to discuss it, but there was no denying it was there.

"If you can't find another sitter, I could watch Danny for you when he's not in preschool."

"I couldn't ask you to do that," she said. So much for her intuition of what he wanted to talk about.

"I have ample time. And I'm going a bit cabin crazy with this enforced inactivity. Unless you don't think I can handle him. Or you don't trust me."

Susan looked at him in surprise.

"It's not that. You're recuperating. You need rest. Not to be running after a four-year-old all day."

"People atrophy if they do nothing. I'm used to working all day almost every day. This sitting around is getting to me."

"You don't think he'll wear you out?"

Zack shook his head. "If I get too tired, I'll nap when he does. But how hard can it be to watch a four-year-old?"

Susan grinned. "Harder than I expect you believe it'll be." She thought about it another moment and then nodded slowly. "You are a lifesaver. I thought I was going to have to take time off from work to watch him. No one seems available tomorrow. I'll take you up on your offer only if you promise to call me if things get out of hand."

"They won't," he said confidently.

Susan hoped he was correct. One of the hardest parts of being a parent was finding child care. Edith had been a lifesaver. The arrangement had worked perfectly for the two of them. But when she was ill, it was hard to get someone on such short notice.

Zack slid a bit closer, put his arm across the back of the sofa and looked at her. His fingers brushed against her hair. Susan resisted the urge to bolt from the room. She leaned back slightly and tried to relax, which was impossible with her heart racing like it was.

"It's supposed to stop raining tonight. Would the park be

too wet for him to play tomorrow?" Zack asked, his caressing fingers causing her great difficulty in thinking straight.

"I'll give you a towel to wipe down the slide if you're the first ones there. After a couple of kids have been on them, they're dry. Are you sure?"

"About what?" he asked, looking into her eyes.

Susan felt her heart rate increase. "About watching Danny."

"Yes."

"Thanks."

"If you keep looking at me like that, I'm going to forget there's a little boy asleep down the hall and a sick woman you need to check and do something that might be construed as moving too fast," he said in his low voice.

Susan reached out to touch his cheek, moving her fingers to his lips. Zack kissed them, sending a shock of awareness through her.

He took her hand and placed a kiss in the palm, closing her fingers over. "Go check on Mrs. Jordan. I'm going home soon. I'll stay here until then."

"About moving too fast?"

"Yes?"

"I don't know if I'm even ready to move on. I loved Tom very much."

"Let's just see what happens. Tell me if I'm pushing too hard," he replied, kissing her fingers.

"I like that," she said softly.

"I do, too," he said, kissing her again.

"I'd better check on Mrs. J and then let you go home. Thanks for the offer. I really appreciate it."

"It'll be my pleasure."

When Susan left, Zack rose and went to see his son again. Danny was asleep, looking angelic. Tomorrow Zack would be able to spend the entire day with him. He smiled, remembering some of the antics and comments the child had made that afternoon. Were all children as endearing or was there a special bond because of their blood ties? He didn't know or care. He loved this child. Tomorrow they'd build on the memories they were making.

He walked back to the living room, standing by the window to watch the rain. It had been challenging to think up activities this afternoon to entertain without any prior experience.

The visit to the park had been easier. Of course he'd let Susan take the lead and she knew more about Danny's likes and activities. Maybe he could get her to show him the pictures of his son from infancy. Zack yearned to learn all he could about Danny.

Zack turned back to look at the room—and all the pictures. Thomas Johnson, obviously, he thought, lifting one of the frames and studying the man who had adopted his son. He looked solid, someone to depend upon. Another showed Tom and Susan at the beach, laughing in the sun. There were several with Tom holding a baby and then a toddler as Danny grew. According to the detective, Danny had been two when Thomas Johnson had been killed by that hit and run drunken driver. The man had been apprehended later and charged with manslaughter. Did that help at all with Susan's loss?

He doubted it. She had that constant hint of sadness in her eyes.

Putting the picture down, he surveyed the rest of the room as he went to sit on the chair near the sofa. It was casually decorated, lots of pictures and books. The television sat unobtrusively in one corner. It was a good room for a little boy.

When he heard the key in the door, he turned.

"She's doing about the same and promised to call her

doctor in the morning. I told her Danny was taken care of and that seemed to take a load off her mind."

"Does she need someone to care for her?" he asked.

"I heated some more soup for her and made some toast. She said that was all she wanted. I made sure she was drinking plenty of fluids. Other than that, I think she wants to be left alone."

"I do when I'm sick."

"Most guys do. I remember Tom—" She stopped abruptly. "Never mind. I hope I don't catch it from her. There's nothing worse than being incapacitated with a four-year-old running around."

"What time should I be here in the morning?" he asked, rising.

"I usually leave around 8:30. Want to come a bit earlier to make sure the transition goes smoothly? It'll be something extraordinary for Danny. I'm sure he'll be delighted, but just to make sure there are no problems."

Zack nodded. He wanted to stay, to talk more to Susan, but it was already after nine and she had to work tomorrow.

"See you then," he said, crossing the room. "Walk me to the door?"

It was only about ten steps, but he wanted to kiss her goodnight. She went with him and looked up expectantly when they reached the door.

"I enjoyed dinner," he said, leaning down to kiss her. He'd only wanted to brush her lips with his, but once they touched, he felt desire rise. He wanted more. Susan was willing and opened her mouth at the first hint from him.

Wrapping her in his arms, he kissed her as he had in the kitchen. Ending the kiss too soon, he rested his forehead against hers. "Thanks again for dinner," he said.

"Thanks for watching my son," she replied, her eyes luminescent.

Zack rode the elevator down to the lobby. He wasn't sure he was going about this the right way. He was beginning to want Susan in a totally different way. And to feel guilty about not telling her about his relationship to Danny. It was becoming complex when all he'd started out to do was catch a glimpse of his son. Now he knew him, knew he was happy and thriving.

Susan had been unexpected—as were the growing emotions and attachment he was feeling for her. How would she take learning he was Danny's biological father? Would she send him packing? Become distant but allow him to continue visiting with them?

Or was she beginning to feel something more for him as he was for her? Could it lead to marriage?

Or would telling her end everything?

Could they make a family? It would be the perfect solution. Only—she'd said she wasn't sure she was ready to move on. The bond between her and Tom apparently had not been broken when he died. As evidenced by all the photos all over the flat and her constant references to him. To see how far they could explore this relationship, she needed to move on.

What could he do to help? He didn't want to feel second best. If their relationship developed, would she ever care for him as much as for her first husband? Would he end up accepting whatever she gave just to stay near?

CHAPTER SIX

By Tuesday, Zack knew he loved being a dad. He and Danny had spent Monday going to the park in the morning. He fixed them both peanut butter and jelly sandwiches for lunch and read him a story before his nap. That afternoon they played at the park again. The more time they spent together, the more Zack knew he was doing the right thing in connecting with his son. What would it be like to be with him until he grew up? To have a part in molding him to manhood?

He looked forward to the evening when Susan returned home. Together they'd prepared dinner. The meals proved lively. Danny hopped from one topic to another. Laughter was common. Zack liked watching Susan when she talked. Her eyes didn't hold as much sadness as he'd once seen. Her laughter was light and delightful. He did his best to keep it going.

And after Danny was in bed, the two adults had a time to talk. Edith was on the mend. She told Susan she'd be ready to watch Danny again in a day or two. Which meant only a couple of more days alone with his son. His scheduled trip to the U.N. to see where Susan worked was postponed while he watched Danny. But he'd make sure to reschedule when things were back to normal. He wanted to see her in her work space, see who she worked with, what her friends were like.

He had the Wednesday meeting at the school to attend, which would give him more insight into her life. Once he had worried he couldn't fit in with her and Danny, but now he was willing to try.

Tuesday while Danny napped, Zack attempted to read. But his gaze was drawn again and again to the many photographs of Tom Johnson that were scattered around the living room. He had also noted an enlargement of one by Danny's bed. Were they there for Danny's sake, or Susan's? Zack wasn't sure.

He was drawn to Susan and she seemed receptive to his kisses. Yet last weekend she had clearly stated she wasn't ready to move on. It was obvious from the pictures that the three of them had been a very happy family. Wistfully, Zack wondered if he'd ever find that kind of happiness.

It was too soon to suggest to Susan that she consider marrying him. He'd only known her a couple of weeks. Yet the rightness wouldn't go away. It all depended upon Susan.

Susan unlocked the door, excited to see the two men in her life these days. Zack had been a huge help these two days. Danny had adored having Zack watch him. That morning he'd gone to preschool and Zack had called to check in with her in the afternoon and told her he'd felt like an elephant in a china shop, but had persevered, running the gauntlet of mothers. She remembered laughing at his recount.

The best time of the day was after she returned home. Being with Zack reminded her of the evenings she and Tom had shared—preparing the meal, talking about their days. But the aching sense of loss she had experienced for the last two years was missing. Being with Zack brought out the best of being a couple with none of the crushing reminders of her dead husband.

"Mommy!" Danny raced down the hall to greet her, flinging his arms around her legs as high as he could reach.

"Hey, sweet thing, how are you?" Susan picked him up to hug, her eyes going to the tall man following him at a more discreet pace.

"Zack and me went to the park."

"I know, he told me he was taking you there." Sharing the look with Zack felt right. When he was close enough, he leaned in and kissed her, then looked at Danny, still in his mother's arms.

"Did you kiss Mommy?" Zack asked.

Danny kissed her then smiled at Zack. He struggled to get down, then ran back toward his room. "I got a ball," he said.

Susan put her purse on the small table and took off her light jacket. "You bought him another toy? Honestly, where is he going to put them all?"

"Hey, a ball, a battery powered car and a kite are hardly going to force you to live elsewhere. Besides, I have as much fun with them as he does."

"I know, two boys at heart."

He pulled her into his arms and gave her a real kiss. "I may be a boy at heart, but around you, I feel all man," he said a moment later.

Danny returned with his ball before Susan could respond. She admired the new ball that was almost as large as Danny. Then said, "I need to change clothes, then who wants to help me with dinner?"

"Me and Zack! Me and Zack!" Danny shouted.

Susan laughed. But as she walked toward her room she began to wonder how her son was going to react when his time with Zack would be curtailed. Or what would happen in a couple of months when Zack moved on? Would he keep in touch? She hoped so. She couldn't imagine never seeing him again.

Once in casual clothes, she hurried out to the kitchen to start dinner.

When Danny had been put to bed and it was just the two of them, Susan became quiet. She was getting too used to this arrangement. Danny wasn't the only one who was going to miss Zack when he wasn't around.

"How about showing me those pictures of Danny when he was younger," Zack suggested when she walked into the living room.

"A great idea to a mother, but you'll be bored after a while."

"I doubt it," he said. He had wanted to see the early pictures for days. He yearned to know all he could about Danny, from if he'd been a fussy baby to when he took his first steps. Surely Susan would like sharing that.

She went to the bookcase and pulled out two bulging albums and carried them to the sofa.

Opening the first, she caught her breath as the memory hit. It showed her holding a bundled up Danny in front of the building where they all used to live. She remembered Tom had wanted to have a picture of Danny's first home in case they moved later. Neither suspected Susan and Danny would be moving without Tom.

"He's about a week old here," she said, pointing to the picture. Slowly she gave a brief comment on each picture as they leafed through the album. To Zack's delight, she noted memorial events. Here was the photo of Danny's first tooth. Looked like a lot of gum to Zack, but Susan assured him that tiny speck on the lower gum was a tooth that had just broken through.

She had several of him standing, looking astonished. "Here's when he took his first step. I wish I had a movie camera. These are just still shots." The little boy had been by the sofa, moving toward the camera. There were four photos shot rapidly showing the steps and the crash landing on his diapered bottom.

There were also locks of hair and handprints and foot-prints from his one-month checkup, notations of his height and weight at each doctor's visit.

Zack studied each photograph, asking her questions through all the pictures. Slowly they moved through almost four years worth of photos in the two albums. There was a gap when Danny first turned two—when Tom had died. It had been weeks before Susan had felt up to taking pictures and able to do so without tears blurring her vision.

The memories were bittersweet, but she went through both albums with Zack. It was her life with Danny recorded, even though Tom was now gone. She was glad she had all the pictures she did.

"My goodness, it's after ten. You weren't bored, were you?" she asked when she closed the second book.

"Not at all. You've done a good job, raising him. It can't be easy as a solo parent. I know he's run me ragged these two days."

She put the book on the coffee table and leaned back against the cushions. "Sometimes I wonder how I can do it, other times I wouldn't change a thing. He's the light of my life."

"Did you ever want more children?"

"Tom and I talked about having three, but it wasn't to be. How about you? How many kids do you want?"

"I never planned on getting married. That might change, however." Zack looked at her. "Would you go out with me Saturday night—to dinner. Maybe dancing if I can find a place. Just you and me."

Susan felt her heart rate increase. This would be a date. No camouflaging it with a little boy as a buffer. No confusing the issue by saying they were just going on a picnic as new acquaintances or bumping into each other at the park. An honest-to-goodness date.

"Yes, I'd like to," she replied. Then a wave of panic doused her. What was she thinking? She glanced at the nearest picture of Tom.

"I hate that," Zack said.

She looked at him. "What?"

"You look at his picture all the time. As if asking permission, or forgiveness for moving on. How long are you going to depend on a dead man? How long are you going to live in the past? He sounds like he was a wonderful person who loved you a lot. But he's gone, never to come back. I wish you would acknowledge that and move on."

Susan felt as if he'd slapped her.

"I don't depend on a dead man as you so crudely put it. He was my husband. I loved him dearly. I miss him." She jumped up and crossed to the window, staring out to the darkness. How dare Zack say she was stuck in the past.

"I know that makes you angry. But look at it from my point of view. Every time I kiss you I feel he's right there in the middle of us. I want to treat you like a woman, yet I feel we have a chaperone in our midst. I know he was a good man. A loving husband and father. But he's gone and you are not. You need to move on. Make a new life for yourself, not be put on hold."

"I know that. He was my husband. Am I supposed to forget he existed? I have made a new life. I have a job, a new apartment. I'm doing the best I can. Maybe if you'd ever been deeply in love and lost, you'd understand. But you seem too afraid to form attachments. Moving around like you do makes it convenient to keep everyone at a distance. Well, I'm coping the best I can."

"It's been two years. Surely you've made some closure. Come to terms with it."

"I have," she said with dignity. Then frowned. "I think."

He rose and moved to stand beside her, not touching, but

close enough to feel the warmth from her body, to smell the sweet scent she wore.

"I'm not sure how close we'll ever become if Tom Johnson is in the middle."

"He's not." Susan realized suddenly it was taking a lot of energy to keep from looking at his picture at this moment. Was she still depending on Tom?

She really enjoyed being with Zack. She looked forward to seeing him, hearing about his day with Danny, learning about his life.

"No one can measure up to him. Especially now that he's gone forever. No man can compete," Zack said.

"And are you trying to compete?"

He hesitated a moment then slowly nodded. "Maybe."

That surprised her. Was he really courting her? Panic flared. She wasn't ready to be more than friends.

"I'd like to think we are friends," she said slowly.

"I think I'm jealous," he admitted.

"Of a dead man?"

"It's hard to compete with a ghost," Zack said wryly.

"You don't have to compete with anyone." She turned, stepped closer, erasing the distance between them. "I think you are very special and I want to go out—just the two of us. As long as I can get a baby-sitter. I don't know if Edith will be up to it by Saturday."

"Then we go if you can get a sitter," he said. "I'll head for home now. I'll be here again in the morning."

He stepped around her and left.

Susan spun around, astonished he hadn't kissed her good-night. Glaring at the door for a moment, she shifted her gaze to Tom's closest picture. She did look at them all the time. They kept her connected. But Zack was right, Tom was dead. Her mother had said clinging to the past wouldn't bring him back.

Tears filled her eyes. Her first love was gone forever. For the millionth time she wished she could turn back the clock. Hold on to what they had. She yearned for his touch, his humor, his love. It had vanished two years ago, never to be again.

Walking over, she picked up her favorite picture and gazed into the dear face she'd never see again. She could hear the echo of his voice, his laugh. She could see the love in his eyes.

"I loved you," she murmured. "It about killed me when you went. If I hadn't had Danny, I don't know how I could have coped. He's such a great kid. You would have enjoyed watching him grow up, and would have taught him so much."

She thought about it for a long moment, then sighed softly.

"Actually, Zack is teaching him things. How to be responsible. How to share. And a bit about families—even though he didn't have one of his own."

She hugged the frame against her chest—it was cold and hard.

With a deep sigh, she went slowly around the room and collected the pictures of Tom, reliving all the memories that flooded when she viewed each one. He would forever be part of her life. But it was time to move on. Maybe to another chapter that could be just as happy.

When she had all the photographs in her arms, she went to the bedroom and placed them in the bottom drawer of the dresser that had been Tom's. She'd let the one stay in Danny's room. And the one by her bed. A child should remember his father. And she wanted to see his dear face a few more mornings when she first woke.

Feeling nostalgic and a bit melancholy, she went to bed. Stretching out her hand, she felt the empty space beside her. Never to be filled, she'd once thought. Now she wondered if Zack would like to pursue their relationship all the way to making love. Closing her eyes, she could almost imagine his strong body pulling her close, his deep voice speaking to her in the night. The joy they'd share making love and sleeping together. Waking up together.

Where once she never expected to share a bed with another, now she wondered if she could imagine not eventually sharing her bed with Zack.

Rolling on her side, she remembered Zack's kisses, his hands caressing her. If things kept on the way they were going, would they fall for each other? Or was she just someone to fill the time while he was on leave? She hoped not. Zack Morgan was a very special man. She closed her eyes. No one could predict the future. But she might just open herself up to whatever came—embracing every new experience.

Wednesday Zack showed up just as Susan was beginning to think he wasn't coming. She had to leave immediately. He had timed it that way, she suspected. But there wasn't enough time to challenge him on the issue. At least he had arrived and she could get to work.

"I'll be home in time to cook a quick dinner so we can leave for the school," she said as she was walking out the door. She looked back. "You are still going?"

"I said I would," he replied, his attention already on Danny.

The day seemed interminable to Susan. She couldn't concentrate on her translations for wondering what Zack and Danny were doing. She hoped he wouldn't regret offering his help. Edith had told her last night when she went to check on her that she felt up to watching Danny for the evening. It would only be for an hour or two and he'd be going to bed at eight.

Torn between wanting to see Zack again, and dreading the confrontation for the churning emotions that filled her, Susan wasn't sure how she felt as she caught the subway for home. Walking in the door just before six, she could smell something delicious cooking.

"I'm home," she called out.

Danny came running from the kitchen. "Zack made dinner," he said, his face full of wonder.

Zack appeared in the doorway, looking as unlike a cook as anyone she'd ever seen. His broad shoulders almost filled the doorway. His attire would be suited to a work site—jeans and a chambray shirt, unbuttoned at the throat with the sleeves rolled up. He looked rugged and handsome. She caught her breath and then smiled.

"What a treat," she said.

"Just burgers and fries," he said.

She didn't correct him. If he thought she meant the food, that was fine by her.

"I'll change and be right out."

"Be ready in about ten. I thought I timed it about right," he said with satisfaction. His gaze moved over her and his eyes seemed to light up.

Feeling flustered, Susan spun around and almost ran to her bedroom. She changed quickly, seeking Tom's photograph. "It is a habit. I hope you won't mind if I break it. If I can," she murmured. Feeling like a soldier going off to war with no armor, she bravely went to have dinner with the most exciting man she'd known.

When they walked over to the school, he took her hand. "I see you put away Tom's pictures."

"Yes." She couldn't say any more. She felt as if she ripped off a Band-Aid. But it was healthy. She would never forget him. Now was time to explore new options and opportunities.

He didn't say anything, either, but the clasp of his hand warmed her.

Promptly at seven the meeting began. Susan had felt extremely self-conscious walking into the school's largest room with Zack at her side. He looked completely out of his element dwarfing the small furniture more suitable to preschoolers than the men and women who had assembled.

The meeting went well, with all parents volunteering for some tasks. There was not a lot of money in the entire group, Susan thought, but they were all parents interested in providing the best for their children.

When Zack volunteered to work on the drywall in two classrooms and the playground upgrade, heads swiveled and questions were whispered as no one recognized him. "I'm here for Danny Johnson," he said.

Speculative glances then moved to Susan from the parents who knew her. She felt awkward. Still, she was glad Danny had someone who could be of more help than she would be. She signed up for painting, both indoors and out. She hoped the weather would cooperate. The first work weekend was in three days. They were scheduled out for a month, then a reassessment would be made to determine how much more work still needed to be done.

"I know most of us have busy lives and can hardly afford the school fees. But working together, we'll pass the city's inspection and keep the school open," the headmistress said at the conclusion of the meeting.

"Thanks again," Susan said to Zack as they rose in preparation to leave. "It's probably minuscule compared to what you normally do."

"It is, but I'll have more direct interaction than I normally do. I'm the boss on the sites. Here I'll get to swing a hammer."

"Oh, fun," she murmured.

"I want to talk to the headmistress. If she hasn't already ordered the supplies, I might be able to help."

They moved toward Mrs. Harper, waiting while two other parents chatted with her for a few minutes. Then it was their turn.

"I'm Zack Morgan."

"I remember seeing you when we had that scare when Danny ran off. So nice of you to volunteer to help us," she said extending her hand and then smiling at Susan.

"If you don't already have your supplies, I might be able to get them at a lower cost." He quickly explained what company he worked for. "One thing the company is always looking for is community projects it can support. I think I can call one of the men in the local office and get supplies at a deep discount."

"Oh, that would be so helpful. We are really stretched on this. We really can't afford these repairs, but if we don't do them, we'll be closed down. I can't let that happen. The hardware store a few blocks away was giving us a ten percent discount. I thought it was the best I could do."

"I'm sure my company will beat that. I'll make some calls in the morning and then let you know."

She smiled and nodded, turning to Susan. "I'm so grateful for your help and your friend's."

"He's in construction, I bet he knows every trick of the trade," she said.

Mrs. Harper's eyes widened. "Oh, perfect. Can you handle the building inspector when he comes? I always feel like he's talking another language."

"Sure," Zack said.

She reached out to shake his hand again. "I can't thank you enough," she said smiling broadly.

On the walk back to Susan's apartment, she glanced at him. He looked as if he were deep in thought.

"Can you really get some bargain rates?" she asked.

He nodded. "Our company is big on supporting local communities, whether here or on location. It builds goodwill."

"This will build a heap of goodwill. As you can imagine, this place runs on a shoestring. Why are you taking such an interest?"

"Told you—"

"There's more to this than you're bored. You could find other things to occupy your time. You hardly know us, why would you do this?"

"It's a good project. And I know you and Danny. Why wouldn't I want to help? It's not much."

"It's a lot."

"Only because no one else there has a construction background. This is sort of like baking cookies for me," Zack said.

Susan laughed aloud. "Baking cookies?"

"Something you do almost without thinking, right?"

She nodded.

"This is nothing compared to building a bridge. Repair a few walls, refurbish some playground equipment. You and the other women will be doing the painting. This is a walk in the park." He reached out and caught her hand in his. "Besides, I get to spend more time with you."

Saturday was bright and clear. Edith had insisted she was well enough to watch Danny while Zack and Susan worked at the school—and that evening when the two of them were going out.

Susan was excited about the date. She had her whole day planned in her mind, including dashing home from the school to shower and change in time for dinner.

When her mother called, she almost blurted it out, but she wasn't up to a thousand questions, which her mother would have had. Instead she kept the conversation short, telling her mother she had to leave soon for the school project. The day started at nine and Mrs. Harper had urged parents to stay until five. Pizza was being ordered in for lunch.

Susan knew several of the mothers of the children in Danny's class. They greeted one another and began the tasks as assigned. Zack gathered tools that had been provided and moved to another room. Two men from his company had also shown up to help. They greeted each other and suddenly Susan felt left out. She watched as they caught up on their lives and observed Zack in his element. All three men were tall, rugged individuals. Competent and assured in their success, but not overblown or arrogant, they quickly set to work and before the morning was finished, it was clear the school had been lucky to get these volunteers. Work procedures were set out and followed. The genial air of camaraderie made it a festive atmosphere.

"Who's your friend," Betsy Singleton asked Susan as they began moving furnishings and scrubbing the stained portion on a wall deemed safe enough to repaint and not repair.

"Zack Morgan. He's only here temporarily," Susan said.

"Too bad. He's a hunk. Bet Danny loves being around him."

Susan nodded. "He does."

"I heard about Danny's running away the other day. That must have been scary."

Susan agreed. "But he seems to have stopped doing that." In the days since they'd met Zack, Danny hadn't run after a stranger once. For that she was grateful, but wondered what he would do when Zack left. She hoped her little boy wouldn't be heartbroken again.

The morning sped by. Susan was glad for the lunch break. Her shoulders hurt from pushing a paint roller. Since the day was nice, the pizza was served in the playground with a long table set up holding the food and beverages.

Zack joined her once they both picked up their plates. They sat on one of the benches lining the playground. Betsy and her husband shared the bench.

"Brad Singleton," he introduced himself to Zack and Susan. She introduced them both and settled in to eat.

"You really know what you're doing," Brad said to Zack.

"I think we'd all be floundering around without you and your buddies helping."

"This is a straight forward project," Zack said. He took a bite of pizza, chewed it and then took a long swallow of the soft drink he'd chosen. "I'm surprised at how many parents turned out. Looks like most of them, would you say?"

Brad glanced around. "At least. And there are two teenagers from our church helping out. Plus your two friends. We might get it all fixed up before the time frame Mrs. Harper set."

"Could. Once some of the men are shown what to do, they manage fine," Zack said.

"Not something we're all used to. You're in construction, I think I heard someone say."

Zack nodded, glancing at Susan. She smiled at him.

"Glad to have someone aboard who knows what to do."

"Apparently Mrs. Harper thinks so," Susan added. "She's asked Zack to be the contact guy for the building inspector."

"Hey, that's cool. I'm sure you know what to do to get us passed first time. We can't afford a different preschool for Bethany. I'd hate for her to lose this chance at getting a jump on schooling."

The discussion veered to talking about the children. Susan was amused to find Zack listening for all he was worth. He didn't contribute much on that topic, but a couple of times agreed when he remembered something Danny had said or done.

Lunch went too fast.

The afternoon turned out better as everyone got into a rhythm. The festive atmosphere continued as everyone knew they were pulling together for their children and the sake of the school.

Promptly at four forty-five, Mrs. Harper began her rounds advising people to finish up so they could leave at five. "Tomorrow we'll start at one to give everyone a chance to sleep in and also go to church. I'm amazed at all that's been done today." She came over to Susan. "And it's all thanks to your friend Zack. He's been a marvel. He works twice as fast as the others and the work is impeccable. And he got all the supplies and tools donated. I can't tell you what that means. It's amazing. We won't be in the red at the end of the school term. And we'll have one of the nicest preschools—and safest—in this area. And so I told him!"

Susan felt a warm glow of pride for Zack's sake. He was volunteering when he should be recuperating. He chose to spend his Saturday helping out a school where he had no one attending. Only the son of a new friend.

Maybe more than a friend?

At five Zack wandered into the classroom, examining the painting. "Did good, ladies," he said with a smile. The other women beamed at his compliment. Susan smiled as well. Forgotten was her tiredness. She was glad she could help.

"Ready to go?" he asked her.

"Yes."

"Not too tired to go out to dinner, are you?" he asked as they began walking toward her apartment.

"No. Are you?"

"I feel fine. Better than fine. Might be the best thing I've done for a while."

"Good."

He stopped outside her apartment building. "I'll go clean up and be back here at seven."

"Okay. See you then." She walked briskly to the elevator and only when the doors closed behind her did she sag against the wall. She was so tired she could scarcely keep her eyes open. But she would not admit that to anyone. She wanted to go out with Zack tonight.

Danny and Edith greeted her. Edith was back to normal and had prepared a small dinner for her and Danny. She asked after the school renovations.

"You went to my school?" Danny asked.

"Yes, Zack and I worked on getting it fixed up. It's going to look terrific before you know it. And it will pass all the inspections the city requires. Zack worked harder than anyone," she told him.

"I want to go with Zack," Danny said.

"On Tuesday when you go to school, you ask the teacher to show you where Zack worked, okay?"

"'Kay."

As Susan prepared for her date, she felt butterflies in her stomach. She had been on two other dates since Tom had died, both a bust in her opinion. The first man was nice enough, but they had so little to talk about. The second had not been especially fond of children and had at one point during the evening asked if she would not talk about her son so much. That had been an instant turnoff.

After those experiences, she'd declined all other invitations to dinner. She was happier with Danny than with men she scarcely knew.

Zack was different. For one thing, he really liked her son. For another, he enticed her like no other. His kisses drove her crazy. And his calm approach to life was like a balm. She worried all the time that she alone wouldn't be able to raise Danny, yet around Zack she felt confident. He had told her more than once she was doing a good job.

The dress she put on was new. Was it sexy enough to get Zack to sit up and take notice? She pictured him with eyes for only her. She made a face at her fantasy and brushed her hair. Putting on her lipstick, she was ready. Taking a deep breath, she tried to quell her nerves. For heaven's sake, she and Zack had spent hours together over the last couple of weeks. This was merely a time for adults, no Danny around. Not so different.

And she vowed she would not talk about her son all night. Though what they would talk about other than Danny was beyond her at the moment. If not for Danny, they never would have met.

Edith was talking with Danny, and Susan could hear the soft murmur of her voice. He was miffed he wasn't included in tonight's outing. While sympathetic, Susan nevertheless had told him that there were some things he didn't get and he needed to learn that young. Edith was reinforcing the sentiment.

She heard the knock at the door as she stepped out of her bedroom. And Danny's "I'll get it!"

She started to protest, but it would do little good.

When she could see the door, she was surprised to find Zack down at Danny's level talking to him. The little boy was nodding, looking solemn.

Zack stood when he saw Susan and smiled. Her heart fluttered. He looked devastatingly handsome in the dark suit and white shirt. His tie was silver and blue. She had never seen him in a suit before. He was dynamite. Every woman who saw him tonight would envy her. Susan smiled. It felt good.

"I'm ready," she said. "What are you up to, Danny?" she asked.

"I'm not going to answer the door without you telling me," he said, his lower lip sticking out suspiciously like a pout.

"That's very good." She looked at Zack with a question in her eyes.

"I told Danny he needs to develop responsibility so he'll be a fine man when he grows up. One way is to mind his mommy when you tell him not to do something."

"Ah." She looked at her son. He seemed resigned. "That is very good advice."

Danny turned and ran back to the living room. He climbed up on the sofa beside Edith and looked at the cartoon movies they'd been watching.

"I'm leaving now." Susan went to kiss Danny goodbye and exchange last minute words with Edith.

"You look lovely, my dear. Do enjoy yourself. Don't worry a mite about me or Danny."

"You're sure you feel up to it?" Susan asked.

"After I put him to bed, I'll do nothing more than sit on this sofa. I'm fine. Still a bit weak, but not so I can't watch this young man."

"I'm gonna be a fine man when I grow up," Danny said. "Like Zack."

"You can't get better than that," Edith said.

Susan silently concurred.

The restaurant Zack took her to was Italian. She savored the aroma of the food when she first stepped in the lobby. "You knew Italian was my favorite, didn't you?" she asked.

"I figured, knowing your mother's Italian. I love Mediterranean cooking. That's one of the things I miss in the Middle East."

They were seated at a small table for two. It was quiet and intimate. The gleaming silverware and crystal sparkled in the subdued lighting. Susan felt like a princess.

The menus were so huge when opened she could not see over hers to Zack. Deciding on the angel hair pasta primavera, she closed it to gaze at Zack. He had already decided on the veal. When their orders had been taken, and wine brought to the table, he proposed a toast.

"To the future, may it give us all we want," he said gravely.

She touched the rim of her glass to his and smiled. "And what is all you want?" she asked after taking a sip.

"A home, a family, a good living and happiness."

"Tall order."

"Do you think so?"

Susan set her glass down carefully and considered her answer. "Maybe not. My parents are still enjoying being married to each other after thirty years. I had a wonderful home life and consider I have a good living now. And Danny makes me so happy." She looked at him.

"As a child, I missed out. No family ties. Not even long-term foster care. I lived in four homes from age four until I turned eighteen. Then I was on my own."

"I thought you said you were still in touch with one family."

"As in we exchange Christmas cards. They've invited me to visit. But I've never gone. They were great, but they aren't blood kin."

"You know what they say—you can choose your friends, but you're stuck with your family. Not being blood kin isn't so bad. There are lots of families and extended families where people aren't related who share their lives. Look at Edith. She's like a devoted aunt to me and Danny. And my parents have friends whom I still see even though we are a generation apart."

Zack was silent for a moment. Now would be the time for her to mention she had adopted Danny and adored him. When she didn't say anything else, he asked "Do you consider blood ties important?"

"Of course. I'm only saying there are other ways to create a family. Look at all the kids who get adopted. Don't you think they're considered part of that family? Or the adopt-a-grandparent project—older people who don't have family and younger ones who need the influence and love older people can give. Some close friends are like family. My aunt Marge and Uncle George aren't blood relatives, but they are closer to us than my mother's sister who lives in North Carolina."

Zack took another sip of his wine and then looked at her. Should he tell her now—that he knew Danny was adopted. And how he knew? He took a breath, and did not.

"I can see your point. But in my case, I have very limited family. I think it's time to put down roots."

She smiled. "That's probably the goal of almost everyone. People marry, have families and want the best for their children. Not everyone, fortunately, ends up in foster care. Roots anchor us, give us a base to always connect to."

"Which is why I want to be there for my child, or children. Things have changed recently. My carefree, footloose days are over. It's time to settle down." He waited for her to confide in him, but she just smiled.

Their salads arrived and Zack used the interruption to change the subject. It was too soon to push for complete revelation. Yet he was growing closer to Susan each time they were together. Could he do as he said—give up his nomadic ways? He had felt alone all his life. Would that change if he married and had a hand in raising Danny?

"Tell me about growing up in New York. How different is it from Chicago? We had the lake, you have the rivers. We had snow, N.Y. has snow. You have Broadway, but we have the Magnificent Mile."

"I was raised in the Upper East Side. We had a nice flat. A park not too far away and a view of the river. Of course, it was between two tall buildings, so a very limited view, but my folks were proud of our sliver of river view. Lots of kids in the building. My best friend, Mary Jane, grew up in the same building. She's with the Peace Corps now in Nigeria. But we're inseparable when she's home. She's like family." Susan grinned at him. "Tell me about your favorite foster home."

"The one where the husband died too young. The Zumwalts were wonderful. He really liked children and played with us every evening after work—even in winter. He said we need not be afraid of the dark, just adapt to lack of light. So we played games like hide-and-seek after dark."

Susan watched as memories came to his mind. He seemed to enjoy remembering the happy times he had with that family. How tragic to lose his biological family and then be wrenched from the foster care that had proved so loving.

"Danny enjoyed playing ball with you. You've been good for him. He needs to see how men are. Mostly he's in a feminine world with me and Edith and his preschool teachers to interact with," Susan said.

"He needs a father figure," Zack said slowly. "Do you think little boys need a male role model more than little girls?"

"Maybe. Or maybe they both need that. Isn't that why normally families have a father and a mother? Each brings something special to the child and balance to a family."

Susan sat back in her chair, wondering if this talk of family was what Zack wanted. This date was to be for the two of them. To enjoy the evening and being with each other.

She smiled wryly. "Guess I'm passionate about families, huh? Tell me more about your work. However did you get into a field that takes you from home so long?"

Zack began to talk about his interest in building, how in college he gravitated toward structural engineering and the path that led him to the work he'd spent more than a decade doing. He painted a picture Susan could readily see about living in deserts with substandard housing and infrastructures until his company built roads and bridges to facilitate transportation and the beginnings of towns with community buildings and office buildings.

Susan enjoyed listening to him, hearing about the travels he'd done when he got leave. It was fun to explore London and Copenhagen through his memories. He even talked about some of his friends. He seemed to have only a few, but they were mentioned frequently when he talked.

She wanted to know more about the land mine, but hesitated to bring it up in case it shattered the mood. How frightening to be going about a normal workday and be injured so severely? And to have a co-worker die.

When the meal ended, the conversation continued.

"Will you miss it if you settle in the States?" she asked, sipping on the after dinner coffee.

"I think I've put in enough time. I'm looking forward to a more normal lifestyle now—home every night, weekends free."

"Home-cooked meals," she inserted with a laugh.

"If they are as good as yours. Your mother must have taught you well."

"I'll tell her that."

CHAPTER SEVEN

SUNDAY Susan slept in late, tired from the work at the pre-school and the late night. Zack had brought her home around midnight. Edith had been asleep on the sofa and Susan hadn't known whether to waken her or let her sleep. Since she looked comfortable enough, Susan left her.

Danny woke her after nine. She smiled at her son as he bounced on her bed. When she moved to get up, she stifled a groan. Her shoulders ached. Flexing her hands, she realized her right hand did as well. Painting demanded muscles not normally used in her regular day.

"Edith is sleeping," Danny whispered.

"I got home late last night. She's probably tired from watching you," Susan said, tickling her son.

His laugher rang out. "Can I wake her up, too?" he asked.

"Not yet. Get a book from your room and you can read in my bed while I take a quick shower. Then if she's still asleep, you can wake her up."

Twenty minutes later when they entered the living room, the sofa was empty. Coffee brewed in the kitchen but when Susan entered, that room was also empty. Probably Edith was grateful to escape before Danny could have wakened her.

Knowing Edith was still recovering from her illness, Susan

wanted to give her as much a break as she could. As soon as breakfast was finished, she took Danny to the park. He ran and played with the other children, scooting down the slide, swooshing high on the swing. Susan watched, glad for the chance to sit in the sun and just relax. Soon enough she'd be at the preschool doing some other task she didn't feel suited for.

Glancing at her watch, she saw it was getting close to twelve-thirty. Zack had told her last night he'd pick her up again to walk to the preschool together. She smiled as she remembered their date. The food had been spectacular. But it was the company she loved the most. They'd talked until the restaurant shut down. Then, instead of taking a cab back home, he'd asked if she'd like to walk. She knew the distance, but it would give them more time together, so she'd said yes.

Ambling along, they looked into shop windows and speculated about inhabitants of the apartment buildings they passed. The streets held little traffic that late and it was nice to feel cocooned from cares as they walked and talked. He'd refused to come in when they reached her apartment, but the kiss they'd shared had unsettled her enough it was hard to fall asleep.

She was falling for Zack. The delight she felt every time she saw him was gradually healing her heart. She enjoyed being with him. She'd never expected to fall in love after her husband's death. But then, she'd never anticipated meeting a man like Zack. A man who seemed to enjoy her company—and that of her son.

Any future she envisioned with a man would have to include Danny. She'd want him to learn to love her son as much as she did. To be willing to be father to the boy throughout his life. To promise never to die before they were old and infirmed.

She knew that last bit was impossible. Tom would never have willingly left them. Would Zack? She couldn't imagine living such a carefree life as he'd known, and then changing so drastically to be part of a typical family, going to work five days a week and doing family tasks on the weekends.

Still, a small part of her began to imagine that Zack did fall in love with her. And she with him. They'd marry and have a wonderful life together. He already liked Danny—maybe more than liked. Why else would he plan activities that included her son? And volunteer his time to help repair the preschool? It was not a come-on to lure the mother. She recognized a growing bond between the two of them.

On the other hand, Zack might be finding this situation novel. He could test drive his commitment to changing after the land mine and see if it were something he'd like. There was nothing stopping him from taking off tomorrow and returning to the Middle East and projects that demanded all his skill and knowledge.

His leaving would break her heart. She swallowed, tears filling her eyes. She was falling for Zack Morgan. And didn't have a clue what to do about it. How could she guard herself and her son from hurt if Zack suddenly decided to leave?

She couldn't. It was already too late. She could only go forward and hope she wasn't making a mistake that would make both her and Danny miserable for years to come.

Zack found his pace quickening as he turned onto Susan's block. Up ahead he could see her and Danny about to enter the apartment building. She must have taken him to the park. At least Danny would sleep part of the afternoon, making it easier on Edith. Zack knew from the days he'd watched his son that the boy seemed to possess the energy of a battalion of men.

And he wouldn't change a single thing about him.

As if attuned to his presence, Susan turned around and looked. Her smile when she saw him could light up the street,

Zack thought as he locked his gaze with hers and walked even faster.

"Zack!" Danny ran down the three steps and raced down the sidewalk toward him, his face beaming in happiness.

Zack picked him up when Danny reached him and swung him high in the air. The little boy laughed aloud. Zack heard Susan's laughter at the same time. For a moment he could scarcely move. He felt truly and completely happy for the first time in years. This felt right.

"Hi," Susan called, coming a few feet down the sidewalk to meet him.

"Hi yourself," he said. Holding Danny with one arm, he drew her closer with the other and kissed her. Not as long as he wanted, but they were on a public street and Danny was only about six inches away.

"Kiss me, too," Danny said, putting his hands on Zack's cheeks and turning his head to face him.

Zack smiled and kissed his plump cheek.

"I'm happy to see you both," he said, his gaze going back to Susan's.

Did he imagine it, or was the sadness so often evident in her eyes gone?

"Ready to work again?"

"I'm so stiff from yesterday. But I'm game," she said as they walked toward the apartment.

"I feel the same way, but it's a good feeling. I'm back in my stride now and want to see if I can get off medical leave sooner than I thought. I'm calling the company's medical doctor on Monday to see when he can see me."

Susan tried to smile, but the anxiety that clutched at her was too strong. If Zack was pronounced ready to return to work, he'd have no reason to remain in New York. Granted, he'd talked about setting down roots. But with the next breath, he'd talked about his foreign assignments and she could hear how much he liked his work.

Where did that leave her?

What did she want? In one thought, she believed she'd never love another like Tom. In another, the idea of Zack leaving, maybe never to be seen again, filled her with anguish. She had come to care for him much more than she realized. The thought of his leaving filled her with panic.

She needed some time to consider all the ramifications. Now it didn't look as if she was going to get what she wanted.

They dropped Danny off with Edith and headed for the school.

"You're really quiet today," Zack said as they walked side by side.

"Sorry. It's really wonderful you feel fully recovered and can return to work."

"But?"

She looked at him. "But what?"

"I don't know, it just sounded like a but should be in there somewhere."

"But I'll miss you," she blurted out.

He slung his arm across her shoulder and drew her closer. "Hey, getting a release just means I'm in working shape again. I told you I'm thinking of looking for something here in the States."

"America is awfully big," she said. "In the States could mean Alaska, which is just about as far from here as the Middle East."

"Don't want me so far away, huh?"

She shook her head, facing forward. The school was in sight. One of the other parents waved and Susan tried to smile as she waved back. She wanted to cry instead.

Zack wasn't sure what to make of Susan's statement. He admitted to himself he wanted her to give him some indication of her feelings for him. Should he suggest staying? Or wait for her to suggest that?

What if she didn't?

He nodded at the other parents as they filed into the old building. The men he'd worked with yesterday greeted him. It felt good to be part of a community effort. He had friends at the work sites, but no one with a normal home life. These men had routine jobs, went home to their families each evening and were working to better circumstances for their children.

"We were thinking of getting together after today's work to celebrate one weekend down," Brad Singleton said as he and Zack started on replacing the last of the drywall in one classroom. "Join us?"

"Sounds like fun. I'll have to check with Susan."

"Yeah, baby-sitters can be a pain. If yours can't stay, bring the kid."

"You bringing yours?"

"We have Betsy's niece staying with us this weekend to watch the rugrats. We'll take her to school in the morning and she'll go home from there, so no worries on our end."

"Lucky." Zack reached for his hammer and began to pound nails. How normal and ordinary the conversation was. Yet for him—extraordinary. If he stayed, if he could build a life with Susan, he would have many encounters like this. Be part of a community that pulled together when things needed doing.

He and Brad talked as they worked and before four, they had finished the second classroom's walls.

"Time for mud and then next week these walls can be painted," he said.

"Jason is the expert on that," Brad said.

"Good, because I'm not," Zack replied.

"But you seem expert in every other aspect."

He grinned. "Well I worked construction through college, and have been on job sites ever since."

"Building a bridge isn't exactly the same thing as repairing a preschool," Brad said.

"We sometimes have to build our own homes while we are on a job site, so I can handle a smattering of plumbing, wiring and drywall."

"Man, you've really lived an exciting life."

Zack shrugged. "It was what I wanted. Now things have changed."

"Susan?" Brad asked as they walked over to Mrs. Hampton's office for the next assignment.

Zack hesitated a minute, glancing at Brad. The question caused him to clarify his feelings. The entire reason he was thinking of changing his lifestyle was because of Susan. The thought kicked him in the gut. He'd been stunned when he received the letter about his son, but had convinced himself once he knew the boy was well cared for, he'd move on and let him have the love and security of his adoptive parents.

Meeting Susan had changed all that. For the first time since he was a kid he began to think about family ties, facing the world united as a couple, leaving his nomadic ways and becoming a man who put down roots and made a difference in a community.

If Susan was there. She made a man long to have her smile at him when he came home at night. Share life's ups and downs. And make a warm and loving home where they could shut away the world and be in a world of their own. Their last kiss flashed into his mind. He couldn't imagine not kissing her. Not having the right to kiss her if she turned to someone else.

"Yeah, I guess because of Susan," he admitted aloud.

"That's cool, man. My sister has three kids and her deadbeat husband left several years ago. She can hardly get a date because of those children. Most men don't want to get involved," Brad said.

"I don't have a lot of experience with kids. Or women, for that matter. Don't you think it would be a privilege to be part of a child's life?" Zack asked.

"Well, of course I do. I have two children myself and can't imagine life without them. Not all men think like that, however."

Zack knew that. Before he'd met Susan, and Danny, he'd been one of them. The thought filled him with panic. He'd been alone most of his life. Now he craved a woman who was still grieving her lost husband.

Mrs. Harper had a large sheet spread out over a table beside her desk. She was leaning over it checking on tasks yet to be done when the two men entered her office.

"Room two complete," Brad said. "What next?"

She looked up and smiled. "This is going so much faster than I anticipated. At this rate, we may finish in only a couple of weekends. The painting is complete in Mrs. Savalack's room. Mrs. Rosa's room and Mrs. Thompkin's rooms now are ready for the next stage. We have the ceilings to repair in two rooms, but there are parents already there. Are you two up for the playground equipment?"

"What's needed?" Zack asked.

"Some of the older equipment is made of wood. It's splintered and deteriorating. It needs to be replaced, bolted in place and then finished so it's safe for the children. And we had two new plastic climbing jungle gyms donated that have to be assembled."

"Zack will be perfect for that—he's used to building bridges. How hard can some playground equipment be?" Brad said.

Mrs. Harper studied him for a moment, smiling in gratitude. "We are fortunate, indeed, to have you helping, Mr. Morgan."

"Zack, please. I'll look at what you have. We already picked up the lumber, right?"

"Yes, it was in the original order you were so helpful in acquiring for us."

As the men headed out to the playground area, Brad asked about the order. Zack explained about the company's policy of helping in local communities.

"That's why those other two guys were here yesterday?" Brad asked.

"Right. They'll be back next Saturday, too."

The entire property in front of the old building was enclosed by a wrought-iron fence. There was a separate area for the playground from the front walkway, and the playground was cross fenced. The double walkway that led from the sidewalk to the front door also had a gate, but it was rusted open.

"If it had been closed that day," Zack said, going to examine it more closely, "Danny would never have been able to run off like he did."

"What's happened?" Brad had not heard the story. When Zack finished, he looked at Zack. "If he hadn't run off, you would never have met Susan and end up here helping out. Sounds like fate to me."

Zack nodded as he assessed what was needed to get the gates in working order again. He had initially planned only to walk down the street, check out the preschool and see if his son was in the playground. He had not planned to stop or introduce himself. He'd never expected to have Susan ask for his help. Maybe it was fate. Did that auger for a positive spin on his idea of family?

"This has rusted pretty good. But I think if we can get it off the hinges and use a solvent to get to bare metal, we can paint and lubricate so it'll work for years." He glanced at Brad.

"Hey, man, I'm up for anything to keep the kids safer. This

is a dangerous world and this isn't the best neighborhood. Just the best we can afford," Brad said.

Zack knew that was true for Susan as well. If they married, he could easily afford to establish them in a better neighborhood in New York City, or even move out to Long Island where they could have a house with a big yard. He paused a moment to try to imagine himself a home owner. It was not something he'd thought about since he'd been a child and had planned to buy the biggest house he could and never leave it.

Obviously the dream had changed as he grew up, but now he wondered if it had just lurked in the back of his mind all these years. He could picture the exact kind of house he wanted.

"Need help?" Brad asked.

Zack looked at the gate he was holding. He struggled a bit to lift it from the hinges and Brad stepped in to help. Together they wrested it from the supports and laid the gate on the walkway. In only moments, with the help of some well placed blows from a hammer, they had the second gate off as well.

"Not in our job descriptions, but something that needs doing," Zack said, studying the rusted hinges. Years of experience paid off; he knew metals and how to care for them. In only a half hour, he and Brad had stripped the rust from each hinge and lightly brushed the gates with a wire brush in preparation for the first coat of paint.

"This will have to do until next workday—we didn't buy wrought-iron paint," Zack said. Maybe he could get some tomorrow and come back during the week. He had nothing else to do until his medical leave ended.

"It's almost five. We'll be winding up soon," Brad said.

"Let's put these back up. I can get them down to paint later," Zack said.

When the gates were back in place, they opened and closed with no effort. When closed, the center latch kept them in place.

Cleaning up the area, Zack returned the tools to the staging area and went to hunt for Susan. He found her with several other mothers, cleaning paintbrushes in one of the bathrooms, the door propped open for ventilation.

He waited opposite the door, listening to the female chatter. The topic was children. He figured he could never learn too much about that so listened as they discussed eating patterns and how to get them to eat enough vegetables. He felt a spurt of pride in Danny. The child never argued with Susan about what to eat. Her nutritious meals were delicious as well as healthful.

She glanced up at one point and looked directly at him. The smile that lit her face reminded him of why he was here. She was not good at hiding her emotions. He nodded, but said nothing.

She murmured something to the woman next to her, who then looked over at him.

"We've been asked to join the others for dinner, can you make it?" she called.

He nodded once, glad the day wasn't going to end soon. He enjoyed being with Susan and the other parents. Samuel at the job site would split a gut laughing if he could see him now. Zack didn't care. This was uncharted territory for him, and he was interested in exploring every facet.

"We're going as is—no one wants to go home first and change," she said, rinsing her hands and then drying them with a paper towel. One of the other mothers gathered all the brushes and shook them in the deep sink, then wrapped them in plastic bags.

Susan came out to the hall, rotating her shoulders a bit. "I won't be able to move tomorrow," she said.

"Turn around," Zack said, and when she complied, he gently massaged her shoulders and neck.

"Ohhh, that feels heavenly," she said, letting her head fall forward.

"Lucky you. Wish Jim would think of something like that for me," the red-haired mother said in passing. "Or I could stand in line and get a turn?" she teased.

Zack grinned at her. "You'd have to ask Susan."

"Hmmm," she said, not offering to share.

The redhead laughed and continued down the hall.

Soon Zack and Susan were alone.

"Do we go?" he said, enjoying the feel of her slight frame in his hands. Her muscles were tense, but he gently worked on them to loosen them up. He knew she wasn't used to this kind of work.

"We go," she said with a sigh. Stepping away, she turned. "Thank you, that feels wonderful."

He leaned over and kissed her.

"That feels wonderful," he said.

In only moments they were out front with the others. Mrs. Harper was opening and closing the gate in delight.

"This is wonderful. We can keep the children in no matter what, and keep out those we don't want wandering in."

Susan looked at Zack. "Did you fix that?"

"I remember Danny running away. What if another child did—without the quick find. It wasn't hard to do."

"But not even on the list of things to repair. As a grateful mother, thank you."

"Brad pointed out that if it had been fixed before, I wouldn't have met you," Zack said.

Her eyes widened at that.

"I can't imagine not knowing you," she said involuntarily.

"Hold that thought for later," he said.

The group who went to dinner together chose to walk to the same pizza place Zack had taken Susan and Danny.

They crowded around two tables pushed together. The conversation was lively and full of laughter. Parents told stories about their children. They all lauded the work of the pre-school. And twice Zack was asked about his own work and how he'd come to volunteer with their group. He found the evening entertaining. He laughed with the others, and kept glancing at Susan. She seemed to be enjoying herself as well.

When they walked home, it was by themselves. He reached out to take her hand, linking their fingers.

"Tired?" he asked.

"Yes. I sure wish I didn't have to go to work tomorrow. I'd love to take a hot bath before bed and then sleep in until noon."

"Take a day off," he suggested.

"No, I have to save my time in case Danny gets sick or something."

"You wouldn't have to do that if you stayed home with him, would you?" Zack said slowly.

"No, but that's not possible."

"It would be if you had a husband to take care of earning the income while you took care of Danny. And the husband, of course," he said, testing the waters. His gaze was fixed on her as they walked. She stared straight ahead.

"But I don't have a husband."

"You would if you marry me."

At Susan's stunned look, Zack began to backpedal.

"Just think about it. No need to answer now." God, how could he have made such a blunder. He hadn't even told her of his relationship to her son. She hadn't confided in him about Danny. They really hardly knew each other.

But he knew down in his gut that marrying Susan would give him all he wanted in life. Had his impetuous proposal ruined everything?

CHAPTER EIGHT

Susan stumbled, grabbed hold of Zack and stared at him in astonishment.

"What did you say?"

"I was going to wait. I should take you out to dinner and maybe a carriage ride around Central Park after dark. That would be more romantic. But it just came out. I know you never thought about it. But think about it now, okay? Just think about it. Don't say no right away."

She listened to him, amazed she could concentrate when her heart raced so. Zack had just asked her to marry him! She didn't know what to say. She kept quiet as he kept explaining away the casual comment as they walked alone. He'd planned to ask her. He'd actually thought about what would be romantic and had planned it. This wasn't some knee-jerk reaction to the thought of her having to work.

At first she couldn't speak. No, was her initial response. Automatic. I love Tom!

But as she watched Zack grow more and more flustered as he tried to explain, her heart blossomed. She had worried about his leaving. Now he was asking her to marry him, to make a home with him.

Suddenly she realized he had stopped talking and was watching her closely.

"Are you all right?" he asked.

"Surprised," she said. Slowly she released the grip on his arm, smoothed the wrinkled shirt watching as she did so, trying to get her reeling senses under control and find an answer. Yes or no? Keep him forever in her life or refuse to share hers with him?

"We haven't known each other long," she began. Don't let me make a mistake here, she prayed.

"You're right. Forget it. It was too soon." He turned and took a step.

Susan remained where she was.

"Forget it? Did you or did you not ask me to marry you?"

He turned, tilting his head slightly as he studied her. "I did. Badly, but I did."

"I never expected to get married again."

"Why not? You're young and pretty and fun to be with. And you have an adorable child who needs a father."

She nodded. "A lot of men don't want to raise someone else's child."

"I'm not a lot of men." He looked back toward the pre-school. "I enjoyed working at Danny's school, using talents I have for something besides earning a living. That's a good group of people, working to make life better for their children." *Tell her,* something inside urged. *She needs to know.*

"That's certain." She glanced at him, glanced away. "I'm not sure I can give you an answer right now."

"Let's keep on as we've been and see what develops," he suggested. *Tell her, tell her.*

She met his gaze. "I won't ever forget. You caught me by surprise, that's all."

He nodded. Taking a deep breath, he turned. Soon they were both walking back to the apartment. Susan knew she'd disappointed him. He'd obviously been thinking about this for a while and had obviously hoped she'd immediately accept.

Why hadn't she? The last weeks had been special. Zack was special. Why was she hesitating? He'd had more excitement in his life than she'd ever see, yet was willing to settle down with her and make a family. At least, that's what she thought.

"Do you plan to quit working abroad?" she asked.

"Yes. I wouldn't marry and leave you," he said.

"Settle here or back in Chicago?" she asked.

"Here. Or in the vicinity at least. I was thinking maybe something in Long Island. I'd like to be near the water after all the desert living I've done. But I'm flexible."

Susan looked ahead, seeing her apartment building in the distance. If she married Zack, it would mean drastic changes. Moving from this neighborhood would not be a problem. It worried her that Danny would have to grow up here. But to marry Zack, make a home with him? It would be different from anything she'd expected.

The question remained: Would she be happy with Zack? Yes!

So what was the problem? Danny? Zack seemed to enjoy being with him as much as with her. And Danny clearly adored Zack. Would they be a perfect match?

She cleared her throat. "Actually you haven't seen Danny when he throws a temper tantrum. He can be less than endearing sometimes."

Zack looked at her. The words ready to be spoken. Would it make a difference? Instead he said, "All kids throw temper tantrums. That doesn't change how we feel about them. Are you worried I won't love him?" *He's my son, I'll always love him.*

"No. I…you caught me by surprise, that's all. Give me a couple of days, please? I don't want to make a spur-of-the-moment decision."

They reached the apartment building.

"I won't come in," Zack said, looking down the street. "I need to get back to the hotel.

"Come tomorrow for dinner?" she asked.

He looked down at her. "How about I treat you to that dinner and carriage ride?"

She smiled. "I'd like that." Reaching up, she brushed her lips against his. "I may even have an answer for you by then." Turning, Susan ran up the three stairs to the lobby and into the apartment building. She hugged Danny when she entered. Looking at Edith, she longed to share the situation, but kept silent. This was one decision she had to make on her own.

Later Susan took a long hot bath to ease tense muscles. She closed her eyes, remembering Zack massaging her shoulders. She wished he were here now. She could use an all-over body massage.

Which she could get if they married.

She sat up, feeling breathless. He'd really asked her to marry him. What was there to debate? She loved him. She longed to be with him, to hear him speak, watch his eyes when they lighted in amusement, or turned soft when kissing her.

He was a good man. Steady and reliable.

He was a stranger. Someone she'd bumped into the day Danny had run away from preschool.

His actions were sound. He could have said no he hadn't seen the child and moved on. Instead everything he'd done had been helpful.

And his kisses were wonderful. She smiled in remembrance. She wouldn't mind a few more of those right now.

How would Danny react to having Zack become part of their family?

How would her parents? Ohmygosh, she'd have to call them in the morning and clue them in that she was considering—marrying Zack Morgan. A man they had never met.

She was truly considering marrying Zack. It took a moment for the truth to sink in. She should have said yes on the sidewalk. If he changed his mind, she'd die.

She loved him. Once she went beyond thinking there would only be one man in her life, she knew Zack was the man for her now.

They would have a short engagement, she hoped. She couldn't wait to start their family life together. Laughing in glee, she sank to her chin, smiling in delight. She was going to marry Zack Morgan.

First thing the next morning Susan called her parents.

"Is everything okay, dear," her mother asked. "It's early for a call. We missed Saturday's chat. How did the work at the preschool go?"

"Everything's fine, Mom. We accomplished more than the headmistress thought we would. And I received a proposal of marriage."

"That's nice, I'm glad—wait! Did you say you got a proposal? For marriage?"

Susan heard her father's exclamation in the background.

"From Zack Morgan. I think I mentioned him before."

"Mentioned is all. I had no idea you were so involved. Isn't this sudden?"

"A bit. But I'm sure. He's sure. You'll like him, Mom. He's steady and thoughtful." And sexy, but she wasn't sure that was something her mother would want to hear. "And he's very good with Danny."

"You aren't marrying him because he likes Danny, are you?" her mother asked sharply.

"No, Mom. I'm marrying Zack because I love him. Very

much. And I hope you and Dad will as well. But it won't matter in the end. It matters only that I love him."

"Your father and I will be up next weekend to meet this young man. We can discuss wedding preparations then."

"I hadn't thought about a wedding. I had such a fairy-tale one with Tom. I don't need another. We can get married at a judge's chambers."

"Is this Zack's first marriage?"

"Yes."

"Then maybe he needs one," her mother suggested gently.

"Oh. You're right. Though, he may not want one. He has no family. He was raised in foster homes."

"But he has a good job?"

"He's a structural engineer and for the last decade has worked major projects in the Middle East. Now he's going to settle down here and find something that will allow him to come home every night. He wants to buy a home in Long Island."

"This seems so sudden."

"I know, he caught me by surprise, too. Tonight he's taking me to dinner and a carriage ride in the park. We'll have lots to discuss." She counted the minutes until she'd see him again.

"Keep me posted. We'll take the ten o'clock flight from Orlando and get there in the early afternoon Saturday."

"We're still scheduled for preschool work. Edith will be here with Danny."

"So your Zack is helping at the preschool renovations."

"He's been a major help. He got all the materials donated by his company, brought a couple of other engineers to help the first day and works harder and faster than any of the parents who've shown up."

"I like the way you stand up for him. Shows you care."

"Of course I do. I love Zack." The more she said it, the

more Susan wondered why she had doubts. She loved him and could envision a long, happy life together.

Susan was scarcely able to concentrate at work. She kept watching the time. Did the clock hands always move so slowly? She wanted to see Zack. Tell him her answer. Discuss their future and kiss him silly.

Finally. She had dashed home, changed into another dress and freshened her makeup. Brushing her hair, she let it fall down her back in waves. A touch of perfume and she was ready.

Edith had agreed to watch Danny. Susan didn't know what she'd do without Edith. Which brought up the question of what would Edith do when they moved?

Some of her happiness dimmed. For two years Edith had stepped in as a surrogate grandmother, watching Danny, helping Susan. She'll be lost, Susan thought.

She went into the living room to visit with Edith until Zack arrived. When he knocked on the door, Danny ran for it, stopping and yelling, "Who is it?" He put his ear against the door. Satisfied with the answer, he opened it.

"I waited until you said Zack," he told the man proudly.

"Good job." Zack smiled at him, his gaze immediately searching for Susan. She rose and came to greet him.

"You look beautiful," he said, taking in her dress and shoes.

"You look wonderful," she murmured, suddenly feeling shy. How did a newly-almost-engaged woman greet her soon to be fiancé?

"You two have a good dinner," Edith said, waving at Zack from the sofa.

"Can I go?" Danny said, clinging to Zack's leg.

"Not this time. You would be bored at the restaurant I've chosen. I hope your mom will like it, though," Zack said.

Susan did. It was the Tavern on the Green. A delightful restaurant in the heart of Central Park. With dining inside and out, it was lit with thousands of tiny lights. It looked like a fairyland.

They were shown a table near the windows, inside where it was warm, but with an unobstructive view of the outside.

Zack ordered champagne and when it had been delivered offered a toast. "To us."

"To us," Susan repeated, the rim of her flute touching his.

Zack said nothing more about his proposal, but proceeded to tell her about calling for a medical release and getting an appointment two weeks from now. "I wanted to be released immediately. I guess to the company, two weeks is immediately."

"So you'll be here for another two weeks, at least."

"Plenty of time to finish the preschool renovations. I talked with Mrs. Harper and I can go over some afternoons when they'll combine classes to give me room to work."

"That's great. But shouldn't you take advantage of the two weeks left to rest up?"

"I'll only be working four hours a day. Hardly enough to give me a problem." His dark eyes gazed into hers. "Tell me about your day."

"I called my parents. They are flying up this weekend to meet you."

"I thought we were working at the preschool."

"I told my mom that. They'll go right to the apartment and visit with Danny until we get there."

"Maybe I'll bring a change of clothes to the school," Zack said.

She laughed. "I think they'll excuse messy clothes knowing you've been helping at their grandson's school. In fact, they'll love you to death for being so nice to me and Danny."

"And you?"

"I'll love you to death, too," she said seriously.

He raised his glass to hers and they both drank a sip.

As soon as dinner was finished, Zack steered them to the
carriage ride concession. They climbed aboard and were
tucked in with a lap robe. It was cool in the evenings. As
the horse started its rounds, Zack pulled Susan closer and
kissed her.

"Susan, will you marry me?" he asked seriously when he
ended the kiss.

"Yes, I will be very happy to marry you," she replied,
reaching up to kiss him again.

She felt giddy and excited and a bit scared. Not about her
relationship with Zack, but the fact life came with no guarantees. She hoped they'd have fifty or sixty years together—
even more. But she'd take whatever time they did have
together and relish every moment. She refused to take
anything for granted again.

Zack couldn't believe she'd said yes. After her reaction
yesterday, he was sure he'd blown it. He wanted to tell the
world. Which, of course, they would do when they got the
marriage license and could get married.

"How soon?" he asked.

She laughed. "Soon. I can't wait to be your wife. And have
you all to myself every night."

"Not as much as I want you for my wife. I will have to fly
back to the Middle East to wind things up. Shouldn't take
more than a few days. I've told the company I'm not returning even when I get the medical release. They're searching for
a replacement for me."

"You're giving up a lot," she said.

"No, nothing worth keeping. Not compared to what I'm
getting."

"Danny's going to be thrilled," she said. "I didn't tell him.
I thought we should be together to do that."

"It's too late tonight," Zack said. It was already past nine and Danny went to bed at eight. "Tomorrow? I can come over after you finish work."

"Perfect."

"Once we're finished with the preschool projects, I'd like to start looking for a place for us. Any preferences?"

"Just close to transit. I do not want to have to drive into the city every day."

"I thought you might like to stay home with Danny. Maybe even consider having more children."

She tried to see him in the dark. His eyes were focused on her.

"It was what I wanted before. I stayed home until I had to go to work when—" She stopped so suddenly Zack knew she'd been about to mention Tom.

"It's okay to talk about him. He was your husband for several years, an important part of your life. Before now." He refused to be jealous of a man dead two years. But he wished he could have been first in Susan's life. He had to settle for being last.

"Now, you are the important part of my life," she said. "I would love to stay home with Danny, at least until he's in school. And if we have other children, I'd want to be home with them when they're young. Then I can decide what to do. I could teach German, you know. If I got a teacher's job, I'd be home when Danny had school breaks."

"You decide. I have enough money that whatever you want is fine."

"I'm worried about Edith," she said slowly.

"Why?"

"She's been such a help to me these last two years, but I've also helped her with the baby-sitting money. She has a very small pension and with prices rising, it's tough."

"Maybe another family will move into your apartment and need her services."

"Maybe. If I keep working, maybe she could get an apartment near us and continue to watch Danny."

"You'd go back to work just to keep her employed?" he asked.

"I like my job, actually. And he'll be in school before long. It's hard to leave her—she's part of the family."

Zack thought about it for a moment. Edith was part of Susan's extended family. She cared more for the woman than as a mere baby-sitter. "Maybe we can find a home with one of those in-law units. Edith could move with us. And be available when you and I want to get away."

Susan beamed at him. "That's a brilliant solution. So you're thinking you and I might want to get away?"

"For dinner some nights. Maybe a few weekends in the city to see a play or something. But I don't plan to be gone from home and family for more than a few days at a time. I'm going to want you all to myself," Zack said, and pulled her closer for another kiss.

The carriage ride was a dream. Zack couldn't believe she'd said yes. The only doubt was telling her about his relationship to Danny. Should he do it now? Or wait until she confessed he was adopted? She had to know. He had to tell her. But the ride was as romantic as he could get. He didn't want to shatter the moment.

He had the hurdle of meeting her parents and passing their inquisition. But even if they didn't approve, he would push to get his way. He wanted Susan more than he ever expected. The future would be bleak indeed if he lost her and Danny.

Susan was almost floating as they returned to her apartment. They had discussed getting married in June, less than six weeks away. Zack hadn't been that sold on a formal wedding, but remembering what her mother had said, Susan suggested a small wedding in a chapel. She would splurge for a new dress and maybe a picture-book hat with a small veil. She wanted to always remember this wedding as special—as special as the man she was marrying.

"I can't wait until we tell Danny," she said as they rode up the elevator. "He's going to be thrilled, I know it.

Edith greeted them and then looked at them both closely. "Something's up," she commented.

"We're getting married," Susan said with a rush, then went to hug her friend. "Be happy for us."

"I'm delighted," Edith said, returning her hug. Then she looked at Zack. "Take good care of this woman…she's very special."

"I will. With your help. We'd like you to consider moving when we do. We're going to look for a house with an in-law unit."

"Oh, my." Edith looked as flustered as Susan had felt when Zack first proposed. "It's so unexpected. Are you sure?"

"His proposal was unexpected, and we're both sure—about getting married and having you move with us. Danny and I will still need you."

"Oh my." The older woman gave a tremulous smile. "I'd be delighted."

She extended her good wishes to them both and left.

Zack glanced at his watch. "It's after eleven," he said, pulling her into his arms again. "I don't want to go, but you have to get up for work tomorrow."

She snuggled closer, savoring his strong arms around her, the beat of his heart against hers. She felt cherished. It had been a long time on her own. She loved this man, loved being half of a couple. She hated to say good-night.

"So before long, you and I won't have to say good-night

and part," he said, practically reading her mind. Or was it he felt the same?

"I can hardly wait," she said, tipping her face up for another kiss.

The next evening, Susan came home to find Zack had arrived a few minutes ahead of her. He was talking with Edith while Danny played with some toys on the floor of the living room.

"Hi," she said, tossing her purse on the small table and shedding her coat.

Zack smiled that sexy smile of his and rose to cross over to kiss her.

Danny ran to greet her, too. After Zack's kiss, Susan picked Danny up and kissed him on the cheek. "Hello to you, my man. How was your day?" She shifted her gaze to Zack.

"Me and Edith went to the park. I went way high on the swing."

"Good for you."

"I'll be running along. Zack and I had a nice chat. I had best get started weeding through things I don't want to move and getting ready," Edith said.

Once she was gone, Susan carried Danny into the living room and sat down, holding him on her lap.

"Zack and I have something to tell you," she said, smiling at Zack.

"What?" Danny asked.

"We are going to get married. Zack will live with us after that and we'll be a family."

Danny swiveled around and looked at Zack. "Are you my new daddy?"

Zack glanced at Susan, then nodded. "I'll be your new daddy," he said.

Danny looked at his mother. "He doesn't look like Daddy. I have a picture. Zack's not my daddy."

"No, he's not Tom. But when we get married, he'll be your new daddy," Susan explained. "Your first daddy went to heaven, remember? Now you'll have a second daddy."

"I'll always love you, Danny. You'll see how good I can take care of you and your mommy," Zack said, reaching to ruffle his hair.

"'Kay," Danny said. He struggled to get down and went to play with his toys.

Susan laughed nervously. "I guess it hasn't sunk in yet. Once we're living together, I think he'll understand better."

As Susan prepared the meal that evening she thought about the changes coming. She had never liked the poky little apartment, but it was the best she could afford. Now Zack was talking about moving to Long Island and buying a house with a yard—and in-law unit for Edith. She wouldn't have to work if she didn't want to.

The idea of spending the day with Danny was extremely appealing. She felt she missed so much while away at work. Little children grew at an amazing rate, learning new things every day exploring their world.

One change would be in preschools. For a moment she felt a wave of sadness. The teachers at his preschool had been wonderful. Working on the renovations made her feel a real connection to the goals of the establishment. They would be leaving that behind when moving.

On the other hand, the neighborhood they'd find would be so much safer for children. She'd make sure they looked for a good school district.

Zack helped with putting Danny to bed that evening by reading him his story. When Danny was asleep, Zack returned to the kitchen where Susan was just finishing the dishes.

"He's out like a light," he said, leaning against the doorjamb, watching her. She was graceful in all she did, including dishes. He felt a contentment at the sight. Being with Susan made him happy. They didn't have to go to fancy nightclubs, constantly seek outside entertainment. Just being with her was enough. He liked to watch her, hear her laughter. He hoped he could make her happy. As happy as she was making him.

He wasn't sure he had it in him to be a good father. But he'd watched George Zumwalt. He knew how a good husband cherished his wife. As he cherished Susan.

He'd risk everything for the chance at making a life with Susan.

Susan turned and gave him a mock frown. "You could come help," she said.

He smiled and let his gaze roam over her. "You're handling that like a pro," he teased.

She folded the dish towel and hung it over the rod nearby. "I want a dishwasher in my new house," she said.

"Done."

"His name could be Zack," she said slyly, turning to grin at him.

He laughed. He hadn't been teased in a long time. It felt good.

"Or its name could be Whirlpool or KitchenAid. Especially if you want all your dishes in one piece by the end of the week."

She sashayed across the room, her gaze never leaving his. He could feel his heart rate increase as she drew near. When her toes almost touched his, she put her hands on her hips and tilted back her head. "I think you are better with your hands than that," she said.

He uncrossed his arms and slowly drew her against him. "I would love to prove the point."

He lowered his mouth to hers, giving her a deep kiss that

rocked her back on her heels. Her arms encircled his neck and she pressed even closer, relishing every inch of him that touched. She couldn't wait until they were married.

Saturday Zack arrived in time for breakfast and brought croissants and coffee from the coffeehouse near his hotel. Susan had prepared pancakes for Danny and he was licking the syrup from his fork when Zack walked into the kitchen.

"I have pancakes," Danny said.

"So I see. I brought your mommy something else." He set his bag and tray of coffee on the table. "Ready to paint again?" he asked, kissing her.

"As I'll ever be," Susan said a minute later. "I checked the flights and my parents are still due to arrive midafternoon. I told Mrs. Harper we'd try to cut out early."

When they found a place to live, he hoped the neighbors would be as friendly and accepting as the parents at Danny's preschool. In fact he hoped all the neighbors would become family friends. Susan would blossom in such a setting. He'd need her help to become comfortable, but was making inroads with Brad and the other fathers working on the preschool projects.

Brad and Betsy Singleton were already at the school when Zack and Susan arrived. Splitting up to go to their separate tasks, Zack watched her walk away. He wished they were working together.

"She's a looker," Brad commented as he watched Zack watching Susan.

"She's agreed to marry me," Zack said quietly. The wonder was still there.

"Hey, man, that's great!" Brad socked him on the arm. "We'll have to celebrate."

In no time everyone helping knew of the new engagement. There were many congratulations, men and women even coming outside to speak with Zack while he and Brad worked on the playground equipment. From the comments flying, Zack knew they were happy for Susan. He was pretty happy himself.

It was after three when he and Susan broke away from the work and headed back to her apartment. He had washed up in the hallway bathroom of the preschool, doing the best he could with limited resources. He wanted to make a good impression on Susan's parents. For a moment he stared at himself in the mirror, remembering back to changing foster houses. He'd always wanted to make a good impression in hopes the people would keep him. It felt almost the same. If her parents didn't approve, would Susan still marry him?

CHAPTER NINE

SUSAN'S parents were at her apartment when Susan and Zack arrived. Edith was talking with them, while Danny sat in his grandma's lap. He struggled off when he spotted his mother.

"Grandma and Poppa are here. They came to visit," he said, jumping up and down. Susan picked him up and gave him a hug. "I see they are. Are you being a good host?"

"What's a host?"

"Someone who has company over. Hi, Mom, Dad."

They had both risen and crossed to greet their daughter and the man who would soon become part of the family.

"This is Zack Morgan. Zack, my parents, Amelia and Tony Molina."

Tony shook Zack's hand. Her mother surprised her by hugging Zack.

"Welcome to our family," she said. "I hope you will always keep my daughter happy."

"I'll do my best," Zack said.

Edith stayed only a little while before leaving. Danny loved being the center of attention and acted up a little until Susan warned him a time-out would be forthcoming if he didn't settle down a little. He looked at Zack.

"Your grandparents are going to be here for a while. There'll be time to spend with just them," he said. Danny nodded and went back to sit in Amelia's lap. Soon he was dozing.

"Edith said he didn't have a nap," Tony said, watching the little boy. "We got here shortly after two—good connections from the airport."

"I'll put him in his bed," Zack said.

Once he'd left the room, Susan looked at her parents. "Well, what do you think?"

"Honey, we just met him. He seems nice, but it'll take a few days to get to know him better," her mother said.

"The question is, what do you think?" her father asked.

"I think he's wonderful. He's patient and kind and is really good with Danny."

"You are not marrying him just to get a father for Danny, are you?"

She shook her head. "No. I'm marrying him for me. It's just a bonus that he wants to be a father to Danny."

When Zack returned, he sat on the sofa beside Susan and looked at her parents.

"Questions, I'm sure."

"How did you two meet?" her mother asked.

For the next hour or so, Zack easily answered all the questions the Molinas asked.

Even when her father asked about his monetary situation and Susan protested.

"I've been working abroad for the last dozen years. The company pays well for hardship locales and provides housing. I've saved quite a bit, and invested it. Susan won't have to worry about money."

"That'll be a switch," Amelia said, glancing around the small room.

"Mom!"

"Will you have to work, or can you stay home with Danny?" her mother asked.

Zack replied, "That's up to Susan. She likes her job, so if she wants to continue, that's fine with me. But I'd be as happy to have her stay home with Danny."

"And any other kids we may have," she said.

They talked about their plans for finding a house. For a small wedding.

"Honeymoon?" her mother asked.

Susan looked at Zack. "We never talked about that."

"We can later," he said. He was getting a bit impatient with all the conversation. What was the verdict? Did the Molinas think he was suitable for their daughter?

Finally her father looked at his watch. "I think we better head for the hotel and check in, Amelia," he said. "We'll meet for dinner at seven?"

"That'll be fine, Dad," Susan said, rising when he did.

"You're not staying here?" Zack asked, also rising.

"Not enough room. And only one bathroom," Amelia said, standing. "If you buy a house on the Island, do get one with more than one bathroom."

When they'd gone, Zack looked at Susan. "What did they say, anything?"

She went to him, oddly touched at his vulnerability. She always thought of him as invincible. "They are happy I'm happy. It's awkward when meeting the first time, I know. But they like you, I can tell."

"You are better at gauging their reaction than I am. Are you sure your father will go along with it?"

She laughed. "Yes. He was worse with Tom. Of course we were still teenagers when we were first dating, but he even asked Tom for his five-year plan. Like a high school kid had such a thing. Relax, Zack. What's not to like?"

"As long as you keep thinking that way," he said, kissing her. "I'll go clean up and change and pick you and Danny up at six-thirty."

"See you then."

While Susan showered she considered the afternoon meeting. Her parents had been more concerned than she expected, but who could blame them. She'd agreed to marry a man she hardly knew, who had no family or even friends in the area.

Yet she knew it was going to be a happy marriage. Zack gave her security and contentment and yet excited her as no man had before. She was looking forward to finding a place together—as she and Tom had. Making a home for their family. Sharing holidays and birthdays. Watching Danny grow to manhood.

She also liked the idea of maybe adopting a child or two to complete their family. She knew Zack would want an older child—as he'd been when available for adoption. He'd never been chosen. Maybe they could change the life of a boy or girl and include them in their family.

The rest of the weekend passed quickly. The Molinas spent as much time with their grandson—and new son-in-law-to-be—as they could. Susan was pleased everyone seemed to get along, but there was no strong bond forged. It would take time. Her parents had known and loved Tom for years. It would take a while for Zack to find his way with them. She hoped they would make every effort. It was important to her that he found acceptance with her family. He'd been without one of his own all his life. She wanted him to be part of hers.

Monday morning her parents flew home. Susan went to work as normal. When she returned home that evening, Zack was home with Danny.

"Where's Edith?" she asked, after appropriate greetings had been exchanged.

"I sent her home about a half hour ago. I came by after my hours at the preschool. Brad also came this afternoon and Phillip Goldstein. We just about have the playground up to code."

"Let me change and I'll start supper."

"We can order in. I want to talk to you about looking for a house. It takes a bit of time after we find a place to close escrow. I'd like to move right in after we get married."

"Sounds fine to me. I'll be right back."

He had brought several sheets of listings in different towns on Long Island. After ordering in a Chinese dinner, they sat together and looked at the different properties. All were waterfront dwellings. Some were huge with matching price tags.

"We can't afford these," Susan said at last. The one in West Islip that was pictured on one leaflet was an ideal home. She'd love to see inside. But no use going there; it was way out of their price range.

"Yes, we can," he said, studying another.

She looked at him. "We can?" Just how much money did this future husband of hers have? The homes were in the millions of dollars.

He glanced at her, caught her gaze. "What?"

"Just how much can we afford?" she asked.

He shrugged. "I'll let you know if we go over budget. None of these will break the bank."

"You've saved more than a million dollars?" she asked in disbelief.

"I earn a lot of money, plus hardship bonuses. I've invested pretty well, and it just keeps growing."

She looked at Danny and then gazed around her apartment. "I can't believe this," she murmured.

"Hey, it's just money."

"You're rich."

"Well-off, I'd say."

"How well-off?"

"I don't know offhand. Do you want me to get my financial advisor to fax you a copy of my portfolio?" he asked whimsically.

"I don't even have a financial advisor. Zack, are you sure about getting married? I'm not bringing much to the union."

He put down the papers and reached for her hands. "You are bringing yourself and Danny, both beyond price. Never let money come between us."

Susan smiled at his reply. Tom had made a good living for them, but it looked as if Zack was in a class by himself. She vowed to do all she could to make sure he was as happy as she was with their marriage.

When the Chinese food arrived, Zack helped Danny wash his hands and soon they were all eating—Zack with chopsticks.

Danny watched, fascinated. "I want sticks," he said.

"You won't be able to eat with them," his mother said.

"Zack can. I can do it, too."

"It takes practice," Zack said. He took another set of chopsticks from the pile in the center of the table. Breaking them apart, he rubbed them together to make sure they were smooth for little boy hands.

"This is how you hold them," he said, patiently showing Danny the way.

Danny dropped everything he tried to pick up. He grew frustrated and before long threw the chopsticks across the room. "They're stupid," he said, his lower lip coming out.

"Go over and pick them up," Zack said.

Danny glared at him. "No."

"Danny," Susan began.

"Please, let me. If he doesn't recognize my authority in some things, it'll make for a bumpy road. Danny we do not throw things in this home. Please go and pick them up—now!" Zack said.

Danny stared at him for a moment longer then grudgingly got off his chair and went across the room to retrieve the chopsticks.

When he put them on the table and climbed back into his chair, Zack said, "Thank you. If something makes you frustrated, you need to find other ways to display that rather than throwing things. Can you remember that?"

Danny nodded, looking at his mother, his eyes filling with tears.

Susan wanted to grab him up and comfort him, but she knew Zack was right and Danny needed to remember that.

"Eat your dinner with your fork. You can learn chopsticks when you're big like Zack."

"I don't like Zack," Danny said.

Susan saw Zack's expression go blank. She knew the childish words had hurt.

"Maybe not right this minute, but you'll like him again soon. Eat your dinner." To Zack, she said, "Kids say that all the time. The first time Danny said he h-a-t-e-d me I thought I'd never stop crying. It broke my heart. But he forgot he said it about ten minutes later. Kids say things they don't mean."

Zack nodded and resumed eating. Susan wished she could go comfort him. But he, like Danny, had lots to learn about making a family. There would always be some hiccups along the way.

Monday night set the stage for the rest of the week. Zack came to the apartment when he finished working at the school. He and Susan would have dinner together, sometimes preparing it themselves, sometimes ordering in. They spent time with Danny and once he was in bed each evening, would look at different real estate offerings, read about school districts and try to agree on the best place to live.

Thursday night when they sat together after Danny went

to bed, Zack put his arm around Susan. "I have to fly to Washington in the morning. They moved up my physical."

"That's short notice."

"I said I'd take any cancellation. Once I'm cleared, I'll talk to the projects director and see what plans they have for any building projects in this area."

"And if not?"

"Then I quit and find something around here."

"That's risky."

"Hey, I'm good at what I do. I'll find a job, don't worry."

"When will you be home?"

"I'll stay in D.C. for the night, get an early flight back on Saturday. It's another workday at the school, and I think the last. Several different parents came during the week to work when I did, which helped move along faster than originally anticipated."

"Your being there is what moved it along faster," she said. "You've been wonderful."

He pulled her closer and kissed her.

Susan loved their quiet evenings together. They talked about everything, from current events, to books they both liked—she mysteries, he biographies. They discussed moving some favorite pieces of furniture with them and getting rid of the rest and buying new. And twice Zack brought up getting a puppy. Susan was not convinced.

"You'll call me after you see the doctor," Susan said when she walked him to the door later.

"Of course. As soon as I know. See you Saturday."

Susan closed the door softly and leaned against it. She would miss him until Saturday. She was getting spoiled with his constant presence. At least Danny had behaved better after his brief tantrum on Monday. She wanted Zack to love him as much as she did.

* * *

Susan, Betsy and other mothers were doing the last of the cleanup on Saturday when Zack strode into the room. He'd called Friday afternoon, but she'd missed the call because she had been in a meeting. Everything was fine, had been his message. She thought he might call last night, but he hadn't. She saw him as soon as he stepped in the room and met him halfway, almost running the last few steps. He caught her in his arms and kissed her.

The calls and clapping of the other mothers ended the kiss. Susan felt embarrassed, but the good-natured teasing had her smiling. Zack looked around dazed.

"He's been gone for sooo long," Betsy said. Then turned to the other mothers and added, "Since Thursday night at eleven."

Laughter followed her statement.

"I remember those days. Now I'd just as soon have the kit and caboodle gone for a weekend to have some me time," one of the mothers said.

"I'd like to stop working weekends," another added.

"We're out of here soon, and doesn't the school look great?" Betsy said.

"Last inspection on Monday. Mrs. Harper said Zack would be our point man," another added.

"Guess I better do a run-through to make sure everything is okay," he said, brushing his fingers against Susan's cheek. She smiled, wishing they could just go off and be alone this instant. Patience was a tough virtue to learn!

"So when's the wedding again?" Betsy asked as they went back to work.

"Last week in June. We're going to look at houses tomorrow," Susan said, polishing one window until not a streak or speck was left.

"We're going to miss you when you move," Betsy said.

"And Zack when other things around here need fixing," someone said.

"He might come back to help," Susan said, wondering if she would see these wonderful people again.

"He'll be needed at Danny's school when he starts kindergarten. You can't imagine all the activities that call for parents' help."

"Right now I can't imagine Danny in kindergarten. He's growing up too fast," Susan said.

"Amy is my fourth and will be starting in the fall. My oldest is already in sixth grade. The years fly by."

Susan had heard that from her own parents. She wished she could keep Danny little forever, but couldn't stop him growing. And she was finding such delight in seeing everything she took for granted being discovered by him. She could double her fun when Zack also got to be involved.

Zack left the school room with the laughter of the women still echoing in his ears. He hadn't cared about making a public display; he'd been anxious to see Susan. He had never expected to miss her so much in the short time they'd been apart. He'd had plenty to do. The physical had been grueling—to make sure he was capable of dealing with the hardships that arose with overseas work. Once he passed that, he'd gone to see the director of International Projects to let him know he was not going back.

When the man expressed dismay, Zack offered to see what they had in New York. Susan had strong ties to New York City and he didn't want to move her any farther away than Long Island. He had enjoyed his weeks in the city and would love the opportunity to discover all New York had to offer.

A new high-rise complex was in the planning stage and the director of Domestic Projects jumped at the chance of having a man of Zack's background and knowledge be a key player. Zack could start work in early June. Time enough for him to return to the job site in the Middle East and wind up his affairs there.

If he missed Susan this much after being gone only over-night, what would a week or longer in the Middle East be like?

He'd soon find out.

"Hey, how did it go?" Brad greeted him when Zack found him in the boiler room.

"I passed."

"So the next step?"

"Head back out to the job site to wind things up. Then I start a new assignment for the company here in New York."

"Man, that's great. I was worried you and Susan would be taking off for one of those far flung countries."

"I wouldn't take a family there. Beside, didn't you hear, we're looking for a house out on the Island."

"Almost as bad. Leaving here, I mean. It's been good working with you."

"Likewise, man."

Together Zack and Brad did an inventory of all the changes made. Zack double-checked that everything had been brought up to code and he had the documentation in order for the building inspector's visit on Monday. The school was in better shape than it had been in a long time.

"Want to go for a beer after this?" Brad asked.

"I heard that," Betsy said, coming into the hall. "What about us?" she asked as Susan stepped up beside her.

"Of course I meant for you two to be with us. How could we bear to be apart?" Brad said dramatically.

She cuffed him lightly on the shoulder. "Good answer. How about it, Susan, got time?"

"Up to Zack. I have a baby-sitter who's there for the entire day if I need her."

"And will be moving with them, when they go," Betsy added for her husband's sake. "We have the Jablonsky twins. And your niece when we need her."

"I know but they'll all graduate from high school before Bethany is old enough to watch herself. So who'll fill in then?"

Zack watched the interaction, enjoying the camaraderie. He'd had that at his work sites, but this was different. Couples with similar goals, working together. Usually when he had paid leave, he'd date the prettiest woman he could find—no strings attached. And certainly no feeling of belonging, of building something for the future together.

"Danny's okay. I checked before I came here," Zack said.

"Devoted daddy already," Betsy said. "Lucky you."

"I know. And not just for that," Susan said, joining Zack.

Several couples went out for a late lunch together. Zack enjoyed spending time with them—no dangers of mines, no endless sand with not a spot of shade to be had. He especially liked being linked to Susan. Everyone liked her and seemed to share in her happiness.

He was almost sorry the job at the school was over.

Not that there wasn't a lot to do in the next six weeks. Changes on every front.

On Sunday Zack rented a car and drove them all to look at houses. Susan sat in the front. A car seat was provided for Danny and he and Edith sat in the back. The older woman had protested she didn't need to go, but Zack had insisted. It was going to be her home as well, and he wanted her to have a vote.

"Well, I never," she said, smiling mistily at him. "Thank you, young man."

Susan grinned, and reached out to hug him. "You're so special," she whispered in his ear.

He'd do all he could to make her happy.

They drove slowly through the little towns to see what amenities they offered. Many had merely a supermarket and gas station. A couple had movie theaters and larger shopping areas. When they reached West Islip, he drove around, finding the schools and the churches from the map the real estate agent had sent him.

At last they met the agent and toured three houses. It was a long day. Danny ran around each one, not understanding the implication. Susan loved each kitchen and couldn't wait to try out some of her mother's recipes in them. Edith was enthusiastic about the in-law suites. One had a pool, which Susan suspected would need to be constantly monitored lest a small child fall in.

On the drive back, Zack asked which she liked best.

"The second one, I think. Which did you like?"

"I liked that one. And the first."

"The first was way too big for our family."

"We may have more children," he reminded her.

"True."

"And I'd be around to help with housekeeping," Edith said from the back seat.

"Which did you like?" Susan asked.

"I liked them all. Each in-law unit is larger than the apartment I have now. And with a lovely garden to work in, how grand is that?"

"I don't know if I'd like gardening. Except for pots on the windowsill, I've never grown anything," Susan mused.

"Nothing much grows where I've been. All that green grass is amazing," Zack said.

"It looks like Central Park."

"We don't have to decide today. We have other listings we can check out," Zack said.

Zack was disappointed Susan hadn't fallen in love with one of the homes. He thought they all were nice. He had no idea how long it took to decide on a house. But he wanted her to pick the one they'd live in.

After dinner, Zack read to Danny. When his son fell asleep, Zack stayed beside him on the bed. Danny had been excited about every house, running up the stairs, stamping his feet with no admonition to keep quiet not to bother the neighbors. He could see his son growing up in every one of them. Having friends over, playing in the pool if they had one. One day he'd be a teenager, and then off to college. Zack closed his eyes for a moment, appreciating all he might have missed out on had he not bumped into Susan that day. He couldn't imagine life now without her in it. Or Danny. He was eternally grateful.

When he rejoined Susan in the living room, she had an array of pamphlets spread out.

"I think I've found the one I like. We'd have to see it, but what do you think?"

She handed him one as he sat beside her. It described a brick colonial. The front lawn was beautiful, sloping gently to the road. He looked at the photographs of the rooms and backyard. There was a swing set already installed, a play area and covered sandbox. A pool was behind the house, surrounded by tall shade trees.

"We can go see it one day this week."

"Or next weekend," she said.

"I won't be here then," he said slowly.

"Where will you be?"

"I have to return to the job site and wind up my part. I'm leaving on Thursday and will be gone at least a week, maybe longer."

"Oh."

Disappointment was evident in her expression. Then worry replaced it.

"I'll be coming back," he said to reassure her.

"Unless you get blown up by another land mine," she said. "Can't you have someone else handle it?"

"It's my responsibility," Zack said.

She sighed. "It sounds so right when you tell Danny about responsibility, but I don't like this."

"Me, either, but I'll be home before you miss me."

"Not possible," she said, leaning against him in contentment.

They were silent for a few moments. Zack took a deep breath. They were growing closer day by day. But the largest obstacle to complete honesty lay before them. He wondered if she would tell him about Danny before they married. He wanted to reassure her why it didn't matter an iota. But so far nothing seemed to lend itself to that discussion.

He wanted all the old life cleared up—his work site in the Middle East, and the truth about Danny's paternity.

"Danny is a wonderful child. You've done a terrific job with him."

"Thanks. It hasn't always been easy. But I wouldn't trade him for anything."

Zack waited a moment. This was as perfect an opening as he could give her. He hoped she'd say something about it being hard to be a mother without the father, that when they had first adopted Danny she and Tom had planned a long life together.

But Susan remained silent.

Time was running out. He had to leave soon and he wanted her to know he knew about Danny and didn't care—in fact he relished the knowledge that she didn't have to raise him alone from now on. And that he was Danny's father.

It would be easier to tell her if she'd bring it up. But Susan continued to snuggle close, obviously content with her own thoughts. Or was she struggling to find a way to tell him? Was she the one who couldn't have children? It didn't have to have been Tom. Was she worried that would impact him someway? He wanted her whether she could have children or not. He didn't love her for her childbearing ability. He loved her for herself, and always would.

"The house you like has five bedrooms and an in-law unit."

"Mmm," she said.

"Could be we'd need to work to fill them up."

"Could be," she said.

"I'm not against adoption, you know," he said easily. "I wish someone had adopted me once my parents were no longer in the picture. But by then I was an older child—no one wanted to."

Now—she'd say how she couldn't bear for that to happen to another child, how they'd joyfully adopted Danny to give him a family and a permanent home.

"I'm sorry you weren't. You couldn't have been much older than Danny is now."

"But maybe not as charming. I can't imagine anyone seeing Danny and not wanting to adopt hm."

"Good thing he's not available," Susan said.

"Not now."

She sat up and looked at him, frowning slightly. "What do you mean? Nothing's going to happen to me."

"I didn't say it was."

"Then why say Danny's not available now?"

"I mean, not now. Earlier, maybe." How much of an opening did she need? His heart sank. Did she not trust him?

"Not ever. Even if something happens to me, my folks would make sure he was loved and taken care of."

"I could do that."

She smiled slightly and nodded.

"Danny's my son," he said.

"I'm so glad you think like that. I've heard stories about

women marrying and the new husband didn't want anything to do with their children."

"I mean, he's really mine. I want to adopt him or change his last name, or something, so the world knows."

She pulled back a bit and tilted her head to better see him, obviously puzzled. "I think he should keep Tom's name. That's all the legacy Tom left him. He would be your son in every way that counts."

"He is my son." Zack stood and walked to the window. "I had a detective find you, to tell me that he was all right, that he was being raised well. I didn't expect to actually meet you and Danny."

"What are you talking about?" Susan also rose and went to stand by him. "What detective?"

"The one I hired to find Danny. I didn't know his name, of course, just that Alesia had given up my baby for adoption."

Susan stared at him for a long moment. "Zack, Danny is Tom's son."

"I know you two adopted him. And that makes him just as much Tom's son as if Tom had fathered him. But you don't have to pretend with me. Together we can explain to Danny."

She stepped back, a look of horror on her face.

"Is that what all this has been about—Danny? You think he's yours? Is that why you insisted in getting to know me, getting to know Danny? You have a child somewhere and thought it was Danny?"

He turned to look at her. "I know it's Danny."

"Just what do you know?"

"Alesia gave up our son, he was adopted by T.J. and Susan Johnson of New York City. I came to New York when I was recuperating to see if I could get a glimpse of Danny. I wasn't planning to stop. But when you asked for my help, every-thing changed."

"Johnson is a very common name. What does T. J. stand for?"

"Thomas, I assume."

"It isn't me," she whispered. "It wasn't Tom. His middle name was Caldwell. I can prove it."

"What do you mean?" Zack asked, not understanding.

"Danny's my child. Mine and Tom's. I have pictures of me pregnant. Me in the hospital with Danny. Us at the christening. Tom and I did not adopt a child. Danny is our child. DNA can prove it in an instant." She stepped back, crossing her arms over her chest, watching him warily.

Zack stared at her in incomprehension. This was turning out all wrong. She was supposed to be relieved he knew the truth, not putting up barriers. "The detective said—"

"Well, I'd ask for my money back if I were you. He got it wrong." She turned her back on him, her hands rubbing her upper arms as if she were cold.

"All this is because you thought Danny's your son," she repeated.

"All what?" He stepped closer, aware he'd made a major blunder. It changed little. He still wanted Susan. It might take a little while to absorb the news she gave. Danny was not his son.

But he could still be Zack's. Once he and Susan were married. For a moment he took a breath. It would come out all right. He took a step closer.

"I'd like you to leave now, Zack," she said, her back still to him.

He took hold of her shoulders, turning her to face him. "I'm not leaving until we hash this out. I obviously made a mistake. So I'll keep looking for the boy Alesia and I had. It changes nothing for us."

"I think it changes everything. Please leave." She pulled away and went down the hall. He heard the bedroom door close.

Stunned, for a moment he couldn't move. *Danny wasn't his?* He loved that little boy. How could he have bonded so quickly with the child if there wasn't a connection?

The same way he had connected with Susan so quickly. He fell in love. For a moment Zack stared ahead without seeing anything. Love didn't recognize biology or blood. Love came from all directions, for all people.

He went down the hall and knocked on her door.

"Susan, talk to me, please."

"No. Go away, Zack. Go away."

He waited a long moment. He should have waited to talk about this. There was a reason she never brought it up—there was nothing to bring up. "Susan, I can explain…"

There was no further sound from her room. Slowly he went to the door. He hesitated, then opened and stepped into the hall, closing the door behind him.

Susan heard the outer door close. She was leaning against her bedroom door, her heart breaking. She'd been so happy just moments before. Now the crushing pain was excruciating. She loved Zack. And he wanted to marry her because he thought Danny was his son. From the very beginning, he'd encouraged their relationship because of a mistaken idea her son was his. She could hardly breathe. Theirs was a relationship based on a lie. There would be no wedding, no new house on Long Island, no Zack in her life any more. She held her breath against the pain, but tears flowed and she crossed to curl up on her bed, sobbing as quietly as she could into her pillow.

After a while the tears ceased. Lying listlessly on the bed she tried to see where she might have realized that Zack hadn't been as in love as she would expect a man to be to get married. Granted, he'd never said he loved her, but she could excuse herself for seeing his every action construed that way.

What other man would take on a woman and her child, plan dates that included activities for Danny, work at the preschool? Only, it wasn't for her. It was all for Danny. Or who he thought Danny was.

She had excused his lack of telling her he loved her due to his background. A child growing up without love might not know to say it. But now she realized that had little to do with his not telling her. He had been honest in that, at least.

It had been so hard to move on, to let herself trust in the future again, to plan to build a new life. But she'd done it—only to have it slap her in the face. She would have done better to never have gotten involved than end up like this. She ached for Zack's arms to hold her. She yearned for his kisses. She would love to just sit beside him, and feel safe and cherished. She would miss planning for a future together. She would always miss *him*!

CHAPTER TEN

SUSAN woke to a splitting headache the next morning. She lay in bed feeling sad and lonely. Hearing Danny running down the hall, she tried to shake off her melancholia so not to upset her son. He would be unhappy enough when he finally realized Zack was out of their lives.

"Hi," he said, peeping around her door.

"Hi, yourself, little man. Come snuggle with me," she said.

He raced across the room and bound up into the bed. They snuggled together for a few minutes—all he could spare from his busy activities.

"I want to go to the park," he said, wiggling around.

"Okay, after we do some tidying of the house."

"'Kay." He struggled to get down. "Let's eat breakfast," he urged.

"I'll be right there. Don't climb up on the counter."

The last thing Susan wanted to do was move an inch. But she couldn't lie in bed the rest of her life. Today would be the first without Zack. She remembered when she'd had the first without Tom. The ache was just as piercing.

She'd have to tell Edith today that they wouldn't be moving. She knew the older woman had been happy with the expectation of change. Life would go along as it had. She'd stay in the poky apartment, fearing for Danny's safety as he grew older and began going outside by himself.

She'd pinch pennies to make ends meet. And sit in lonely silence in the evening hours once Danny was in bed.

Tears welled again. How could she stand it?

"Oh, Zack, why wasn't I enough?" she said softly, getting up to get dressed.

Once breakfast was finished, the apartment had been vacuumed and dusted and Danny dressed, Susan gathered their things for a trip to the park. She would not disrupt her son's routines. He asked for so little and she wished she could shower him with all things good.

The day was already warm and would probably be uncomfortably hot by midafternoon. But at this early hour it was comfortable and pleasant.

Susan held Danny's hand until they reached the park. He took off running to play with the children at the playground. She crossed the grass more slowly and sat on one end of a bench that held an older man who was watching the children. Probably a proud grandfather, she thought, smiling politely as she sat down. Her father loved to take Danny to the playground when her parents visited.

Time seemed to pass slowly as she mindlessly watched her son. If he needed her, she'd be there in an instant. Otherwise, she was content to let him interact with the other children. He'd look over occasionally and she'd wave. He played well with other children and from the shrieks of laughter, she knew they were all enjoying themselves.

Suddenly he got off the slide and began running across the grass. Susan jumped up. Was he chasing after someone who looked like Tom again? She passed the older gentleman and stopped, recognizing Zack heading toward her. Danny ran to him and Zack leaned over and picked him up, tossing him into the air. Susan could hear his laughter from where she stood.

Her heart began to pound. What was Zack doing here? Why had he come?

He settled Danny on one arm, talking to him as they walked steadily toward Susan. She wanted to run away and hide. Or stay and rail against him for letting her fall in love with him when he hadn't fallen in love with her. For raising her hopes and dreams only to have them smashed into dust.

When he drew closer, he put Danny on his feet and urged him back to the playground. His gaze caught hers and he walked purposefully toward her.

"Hi," he said.

She couldn't respond. She turned and went back to sit down, ignoring him completely. She was afraid to say anything lest tears began and never stopped.

Not deterred, Zack came and sat beside her. The older man glanced at them, then resumed watching the children.

"We need to talk," he said.

She shot him a look and shook her head. "I think we said all we needed to say last night."

"Not by a long shot," he said.

She shifted slightly, turning her shoulder to him. Maybe she should get Danny and return home.

He reached out and took her hand. When she tried to snatch it away, he held firmly.

"I want you to marry me. I want us to be a family. I want to raise Danny as my own."

"He's not yours."

"I didn't say he was, I said as my own."

"Go find your own son."

"Maybe. In time."

She looked at him, curious. "Why not now?"

"I have to get this straightened out first. Time enough later to see if that boy is happy and doing well. Which is what I started out doing here. I was only going to walk by the school, see Danny and then move on. Fate, angels, whatever changed that when you asked me for help. One thing led to another."

She looked away, thinking how she had fallen in love with the man and he'd been there for a different reason.

"When Danny ran to greet me just a moment ago, love pure and simple shone from his eyes."

"He loves you."

"And you love me. Funny. All my life I wanted someone to love me, really love me. And when it happened, I didn't even see it."

Susan felt her eyes moisten with tears again. How sad to long for love. Every child should at least have that. Zack hadn't.

"Love grows best when it's returned," she mumbled, swallowing hard, trying to prevent the tears from spilling over.

"I walked all the way back to my hotel last night, stunned that you'd turned me out. It gave me a taste of what life would be like without you in it forever. I can't do it."

"Do what?"

"Face life without you. I'm not good at this, Susan, but I love you. The feelings I have for you are stronger than any I've ever had before. I may not be good at it, but I think these feelings will last a lifetime."

"You're just saying that. You managed fine all your life before finding me, you'll do fine the rest of your life without me," she said.

"But why should I? I love you. You love me. Let's get married. Build on the future together. Grow old together."

"Good idea," the older man said. "Love doesn't come to everyone more than once. By the child you have, I'm guessing this is your second chance, ma'am. I never got it. My wife died thirty years ago. My one daughter and now her children are all I have. I wish I'd met another woman I wanted to spend my life with."

Susan looked around Zack at the man.

"He only wanted me because he thought Danny was his son."

"Doesn't sound like it now," the man countered.

She blinked and looked at Zack. "Do you really love me?"

"Oh God, you don't know how much," he said, drawing her into his arms and kissing her soundly.

Danny called something from the playground, but Susan couldn't hear him. She only heard the beating of her heart as she returned Zack's kisses. From the depths of despair to the heights of joy in an instant. Was this real?

"So you'll marry me as planned?" Zack asked a moment later.

She hesitated only a second then nodded, feeling fearful and excited at the same time.

"Let me be the first to wish you both a long and happy life together," the older man said. He smiled at them, then rose and beckoned to two children. They ran to him, calling him Grandpa, and the trio walked away from the park.

"I do love you," Zack said, holding her close. "I'll do anything to make up for the heartache of last night."

"You don't need to do anything—not if you truly love me. That's all I wanted. But what about your quest for your child?"

"Maybe together we can find him and make sure he's okay. Families are formed by love, not only biology. If he's happy in his adoptive home, why would I want to wrest that from him? Maybe later we can approach them and let them know who we are and that we would always be available if he wants some kind of relationship. His parents may not wish that. Which, hard as it is to think about, would be okay. I would not rock his security for anything. Look at what happened to Danny when Tom died. I never want another child to go through something like that."

"Danny adores you. I was so scared for him when I thought you were out of our lives. Those hours last night were the worst I've had in years," Susan said.

"I never expected to find a woman like you. Never thought of myself as a married man. But now I can't wait. I'll be getting a wife and son all at once. And maybe we can add to our family when the time is right."

"Works for me. I always wanted several children. I'd love to have a baby with you."

"I would, too, but I would never love it more than Danny."

"No, the good thing about love is that it's infinite. You'll love our next child as much, and the one after that as well."

"How many are we going to have?" Zack asked.

"As many as we want and can afford. I would not mind adopting one or two, either, and having some of our own."

"Then the sky's the limit, my love." He kissed her.

EPILOGUE

ZACK read the report from the detective. He slid it across the dining room table to Susan.

"Think he's got it right this time?" she asked, picking it up to read. Dinner had ended a little while ago. Danny was outside in the backyard playing with the puppy. Edith had gone to fuss in the garden while it was still daylight. Twilight came earlier each day in September.

"Maybe. This T.J. Johnson lives in Queens and works as an accountant. His wife's a librarian. They have a nice apartment and the child's name is Tommy, Junior. What do you think?" Zack asked, pointing to the photograph of a family at a company picnic somewhere.

"They look happy," she said, glancing up at her husband. "What do you think?"

"I hope they're as happy as we are. It's what I wanted, to know that he was well cared for and happy."

"Now what?"

"I think I'll ask Josh for his advice. Maybe have him contact them just to see if they need anything, to let them know I'm here if they do." Josh was their new next door neighbor, fast becoming a friend. He was an attorney specializing in family law.

"Sounds like a plan. I'm happy with whatever you decide," Susan said. "If you want to go meet them, I'll go with you."

"If they want that. Or maybe just knowing we're in the background will make things easier for them."

Zack rose and came around the table, taking her hand and helping her up. "I'll help with the dishes if you want," he said, leaning over to kiss her.

"He's not your only child, you know," she said smiling up at him.

"No, Danny's mine in every way that counts."

"And he's not your only one, either," Susan said. "We're pregnant. I think it happened on our honeymoon."

Zack stared at the woman he loved in disbelief. "We're going to have a baby?"

She nodded, her happiness shining from her eyes. "And I got brochures from the adoption agency in town. Honey, if you want, we could have a house full before much longer."

Zack hugged her, lifting her off her feet and twirling around. Susan laughed and reached up to kiss him when he set her back on the ground.

"I love you, Zack," she said.

"I love you, sweetheart, now and forever." He sealed his vow with a kiss. In his quest for his son, he'd found the only woman he had ever loved. And she'd given him the family he'd never had. Amazing.

CONFIDENTIAL: EXPECTING!

BY
JACKIE BRAUN

Jackie Braun is a three-time RITA finalist, three-time National Readers' Choice Award finalist, and a past winner of the Rising Star award. She lives in Michigan, with her husband and two sons, and can be reached through her website at www.jackiebraun.com.

'Unlike my heroine, I'd never be able to keep the news of a baby confidential. I think half the free world knew my husband and I were adopting a second child before the agency received our application.'
—*Jackie Braun*

For Don and Jean Fridline,
who lived a love story. I miss you both.

CHAPTER ONE

"Is THIS seat taken?"

Mallory Stevens knew that deep, seductive voice. As best she could, she braced herself before looking up into a pair of smiling gray-green eyes and a face that would have made Adonis seem homely by comparison. It was no use.

Zip, zap, zing!

Just that fast, her hormones snapped to attention and her limbs turned liquid. It was a bizarre reaction, though she'd be lying if she labeled it unpleasant. Nor was it unprecedented. She'd experienced its twin a week earlier when she'd met Logan Bartholomew for the first time.

They'd been in his office, and she'd written it off then as a fluke. She'd been working too many hours. She'd barely slept the night before. She'd gone without the company of a man for *way, way* too long.

But a fluke didn't happen twice. When it did, and it involved a member of the opposite sex, it was called something else: attraction.

Mallory sucked in a breath before letting it out slowly between her teeth. She certainly had nothing against mingling with members of the opposite sex. She liked men, but she had a rule about mixing business with pleasure. It was a no-no. Logan Batholomew was business, even if everything about him made her body hum with pleasure.

"You're welcome to join me, Doctor," she told him. Though it took an effort, her tone was blessedly non-chalant. She hoped the smile she sent him was the same.

He folded his athletic frame into the chair, managing to look both elegant and masculine. For the umpteenth time in their short acquaintance, she found herself thinking his gorgeous looks were wasted on the radio. He hosted a call-in program that had all of Chicago talking.

"I thought we'd agreed it was just Logan," he said.

Mallory knew he was wrong. Even though, now that *he* was here, sitting through the Windy City Women of Action luncheon she'd been assigned to cover held far more appeal, a qualifier such as *just* didn't apply when it came to Logan. Everything about the guy was off the charts, from his leading-man looks and tri-athlete physique to the way his show had burned its way to the top of the ratings in a little over a year. It was no wonder he'd been voted Chicago's most eligible bachelor in a recent poll sponsored by her newspaper.

As a reporter, Mallory reminded herself that she was interested in more than his heart-palpitating appeal and sigh-worthy exterior. She was interested in a story and she smelled one here. Not necessarily the sort that went with his sophisticated cologne and designer tie, and certainly not the trivial one that had landed her in his office the week before.

In her experience, no one was ever as perfect as this guy appeared to be with his Harvard degree and penchant for supporting worthwhile causes. She intended to unearth the skeletons in his closet and then expose each and every one of them. Maybe then her editor would forgive her for the embarrassing faux pas that had the newspaper's lawyers fending off a libel suit and Mallory writing the kind of general assignment fluff that usually went to the college interns.

"I should thank you for the article you did on my commencement address to the students and faculty at Chesterfield Alternative High School," he said.

Fluff, definitely. So much so that the airy advance had wound up buried in the bowels of the *Chicago Herald*'s Lifestyles section.

"You read it?" she asked, equally surprised that he'd found it.

"All four paragraphs," came his dry reply.

Truth be told, Mallory had had to pad it with his background to make it that long. God, she missed her city hall beat. Two months of writing nonsense had her feeling like a carnivore at a vegetarians' convention. She needed meat, the rarer the better, and unless her instincts were wrong, Logan was prime rib.

Angling her head to one side, she said, "So, any truth to the rumor I heard that *Doctor in the Know* might go national? Or that a certain cable television network has made you an offer for a prime-time program?"

If he was surprised by her questions, it didn't show. He didn't so much as blink. Rather, in a bland voice, he inquired, "On the record or off?"

"On, of course," she replied.

"Well then, no."

She lifted one brow. "And off the record?"

Logan leaned toward her, close enough that she could feel the heat radiating from his skin. She pictured his mouth, lips barely an inch from making contact with her earlobe when he whispered, "No comment."

In spite of herself, Mallory shivered. The man was downright lethal, a straight shot of sex outfitted in a suit that probably cost the equivalent of a month's worth of her take-home pay. She'd splurged on the black pencil skirt and tan fitted jacket she was wearing, but they were hardly designer label. Clearly, she was in the wrong profession, not that she had any plans to change. She loved her job. Until lately, it had been by far the most satisfying and reliable thing in her life. She intended it to be that way again.

Leaning back in her chair, Mallory smiled at Logan. "I'll find out eventually, you know. Ferreting out people's secrets is what I do best."

"I'd heard that about you," he replied amiably. "In fact, my agent called to warn me to be on my toes before you came to my office for the interview last week. She said you were a regular pit bull."

"A pit bull, hmm?" Mallory ran her tongue over her teeth.

"Actually, she called you a *rabid* pit bull." Logan chuckled as if to soften the description and added, "I hope I haven't offended you."

"Offended me?" She exhaled sharply. "Please. I'm flattered by her description."

"I don't think she meant it as a compliment."

"I'm sure she didn't." Still Mallory shrugged. "I'll take it as one, anyway. In my line of work I believe in going for the throat. It's what yields the best results."

Her gaze lowered as she said this. Loosen that silk tie and undo the top button at his collar and Logan Bartholomew had one very delicious-looking neck.

"What about outside of work?"

His question startled her from her musings. Mallory's gaze shot back to his face, where a potent and very male smile greeted her.

"Wh-what do you mean?" She hated that she'd actually stammered like a shy schoolgirl conversing with the football team's star quarterback.

"What do you do after hours? You know, to unwind?" His expression was just this side of challenging.

"I tend to work late." Then she went home alone, picking up some takeout on the way to her walk-up half a block from an El stop. Once she'd changed out of her work attire, she usually ate while watching the television before crashing for the night on the queen-size bed in her room. Alone.

"No…boyfriend?" he inquired.

Her eyes narrowed. "Not at the moment." Though not
for two years was closer to reality.

"Hmm."

"Are you analyzing me, Doctor?" Mallory asked.

"Logan," he reminded her with an affable grin.

"Yes, but at the moment you're sounding an awful lot
like someone with a degree in psychiatry."

"Ah." He grimaced, seemingly for effect. "Sorry
about that. A hazard of my profession, I'm afraid. I just
find it hard to believe that someone as bright, interesting and, well, attractive as you are isn't in a serious relationship."

"Good save." She said it dryly in the hope of camouflaging the spurt of pleasure she'd experienced upon
hearing his compliments.

Bright, interesting, attractive. What woman wouldn't
want to be considered all three, especially by a man who
looked like this one?

The servers came around then with their salads and
baskets of bread. Mallory selected a hard roll. At their
first meeting, Logan's time had been limited, so she'd
only had the opportunity to ask him questions related
to the commencement address. Now, under the guise of
small talk, she asked him, "What about you? What do
you do when you're not at the radio station?"

"Well, for starters, I like to eat." He forked up some
mixed baby greens that were coated in raspberry vinai-
grette.

"Yes, you look it." Logan was a walking advertise-
ment for physical fitness. If the man looked this good

with his clothes on, she could only imagine how he appeared sans his professional attire. The thought had her coughing.

He swatted her back. "Are you all right?"

"Fine," she managed. "Never better. You were saying something about eating?"

"I like food. For that reason, I learned how to cook."

Mallory squinted at him. "Learned how to cook as in learned how to work the microwave oven or learned how to cook as in—"

"I know my way around the kitchen," he inserted. "For instance, tonight I'm planning to grill a marinated flank steak and then pair it with rice noodles and a simple green salad."

Her mouth watered. "Just for you?"

"Most likely."

"I'm impressed." And she was. "I've never gotten much beyond boiling water, which is actually pretty handy considering it's one of the most important steps in making macaroni and cheese."

"From a box," he acknowledged. "There are other ways, you know."

No, she didn't know. In her albeit limited experience, all that was necessary was to bring the water to a boil and add the elbow noodles. When they were cooked, she drained the water, drizzled in a quarter cup of milk and stirred in the packet of a dry, cheeselike substance. *Voilà.* Dinner.

Logan was saying, "I've found cooking to be a surprising release for my creative energy."

She found his admission surprising, as well, but as secrets went, well, news that Chicago's new favorite son liked to play chef in his off hours wasn't likely to score Mallory many points with her editor.

So, she asked, "What else do you do in your spare time? I know you don't frequent the hot night spots."

She'd checked.

"I'm a little old for that."

"Thirty-six isn't exactly ancient." Especially when it came packaged in broad shoulders, narrow hips and topped off with a full head of gorgeous sandy hair.

The shoulders in question rose. "Night clubs aren't really my thing."

They weren't Mallory's, either. Sure, she liked to dance, sip a cocktail and have a good time every now and then, but she'd long ago grown out of the meat-market scene so many of the city's hottest spots promoted. These days when she went out it was usually with a former college roommate for margaritas at a little Mexican restaurant that was one step above dive status.

"So, what is your thing?" she asked.

Logan said nothing for a long moment. Rather, he studied her with a gaze that was both challenging and assessing. Which is why Mallory found herself holding her breath until he finally replied, "I like to sail."

The air whooshed from her lungs. "Sail. As in boats?" Mallory couldn't help feeling disappointed. Unless he was going to tell her he kept narcotics in the hold this revelation was as newsworthy as the tidbit about playing chef.

"Is there any other kind?" He was smiling. "My parents had a catamaran when I was a boy. I loved being out on it. So, I bought a thirty-one-footer a few years back. I take her out on Lake Michigan as often as I can. Even so, the season's just too damn short here."

Mallory didn't consider herself to be the romantic sort, yet she had no problem picturing Logan standing on a teak deck, manning the helm of a sailboat as the Chicago skyline grew small at his back and the deep aquamarine waters of the great lake beckoned.

"Sounds nice," she said in a voice just this side of wispy. Good Lord, what was wrong with her?

"It is. Especially first thing in morning. There's nothing like sitting on deck, drinking a cup of coffee and watching the sun crest the horizon."

Mallory swallowed. Focus, she coached herself, when her mind threatened to meander a second time. "You make it sound like you sleep on your boat."

"I've been known to. It's peaceful out there, you know? None of the city noise. Only lapping water and the occasional cry of gulls."

She thought about the El train that rumbled past her apartment at regular intervals. As far as she was concerned, what he spoke of was heaven. That was before she pictured him clad in…hmm…what did the good doctor wear to bed? That question brought another one to mind.

"Do you sleep there alone?" When his brows rose, she amended her query. "Who do you go sailing with?"

Logan's laughter rumbled, deep and rich, dancing up

her spine like a flat stone skipping over water. "Are you asking if I'm involved with someone?"

She cleared her throat, kept her tone reporter-neutral. "A lot of single women who read the *Herald* are dying to know just how eligible of a bachelor you are."

"It's that damned poll."

"Yes," she said dryly. "Every man in Chicago wishes he were so lucky as to find his name on it."

"Do I have you to thank for my…providence?" he inquired.

Mallory shook her head. "I wasn't part of the Lifestyles team then."

He was undeterred. "But are you one of them? You know, the voters, those women interested in my personal life?"

"Not a voter, no. But you bet I am interested in your personal life." She pulled a pen and slim notepad from the purse hanging over the back of her chair. "So?"

Some of the good humor leaked out of Logan's expression when he said, "I didn't realize that you were sent to this luncheon to cover me."

Was that censure she spied in his gaze or disappointment? Mallory didn't like seeing either one, but neither was she willing to back down. "Rabid pit bull," Logan's agent had called her. Well, she'd earned the reputation for a reason.

"Sorry. Hazard of my profession. And I can't help thinking you make a far more interesting story than the winner of this year's Action Award." She tilted her head in the direction of the head table. "You're a local celeb-

rity, Logan. Homegrown, self-made and very successful. You're also a bit mysterious. Other than where you
earned your degree and some of your vital statistics, not
much is known about you."

He folded his arms over his chest. "I like my privacy."

"Yes, and readers like to invade it." Mallory angled
her head to one side. "It's good public relations to toss
them a bone every now and then. You know, since
they're the ones who tune in to your radio program and
all." Going for the jugular, she added, "In a very real
sense, you could say you owe your success to them."

"Well, when you put it that way." A smile spread
slowly across his face. Lethal, Mallory thought again,
as her hormones popped around inside her like the
numbered balls in a bingo machine. She found herself
actually leaning toward him, drawn the way a moth is
to a flame. And so it came as little surprise when heat
began to spiral through her.

"Well?" Was that her voice that sounded so breathless, so damned eager?

"I'm not…in a relationship."

She moistened her lips, leaned back. "Ah."

What exactly did that mean? Men, she knew first-
hand, defined relationships differently than women did.

"Any other questions?" Logan asked.

Mallory had dozens of them, and the man, her prime-
rib ticket to workplace redemption, was offering her
the opportunity to ask them. Unfortunately, with him
looking at her in that assessing way, her mind had gone
blank. She shook her head slowly, thankful when their

entrees arrived and saved her from appearing tongue-tied, which, for the first time in her professional life, she was.

They ate their rubber chicken and overcooked rice pilaf in virtual silence; all the while Mallory recalled his mention of grilled marinated flank steak. It was almost a relief when the servers cleared away their plates and the award program began. Except that, as the president of the women's club blathered on about the recipient's many virtues, from the corner of her eye, Mallory spied Logan watching her.

What on earth was he thinking?

Logan studied Mallory. He'd meant it when he'd told her she was bright, interesting and attractive.

Attractive. Hell, she was downright lovely with all that rich brown hair framing an oval face that was dominated by the most amazing pair of big dark eyes he'd ever seen. Despite her physical beauty, it was her personality that captivated him. He liked smart women. The smarter the better. Add in pretty and, well, it was a lethal combination as far as he was concerned. Mallory certainly hit the mark. That in itself was a problem.

Logan had met her kind once before, years ago. He'd fallen hard at the time, so hard he'd almost made it to the altar, ready and willing to promise his undying love and devotion. A month before their nuptials, however, his fiancée had called off the wedding. Felicia had claimed to need time and space. She'd needed to think, to reflect. What became clear was she hadn't needed him. She married someone else.

It had been nearly a decade since then. Logan had heard from her only once, just after her wedding. She'd sent him a letter, the postmark read Portland, Oregon. In the brief note, she'd asked him to forgive her, but even if he'd wanted to, he couldn't. She'd included no forwarding address or phone number. He'd taken the hint. He'd been wary of commitment ever since.

That didn't mean he didn't like women or spending time with them. It just meant he didn't let things progress into anything serious.

He glanced over at Mallory. She was scribbling down notes, seemingly absorbed in the award recipient's less-than-exciting speech. As he watched her, his interest, among other things, was definitely piqued.

Rabid pit bull.

Logan's agent had been adamant that he should steer clear of this particular reporter. Mallory had a reputation for ruining people, Nina Lowman insisted. Maybe it was the masochist in him that considered her reputation a challenge. Besides, he could handle himself around reporters. He'd been doing it enough since his radio call-in program had staked out the top spot in the ratings.

So, as the luncheon wrapped up, Logan leaned over to Mallory and asked, "Since turnabout is fair play, I have a question for you."

"Oh?"

"What are you doing later this afternoon?"

She blinked, before her eyes narrowed. Why was it he found her suspicion sexy?

"Filing a story. Why?"

"How long will that take?"

"For this?" Her lips twisted, showing her distaste. It wasn't the first time he wondered why a reporter with her reputation had been sent to cover a minor story. "I need a couple of quotes from the winner, a quote from someone on the award committee and to tap out a couple of paragraphs summing up why the winner was selected."

"In other words, you could write it in your sleep," he concluded.

She rewarded his blunt assessment with a smile. "Once I do a couple of brief interviews it should take me half an hour, tops. Why?"

Logan was playing with fire, which wasn't like him. While he liked challenges, he wasn't one to take unnecessary risks. Still, he heard himself ask, "Have you ever seen the city from the water?"

"No," she said slowly.

"Well, if you want to, I dock my sailboat, the *Tangled Sheets*, at the yacht club. I'm planning to take her out around five."

Something flashed in her dark eyes. Interest? Excitement? Briefly he wondered whether it was the reporter or the woman responsible for whatever emotion it was. To his surprise, he found he didn't care.

"Which yacht club?" she asked.

Logan wasn't willing to make it too easy for her. So

he stood and, giving her a salute, walked backward a few steps toward the exit.

Just before turning he called, "You're a reporter, Mallory. If you really want to meet me, you'll figure it out."

CHAPTER TWO

DESPITE changing into a lightweight blouse and a pair of cropped trousers, Mallory was wilting in the late-afternoon heat by the time she arrived at Logan's slip at the Chicago Yacht Club. It didn't help that she'd nearly jogged the half-dozen blocks from the El stop. She had a car, but she often found public transportation less of a hassle than trying to find a place to park.

After leaving the luncheon, she'd hurried through her story, filing it after only a cursory second read and a run of her computer's spellchecker. It wasn't like her to rush, especially for a man. But then Logan was far more than that to her. He was a story.

Her *story* took her breath away when she caught sight of him standing with his feet planted shoulder-width apart on the deck of a sailboat. Behind him sunlight reflected off the smooth, aquamarine surface of the lake, making him look like something straight out of a fantasy.

His back was to her, a cell phone tucked between his ear and shoulder, so she took her time studying him.

He'd changed his clothing, too. Instead of the pricy suit he'd worn earlier, he was attired in a short-sleeved shirt that showed off a pair of muscled arms and casual tan slacks that fit nicely across a very fine and firm-looking butt. Mallory fanned herself. Damned heat. Though it was only June, the mercury had to be pushing one hundred degrees Fahrenheit in the shade.

On the barest wisp of a breeze, Logan's side of the conversation floated to her.

"You don't need to worry… No. Really. Do you know the saying 'Keep your friends close and your enemies closer'?" His laughter rumbled deep and rich before he continued. "Exactly… Yeah, I'll call you."

He said goodbye and flipped his phone closed. As soon as he turned and spotted Mallory, male interest lit up his eyes and a flush of embarrassment stained his cheeks.

He coughed. "I didn't realize you were here."

"Obviously."

His flush deepened.

Mallory could have pretended not to have overheard anything. That would have been the polite thing to do. But she was a reporter, which meant curiosity trumped politeness.

"So, which one am I?" When he frowned, she added helpfully, "Friend or enemy?"

She gave him credit. Logan pulled out of his flaming, death spiral with amazing speed and agility. But then, he was a veteran of talk radio and live broadcasts, which meant he was good at thinking on his feet.

Walking to the rail, he asked, "Which one do you consider yourself?"

"Ah. Very clever, turning the question around. Is that what they teach you to do in psychiatry school?"

"Among other things," he allowed.

Whatever remained of his embarrassment had evaporated completely by the time his hand clasped Mallory's to help her aboard. His palm was warm against hers, pleasantly so despite the heat. It seemed a shame when he removed it, though she supposed it would have been awkward if he had continued the contact.

"So," she said, filling in the silence.

"So." One side of his mouth lifted, but he backed up a step, and she liked knowing that she could keep him as off balance as he made her. Tucking his hands into the front pockets of his trousers, he said, "I wasn't sure you were coming or that you'd be able to find me."

Though the city had more than one yacht club, it hadn't taken much effort. His boat was registered. Besides, the Chicago Yacht Club, which dated to the late eighteen hundreds, was exclusive. It seemed the most likely spot for an up-and-coming celebrity who cherished his privacy.

Mallory nodded toward the bottle of red wine that was open and breathing on a small table topside. "I'd say you knew that I would."

He shrugged. "I was hopeful. Besides, I was banking on your journalistic instincts."

"I bank on them, too, since they rarely fail me."

"Should I be nervous?"

"You tell me," she replied.

"I guess that depends on why you're here."

"I was invited," she reminded him.

"So you were."

In truth, Mallory was still perplexed by Logan's spontaneous offer of an afternoon sail. It was one of the reasons she'd come. What exactly did the man have in mind?

"Why?" The question rent the silence with all the delicacy of a gull's cry.

"Excuse me?"

"Why did you invite me?"

"Well, that's blunt." He chuckled.

Mallory shrugged. "I don't believe in beating around the bush."

"No, I don't suppose you would." With an index finger, he tapped his cell phone. "You know, my agent wanted to know the answer to that very question, too."

"What did you tell her, besides not to worry?"

His brows furrowed. "Actually, I didn't have an answer for her."

"Besides the friends-and-enemies adage," Mallory remarked.

"Besides that," he agreed. "So, why did you come? And, yes, I'm turning the question around."

"Curiosity," she replied honestly. "How could I decline when I find you so intriguing?"

"I'm flattered, I think. Especially if that's the woman speaking rather than the reporter."

"They're one and the same, remember?"

Logan's gaze intensified. "Are you sure about that?"

She was, or at least she had been until he'd pinned her with that stare and baldly asked. The boat moved under her feet, a slight rolling motion that reminded her of the water bed she'd had as a teenager. She'd slept like a baby back then. These days she was lucky to snatch a few hours of uninterrupted slumber before her eyes snapped open and her mind began clicking away like a slide projector, flashing the items on her current to-do list at work along with the goals related to her long-range career plans.

"I'd love a glass of that wine," she said, opting to change the subject.

"I wouldn't mind some myself." As he poured it, he said, "How exactly did you find me? I only ask so I can prevent others from doing the same."

"Sorry." She shook her head and, after a sip of the Merlot, added, "As much as I'd like to help you out—not to mention, keep other reporters away—I can't reveal my sources."

He nodded sagely. "Bad form?"

"Right up there with a magician giving away the secret to how he saws his assistant in half," she said with sham seriousness.

His smile turned boyish and was all the more charming for it. "I've always wanted to know how that's done."

"I do," she couldn't help bragging. "Just after college I was assigned to do a feature on a guy who did a magic act at a local nightclub. After the interview, he showed me."

"But you won't tell me, will you?" Logan guessed.

"And ruin the illusion?"

"Right." Logan chuckled. "So, are you hungry?"

"I'm getting there," she replied casually.

In fact, Mallory was famished. She'd barely picked at her lunch, and breakfast—a toasted bagel with cream cheese eaten at her desk just after dawn—was a distant memory now.

"Good. I went ahead and made dinner."

Her mouth actually watered. "The marinated flank steak you mentioned at the luncheon?" When he nodded, she said, "Do you mean you actually cooked it here?"

"I cooked the meat topside on that portable gas grill, and the rest was prepared below deck."

The meal he'd described earlier seemed the sort one would make in a gourmet kitchen, so her tone was dubious when she asked, "You have an actual stove down there?"

He smiled. "Quarters may be a bit tight, but you'll find my boat has all the amenities of home."

Why did that simple sentence send heat curling through her veins?

"A-all?" she stammered, then cleared her throat. In a more professional tone, she inquired, "How is that possible? I mean, this thing is just—what?—thirty feet long."

"Thirty-one, actually. But you'd be surprised what can be fitted into that amount of space using a bit of ingenuity. Want a tour?"

"I'd love one," she said, even though the idea of moving below deck with him suddenly made her nervous. It wasn't Logan who made her wary. Her concern had more to do with herself. Story, she reminded herself for what seemed like the millionth time since meeting him.

Luckily she was given a reprieve. "Can you wait until after dinner?"

"Sure." She shrugged. "I'm in no hurry."

Mallory sat at the table and let Logan serve her since he seemed to have everything under control. More than under control, she decided, when he reappeared from below deck a few minutes later carrying two plates of artfully arranged food. The meal looked like something that would be right at home on the cover of *Bon Appetit*.

"Wow. If this tastes as good as it looks, I'll be in heaven."

She meant it. Even though unmasking Logan's qualifications in the kitchen would never earn her a Pulitzer, much less her editor's forgiveness, it was hard not to admire a man who could whip up a five-star meal aboard a boat in the late afternoon heat and barely break a sweat as evidenced by his dry brow.

Logan settled onto the chair opposite hers. "Thanks."

"Mmm. Heaven, definitely," Mallory remarked after her first bite of the marinated meat. It melted in her mouth like butter. Afterward, she raised her glass. "I have to toast the chef. I'm impressed."

"That's quite a compliment coming from you. I get

the feeling you're not the type of woman who is quick with the accolades."

"Only when they're earned."

He smiled and sipped his wine. After setting it aside, he said, "Then, I can't wait until you taste the cinnamon apple torte I made for dessert."

"That good?"

"Better," he assured her with a wink that scored a direct hit on her libido. "Forget accolades. You just might be rendered speechless."

"That would be a first." She laughed. "But then, you've already proved you're a man of many talents."

"Yes, and I'm looking forward to introducing you to another one of them later."

Heat began to build again. "Oh?"

"The sail." But Logan's crooked smile told Mallory he knew exactly which direction her thoughts had taken and that he enjoyed knowing he could inspire such a detour.

As their meal progressed, the conversation veered—or was it steered?—to her personal life. Mallory didn't like to talk about herself, but as a reporter she'd found that divulging a few details about her past often helped her sources loosen up. So, when he asked if she was a Chicago native, she told him, "No. Actually, I'm not a Midwestern girl at all. I grew up in a small town in Massachusetts."

"That explains the flattened vowels." He smiled. "What brought you to Chicago?"

Nothing too personal here. So she said, "College. I attended Northwestern on a scholarship."

"And then you were hired in at the *Herald*," he assumed.

"Eventually. I spent the first three months after I graduated working gratis as an intern in the hope the editors would notice my work and offer me a full-time job. At the time, even though the *Herald* had no posted openings in its newsroom, competition in general was fierce."

"You wanted to be sure you had a foot in the door. That was very industrious, if a bit risky." Still, he nodded in appreciation. "What did your parents think of your decision to work for free?"

She sipped her wine. "It's just my mom and she thought I'd lost my mind."

"Why would she think that?"

Laughter scratched her throat. "I didn't mean that literally, Doctor."

"Good, because I'm not on the clock. Well?"

More than being direct, his gaze made her feel...safe. That brought heat of a different sort. She felt as if she could tell him anything and he wouldn't judge her the way her mother always had. And still did.

"My mother thought I was being a fool. She wanted me to be financially independent and she didn't see how working for free was going to get me anywhere."

"Reasonable goal," he allowed.

"Yeah, except it was a mantra she beat me over the head with after my folks divorced."

"I...I guess I thought your father was no longer around. When I asked what your folks thought, you said it was just your mom."

"It is and has been." She had to work to keep the bitterness out of her tone. "My dad's not dead. He's a deadbeat."

"Ohh." He grimaced. "Sorry. How old were you?"

"Eleven. My mother had been a stay-at-home mom with no marketable job skills when their marriage ended. She had a hard time finding work. She didn't want me to wind up depending on a man."

Mallory reached for her wine, if for no other reason than that taking a sip would shut her up. The only other person she'd ever mentioned this to was Vicki, her college roommate, and then only after a few too many margaritas.

Because she had a good idea what Logan must be thinking, she decided to say it first. "That's not the reason I'm married to my job, though. I happen to really enjoy what I do."

"I don't doubt it." He sipped his wine, too.

It was time to shift the conversation's focus. "What about your family? Siblings?"

"One of each, both younger than me."

"And your parents? Are they still together?" She knew that they were, but saying so would make it seem like she'd done a background check on him. Which she had.

"Yep." Nostalgia warmed his smile. "They're going on forty years and they still hold hands."

The answer prompted a question she was only too happy to ask, since it would turn the spotlight away from her life. "And yet you're thirty-six and single. Why is that?"

A shadow fell across his face, there and gone so quickly she almost wondered if she'd imagined it. But then he offered a disarming smile—a defense mechanism?—that made her all the more curious.

"I guess you could say after the apple fell, it rolled far away from the tree."

This apple had, too, Mallory thought, stuffing memories of her childhood back into their cubbyhole. And for good reason in her case. But why would someone whose parents had what sounded like the perfect union be gun-shy when it came to commitment? It bore looking into. Later.

Now, she said, "Do your siblings still live in Chicago?"

She knew his parents did. The elder Bartholomews were no strangers to the newspaper's society pages.

"Yes. My sister, Laurel, attends Loyola. She's pushing thirty, has been taking classes for more than a decade and has yet to settle on a major. It drives my parents crazy. Luke, my brother, owns a restaurant."

"Locally?"

He nodded. "The Berkley Grill just a few blocks up from Navy Pier."

"I love that place!" Mallory exclaimed. "Especially the grilled portabella mushroom sandwich topped with provolone cheese."

"That's one of my favorites, too."

"Is your brother a chef, then?" she asked.

"No. Like me he can hold his own in the kitchen, but he's a businessman by trade, and he has a good eye for spotting potential." His voice was tinged with pride. "The restaurant needed a fresh menu, updated dining room and better marketing to capitalize on tourist traffic. Since he bought it and made the upgrades, the place has done pretty well, even in this economy, and earned free publicity with a spot in a Food Network special."

"Do you ever plug his place on your radio program?"

"That would be a conflict of interest and not terribly ethical. Besides, he doesn't need my help."

Mallory nodded.

His gaze narrowed. "Are you disappointed with my answer?"

"Of course not. Why would I be?"

He didn't reply directly. Instead, he lobbed a question of his own. "What made you decide to become a journalist?"

"Curiosity," she said again. "I like knowing why things happen the way they do. Why people make the choices they make. I'm rarely happy unless I'm getting to the bottom of things."

"Then what were you doing covering today's luncheon? Not much dirt to uncover there."

"Penance," Mallory muttered before she could think better of it.

She expected him to pounce on that, since getting to the bottom of things was one of the hallmarks of his pro-

fession, too. But just as he'd knocked her off balance
with the offer of a sail, he surprised her now by changing
the subject.

Rising from his seat he asked, "Are you ready for
coffee and dessert?"

"Maybe just coffee." She stood, as well, and helped
him collect the dishes.

"A rain check on the dessert, then?"

Mallory liked the sound of that. It would give her an
excuse to contact him again. Another chance to dig for
a story that had to be in his past somewhere. "Okay."

Five steps led from the sailboat's deck to the cozy
main cabin that was filled with the amenities Logan
had mentioned. The small kitchen area boasted a sink,
cooktop, oven, microwave and wood cabinetry that
deserved points for both function and form. Upholstered
benches flanked a table on the opposite wall. Further
back was a comfortable seating area and a door that she
guessed led to a bedroom, since the bathroom's door
was clearly marked with the word Head.

"This is nice," she commented.

She meant it. Mallory didn't know much about
sailing. For that matter, she'd never been inside a boat
like this one. But the glossy hardwood and soft-hued
fabrics and upholstery were homey and inviting. The
gentle swaying motion didn't hurt, either.

"I like it."

"This is an older boat, right?"

"She dates to the 1970s," he agreed.

"She." Her lips twisted.

Logan was grinning when he took the dishes from her hands and set them in the sink. "I'm guessing you consider it sexist that boats are referred to using female pronouns."

"Not sexist necessarily. Just…annoying."

"Right. From now on I'll call my boat Bob," he deadpanned. "Better?"

"I don't know." She shrugged. "He seems more like a Duke. Besides, it has a name."

"*Tangled Sheets.*" He grinned and she fought the urge to fan herself.

"That's an interesting name for a boat. One might even call it a bit risqué."

"Why? A sheet is another name for a sail, Mallory." His face was the picture of innocence now, but it was plain he understood the double entendre because when he turned to retrieve two coffee cups from a cupboard the grin returned.

"Well, someone has either taken excellent care of this boat or it's been restored."

"The latter," Logan confirmed. Over his shoulder, he asked, "Cream or sugar?"

"Black."

He handed her a steaming cup and poured one for himself. Leaning back against the sink, he said, "It took me an entire winter's worth of weekends after I purchased her—" he cleared his throat "—I mean, Duke, to finish the overhaul. I basically gutted the place and started over. And I'm still puttering most weekends."

He glanced around the salon and nodded. Puttering

still or not, his expression made it clear he was pleased with his progress so far. Mallory could understand why. Logan might not look like the sort of man who would know a hammer from a ham sandwich, but obviously he could hold his own with the guys on HGTV. Power suits and power tools didn't normally go together. Questions bubbled.

"Where did you learn carpentry and—" she motioned with her hand "—how to do repair and maintenance?"

"One of my dad's hobbies is woodworking, and he's always been good at home repair. My brother and I spent a lot of time with him in his workshop, helping him put things together. I picked up a few tips along the way."

"I guess *so.*"

"You're surprised."

"Maybe a little. You don't look like the sort of man who would be…"

"Good with his hands?" he finished.

He set his coffee aside and held up both hands palm side out. His fingers were long, elegant, but the palms were calloused. The man was definitely hard to figure out, but she wasn't trying at the moment. She was staring at those work-roughened hands and wondering how they would feel…on her skin.

Mallory swallowed and ordered herself to stay focused. "Why not just buy something brand-new?"

"I don't know. I guess you could say I prefer a challenge."

The way his eyes lit made Mallory wonder if that was what he considered her to be.

Logan was saying, "Besides, she had great bones and an even better history. Her previous owner had sailed her from Massachusetts all the way to Saint Thomas the year before I got her and nearly lost her to a hurricane along the way."

"So, your boat is a survivor and you had a hand in resurrecting her...him."

"Duke."

"Duke," she repeated.

His laughter was dry. "Yes, but I can assure you I don't suffer from a God complex."

"Then why did you get into psychiatry? Didn't you want to save people?"

"I wanted to *help* people." Oddly, he frowned after saying so. He sipped his coffee. The frown was gone when he added, "Most people have the tools to turn their lives around all on their own. They just need a little guidance recognizing those tools and learning how to use them."

"Good analogy. I guess you really are the son of a carpenter."

"Yeah." He laughed and was once again his sexy self when he asked, "Ready for that sail?"

"Of course. That's why I came."

CHAPTER THREE

LOGAN used the motor to maneuver the boat out of its slip at the yacht club. Once away from the shore, he cut the engine and enlisted Mallory to help him hoist the sails. He could have done it by himself. That's what he usually did, even though it was a lot of work for one person and took some of the pleasure out of the pastime.

Pleasure.

That's what he was experiencing now as he and Mallory stood together on the deck while the boat sliced neatly through the water. He rarely shared *Tangled Sheets* with anyone. It was his private retreat, his getaway from not only the hustle of the city, but from the fame he'd chased so successfully and the reporters who now chased him. Reporters who were much less dangerous than Mallory Stevens was…at least to hear his agent tell it. Nina Lowman had made Logan promise to call him later in the evening, apparently as proof that he'd survived the encounter. Even so, he didn't regret his decision to ask Mallory aboard.

He attributed the invitation to the fact that he'd been

without the company of a woman for several months. Scratch that. He'd been without the company of an *interesting* woman for several months, maybe even for several years. Logan's last fling, and *fling* was almost too generous a term for it, had been with a socialite who'd turned out to be every bit as vapid and vacant as she was gorgeous. Tonya may have been stimulating in many regards, but conversation wasn't one of them. Logan enjoyed smart women. He enjoyed savvy women. Women who were as adept at playing chess as they were strip poker. Logan would bet his last stitch of clothing that Mallory could hold her own in both games.

So it really was no surprise he was enjoying himself this evening. The bonus was that the feeling appeared to be mutual. Glancing over, he noticed that Mallory was leaning against the rail. Her eyes were closed, and the fine line between her brows had disappeared. Even with her face turned to the wind, a smile tugged at the corners of her lips.

For the first time since he'd met her, she looked truly relaxed. And all the more lovely for it, which was saying a lot. The woman was naturally beautiful to begin with: fresh-faced, unmade, unpretentiously pretty. Of course, she could afford to have a light hand with makeup. Her lashes were dark and ridiculously thick and long. They fringed a set of eyes that were rich with secrets. No other adornment was necessary.

A man could get sucked into those eyes if he wasn't careful. It was a good thing Logan had no intention of being lulled into complacency, even if he did enjoy the challenge of staying one step ahead of her.

The eyes in question opened. If Mallory was unnerved to find him studying her, it didn't show. She regarded him in return—boldly, bluntly and not the least bit embarrassed or uncomfortable. Logan swallowed, experiencing again that low tug of interest that seemed to define the time he spent in her presence.

"I probably should apologize for staring," he admitted. He waited a beat before adding, "And if you were another kind of woman, I would."

Her brows rose fractionally. "Another kind of woman?"

"The coy sort."

"Coy." Her lips pursed. "That's not a word one hears often nowadays. It's rather old-fashioned."

"Exactly."

"I'm not old-fashioned."

No, indeed. Mallory was worldly, at least in the sense that she grasped nuances, gestures. She wasn't hard, though. He recalled the way she'd looked when speaking about her parents' divorce. Then she had seemed almost vulnerable.

"Nor am I coy," she continued now.

It was impossible to tell from her tone whether she was insulted or not. Logan decided she wasn't. "Which is why I don't feel the need to stand on pretense around you. I can say what I mean."

"Hmm." It was an arousing sound that drew his gaze to her mouth. "Is that a good thing or a bad thing?" she asked. When he glanced up and met her gaze, the amusement shimmering in her eyes told him she'd already made up her mind.

"A good thing. Definitely a good thing."

She laughed. The sound was low and throaty. "I don't know. I think I might prefer some pretense every now and then. I get so little of it. Subterfuge, sure." She exhaled. "That's par for the course in my line of work."

"But we're not talking about your work." Interesting, Logan thought, how it kept coming back to that. Interesting and a little unnerving.

Mallory smiled. "Oh, that's right. We're talking about pretense."

Not just talking about it, he thought. Well, two could play the game. Logan decided to up the ante. "Are you saying you *want* me to pretend that I don't find you as sexy as hell?"

She blinked. He'd caught her off guard. He'd done it a few times in their relatively short acquaintance. Perhaps it was his male ego talking, but he liked knowing he could manage it.

"Well?" he prodded when she remained quiet.

"I'm trying to think of a response."

"And you can't?" That came as a surprise.

Mallory cleared her throat. "Well, you have to admit, Doc, yours is a loaded question."

Just the sort of question she was very good at asking, but he kept the observation to himself. Instead, Logan snorted. "And here I thought you weren't one to act coy."

"Well, if I tell you no, you'll think I'm playing games, but if I say yes, you'll accuse me of being vain."

"Will I?"

She ignored his question. "You've painted me into a corner. I don't like corners."

"Sorry. I didn't realize."

"Yes, you did."

He flashed a grin. "Okay, maybe I did. But in my defense, I find myself immensely curious as to what your answer will be."

The wind tugged at her hair, sending several strands of it across her face. Mallory pushed them aside with the palm of her hand. The gesture was practical and... "Tell me, Doc, what woman doesn't enjoy being called sexy?"

It was a question rather than an actual answer, but Logan let it pass.

"For the record, I believe I said 'sexy as hell.' If you're going to quote me..." He left the sentence unfinished in part because the words were unnecessary, but mostly because her complexion paled. When she stumbled back a step, he reached out to steady her. "Mallory? Are you all right?"

"Fine." She moved back another step to lean against the rail, forcing him to release her arm. "I...I guess I don't have my sea legs yet." He didn't think that was what had caused her momentary weakness, but she was saying, "In response to your finding me 'sexy as hell,' what am I supposed to do?"

"I have a couple of suggestions." He bobbed his

brows to lighten the moment and was rewarded with a laugh.

"I hate to break it to you, but *coy* isn't another word for *promiscuous*."

Logan snapped his fingers in a show of disappointment. "Damn."

"You know, if I thought you really meant that, I'd have to toss you overboard."

He had little doubt she would try and perhaps even succeed despite the fact she was no match for him physically. "How would you get back to the yacht club then?"

She folded her arms across her chest. "Oh, I'd manage."

Even from their short acquaintance, Logan could tell that about her. Mallory was a survivor. That caused him to sober. He'd met survivors before. He'd counseled a good number of them in his private practice before he'd taken his profession to the airwaves. While he admired their ability to persevere and overcome, in some cases survivors could be very solitary. They didn't need anyone.

"It's time to head back."

"Already? You know, I was just kidding about leaving you bobbing in Lake Michigan." She laughed again.

Logan joined in. "I know."

"But I've made you nervous." The line returned between her brows.

"Not because of that remark," he admitted.

"Hmm." There was that sexy sound again.

"There's not much daylight left and I'm not a fan of

sailing in the dark. Besides, I have some prep work to finish for tomorrow morning's show." It wasn't a complete fabrication. In addition to taking listeners' calls, Logan included a segment on general mental-health topics. Tomorrow's, appropriately enough, was panic attacks.

He prepared to bring the boat around. Mallory helped. In fact, she insisted on lending a hand, as if it was vital that she know what to do to return to the safety of the shore. Survivor, he thought again.

"Watch for the boom," he called. "Or you'll be the one overboard."

"Aye-aye," she called, offering a salute even as she ducked to avoid being struck.

When the Chicago skyline with the sun peeking around the skyscrapers was before them, she whistled. "Talk about a million-dollar view."

"It's something all right. Want to take a turn at the helm?"

"Are you kidding?"

"I never kid when it comes to my boat."

"Then, yes." She stepped into place, legs splayed shoulder width apart, hands at the ten and two positions on the wooden wheel he'd spent hours sanding and staining. Though there was no need, Logan moved in behind her and set his hands over hers.

"Don't you trust me?" she asked.

"Sure." He dipped his head low enough so his jaw scraped her cheek and whispered into her ear, "I'm just looking for a good excuse to touch you."

Was that a shiver he felt? It was hard to say since Mallory's voice sounded perfectly normal when she asked, "Do you need an excuse to do that?"

"Apparently."

"Sad." She made a tsking sound. "Perhaps you should see someone about your…hang-up around competent women."

"Hang-up?"

She shrugged. "I know this famous doctor who might be able to offer some advice."

"Really?" He let his cheek brush against hers. "Should I make an appointment?"

"No. He's much too busy to take appointments these days. Famous, remember?"

"Ah. Right."

"But you could place a call to his radio program. It airs weekday mornings, top of the FM dial. All of Chi-town tunes in to listen to it."

"Don't forget the rest of the greater metropolitan area," he added.

"How could I? He's the savior of their maddening morning commute. Who knows how many cases of road rage he's nipped in the bud with his calming words of wisdom. Hundreds would be my guess."

"I'd venture thousands," Logan said. "No wonder he's said to be in contract negotiations for a nationally syndicated television show."

Mallory went still. The teasing humor was gone from her tone when she said, "Really?"

God, was the woman ever off the clock? "That's the rumor, anyway. Sadly, it's unconfirmed."

Logan felt a little guilty for baiting Mallory until she leaned back against his chest. Then he just felt…her. More precisely, he felt the vibration of her laughter. "Well, I'm sure the doctor can help you."

Dark hair tickled his jaw. "Why are you sure?"

"From the press releases I've read on this guy, he can all but walk on water."

He'd seen those releases, which had come courtesy of his agent and the station's marketing team. He knew what Mallory meant. The accolades were true but they made him uneasy, for the very fact that while he'd once believed he truly had a gift for helping people, these days he sometimes felt all he did was entertain them for a few hours of product-sponsored programming.

"What if the renowned Dr. Bartholomew is just a man?" he asked quietly.

"Just a man?"

"Human," Logan clarified.

"Are you saying he's fallible?"

"Would that be so hard to believe?"

Mallory laughed again. "After reading those press releases, yes."

"Forget what you've read," he said seriously. "Make up your own mind."

She turned halfway around, bracketed in his arms, her lithe body trapped between his larger, harder one and the wheel. The late-day sun sparked off the highlights in her hair and turned her eyes ethereal. "I always make up my own mind, Logan."

"I'm glad to hear it."

The moment stretched as they regarded each other. Something flickered in her gaze. He needed to believe it was the same damnable attraction he was suffering. When Logan finally managed to drag his gaze away, it came as a surprise to realize they were almost back at the yacht club.

"We need to lower the sails," he said, backing away.

"Timing is everything," he thought he heard her say.

Once they were docked, Logan helped Mallory step onto the wooden planks. She didn't require assistance. Come right down to it, she was the sort of woman who would never require assistance, or at least never ask for it. But he wanted to touch her and was pleased when she took the hand he offered.

It was odd to be saying goodbye on a dock. Logan was the sort of man who walked a woman to her door. Mallory might not be old-fashioned, but he found he still wanted to and he said as much.

"That's all right. I got here under my own steam."

"But the El? This time of night. If you wait, I can drive you home."

"I don't mind the El. Don't worry about me. I can make it to my apartment alone." She tilted her head to one side. "But, thanks. Your offer is…sweet."

"And no less than you deserve," he said.

"Yeah." She tucked some hair behind one ear. Flattered? Shaken? "Well, thank you for this evening.

Dinner was excellent and the sail was an experience I won't soon forget."

"Glad to hear it."

She motioned beyond him to where the setting sun played peekaboo around the skyscrapers. "I like the city. I love it, in fact. I think I feed off its endless energy." She laughed. "But tonight…I didn't expect to enjoy being away from it as much as I did, being able to see it, yet remain separate."

He knew exactly what she meant. "You're welcome."

She smiled and backed up, offering a little wave. "Good night, Logan."

"Good night." Part of him didn't want the evening to end. When she started to turn, he called out, "I'd like to see you again."

That stopped her. "You would?" The line deepened between her brows, even though she grinned. "To keep an enemy close?"

Logan didn't smile. "No."

"Then why?" Her head angled in challenge.

The ball was in his court. He was grimly serious when he said, "Because of this."

He closed the distance between them as he spoke and pulled her into his arms before he could think better of it. His mouth found hers before she could mount a protest. He should have known Mallory wouldn't protest. Hadn't they already established that she wasn't coy? Instead, she rose on tiptoe and boldly kissed him back. When he would have ended it, she was just getting started, tilting her head in the opposite direction and deepening the contact.

Zip. Zap. Zing. He dove back in.

The woman might well be the death of him, but Logan didn't care. He hadn't felt this alive in years.

CHAPTER FOUR

THE encounter with Logan played on Mallory's mind as she waited for her train to arrive. Actually, it more than played on her mind. It obliterated all other thoughts.

The man sure knew how to kiss.

But then, she'd expected more than mere competency from someone who looked like Logan. What she hadn't expected were fireworks. These weren't some piddling display, either, but the kind that lit up the sky for a citywide Independence Day celebration. God help her, they were still going off, raining down sparks on her heated skin, especially when she recalled the wanton way in which she'd responded to him.

She'd wrapped her arms around him, clinging like some sort of human ivy.

The man was a story, she reminded herself yet again. Dinner and an evening sail on his boat had been borderline unprofessional, but Mallory had bypassed her conscience, telling herself she was meeting him in the name of research. Research didn't include getting physical. She'd crossed the line big-time with that kiss.

Though the sun had set, the temperature hadn't dipped much, and she was too keyed up to go home, where her air-conditioning was on the blink. There was no way she wanted to sit alone in her hot little box of an apartment and ruminate about Logan's masterful mouth and her appalling lack of restraint and professionalism. She opted to return to the office.

This wasn't the first evening that had found Mallory in the *Herald*'s multistoried Art Deco building on Grand Avenue. She'd been known to sleep on the lumpy sofa in the women's lounge when a story kept her late. When she entered the lobby this evening, the second-shift security guard smiled and sent her a friendly wave.

"Hey, kiddo."

Kiddo. Sometimes Mallory felt positively ancient despite not having yet reached her thirtieth birthday. Tonight was one such time.

"Hi, Joe."

"Cubs are up by three runs in the bottom of the seventh," he informed her as she waited for the elevator to arrive. "A win tonight will put them three games ahead of the Sox."

"I'm not switching my allegiance," she said of her beloved baseball team. She'd been a fan even before moving to Chicago, which was one of only a couple cities to have more than one Major League franchise. "Even if my guys wind up dead last and the Cubs go all the way to the World Series, you won't find me cheering them on. There's still such a thing as loyalty, you know."

The older man merely winked. "You'll come around, kiddo."

"Not in this lifetime," she replied as she stepped into the lift.

Relative silence greeted Mallory when she stepped off on the fourth floor. The *Herald* was an afternoon paper, which meant it went to press before noon. At this time of the evening only a couple of overnight city desk editors and a smattering of reporters, including the one working the night-cops beat, were at their desks. The television was on, tuned to a cable news channel, and static-laced conversations could be heard coming from the omnipresent police scanner. She breathed in the earthy scent of newsprint and the underlying odor of stale cigarette smoke. Smoking had been banned building wide a few years earlier, but even a fresh coat of paint on the walls and new carpet tiles on the floor hadn't managed to completely banish the smell.

Careers had been made in this newsroom. Mallory would be damned if she would give up hers without a fight.

Pushing Logan's kiss to the recesses of her mind, she grabbed a bottle of diet cola from the cafeteria vending machine and headed to the second-floor library. In newspaper jargon the library was also known as the morgue. It was as quiet as one tonight when she flipped on the overhead lights and stepped inside.

These days technology made it possible to access every story, photo and caption that ran in each day's edition from the computer at her desk, which was one of the reasons the library's staff of six had been pared down to two, one of whom worked only part-time. The computer system had been in place for a while now, but everything that predated it was stored in this room, either on microfilm or in individual files of clippings that were categorized by both the reporter's byline and the story's subject matter.

Mallory started with the clip files, grabbing a handful by a senior lifestyles reporter who'd covered the city's social scene at the *Herald* for more than three decades. Logan was a born and bred Chicagoan, and his wealthy parents regularly made headlines for charity work and other good deeds. Maybe, just maybe, she'd get lucky.

Two hours later Mallory rubbed her bleary eyes and finished off the last of her now warm diet cola. She'd gone back through several years' worth of clippings and had found nothing more controversial than a photograph of his father christening a sightseeing boat for a company that was the top competitor of one that now regularly advertised on Logan's program.

She was ready to call it a night when she spied a folder titled Engagement Announcements that had accidentally been filed with the other. A light bulb clicked on. Logan wasn't married now, but had he ever been?

Her question was answered forty-five minutes later when she opened a folded yellow clipping that announced the engagement of Logan Reed Bartholomew and Felicia Ann Gable. He was nearly a decade younger in the photo, but he looked the same even though his hair was a little longer and his face less angular. The woman standing at his side smiled adoringly at him. She also was stunning and Mallory's polar opposite with long blond hair and classical features.

Mallory's stomach knotted. She passed it off as excitement though it felt suspiciously like disappointment or, more ominously, dread. But that was ridiculous. She *wanted* to find dirt. That's why she was in the newspaper's morgue scouring clip files for leads. It was why she'd accepted Logan's invitation for dinner and a sail. Of course, the fact he had been married wasn't exactly dirt. His wife could have died. Or he could be divorced. A lot of marriages failed. Statistically speaking, half of them, as her mother liked to remind her. Divorce wasn't a story…unless it was the result of something serious such as spousal abuse or some kind of addiction.

Logan an abuser…either of women or substances? That didn't seem possible. But during her years of reporting, Mallory had encountered people every bit as seemingly upstanding as Logan with even darker secrets to hide.

"A fall wedding is planned," the notice read.

"Now we're getting somewhere," she murmured half under her breath.

From a filing cabinet at the back of the room she pulled out a stack of files of wedding announcements starting in late September of the same year and running through March of the following one. Sometimes it took newlyweds months to turn in the notice, especially if they were waiting to receive proofs from their photographers.

She'd just settled back in her seat when the door opened.

Sandra Hutchens eyed Mallory in surprise. "You're here kind of late, aren't you, Stevens? Or has another screw-up caused you to be busted back to night file clerk?"

"Funny," Mallory muttered between gritted teeth. "What are you doing here?"

"Gathering a little background for an investigative piece I'm working on with Tom Gerard." Tom was one of the reporters assigned to district court. "You remember those?"

Did she ever. God, she missed real news.

"All the Freedom of Information Act requests we had to file are finally paying off. Heads are going to roll after this story runs."

It was all Mallory could do not to salivate, especially since she knew her demotion was the only reason a hack like Sandra was now working on such a meaty story with Tom.

"Enjoy it while it lasts," Mallory muttered, knowing an explanation of "it" was unnecessary.

Sandra grinned. "Oh, I intend to."

It was all Mallory could do not to snarl. She and Sandra tolerated each other in a professional setting, but it was an open secret that no love was lost between them. Their adversarial relationship dated to Mallory's days as an unpaid intern at the paper. Sandra, who had been at the *Herald* for nearly a decade by that time, had covered Chicago government, and she'd balked at having to take a rookie around on her beat. Not long after, that "rookie" had made a fool of her.

After a seemingly mundane city council meeting, they had returned to the newsroom where Sandra had filed a straightforward story about the city not renewing its contract with the current waste management company. Mallory, however, had acted on a hunch and done a little more digging.

Two months later, her piece exposing a scandal involving three aldermen receiving kickbacks from the new firm ran across the top of page one. Then it was picked up by the Associated Press wire service and printed in newspapers from coast to coast. Sandra had hated Mallory ever since, and she had celebrated Mallory's fall from grace by buying a round of drinks for patrons at the Torch, a hole-in-wall pub that catered to reporters and other working stiffs rather than tourists.

"Wedding announcements." Sandra's eyes narrowed. "What are you up to?"

"You know those fluff pieces we get to do for the Lifestyles section," Mallory evaded. "Who cares what styles of dress were in fashion a decade ago?"

Sandra snorted out a laugh. "Wedding fashions. My how the mighty have fallen."

Offering a brittle smile, Mallory rose to her feet and raked the files into a pile, intending to leave.

Sandra laid a hand on her arm. "Have you filled out the form to check those out?"

"I'm just taking them to my desk." Actually, Mallory

was planning to take them home. Per usual, she had no
other plans for the weekend.

"It doesn't matter. If you're taking clip files out of
this room, you need to fill out a form," the other woman
insisted and pointed to the stack of papers on a high
counter next to the door.

Mallory snorted. "Right. And you do that every
single time you walk out of here with clips."

"No." Sandra's smile was smug. "But we're not
talking about me. We're talking about you. And for
someone who's basically on probation, I'd think you'd
be eager to follow the rules."

"How kind of you to remind me of that," Mallory
muttered.

"Don't mention it." She smirked. "Really, it's my
pleasure."

Mallory filled out the necessary form, jotting down
the file numbers, the date and, because she was feeling
peevish, she put Sandra's name down as the person
checking them out.

Logan's apartment was quiet when he arrived home.
He'd loitered on his boat for a couple of hours after
Mallory left, thinking as much as puttering. As he'd
washed the dinner dishes, stowed the small barbecue
grill in the hold and checked the rigging, he'd tried to
figure out what his next move with Mallory should be.

He still hadn't reached a conclusion, though he knew
he shouldn't have kissed her. Hell, even as he'd drawn
her into his arms, he'd known that. But just as he hadn't

been able to resist the temptation she'd posed then, he couldn't muster any regret now.

At home he prowled his penthouse, which offered stunning views of the lake from the living room's large windows and a generously proportioned patio. Where once he'd welcomed the high-rise's solitude and privacy, it just seemed lonely now. He poured himself a drink and headed outside.

Part of him had hoped that whatever magic spell Mallory had cast on him would wear off with that kiss. It hadn't and the other half of him was damned relieved. Despite all of his uncertainty, one thing was clear: tonight wasn't the end of it.

The phone on the bedside table rang before eight the following morning. Logan grabbed for it, muttering a sleepy hello even as he folded the other arm over his eyes to block the light coming from the window.

"You didn't call last night," the woman on the other end of the line accused without the courtesy of a greeting.

"Sorry." Squinting, he levered up on one elbow, more amused than irritated. "Am I grounded?"

His agent dismissed the teasing question with an audible huff. "What happened with Mallory Stevens? I want to know everything."

That statement cut deeply into amusement's lead over irritation. "I don't believe in kissing and telling."

Logan regretted the words instantly.

"Dear God!" Nina exclaimed. "Please tell me nothing happened between the two of you."

"Nothing happened," he repeated in monotone.

"This isn't funny, Logan."

"No, it's not." But Nina failed to detect the edge in his voice.

"You can't trust her," she went on. "Reporters like her are sharks. They get one whiff of blood in the water and they go on the attack."

"That's rather dramatic," he drawled. "Besides, I thought you said Mallory was a pit bull? Sharks and dogs are two different species, you know."

"Logan—"

He sat up fully and swung his legs over the side of the bed. "Look, Nina, as touching as I find your concern, my personal life is just that…personal."

"I guarantee you that Mallory doesn't see it the same way. If she finds out something about you that can help sell newspapers, she's going to use it. And unless it's out and out false and maliciously published, we won't be able to do a damned thing about it because you're a public figure."

His agent was right, of course. As a celebrity, he was fair game. If Mallory sniffed out a story, she would write it. What did it say about him that he didn't care? Besides, he rationalized, what did he have to hide?

So he told his agent, "There's no need to worry. She's curious about the syndication deal. She's not the only reporter who is."

Maybe he would give her an exclusive when the terms of the contract had been hammered out.

"In the meantime," he continued, "there's nothing Mallory Stevens is going to discover about me personally that's exciting enough to grace the front page of her newspaper or any other. As much as I hate to admit it, Nina, my life is pretty damned pedestrian."

"Are you sure about that?"

"I'm positive."

CHAPTER FIVE

NOTHING.

After scouring the clip files that was exactly what Mallory had found. She'd even returned to the newspaper morgue late Saturday for wedding announcements through the end of that calendar year. Again she came up empty-handed. Even if Logan and Felicia's planned fall wedding had wound up delayed for several months—and why would that happen?—no record of it appeared in the *Herald*.

Record or no record, something told Mallory she was on the right track. She decided to press on. Monday morning, between writing advances for a couple of alternative-art exhibits, she searched the state's vital records for a certificate of marriage. *Nada.* If the couple had married, they had not done so in the state of Illinois.

On a hunch, Mallory checked the records for Felicia's name alone. *Bingo!*

She could have saved herself a lot of time and effort if she'd done so first, she realized. Miss Felicia Ann Gable had been a fall bride after all. She'd wed another man, Nigel Paul Getty. The nuptials were performed by a justice of the peace. This probably explained why no wedding announcement had appeared in the newspaper. When a bride threw over her groom for another man just before they were to say I do, flaunting it in the media was bad form.

Poor Logan.

The sympathy Mallory felt for him far outpaced her excitement over the discovery. She told herself it was because she didn't yet know if this lead would pan out. Besides, she knew how it felt to find out your significant other was cheating. Two years post-Vince, Mallory still felt like a fool for not having put two and two together sooner. It would have helped her save face among their mutual friends, many of whom apparently were privy to the fact he was two-timing.

Her telephone rang as she mulled over what to do next. "Mallory Stevens," she said distractedly into the receiver.

"Just the person I was hoping to reach."

The aggrieved groom in question was on the other end of the line. Mallory stared at the photograph of his lovely former fiancée, feeling oddly guilty and fighting the urge to apologize.

"Logan, hi. What…why are you calling?"

"I need a favor," he replied.

"What sort of favor?"

"I've been invited to a dinner this Thursday evening at the Cumberland Hotel. It's a benefit to raise funds to send children with life-threatening illnesses to summer camp."

"And you're hoping to get a mention of it in the *Herald*," she guessed.

"Actually, I was hoping you'd agree to come with me." He chuckled dryly. "Good cause notwithstanding, these things can be tedious."

"You want me to go with you," she repeated in surprise.

"Not interested?"

"I didn't say that."

"No. But neither have you said yes," Logan pointed out.

"Yes." Even though Mallory had spent the weekend reminding herself of ethical boundaries and the danger of mixing business with pleasure, the answer slipped easily from her lips.

"Terrific. Dinner is at seven with cocktails and appetizers starting at six. Would five-thirty be too early for me to come by and collect you?"

She'd have to leave work a bit before her usual quitting time to reach her apartment and be ready on time, but she didn't hesitate before saying, "That's fine."

"Good. And, Mallory?"

"Yes?"

"I'm looking forward to it."

She pictured him grinning and her skin grew warm. Despite all of her internal lectures to focus and be professional, Mallory knew Logan wasn't the only one filled with anticipation.

* * *

Between Monday and Thursday, Mallory put in more than a dozen hours fleshing out what she knew about Logan's failed relationship. Felicia not only had hurriedly remarried, she'd moved out of state a few months later. She and her husband relocated to Portland, Oregon, where they'd had a son, who was either premature or conceived before they were wed. This, Mallory figured, was the reason for Felicia's defection.

A year after that, Felicia and Nigel Getty were divorced. These days, Felicia was a businesswoman, though perhaps not for much longer. Barring an infusion of cash, her upscale fragrance boutique would soon be in Chapter Eleven.

What went around came around.

Thursday started out bad and continued downhill for the rest of the day. Mallory forgot to set her alarm clock, missed her El train and then spilled half of her first cup of coffee down the leg of her ecru trousers while waiting for the next one. Unfortunately, she had no time to return home to change clothes, so she arrived at the *Herald* wearing spotted pants that smelled like Arabica beans.

As Mallory slunk to her desk, Ruth Winslow, the Lifestyles section editor glanced up from her computer and then consulted the large wall clock.

"I wasn't aware you had an interview this morning," Ruth remarked.

"I didn't. My alarm clock..." Ruth's steel-colored eyebrows rose, cutting off the rest of Mallory's explanation. "Sorry."

"I'll expect a list of story ideas by noon for the special

pullout tab on street festivals that's going to run next Sunday, and I've got a couple of advances for you to write. I need both by the end of the day."

"Sure." Now would not be a good time to ask to leave early, Mallory decided.

When Mallory spilled a second cup of coffee on her clothes half an hour later, she began to wonder if Logan's ex wasn't the only one getting smacked by karma.

Given the way her day had gone, she didn't find it surprising that she was running late. Logan was leaning against her apartment door when she arrived home.

"Have you been here long?" she asked as she balanced her oversize shoulder bag on one knee and dug through it for her keys.

"Fifteen minutes or so."

Mallory glanced up and winced. "Sorry."

He cast a considering look. "That's all right. I'm guessing you've had a bad day."

"That obvious?"

A smile played around the corners of his mouth. "Let's just say your clothes tell a story."

When her fingers wrapped around the keys, she sighed. "They only offer the abridged version, believe me. I felt like the poster child for Murphy's Law today."

"Sorry to hear that. If you want to cancel, I'll understand."

As tempting as she found his offer, she waved it aside. "That's kind of you, but no. Of course, if a natural disaster strikes while we're out tonight don't say that I didn't give you fair warning."

"I won't," he replied on a laugh.

Mallory opened the door and invited Logan inside, grateful that the place looked presentable. Housework tended to rank low on her list of priorities, especially when she was in hot pursuit of a story.

"I have a decent bottle of Merlot in the kitchen if you'd care for a glass while I'm getting ready," she told him as she toed off her shoes.

"Should I pour some for you?"

She sent him a wry look. "Given my track record today with beverages that stain, I think I'd better pass."

Mallory's apartment was small, easily a third the size of Logan's condo, but glancing around, he decided it offered a huge insight into the woman. Her music collection included CDs by Duke Ellington, Miles Davis and Fats Waller, making her a fan of jazz. The bold red wall that served as a backdrop for a piece of oversize geometric art said she wasn't afraid of color. And her eclectic sense of style—Asian-inspired pieces were mixed in with a boxy modern couch and more traditional leather recliner—told him she didn't believe in following someone else's rules.

She also liked to read. A built-in bookshelf to the left of the television boasted lengthy tomes by some of the country's leading political commentators, classic literature by the likes of E. M. Forster, William Faulkner and Sylvia Plath, as well as the newest thriller from Tami Hoag. There were no self-help books, he noted, unless he lumped the one on basic home repair into that category. No surprise there. Mallory was self-reliant, self-sufficient.

A survivor.

When the uncertainty he'd experienced on his sailboat niggled again, Logan decided to take her up on the offer of wine.

Her kitchen wasn't much bigger than the galley on his boat, but since Mallory had already admitted she didn't cook, he doubted she thought it deficient. He found a corkscrew in one of the drawers and located a wineglass in a top cupboard. As he sipped Merlot, he glanced at the snapshots and other clutter stuck to the front of her refrigerator. One in particular caught his attention. It was of Mallory and another young woman. They were sitting on a split-rail fence wearing cowboy hats and silly grins. Mountains peaked in the background, making it clear the photo had not been taken locally. A vacation? Whatever the occasion, she looked so open and uncalculating. No questions to be asked. No agenda.

Would she ever be that way around him?

"That's my college roommate, Vicki."

Logan turned at the sound of Mallory's voice and nearly fumbled his wine at the vision that greeted him. "Roommate?" he managed.

"Yes. She lives in Chicago, too, and we've remained close since graduation. Once a year she talks me into going on some wild adventure. She claims it's good for me."

"I think I like her already."

"Last year, it was working a cattle drive. That picture was taken before our first grueling day in the saddle. Hence our smiles."

She motioned toward the photograph, but Logan's gaze was taking in the pale-gold cocktail dress she wore. Cap sleeves showed off a pair of toned arms and a short hem highlighted her killer legs. The flirty jeweled sandals on her feet caught the light and shot off sparks.

Logan swore he felt some of them land on him.

"You look amazing."

It was no empty compliment he paid. In the amount of time it took most of the women he knew to apply their makeup, Mallory had changed clothes, done something sexy with her hair and added a bit of drama to her eyes. She was pretty before, lovely. She was dangerously gorgeous now, and he wasn't sure whether he should be grateful or nervous.

"Thanks."

"I'll be the envy of every man there." He meant that, too. Her unconventional looks turned heads even when she wasn't also wearing something sexy.

Mallory brushed the compliment aside. "Let's not get carried away."

Because he wasn't a man given to hyperbole, Logan persisted. "You're gorgeous."

"I'm not." She expelled a breath, not so much exasperated as flustered, which he found interesting, endearing.

"Who told you that?" he asked.

Her brows beetled. "No one told me that. I'm not

fishing for a compliment here. I'm not ugly. I'd even go so far as to say I'm attractive. But gorgeous? No."

"Why?" he countered.

"I have a mirror."

Logan didn't care for her explanation. Generally speaking, Mallory didn't suffer from low self-esteem. Hell, he'd never met a more confident, self-possessed woman…when it came to her profession. But someone definitely had made her feel lacking when it came to her appearance. Who? Why? The answers would have to wait. But this couldn't.

"Then you must not look in it very often." He took her by the shoulders and steered her to the foyer, where an oval-shaped one hung on the wall over a small table that was stacked with junk mail. "See?"

Mallory studied herself for a moment, but then offered a dismissive shrug. "I'll have to take your word for it."

"Will you?"

This time it was his reflection she surveyed. Logan let his hands slide from her shoulders to her hands, releasing one so he could turn her around.

"Well?"

She leaned forward slightly before stepping away. "We'd better get going. We're already late for your party."

"Fashionably so," he assured her, even though generally speaking Logan was a stickler for punctuality. "A few more minutes won't hurt."

But she shook her head. "I just need to go grab my

handbag and a shawl. You go on ahead. I'll meet you downstairs."

Logan was still standing in the foyer when she returned from her bedroom. After taking the gauzy wrap from her hands and settling it around her shoulders, he took her arm and escorted her downstairs to his waiting car.

The hotel's ballroom was crowded with people—entrepreneurs, politicians, celebrities and members of Chicago's social elite. Some had come out to support a worthy cause. Others had come out to be *seen* supporting a worthy cause. Mallory recognized many of them, including the alderman who was rumored to be taking bribes from a development firm. Another time she would have been tempted to corner him and ask a few questions to see what she could get him to say on the record. This evening, however, the only person she found herself curious about was Logan...and it had nothing to do with a story.

He looked incredible. No surprise there, of course. The man not only could afford to wear Armani, his broad shoulders and lean, muscular build did the suit justice. But there was more to Logan than Hollywood good looks. She'd never doubted his intelligence, but he was deeper and far more complex than she'd first realized.

He fascinated her not because she was a reporter, but because she was a woman.

Gorgeous? Did he really think so? And those manners of his, opening doors, helping her with her shawl. He made her feel as if she'd just fallen into a fairy tale.

"Mallory?"

She blinked, becoming aware that the man in question had been speaking to her while she'd been gazing at him. She could only hope she wasn't wearing some sappy expression on her face.

"Sorry. My mind strayed."

"And here I thought you were hanging on my every word," he teased. "I was just saying that the seating isn't assigned. Do you have a preference?"

She glanced around. At this point all of the tables had at least two or more occupants, which meant introductions would be necessary, small talk, too. Usually she enjoyed meeting new people. As for small talk, Mallory was good at it, and even better at getting folks to open up about themselves. But suddenly she didn't want to socialize or chat or look for possible stories. She wanted to be alone with Logan, picking up where they'd left off in her foyer.

"Would you mind sitting at a table near the back of the ballroom?" she asked.

His brows notched up at the suggestion. "So we can leave early without causing much of a disturbance?"

"Exactly."

When he smiled, it caused another sort of disturbance, especially when he asked Mallory, "Am I to assume you have something in mind for us later?"

"Maybe," she allowed.

What was she getting herself into? She didn't know. She didn't care, which was totally unlike her.

She was off her game completely, she realized a moment later when she failed to notice Sandra Hutchens until it was too late to avoid her.

"Hello, Mallory. I wondered who was here for the *Herald*."

The other woman's gloating snarl turned to bewilderment, however, the moment she recognized Mallory's escort.

"You're...aren't you...?"

"Yes." Logan took the hand Sandra was pointing in his direction and shook it politely. "I'm Logan Bartholomew. And you are?"

"A pain in my butt," Mallory muttered at the same time Sandra gave her name.

"Mallory and I work together."

"Are you here covering the benefit?" Logan asked, unaware—or was he?—of how insulting the senior reporter found the question.

"No. I have a beat that allows me to write actual news stories." Sandra sniffed. Her gaze shifted to Mallory then, and the malicious triumph in her expression was impossible to miss. "I'm here tonight as the guest of Larry Byram. You remember him, don't you Mallory."

Oh, she remembered Larry, all right. Her teeth clenched. Larry was one of the mayor's top aides and the weasel who'd fed Mallory the bogus story and quotes that ultimately had led to her demise.

"How is Larry?" she asked sweetly.

"He's good. And enjoying a promotion."

No doubt he was also enjoying Mallory's demotion. "How nice for him," she managed.

"I'll tell him you said hello," Sandra offered with ill-concealed delight.

"Yes, please do."

"Would you excuse us for just a moment?" Sandra said to Logan. She grabbed Mallory's arm and dragged her a couple of feet away without waiting for his reply. "I don't know what you're up to, Stevens," she hissed the moment they were out of earshot.

"Up to?"

"Don't play games with me. You're with Logan Bartholomew."

"I know."

"Why?"

"I should think that's obvious."

"Not in your case," Sandra snapped. "You don't have a real social life, so I know whatever is going on between you two has got to be work related."

She wanted to deny it and was a little troubled that she couldn't, not completely. "Your point?"

"Unless it's something an intern could write in her sleep, *you* shouldn't be working on it."

"What? Are you my editor now?" Mallory asked. "If so, I missed the memo."

"Leave the real stories to those who can do them without costing the newspaper a bundle."

Sandra's remark posted a direct hit. Mallory felt her

face heat, partly from irritation but mostly from embarrassment. She couldn't prove it, but she knew she'd been set up. Still, it was her own fault. Even if she was able to return to her beat eventually, would she ever be able to live down her costly mistake?

"I've got to go."

When she attempted to walk past Sandra, the other woman blocked her path and pointed a finger in her face. "Just so you know, I'm watching you. One more screw-up and you'll be gone."

"You'd like that, wouldn't you?"

"I live for the day."

Mallory managed to sound bored when she said, "Then you need to get a life, Sandra."

"Charming woman," Logan remarked when Mallory rejoined him.

"Yes, we're the best of friends."

"As tight as Brutus and Caesar, I'd say."

"Exactly, which is why I watch my back whenever she's around."

"How about if I keep an eye on your back…and other things…tonight?"

His brows lifted and so did the pall the encounter with Sandra had cast over Mallory's mood.

"I see a table over there." She pointed to one that was adjacent to a side entrance.

"Good choice," he replied, nodding toward the doors.

"I thought so."

She changed her mind a moment later. Two other couples already were seated there sipping cocktails and sharing a plate of appetizers. Introductions were made, although both of the women knew Logan—or, rather, knew who he was—even before he gave his name.

So much for Mallory's hope that the two of them could just chat between themselves until the opportunity to leave arrived.

"Oh, my God! You're Logan Bartholomew! *The* Logan Bartholomew!" the bustier of the two brunettes shouted. "I just love your show. I listen to it every morning while I'm getting ready for work."

"Thank you."

"My name is Anita, by the way. And this is my husband, Victor."

"It's nice to meet you, Anita." Logan turned to shake Victor's hand. "And you, too."

"The same," Victor replied, although he didn't appear to be nearly as starstruck as his wife.

"I feel like I already know you." When Anita winked flirtatiously, Mallory gritted her teeth, feeling oddly possessive.

The other brunette piped up then. "I'm your biggest fan, Dr. Bartholomew. I never miss your show."

"Please, it's just Logan."

"Logan." She actually giggled. "I'm Julia Richmond." Motioning to the irritated-looking man sitting beside her, she added, "Thanks to you, Darin and I have been able to work out some of our differences and keep our relationship moving forward. We're getting married in the fall."

She extended her left hand, showing off a diamond

engagement ring big enough that it should have required an escort of armed guards.

"Wow," Mallory said. "That's some rock."

"Tell me about it," Darin muttered.

Logan cleared his throat and offered a diplomatic "Congratulations to you both."

"Thanks. We owe it all to you, don't we, honey?" Julia wrapped an arm around Darin, who said nothing. Instead, he hoisted his drink in a mock toast and took a liberal swig. Mallory gave their marriage a year, tops, assuming they even made it to the nuptials, which at this point looked dicey.

Julia was saying, "The advice you give on your show, especially to couples who are having problems, is right on the money. It's like you wrote the book on relationships or something."

"Yes. You're very insightful, especially when it comes to understanding women and what we need from the men in our lives," Anita chimed in.

Darin wasn't the only one who looked irritated now. A muscle had begun to twitch in Victor's jaw. It was clear neither man appreciated the attention Logan was receiving. Mallory wasn't thrilled with it, either.

"I'm glad you found something I've said to be of help," he replied modestly.

Far from basking in the women's profuse praise, Logan shifted uncomfortably in his seat. And no wonder, given his personal history, Mallory thought. If he'd written the manual on relationships, as Anita claimed, he wouldn't have been blind-sided by his fiancée's infidelity and virtually left at the altar.

Mallory decided it was time to steer the conversation to a neutral topic.

"So, how 'bout those White Sox last night?" she said, earning black looks from the women and a sneer from Darin, who was obviously a Cubs fan.

Logan, however, latched on to the new subject. "Did you see that play at third base in the bottom of the seventh inning?"

Because she could tell that all of his enthusiasm wasn't manufactured, Mallory grinned. A Sox man. Who knew? Another reason to like him.

"See it? I screamed so loud I woke up half my building. Detroit thought they had the game sewed up till that play, then our boys rallied," she said with the kind of pride only other diehard fans could understand.

Victor apparently was one of them. Either that or he was just eager to talk about something other than relationships. He began rattling off the standings for the teams in the American League Central. Darin entered the discussion a moment later and for the next several minutes a spirited debate on the designated-hitter rule ensued. Anita and Julia didn't look all that pleased that sports were now dominating the conversation, but they began to chat between themselves about Julia's upcoming wedding, so all was well. Beneath the table, Mallory felt Logan's hand brush her knee. When she glanced over, he mouthed the word "Thanks."

"No problem," she mouthed back.

Several minutes later, Buck Warren, the head of the charity, took to the podium to welcome everyone and thank them for coming. He also made a not-so-subtle request for donations with the reminder that such gifts were tax deductible. Afterward, dinner was served. No rubber chicken, thank goodness, but Mallory couldn't help thinking the pork tenderloin was on the dry side and the steamed green beans were undercooked.

"They should hire you," she informed Logan after washing down a bite of the tenderloin with some wine.

He shrugged off the compliment. "It's easier to cook dinner for two than it is for two hundred."

"True. I wonder what the dessert will be. I hope it's chocolate."

He leaned over and whispered, "In the mood for a little decadence tonight?"

"As a matter of fact…" Heat shimmied up her spine as she returned his smile.

Dessert turned out to be apple pie with a side of vanilla ice cream that came largely melted.

"How disappointed are you?" Logan asked.

"Very." But something occurred to her then. "You know, this might be a good time to claim my rain check."

"You want me to make you dessert?"

She nodded. "Something with a sinful amount of chocolate in it. What do you say?"

"And leave before the dancing even starts?" He looked comically appalled.

Chocolate was momentarily forgotten. "You dance?"

"Slow only. I made a point of learning how in junior high school when I figured out it was a good excuse to put my arms around a girl without getting smacked for my trouble."

"Very calculating." But she laughed. "Well, we have to stay now."

"Eager to be in my arms?"

Though she was, she said, "I'm more eager to find out how good you are." When his brows rose, Mallory added dryly, "At dancing."

A local band had been hired for the event. Its female singer was dressed in a vintage floor-length gown, her hairstyle reminiscent of something from the 1940s. Mallory almost expected to hear "Boogie Woogie Bugle Boy" when the band started its first tune, but the song turned out to be a modern ballad. The small dance floor filled up quickly. Even so, Logan rose from his seat and held out one hand.

His lips were twitching, but his eyes glittered with a dare when he asked, "Shall we?"

"Oh, by all means."

Their hands remained clasped as they weaved their way through the tables to the dance floor. Even that minor bit of physical contact had Mallory's hormones starting to hop and hum. When they reached their destination and he pulled her into his arms, it was all she could do not to moan. Their bodies bumped, separated and brushed, but only occasionally as they swayed and circled to the music. Mallory forgot about moaning. Now she wanted to scream with need. The eagerness

Logan had spoken of earlier mocked her now. She was pretty sure he knew it, too.

He dipped his head lower. "Mmm. You smell good." The words vibrated against her ear.

"So do you." Though, of her five senses, touch was the one she was focusing on now. She turned her head slightly and their cheeks collided.

"Mmm," he said again.

"The song is almost over." And with it this sweet torture would end.

"I know. But there's still dessert."

"Yeah." She sighed. Her mouth was watering, though the hunger she hoped to satisfy had nothing to do with food.

"Do you have something in particular in mind?" he asked.

"You're open to requests?"

"Always and especially from you."

She smiled. "I'll have to think about it. Maybe you can tell me what your specialties are."

"Sure. I'll list them after we leave. But I'm open to trying new things, too."

"In the kitchen," she clarified.

"Right. In the kitchen." He nibbled her neck. "That's where I do my best cooking."

"Yeah?"

His hand stroked her lower back, causing her to tremble. "I'll show you."

"Mmm. Looking forward to it," she said.

The music stopped. The floor began to clear.

"Want to stay out here for another dance?" Logan asked.

"I'd rather go."

"Okay." His hand found the small of her back as they started for their seats.

"Home," Mallory added.

He stopped walking, turned toward her. His slow, conspiratorial smile further stirred her agitated hormones.

CHAPTER SIX

LOGAN drove the speed limit and took a detour after leaving the party, trying to give both of them time to come to their senses. They couldn't do this.

Well, they could, obviously, and he figured with mutually satisfying results. But they shouldn't.

His body demanded a reason why not. Unfortunately, he was damned if he could come up with one. Still, he was sure one existed. Probably several, for that matter. His agent could tell him, but he wasn't interested in calling Nina Lowman right now.

That's when he realized it. He didn't want reasons. He didn't want to come to his senses. He wanted this night with this woman. If there were consequences to be paid afterward, he'd pay them. With interest if need be. But tonight, even if just for tonight, she would be his.

He depressed the accelerator and the car shot forward. Mallory glanced sideways at him. God help him, he thought he saw her smile.

He'd planned to take her to his penthouse. He had

a spacious bedroom, including a king-size bed. Given the way he felt, extra room seemed a good idea. But as he moved through traffic, accelerating through yellow lights, he decided against it. Her place made more sense.

First of all, taking her to the condo seemed too presumptuous, even though the signals she'd given off all evening pretty well confirmed they were on the same wavelength. Secondly, it wouldn't allow either one of them a graceful out if they changed their mind. A doubtful scenario, that. But still. And third, it would save him from having to run her home in the wee hours of the morning.

Yeah, the conclusion that their lovemaking would last for hours was presumptuous, too, but surely one primal encounter wouldn't be enough.

He pulled to a stop outside her building, lucky enough to find a parking space, although at this point he would have left his car in the fire lane if necessary.

"Well, here we are." It was all he could do to keep from thumping his head on the steering wheel after making that hackneyed observation. Worse than sounding eager, he sounded nervous. And he was. He was hardly an inexperienced teenager, but his hormones didn't seem to know that. He felt eager and nervous and, hell, just plain desperate. God help him, his palms were even damp.

In the dim light of the car's interior, he thought he saw Mallory's lips twitch.

"Yep. Here we are." He heard the latch on her seat

belt unhitch. "You're coming up, right? I have that wine. It seems a shame to drink a glass alone."

"Well, in that case..."

Mallory was apprehensive, though need trumped her nerves. It was obvious Logan felt the same. Gone was his sexy swagger and confident radio voice. Out of the corner of her eye, she saw him rub his palm on the leg of his trousers before taking her hand. Even so, it felt hot to the touch and telltale moist. She found his sudden lack of polish endearing and every bit of a turn-on as the way he'd held her in his arms when they'd danced earlier.

At her apartment door, she handed him the key, which she'd thought to have out in advance. Since he seemed to like doing these small courteous things, she would let him. Truth was, she liked his manners.

The apartment was dark and quiet, though she thought she could hear her heart beating. She hadn't left a light on. She walked to the lamp on the table next to the couch and switched it on.

"So, some wine?" she inquired.

He was still standing just inside the door. "If you're having some."

"You're not worried about driving, are you?" She raised one eyebrow in subtle challenge.

"Should I be?" The corner of his mouth lifted.

"No." But then Mallory shrugged. "Although I have heard that even small amounts can impair one's ability to drive...among other things."

Logan crossed to where she stood. "Then I shouldn't chance it. I want to be fully…able."

His hands found her hips and he pulled her into closer proximity. As his head dipped low, she whispered, "I'd prefer that as well."

He bypassed her mouth and started with her neck. The first nibble sent a series of shocks through her system.

Zip, zap, zing.

She enjoyed every one of them, no longer trying to determine why she felt the way she did. Some things defied explanation.

"Mmm." The sound vibrated out on a moan.

"You like that?"

Logan's voice had taken on a cocky air. Apparently he'd found his footing again. She didn't know whether to be glad or disappointed. Glad, she decided when his mouth began to explore the other side of her neck.

"You have to ask?"

"Not really."

Cocky, definitely. It was time to level the playing field. She backed up a step, creating just enough distance between their bodies that he was forced to stop exploring her collarbone. He looked at her in question.

"I probably shouldn't tell you this, but whenever we're together, I get this…this sensation."

"Sensation?"

"Uh-huh." She nodded solemnly.

"Really? Where?"

"I don't know if I should say."

"You can tell me," he coaxed.

"That's right. You're a doctor." Mallory's smile was bold. He returned it in kind.

"Exactly," Logan told her.

"It starts about here." She laid her right hand on her chest.

"Here?" His fingertips skimmed her exposed collarbone in a sensual caress.

"A little lower, actually," she managed in a voice that verged on studious.

"Lower?"

"Yes."

"Hmm." His gaze turned from considering to smoldering as his hand slowly meandered south, where it kneaded the upper curve of her breast through the satiny fabric of the cocktail dress.

"Here?" he asked.

"Still lower," she managed. This time her voice was a breathy whisper. She decided to show him rather than use words. Placing her hand over his, she guided it down until the fullest part of her breast filled his palm. "Right here."

His head dipped down and he whispered her name against her cheek as his hand's gentle movement had her knees threatening to buckle. But she wasn't through.

"That's where it starts, Doctor. But that's only where it starts."

Mallory thought she heard Logan swallow, though it was hard to tell over the loud thudding of her heart. As for her, she had nothing to swallow. Her mouth had gone dry. So much for leveling the playing field.

"Where does it end?" he asked.

She should have been nervous. She had been. Now, she was anything but. She felt powerful, empowered. For the first time in her life, she knew exactly what she wanted and it had nothing to do with news beats or stories or journalism awards.

"Let me show you." She took his hand and turned, pulling him in the direction she wanted to take him. The direction she wanted to go, despite the lines that would be crossed on the way to her final destination.

Logan glanced past her to the hallway that led to her bedroom. He didn't move and she was forced to stop, as well. "Are you sure, Mallory?" His hand squeezed hers. "I want you to be sure."

Mallory swallowed. Something inside of her warmed. Logan was ever the gentleman, even at a time like this. He really was a special, special man.

I'm positive, she thought, but what she told him was, "If you want to find out exactly how sure I am, you'll have to come with me."

Logan stayed the night. The *entire* night. Leaving just after dawn the next morning with his suit coat slung over one arm, his tie peeking out of his trouser pocket, stubble shading his jaw and a smile of satisfaction lifting the corners of his mouth.

"I've got to go."

"Me, too," Mallory said. She couldn't afford to be

late to work for the second time in two days, not with Ruth watching the clock and Sandra gunning for her back.

"Bye."

"Bye."

Even so, they lingered in the doorway of her apartment for another fifteen minutes kissing farewell.

"I'll call you later today," Logan said when they finally broke apart.

He did, though it was much, much later.

Mallory scrubbed off her makeup and brushed her teeth, going about her nighttime routine as if nothing had happened when in fact nothing was the same. Her well-ordered world had rocked on its axis.

She had been able to think of nothing else all day except for Logan…and last night.

What a night it had been. It wasn't only what had transpired in her bedroom that had her mind straying from work all day. She couldn't stop recalling the hours that had led up to it.

She kept trying to pinpoint the moment everything had changed. It was the look, she decided. The look on Logan's face when he'd turned around in her tiny kitchen to find her dressed and ready for their evening out. His reaction had made her knees weak.

Mallory still couldn't believe that he thought she was gorgeous. Pretty? Oh, sure. She'd been called that on occasion. More often than not, though, with her oversize eyes and blunt chin, she'd been labeled cute. Add in her personality, especially while on assignment, and *ruthless* was the adjective that most often had been hurled. She'd taken it as a compliment, though obviously the sources who'd issued it hadn't intended it that way.

But *gorgeous*?

She stared at her reflection now, both amazed and intrigued that Logan could see her that way. She'd barely managed to wrap her mind around the compliment when he'd all but seduced her while they'd circled the crowded dance floor. To be fair—and Mallory was a firm believer in fairness—she'd been only too happy to return the favor. And later she had.

She dabbed moisturizer on her face and, rubbing it in, sighed. He'd said he would call today, but he hadn't. Not while she'd been at work, not on her cell phone and not since she'd been home. It was now past eleven o'clock, the last hour of the day ticking away. She tried to remain optimistic, which was something in itself. Even two years into her relationship with her last boyfriend, Mallory had taken every vow Vince made with a grain of salt:

"The next time my boss invites everyone out to dinner, I'll invite you along." "When my parents come to town next time, I'll introduce you." "I've got a buddy who says he'll get us some prime Sox seats for the next game."

Yeah, right. Whatever. Mallory hadn't pinned her hopes on any of her ex's promises. She'd known he would break them. Just as when she was a kid she'd known her father would fail to honor his word the few times he'd actually made plans to visit with her after the divorce.

For reasons she couldn't quite comprehend, she wanted to believe Logan. She didn't want him to disappoint her.

She moved to her bedroom, where she slipped into a tank top and boxer shorts. Pulling back the comforter on the antique four-poster she'd purchased at an estate sale in Lake Forest, she knew there would be no need for down tonight. Even the cotton sheet would be overkill. The air-conditioning unit had been fixed, but even with it blasting on high her skin felt heated.

She was fanning herself and considering a cold shower when the telephone rang. Even before she glimpsed the Caller ID readout she knew who it was. Her heart did a crazy thump and she was glad no one was around to see her foolish smile.

"I was just thinking about you," she said in lieu of the standard greeting.

"I guess that means I didn't wake you. Are you in bed?" His voice was low and all the sexier for it as he asked the question.

"As a matter of fact, I just climbed under the covers." Mallory lowered herself onto the mattress as she made the claim.

"Imagine that. So am I."

Her already elevated body temperature shot to the combustible range as she pictured Logan stretched out on his mattress wearing what he'd had on late last night…nothing. "Mmm."

"What was that?" he asked.

"Nothing." She smiled at the memory. "Nothing at all."

"I'm sorry to call you so late. It was a crazy day. After my show I spent a few hours taping promotional spots to run during other programs and then…it doesn't matter. Suffice it to say it was a really long and tedious day."

"Sorry. We can talk tomorrow if you'd like. For that matter, you needn't have called at all." Though she was so glad he had.

"I told you I'd call. I'm a man of my word."

Logan said it simply, stating it as fact. Her heart did that funny thump thing again. She wasn't sure which she found more disconcerting, the flash of fire he could provoke with a look or this new physical reaction.

"I like knowing that you try to keep your promises," she admitted.

"Everyone should."

"But everyone doesn't."

"You've been hurt," he said.

"Haven't we all?" Mallory waited a beat, wondering if he might mention his own breakup, and not just because she wanted a story and still smelled one here. But because she wanted to know more about Logan for herself.

He made a sound of agreement, but didn't expound on it. Instead he said, "It's pretty much a given that by the time you get to our age someone will have broken your heart or breached your trust. It's the human condition. Of course, that doesn't make it hurt any less."

"No."

She heard him sigh. "It's late. I should let you go."

"Is that a polite way of telling me I need my beauty sleep?" Mallory asked lightly.

"No. You're already gorgeous. Remember?"

Thump!

"So you say." She wrapped her free arm around her middle, hugging herself in an attempt to keep the pleasure his words generated from escaping.

"Still don't believe me." It wasn't a question. "I guess I'll just have to keep telling you until you become a believer."

Because she could think of nothing to say to that, she changed the subject. "What time do you need to be at the radio station?"

"I usually try to get there about an hour before I go on the air." Which meant he would be getting up in about five hours, given his commute. "What about you? What time do you have to be at the *Herald*?"

There had been a time in the not-so-distant past when Mallory had beaten in the copy editors, who were traditionally among the first to arrive in the newsroom. She'd stayed late in the day, too. A fifteen-hour shift wasn't an anomaly, even when she'd had nothing more pressing to do than scroll the national news wires and read the stories. She'd considered it a badge of honor then, a display of her dedication. It seemed a little pathetic now.

"My start time varies depending on what I'm covering. These days, though, it's a pretty safe bet I don't need to be at my desk till eight. You know, about the time the lonely and unemployed start phoning your show," she finished on a laugh.

"They need help, too."

Something in Logan's tone prompted Mallory to ask, "Is this how you expected your life to turn out when you graduated from medical school?"

"No."

Silence stretched after his startlingly candid answer. The reporter in her would have pounced on it, following up his admission with half a dozen questions intended to reveal more. But all Mallory said was, "I'm sorry."

More silence ensued. When she could stand it no longer, she said, "Logan? Are you there?"

"Yeah. I'm here."

"We're off the record, you know," she felt the need to point out. "It's just the two of us…talking."

"The two of us." He still sounded doubtful.

And though part of her wasn't sure it was the wisest course to take, she further clarified, "Just a man and a woman. Not a potential story and the reporter interested in writing it."

"Really?"

"Really."

"What I just said could make one hell of a story, especially with a nationally syndicated television talk show in the works." He swore ripely after the words slipped out.

Another exclusive gem and Mallory was privy to it.

But what she asked was, "Have you talked to anyone about this?"

He laughed. "Do you mean a professional? Now that would put your byline on the *Herald*'s front page. Chicago's Doctor-in-the-Know seeks counseling over career crisis."

His comment stung, but even more so, she felt for him. Here was a man who helped thousands with his advice, yet he had nowhere to turn when he needed guidance.

"You know, I'm here if you ever need someone to talk to, Logan. I'm not sure what kind of advice I can offer. Helping people is a little beyond my degree. But I'm a pretty good listener," she added. "Even when the content of the conversation isn't for publication."

"You really mean that."

"Yeah."

"Thanks." He laughed then, though without much humor. "I still can't believe I told you that."

"Because I'm a reporter?" Mallory asked, the lead weight returning to her stomach.

"No. Because I've never so much as hinted about that to my folks. They're usually the first people I go to when I need to hash things out."

What a luxury, she thought, to have parents you could confide in and seek counsel from. "Why haven't you said something to them, then?" she asked.

"I don't know. I guess I haven't wanted to worry them. Besides, they're so proud of me."

"But you have to be proud of yourself," she said

softly. "You have to be happy doing what you're doing or their pride won't matter."

Soft laughter filtered through the line. "And you said you're not good at this. Maybe you could take a turn guest hosting my show."

"Nah. Not my thing." She kicked the sheet to the bottom of the mattress. She was alone in bed, and yet she couldn't think of a more intimate conversation she'd shared with a man while being horizontal. Heaven knew, last night the pair of them hadn't spent much time talking. "Logan?"

"Yeah?"

She felt so privileged that he'd told her what he had, and she was determined to show him his trust wasn't misplaced. "Let's make things even between us."

"What do you mean?" he inquired on a sleepy yawn.

"Ask me anything you want to know."

"Anything?"

He didn't sound sleepy now. Indeed, his probing tone raised gooseflesh on Mallory's skin despite the Chicago night's sweltering heat.

"Yes. Anything."

"Okay." He made a humming noise, apparently considering his options. But he didn't keep her in suspense for long. "Tell me something about you that no one knows."

"No one?"

"A deep, dark secret. That will make us even."

"Something no one else knows," she repeated, thinking. The memory came, rising up from the recesses of her mind with all the unpleasantness of bile. As such, it nearly gagged her. For a moment she considered telling Logan something else. But honesty demanded honesty. She swallowed and began.

"I told you that I hadn't seen my dad since my parents divorced. But that's not true. I ran into him a few years ago."

"In Chicago?"

"Yes. Well, sort of. We were at O'Hare. I'd been out of town covering a story for the newspaper and I'd just returned home when I spotted him in the baggage claim area at the airport."

She squeezed her eyes closed, girded her heart. Not that any measure she took did any good. The pain trickled through her system as painful as acid. Three years had passed, but the memory remained fresh. The wound was still festering.

"And?" Logan prompted when she said nothing more.

"He looked the same as I remembered." She cleared her throat, hoping to make her voice sound more nonchalant. "He had a little more gray at his temples and a few more inches around his waist, but overall he was exactly the same. Tall and imposing and looking like he'd rather be anywhere but the place he was."

She remembered that look well. He'd worn it during holiday gatherings, during her dance recitals, on those few evenings when he'd been home and she'd asked him to read stories.

Mallory had to swallow again before she could

continue. "I saw him, and even with thirty feet and half a dozen people between us, I knew him at a glance. I guess I must have changed a lot, though."

"He didn't recognize you," Logan guessed.

"No." It was worse than that, though. "Actually, he thought I was a porter."

"Aw, Mallory."

"After I tapped on his shoulder, he turned and smiled. But before I could even say, 'Hi, Dad,' he handed me a couple of bucks and pointed to his bags." What started as a laugh ended in a sob. "He expected me to load them on the cart I'd just rented for my own luggage."

"What did you do?"

Even after three years, shame washed through her. Thankfully, anger followed swiftly on its heels. "I should have told him to go to hell, but I was a little too stunned."

"He deserved no less, you know." Logan said it with such conviction that it lessened some of her remaining heartache.

"He had three bags, two of them well over the weight limit. Mom always said he didn't know how to pack light. You know, in addition to being a lousy father, that day he proved he's also a lousy tipper. Three stinking bucks." She snorted. "He should have paid me triple that for the near hernia I suffered."

"Did you ever tell him who you were?" Logan asked.

"Nah." Though Logan wasn't there to see her, Mallory shook her head. "It was too humiliating, especially since I'd already loaded his luggage and he'd handed me the tip."

"What about your mother? Did you tell her?" he asked.

"And give Maude another reason to gripe to me about him? Nah." Mallory ran a hand over her cheeks, surprised to find them damp from tears. She hadn't cried over her father in years, not even after the O'Hare incident. She hadn't thought herself capable of tears any longer where the man was concerned.

"You chose to protect her," Logan said.

She didn't view her actions as altruistic. "He did it to me, Logan. He didn't do it to my mom."

"But she would have commiserated and understood."

"No. Our relationship isn't like that. My mother never would have let me hear the end of it."

"I'm sorry." After a moment of silence, he added, "Thanks for sharing that."

"You know, it felt good," she admitted. "Maybe there's something to therapy."

"I'm not sure I'd classify this as an actual session," Logan began. "But it felt good to tell you what I did, too." He snorted out a laugh then. "And it was a good reminder, too, since I'm always telling my listeners that it's not healthy to bottle up their emotions."

"Do as I say, not as I do?"

"I guess you're right." His tone was rueful. "But no longer. Nothing gets resolved that way."

"You have to face things, don't you?" she said.

"Yes. You do."

Cradling the phone to her ear, Mallory rolled to her side and caught sight of the clock. "Oh, my God, Logan. It's nearly one o'clock."

"I know."

"I really should let you get some sleep."

"I'm not tired. If you hang up now, I'll just lie here awake." She heard his breath hiss through the line a moment before he asked, "Stay with me, Mallory?"

"Okay. I won't go anywhere." Cradling the phone to her ear, she turned on her side, and though he was far away, she felt him beside her, filling up a vast emptiness she hadn't even been aware existed.

CHAPTER SEVEN

MALLORY wasn't sure how she would feel during her next face-to-face encounter with Logan. Excited? Embarrassed? Both? She'd bared her body to him and then a little bit of her soul. They'd spent two nights together, and though miles had separated them during the second one, it had been every bit as intimate as the first. She'd never felt closer to anyone than she'd been with him during those long hours they'd spent talking in hushed tones and sharing secrets until just before the morning sun turned the horizon pink.

When it came right down to it, she and Logan barely knew each other. Yet he already seemed to understand her far better than anyone else. And that was why she knew a moment of uncertainty the following afternoon when she spied him standing outside the *Herald* as she walked out the building's grand front entrance.

"Hello, Mallory."

"Logan."

The strap of the bag carrying her laptop slipped down

her arm. The computer would have crashed to the sidewalk had he not rushed forward to grab it.

She tried to keep a foolish smile corralled as she inquired, "What are you doing here?"

"Besides rescuing your computer, you mean?"

"Yeah, besides that. Thanks, by the way."

"You're welcome." When she held out her hand for the heavy bag, he looped the strap over his shoulder instead. "I wanted to see you."

That foolish smile unfurled. She ducked her head in an effort to get it under control.

"I probably should have called, rather than just showing up at your workplace."

"I don't mind. It's a nice surprise."

"Do you have any plans for this evening?"

She didn't, but even if she had, they would have escaped her now. She couldn't seem to think when he was looking at her like that, all interested and sexy.

"None that I can think of. Why?"

"Good. I thought I'd take you to a jazz club."

Though she couldn't have said why, that brought Mallory up short. "You like jazz?"

"No, but you do. So…" He shrugged, as if that explained everything, and in a way it did.

Heaven help her, Mallory wanted to kiss him right then as they stood on the sidewalk in front of the *Herald*. To hell with the purpose-driven professionals and camera-toting tourists who were streaming around them. She couldn't think of another man—her father included—who'd put what she liked, what she wanted ahead of his own needs or preferences.

"Thank you."

His brow furrowed. "For what?"

"For…the good time I'm going to have this evening," she said. "Would it be okay if we swing by my apartment first so I can change clothes?"

She had on an ivory linen suit that was wrinkled from a full day of wear, and her feet were begging to be freed from a pair of peep-toe pumps that required a little more breaking in to be comfortable. This wasn't what one wore to a club, especially when Logan was clad in denim jeans, Italian loafers and a short-sleeved shirt whose tails he'd left untucked.

"No problem, though I really like those heels. They do sinful things for your legs." He took a step toward her, close enough that there was no mistaking the interest brewing in his eyes.

"You think so?"

"Oh, yeah."

The outside world melted away, just as it had when they'd held each other on the dance floor…and later in her apartment.

"Then you should see me in stilettos," she announced boldly, bluntly and with just a hint of challenge.

"Something to look forward to." His words and the smoldering expression that accompanied them caused Mallory's breath to catch. "Are you ready?"

"Ready?" The question had her blinking.

"To go." He smiled knowingly. "My car's parked just down the street."

"Lead the way."

The Swing Shop was small, dark and smoky. It drew an eclectic crowd—college students, couples young and old, tourists, suit-wearing businessmen and even interns and residents from the nearby hospital, who were still outfitted in scrubs.

Everyone was equal here. At the French restaurant up the block a discreetly passed tip might garner a better table or less time spent on the waiting list, but at the Swing Shop seating was first-come, first-served. Patrons who hoped to get a table came early, often right from work when their day ended. And they tended to stay late, buying drinks and ordering the kitchen's greasy offerings as their feet tapped and their bodies swayed to wailing saxophones and weeping coronets.

Yes, getting a seat was tricky, but a little aggressive maneuvering through the crowd helped. That's why as soon as Mallory spied an older couple rising from a table near the stage, she elbowed her way past two legal-eagle types and a plus-size woman wearing an I Love Chicago T-shirt to plant her beer on the scuffed Formica. Logan caught up with her a couple of minutes and half a dozen *pardon-me*s later.

"That was amazing." He lowered himself into the chair opposite hers. "Professional football players running for a game-winning touchdown could take tips from you."

Mallory merely shrugged. "You know the saying—he who hesitates is lost."

He chuckled. "I take it you've been here before."

"This club is one of my favorites."

"And I thought I was going to be treating you to a new experience."

"That's sweet." And it was.

"This is my first time coming here," Logan confessed.

She stifled her laughter. "Yes. I thought that might be the case when you stood at the door and politely held it open for the large party of tourists who entered just behind us." She glanced meaningfully in the direction of a boisterous bunch of middle-aged women who'd pushed together three of the club's highly prized tables to accommodate their party, not all of whom had arrived yet.

"Now that we have a table, do you want to order something to eat?" he asked.

Mallory crinkled her nose. "The food's not really all that good here, but I tell you what, if you can make do with an appetizer or two until the main attraction finishes, dinner will be on me."

"Do I get to pick the place?" His brows bobbed.

"It sounds like you might have somewhere in mind."

"I might." He pulled a plastic-coated menu from between the salt and pepper shakers in the center of the table. After a cursory glance, he asked, "Do nachos work for you?"

Mallory grinned, enjoying the fact that even though

Logan possessed the skill of a gourmet chef, he harbored no prejudice against more pedestrian fare. "Heavy on the jalapeños, hold the onions."

"Got it." He raised his hand to catch the attention of a harried-looking waitress.

They stayed three hours and might have remained longer if Mallory's stomach hadn't protested. She'd switched to coffee after her second glass of wine, since it seemed to be going right to her head. And she couldn't bring herself to eat another bite of nachos. She was already regretting her heavy-on-the-jalapeños request.

Outside, the night air had cooled considerably from the afternoon high temperature of nearly ninety degrees, but with the heat still radiating from the sidewalk, the change was negligible, especially since Mallory was with Logan and even the casual way he clasped her hand in his had her feeling feverish.

"You said something about treating me to a meal," he reminded her as they made their way to his car.

"Yes, I did. What are you in the mood for?" she asked.

He stopped walking, turned and her question took on a whole new meaning.

"You."

Logan released her hand, but only so he could use both of his to frame her face. His hands were big. His palms warm even to her heated skin. Though she was probably being ridiculous, she thought she could feel the calluses he'd earned tending to his boat.

He'd kissed her before, done much more than that.

But each encounter had struck her as something new, unique. As she had before, she lost herself in his embrace, sucked under and in no hurry to resurface.

The kiss might have lasted seconds or it might have lasted several minutes. Mallory had no clue. Slowly she became aware of the traffic passing, of horns blasting in the distance and of snippets of the conversations from the people walking by them.

She was pressed up against Logan, her body flush with his, making her fully aware of his reaction to the contact. His breathing was heavy and ragged. The hands still bracketing her face trembled. Mallory wasn't one given to public displays. She couldn't seem to help herself around Logan.

"Food is the last thing on my mind after that," he murmured. "You?"

"Who needs to eat?"

He chuckled, but then turned serious. "I want you, Mallory."

"That was obvious," she replied. "I want you, too."

Suddenly, though, she wanted more than sex. Though they had been together for barely a handful of dates, she found herself yearning for a long-term, committed relationship. The kind she'd never had with a man. The kind she'd stopped believing in when her father had packed his bags and gone.

"Where is this heading?" The question slipped out before she could stop it.

Logan blinked. In the scant glow of the streetlights she watched his expression turn guarded.

"I'm not sure," he admitted after an excruciatingly long pause. "I like you a lot, Mallory. That much you should know by now. But if you're asking for promises…I don't know that I can make them."

Now or ever? Thankfully she managed to keep that question to herself. She lifted her shoulders in a negligent shrug.

"No need for promises, Logan. This is what it is." She forced herself to smile and added in a seductive whisper, "And I plan to enjoy every moment of it."

She'd hoped that would be the end of it, but now he was frowning. "What exactly *is* this?"

Words were her refuge and, at times, a trusted defense mechanism. They failed Mallory now, though, leaving her to babble incoherently before she finally managed to say, "I don't know, but we're good together."

"The sexual chemistry, you mean?"

"Yes. That's what I mean." Only it wasn't. Not completely. And she couldn't help wondering why that suddenly bothered her so much. "You probably studied stuff like that when you were getting your degree."

Logan massaged his forehead. Not that he could recall, and God knew he was trying to remember. He was a man of science, but some things defied academic explanation. His intense, over-the-top physical reaction to Mallory was one such thing.

He lifted one hand but stopped before his fingers made contact with her cheek. "That's got to be why I haven't been able to get you out of my head."

Her eyes widened and her lips curved. The traces of

vulnerability she'd tried to disguise with bravado vanished. "You haven't been able to get me out of your head?"

"Don't look so damned pleased," he muttered, even though she didn't look pleased. Rather, she appeared to be surprised. And hopeful? "I've never had this response to a woman before."

"Never?" It wasn't only her expression that held bafflement this time. Her tone was ripe with it.

Recalling the way she'd reacted before the charity event when he'd complimented her appearance, Logan gave in to the temptation to touch her and framed her face with his hands. "In addition to thinking you're gorgeous—and don't try to argue with me this time," he added when her mouth opened, presumably to do just that. "I find you incredibly sexy, Mallory."

She didn't argue. She didn't so much as blink, even when he leaned down and kissed her lightly on her lips. She studied him with dark, watchful eyes. The woman who had a well-earned reputation for being shrewd and intuitive only looked vulnerable now.

"Are we going to stand out here on the street all night or are you going to take me home and make love to me?"

Logan chuckled at her question. Okay, maybe she wasn't *completely* vulnerable.

"Let's go."

His car was half a block up the street. With a press of the key fob, the lights flashed and the doors unlocked. When they reached it, Logan opened Mallory's for her, as was his habit. As they drove, she was quiet.

"Is something wrong?" Logan asked.

"No. Not really." She smiled at him. "You're always opening doors for me, even my car door. You're a gentleman."

"My mother's doing."

"Then I like your mother."

His laughter rumbled low. "That makes two of us." He sobered. "You sound surprised, about me being a gentleman, I mean."

"I've never dated anyone quite like you."

"Why?"

His question had her shrugging. "I don't know. I just…haven't."

As Logan maneuvered the car through traffic, he commented, "You know, it's funny how a lot of people confuse basic courtesy with being condescending. I open your door as a sign of respect. I suppose you could do the same for me. Either way, it's not a gesture intended to display dominance."

"No."

He cast a glance sideways when they reached a red light. "You'd be pretty damned hard to dominate, anyway. You're too strong-willed for that and far too outspoken."

She smiled. "Is that how you see me?"

"More or less." Logan nodded. The light changed and he returned his attention to the road. It was a moment before he glanced sideways again and asked, "How do you see yourself?"

"I don't know." She fussed with her hands in her lap.

"But I've been called worse things than strong and out-spoken. In fact, I'd consider both as compliments."

"I'm glad. You should. But that's not an answer, Mallory. How do you see yourself?"

She laughed.

"I'm serious. I'd really like to know."

"Okay. I see myself as determined."

"Come on," he challenged. "You can do better than that."

"There's nothing wrong with determination," she returned, sounding slightly defensive.

"You're right. There's nothing wrong with it." God knew, determination was probably what had seen Mallory through her rough childhood and into a much brighter future. "But surely you can come up with more adjectives than that."

"I'm hardworking," she told him.

Logan blew out a breath, unimpressed. "That's just another label for the same thing. Is that the best you can do?"

"It's enough. It should be enough." Her voice rose.

He reached over for one of her hands. "I haven't known you very long, Mallory, and already I see so much more than that. You sell yourself short."

Even in the dimly lit car he could see her throat work. "Well, do tell."

He wasn't offended by her attempt at sarcasm. He squeezed the hand he still held in his. "No. It's for you to see. Not for me to tell you. It won't have the same impact then. And before you accuse me of analyzing you, how about we change the subject?"

"Okay." She blew out a breath, clearly trying to rally. Determined. Yes, she was definitely that. "So, what do you think of jazz?"

"I like it."

"You sound a little surprised."

"I am. Maybe it was the live performance tonight or the company." He flashed her a grin. "But I really enjoyed myself. I may have to go out and buy a jazz CD. Or you could lend me a couple of yours until I'm sure I like the genre?"

"Maybe," she allowed.

They reached her apartment building. Logan found a parking spot half a block past the front entrance and pulled the car to the curb. Switching off the ignition, he turned to her and asked, "So, are you still mad at me?"

"Mad? Why would I be mad?" But she crossed her arms over her chest. He thought he saw a flicker of challenge in her expression.

He played along. Nodding, he said, "You are, but you know, this could be a blessing in disguise."

Mallory's brow crinkled. "How do you figure that, Doc?"

"Everyone knows that make-up sex is the best kind." He waited a moment before bobbing his eyebrows.

Mallory didn't so much as smile.

"You look skeptical."

And a little amused. Her lips had begun to twitch

despite her effort to remain stoic. "I may need some convincing," she said.

Logan opened his car door and came around to her side. As he helped her out, he said, "Come on, then. Let's get started."

CHAPTER EIGHT

"So, who is he?" Vicki Storm asked.

Their drinks, tortilla chips and a bowl of salsa had just arrived at their table at Tia Lenore when Mallory's best friend and former college roommate asked the question. Vicki wasn't one to beat around the bush. It was one of the things Mallory liked about the other woman, but she didn't appreciate it tonight. For reasons she couldn't quite explain, she hadn't told her friend about Logan.

"Who is who?"

"The man who has kept you so busy that you've skipped not one but two of our margarita dates? And tonight doesn't really count as a margarita night, either." Her friend's nose wrinkled. "You're drinking plain old water."

"I didn't feel like tequila tonight." The truth was, salsa was low on her list, too. She'd been battling a bad case of indigestion for the past week.

When silence ensued, Vicki followed up with an impatient, "Well?"

Vicki worked as an interior designer, decorating the palatial penthouses and estates of some of the area's wealthiest people. She was good at her profession. Downright gifted, in fact. But Mallory still thought the woman should have gone into journalism. She'd make one hell of a reporter. Or a formidable interrogator with the Chicago police department.

"His name is Logan, okay?"

"Does he have a last name or is this some sort of kinky Internet thing?"

The moment of truth had arrived. "It's Bartholomew."

"Logan Bartholomew." Her friend's eyes widened then. "As in the hunky radio doctor?"

"That's the one." Mallory couldn't help the smug smile that accompanied her words.

"There's an ad promoting his show at my El stop. Is he as gorgeous in person or was he Photoshopped to male perfection?"

"He's that good-looking." It came out a near sigh.

Vicki whistled between her teeth. "Well, no wonder you've fallen off the radar. When did this happen? How? Where? Why? Etcetera. And don't even think about skimping on the details," her friend warned, taking a chip from the basket in the center of their table to dip in the salsa.

"We've been seeing each other for about six weeks," Mallory began, using her index finger to follow the path of a bead of condensation on the outside of her glass of ice water.

"Uh-oh."

She glanced up sharply. "What?"

"It's serious, isn't it?"

"We're just dating." Mallory attempted a shrug.

Vicki appeared unconvinced. "So, tell me about this famous hunk you're *just* dating."

No doubt her friend was regretting her offer when, half an hour later, Mallory ended her monologue. She hadn't been able to help herself. Nor had she been able to prevent smiling.

It was no surprise when Vicki plunked back in her seat on an oath. "I think I need another drink. I've never heard you go on about a guy the way you do this one."

Mallory folded her arms. "Gee, sorry if I've bored you."

"You know you haven't. Sadly, given the state of my love life lately, listening to yours is more exciting." Her friend sighed again.

"What about that accountant, John?"

"Jerry. And it turns out he's married."

"Sorry, Vicki. Want to talk about it?"

"Thanks, but we'll save my man troubles for another girls' night out. Back to my point. You dated Vince for what, three years?"

"Technically, three and a half," Mallory said, forgoing the salsa to munch on a plain tortilla chip.

"Yet whenever we got together for margaritas and girl talk his name rarely came up in conversation," Vicki pointed out.

"Vince was a jerk," Mallory said succinctly.

"I'm glad you realize that."

"What was to realize? He cheated on me." Four words that said it all but barely scraped the surface of the pain Mallory had experienced when she'd dropped by his apartment unexpectedly one Saturday and had come face-to-face with the half-naked proof of his betrayal.

"Yes, but he was a jerk even before he stepped out," Vicki said. "He was a real pro at putting himself first and you last and getting you to think it was your idea."

If it were anyone but Vicki saying this, Mallory would have felt ashamed. Since it was Vicki, she pulled a face. "I hate it when you're right."

"And I love it that you've finally met a great guy, one who opens car doors for you and takes you to places that he knows will be of interest to you."

"Logan is great. The more time I spend with him…" She shrugged, smiled.

"You're hooked."

Her friend's smug pronouncement had Mallory straightening in her seat. *Hooked* was just another name for a really big emotion. "Oh, no. No, no, no." She shook her head. "I'm not hooked."

Vicki blinked. "What?"

"I can't be hooked."

Her friend's eyes narrowed and her tone took on an edge. "But you said you'd already decided Logan wasn't a potential story."

"I have." Indeed, Mallory had given up on that idea while lying in bed with a telephone receiver tucked under her ear, listening to him talk and giving voice to some of her private demons. "I'll find another way to free myself from pabulum-writing hell."

Then she frowned. Odd, but for weeks now her career had stopped being the center of her existence. She'd been too focused on Logan. Not the man, but the relationship that was developing between them. For her at least, it was moving well beyond the sex.

Sex…for weeks…without interruption from—

Another thought niggled as she contemplated that time frame, and nausea rose up to taunt her. Mallory pressed a hand to one temple. The room seemed to spin. She wished she could blame it on tequila, but she'd sipped nothing stronger than water. And thank God for that, given what she was thinking right now.

"Oh, no," she moaned, and slumped back in her seat.

Vicki's eyes widened. "Mal, you okay? You're as pale as a ghost."

Mallory shook her head. "I'm not okay."

"Are you going to be sick?" Vicki glanced around in a panic for their waitress. "I'll get the check and meet you outside."

"No, no." She waved off the suggestion, though a little fresh air wouldn't have hurt. "I'm not sick, Vicki. I'm… I'm…"

Her friend leaned forward. "You're what, hon?"

Pregnant? In love?

She couldn't bring herself to say either aloud. Instead she murmured, "I think I may be heading toward hooked."

* * *

Later that evening, alone in her apartment, she read the display on the early test kit she'd purchased on the way home. She was indeed going to have a baby. Logan's baby.

Slumping down on the closed lid of the toilet, she let out a long breath. She was scared to death and excited beyond measure.

She'd been physically attracted to Logan from the very start, but she'd suspected for a while now that so much more was at stake. Maybe that was why she hadn't told Vicki or anyone else about the relationship. She hadn't been ready to face what was happening.

Her heart was on the line, the same heart the other men in her life—the really important ones—had made a bad habit of breaking.

Now even more was on the line than that.

How was Logan going to feel when she told him he was going to be a father?

Logan whistled as he wrapped up his work at the radio station for the day. His Doctor-in-the-Know program had ended an hour ago and on a professional high note. For once he'd felt as if he really was doing some good. A caller had complained about her elderly mother's recent odd behavior. Sadly, it sounded like the early signs of dementia, although it could have been a drug interaction or even a vitamin deficiency. Off-air, he'd stayed on the line with her, suggesting a list of questions the woman should ask her mother's doctor.

Perhaps reaching out to people who felt they had

nowhere else to turn for advice was every bit as important as serving clients in a private practice. Perhaps even more so.

All he had to do before leaving for the weekend was finish some paperwork and catch up on correspondence from fans. Logan made a point of clearing his e-mail at the end of each week and selecting a few from listeners who'd been unable to contact him on-air, which he then discussed in his Monday morning "mailbag" segment.

As he sifted through the e-mails, though, his mind was on Mallory. They had plans for the evening. There was nothing especially new in that. They'd spent time together almost every day, meeting for lunch, going out for dinner, taking evening sails on *Tangled Sheets*.

He couldn't seem to get enough of her. He didn't want to. The more time he spent with the woman, the more time he wanted to spend with her. She was one of the most fascinating people he'd ever met. So many damned layers. And he was enjoying peeling back each one to see what was revealed.

His interest was not that of a psychiatrist, though his training made it easier to understand why she could be so confident in some aspects of her life and so utterly vulnerable in others. If he ever met her father—not that it looked like there was much chance of that—Logan was more likely to sock the guy in the jaw than to shake his hand. That was saying a lot, since generally he frowned on violence and considered it a poor substitute for civilized discourse. But give him ten minutes alone with Mitchell Stevens and Logan would put his fists to good use.

Divorce or no divorce, what kind of man walked away from his children and failed to provide for them, not only financially but emotionally? Perhaps because of his own loving upbringing, Logan found it inconceivable and unforgivable. He ached for Mallory and detested the harm such an elemental rejection had done to her psyche. But his interest in her was not that of a doctor or counselor. His interest in Mallory was purely that of a man…a man who was having a damned hard time keeping his hands to himself.

The only stumbling block to total peace of mind was that he didn't quite trust her. Not completely and without reservation. He needed to believe that Mallory's only reason for seeing him was personal. He almost did.

Almost.

His hesitation had less to do with her reputation—which his agent called to remind him of daily—than it did with his past. Nearly a decade after Felicia's bombshell that she'd found someone else and was leaving, his heart finally had healed. It was perfectly whole now, every last fissure mended. Not surprisingly, he wanted to keep it that way. But relationships—the serious and long-term variety, at least—required one to take a risk. Logan wasn't sure he was ready to do so, even if that was exactly what he regularly advised some of his lovelorn callers to do.

Case in point, Emily in Elmhurst, whose e-mail was on his computer screen at the moment.

Dear Doctor,

I've been dating my current boyfriend for nearly a year. I would classify our relationship as serious, though he hasn't mentioned marriage. We are both in our thirties and we both have suffered bad breakups in the past. My concern is this: I have yet to meet his family. They live nearby and he sees them regularly, but I have never been invited along. Could he be trying to tell me something?

"Confront him about the matter, but without hostility. Discuss the situation calmly," Logan wrote. "Your boyfriend may not think the relationship as serious as you do, or it may be something else entirely at the crux of his hesitation. Something such as…"

He frowned at the computer screen as his own experience juxtaposed with that of Emily's beau. He understood the man's hesitation. He understood it perfectly.

Logan hadn't brought a woman around his family since his breakup with Felicia. They had accepted his ex-fiancée, loved her and when she betrayed him, they had felt betrayed, as well. So, just as he'd guarded his own heart these past years, he was careful with theirs.

He was contemplating the wording of his advice to Emily—advice he wasn't sure he would be ready to heed—when his cell phone trilled. It was his brother.

"Finally," Luke groused upon hearing Logan's greeting. "You've been a hard man to reach lately. If it weren't for hearing your voice on the radio, I might think something bad had happened to you."

"Sorry. I got your messages." Luke had left three in the past week. None had seemed urgent, or Logan would have returned them immediately. "I was going to call you today."

"I've tried you day and night. Where have you been?"

"Out."

Logan's monosyllabic response earned laughter from the other end of the line. "No kidding." Luke sobered somewhat when he asked, "Is everything okay?"

"Better than okay, actually."

"Hmm." More laughter followed. "So, what does she look like?"

"Funny," Logan evaded. "Is there a point to this call?"

"Beyond my being concerned about my big brother's welfare, you mean?" Barely fifteen months separated them in age. When they were boys, they'd fought unmercifully. As men, they had become the best of friends.

"Yeah. Beyond that," he said dryly.

"Fine. I need your taste buds. Even though you'll never be able to hold a candle to me in the kitchen, I trust your judgment."

"Gee, thanks." Logan leaned back in his chair and doodled on the edge of the desk blotter with his pen. "For what exactly?"

"I want to expand the Grill's menu," Luke replied, referring to his restaurant. "We offer a terrific selection at lunchtime. The diverse crowd we pull in reflects that.

But traffic falls off significantly in the evening. The same patrons who faithfully come in at noon for our sandwiches, soups and salads, forget all about us when the sun sets."

"Is business bad?" Logan asked. The economy being what it was, a lot of establishments that relied on people's disposable incomes were foundering. If Luke needed cash to see him through to better times, Logan would offer it. No questions asked, no strings attached. They were family.

"I wouldn't classify it as bad," Luke hedged. "We do well enough thanks to eat-in and takeout lunch orders, but I'd be able to make a couple of my servers full-time if we brought in a better dinner crowd."

Logan set his pen aside and rubbed his chin. "So, what kind of dishes are you considering?"

"Nothing five-star."

"You're too casual an establishment for that," Logan agreed, thinking of the Grill's comfortable interior. It boasted no linen tablecloths, chandeliers or fancy flatware, but with its framed vintage posters and brightly colored stoneware plates it was hardly on a par with a fast-food stop.

"Exactly. I have a few pasta dishes that I think would enjoy broad appeal, and I'm toying with the idea of a catch-of-the-day fish special to play off our proximity to the lake."

"That sounds like a good idea. What about chicken or beef?"

"I put smothered chicken on the dinner special board

last week and it did pretty well. Beef?" Luke blew out a breath. "Other than my burgers I'm undecided."

"I've got a couple ideas."

"That's what I was hoping. So, do you think you could sample a few recipes and give me some advice?" Luke asked.

"Sure. Glad to. Just say when and where."

"Tonight at the restaurant. Say around eight. The dinner rush will be done by then."

"Tonight?" Logan's heart sank. He and Mallory had reservations at an exclusive, celebrity chef–owned restaurant. It had taken nearly two weeks to secure them. "I already have plans."

"That's all right," Luke said. No disappointment was audible in his brother's voice.

"I'm glad you understand."

"Oh, sure. No problem. I don't mind if you bring her along. Just make sure she's hungry."

"Luke," Logan began, but he was already talking to a dial tone.

Mallory opened her apartment door that evening wearing a strapless black dress. The satin ribbon spanning her waist made her look like a present—one Logan was eager to unwrap.

After sucking in a breath, he said, "Look at you."

"And look at *you*." Her gaze meandered down. Logan had forgotten all about the jeans and T-shirt he'd thrown on. "It would appear one of us didn't get the memo. The last I heard formal attire was required at Romeo's."

"It is." He winced. "There's been a change in plans. I should have called, but…" He let the words trail off.

Her gaze skittered just to the left of his shoulder. "You're canceling our date," she guessed.

That had been his plan, and he could still do it. Mallory was giving him the out, already expecting him to disappoint her. Had he really thought their trust issues were all one-sided?

"Not exactly."

The line appeared between her eyes as she continued to study the wall. She looked a little pale, he thought. And the vulnerability she tried to hide made an appearance. "What does that mean?"

"I promised my brother I'd come by his restaurant tonight. He's thinking about adding a few new items to his dinner menu and he wants my input." He swallowed hard. Once the invitation was tendered, there would be no going back. Is that what he wanted, for her to meet a member of his family? He answered the question by asking one of her. "Will you come with me?"

Mallory's gaze veered back to his. "Are you sure? I'll understand if you want to go alone."

She would, too. She would understand his defection, because she was so damned used to it. Logan forgot about guarding his own heart. It was hers that required protection.

"Come with me tonight, Mallory." He reached for her hand. "Please. I want you there."

The smile that bloomed on her face was almost his undoing. "Okay. Just let me change my clothes."

CHAPTER NINE

THE Berkley Grill was in a prime location just blocks from Navy Pier. Logan managed to find a parking spot on the street just up from the restaurant. As he escorted Mallory to the door, his nerves jangled. He was anxious about introducing her to his brother. Luke would like her and vice versa, but he hoped neither would read too much into tonight.

One step inside the bustling restaurant and Logan knew his brother had. The Grill was sparse on square footage, sporting no more than twenty tables and half a dozen booths that lined the walls. Almost every seat was filled with diners, including the one just outside the kitchen doors. At it sat his mother, father and sister, Laurel.

God help him. God help him and Mallory both.

He might have been tempted to grab her hand and head back through the door, but his mom was already rising to her feet and waving her arms.

"Logan, over here." Her voice could be heard over the din of conversation and background music.

Mallory glanced at him in question. "It looks like my folks came tonight, too." He had to clear his throat before he could add, "And my sister."

"Apparently your brother wants them to sample some recipes, too."

But her tight smile said she knew better. The Bartholomew clan had gathered to form and offer opinions, but none of them had to do with the Grill's new menu plans.

"If you'd rather not stay, I'll understand," Logan began. "We can stop somewhere else for dinner."

"I have no problem meeting your parents." The line reappeared between her brows then. "But maybe that's not what you mean. Maybe you don't want them to meet me."

"Generally speaking, I don't bring my dates around my family," he admitted, and watched the line deepen into a groove.

"Okay." She started to back toward the door, but he grabbed her hand, tugged her to his side.

"You didn't let me finish. I said, generally speaking I don't introduce the women I date to my family, but I want them to meet you, Mallory."

He watched her swallow. "You do?"

It scared him a bit that he meant it when he replied, "Yes."

The groove disappeared and a smile lit up her eyes. She looked so beautiful just then it was all he could do not to pull her into his arms and kiss her. "I want to meet them, too."

"Good." He squeezed her hand, grinned. "Later, when they're still picking over your bones, remember that I offered you a way out."

"I don't mind questions. I'm a reporter."

"Take notes, then. My mother will make you look like an amateur."

Mallory walked hand in hand with Logan through the restaurant. Outwardly, she knew she looked composed. Inside, she was a quivering bundle of nerves. Logan's family. Was she ready for this? She could only imagine what they were going to think of her.

She swallowed and recalled the photograph of Logan and Felicia. Even in grainy black-and-white the other woman's classical beauty had been undeniable. And her background had been much more in line with the Bartholomews' social standing. Logan insisted that he found Mallory gorgeous, a fact that went a long way toward buoying her confidence now, but she knew she was a diamond in the rough compared to Felicia's highly polished gem. What's more, even though logically she knew no one could tell she was pregnant, Mallory still felt like she had a flashing neon sign on her forehead that read: Expecting.

Mallory had been in the Berkley Grill before, though never in the evening. It was crowded with customers—families, couples, friends out for a quick bite, tourists pouring over El train maps. The only people she was paying attention to were not so subtly sizing her up, as well.

When they reached the table, Logan pressed a kiss

to his mother's cheek, shook his father's hand and sent a wink in his sister's direction.

"Hey, everyone, I have someone I'd like you to meet." His hand was on Mallory's lower back, the pressure firm and reassuring. "This is Mallory Stevens. Mallory, these are my parents, Douglas and Melinda Bartholomew, and my kid sister, Laurel."

"Kid." Laurel sniffed. "I'm thirty-two. As Mom likes to point out, my biological clock is ticking like a time bomb with each passing day."

Logan shrugged. "Until you graduate from college with an actual degree, move out of Mom and Dad's house, and get a paying job, I'll consider you a kid."

"It's nice to meet you, Mallory." The young woman shook her hand before tagging on, "Even if I do question your taste in men."

"Laurel," their mother said evenly before turning her gaze on Mallory. Though the woman's smile was benign Mallory still felt as if she'd just wound up in a sniper's crosshairs. And for good reason, she decided, when Melinda said, "We didn't realize our son was seeing anyone until his brother called us this afternoon and mentioned that Logan and his girlfriend were coming by the restaurant."

Girlfriend. The moniker popped around in Mallory's head with the surprising effervescence of champagne bubbles. She wanted to turn and try to gauge Logan's reaction. Perhaps it would offer a key to how he was going to feel when she told him about the baby. But she didn't dare. Not with this attentive audience.

"She's not going to want to see me again if you guys don't stop interrogating her," he groused good-naturedly.

"We're not interrogating her. Yet," his father added in a comically ominous tone. Douglas patted the empty chair next to his. "Have a seat next to me, Mallory."

"I tried to warn you," she heard Logan mumble before he sat in a chair between his mother and sister.

Mallory found his family…interesting.

Half an hour in their company and she still couldn't quite figure them out. Usually she was good at sizing people up, but like Logan, the rest of the Bartholomew clan didn't fit into any of her preconceived notions. For instance, they were wealthy, but they didn't flaunt their status. Passing them on the street one wouldn't guess they ranked among the country's richest families.

Melinda's fingers sported only two rings, a tasteful gold wedding band on her left hand and what Mallory assumed to be a mother's ring, given its trio of birthstone gems, on the right one. Melinda was a lovely woman, but not an overly vain one. Her dark hair was streaked with silver in the front and the fine lines around her eyes crinkled into deeper creases when she smiled or laughed. No Botox for her.

Douglas's hair was a mix of dark blond and gray. It had a natural curl like his son's, though he wore it shorter and tamer. His build wasn't as athletic as Logan's, but he was hardly out of shape. Indeed, even though he had to be in his late sixties he could turn female heads. But it was clear, touchingly so, that he only had eyes for Melinda, his wife of forty years.

Like his father and older brother, Luke was a head turner. He stood taller than Logan and had a stockier build. His smile was easy and engaging. He'd popped out of the kitchen not long after their arrival and apologized for keeping them all waiting. The crowd was heavier than he'd anticipated and they were short a waitress. It would be a while yet before he could join them. He'd brought out more wine and a tray of appetizers. Mallory wondered if Logan noticed she hadn't touched the glass he'd poured for her earlier. Before returning to the kitchen, Luke had grinned at Mallory and bobbed his eyebrows in Logan's direction.

As for Laurel, she was a bit of a wild card. She had inherited her mother's dark hair and cheekbones, her father's long limbs and height, but none of their tact. She eyed Mallory with outright curiosity and just enough skepticism to make Mallory choose her words carefully whenever she spoke.

Even so, she was enjoying herself. Logan's family helped to explain a lot about him—his easy smile, for instance, and self-confident nature. Both came from a lifetime of his parents' love and support. Since he was a psychiatrist, she figured he understood the effect those things had on a person, but she wondered if he was as grateful for his good fortune as she found herself envious of it. Even now, her mother's love remained tainted by the bitterness of having to raise her daughter alone. As for support, Mallory's happiness and self-fulfillment came a distant second to her mother's desire to ensure her daughter was independent and self-sufficient.

"So, what do you do for a living?" Melinda asked. "Do you work at the radio station, too?"

"No. I'm a reporter with the *Herald*."

"A reporter." Douglas's eyebrows rose and he whistled through his teeth.

"At the *Herald*, you said?" This from Laurel. Something in her eyes put Mallory on guard.

"That's right," she said slowly.

"You cover city hall," his sister said.

"I did."

"She works in the Lifestyles section now," Logan inserted. "That's actually how we met. Mallory interviewed me for an advance on a speech I was giving."

"News reporting seems like such an exciting career," Melinda said. "I'd imagine you've met a lot of interesting people through your work."

"I have," she agreed.

"Me, for instance," Logan added, inducing a round of laughter that helped dilute Mallory's edginess.

It was back at full strength when Laurel said, "It seems an odd change of pace for someone to go from covering city politics to writing up lightweight feature stories."

"Laurel." Melinda's tone was disapproving. "You're being rude."

The younger woman shrugged. "I'm not trying to be. I just find it strange." Her gaze connected with Mallory's. "What prompted you to ask to be reassigned? If you don't mind my asking, that is," she added, presumably to appease her mother, who was glaring daggers at her. As for Logan, he looked as though he could have cheerfully wrung his sister's neck.

Mallory didn't care to be put in the hot seat, though she admired Laurel's go-for-the-throat technique. Bluntness was best met with honesty. Evasiveness would only raise more questions.

"Features, as you rightly note, are not my forte." She glanced at Logan then. "Although I have to admit that writing some of them has proven to be unexpectedly rewarding."

He smiled and that gave her courage. "The truth is I didn't ask to be reassigned from my city hall beat. I was removed from it. I screwed up." Admitting so in front of Logan wasn't as embarrassing as Mallory had thought it would be, perhaps because her job was no longer the epicenter of her life.

"There was a lawsuit," Laurel murmured, though her tone said she couldn't put a finger on the details.

Mallory decided to offer them now. "Yes. A big one that cost the newspaper a bundle in an out-of-court settlement. And it was my fault. I received information about suspected corruption from someone I considered a reliable source. I ran with it, even though I should have cross-checked the facts with other sources. I even used a quote from the mayor that came secondhand through one of his aides."

She'd been so eager to be the first to break the news, especially when her source claimed that reporters from other news agencies were sniffing around. She'd been a fool to believe him and then hung out to dry when he claimed under oath during a deposition that he'd never said the things Mallory claimed.

She had no tape recordings of their conversation, only hastily scribbled notes. It was her word against his, and though her editor would have supported her on that score, the lack of other sources and her insistence that they rush to print had sealed her fate.

"I let ambition cloud my judgment," she finished.

"That happens to us all from time to time," Douglas allowed with a sympathetic nod.

Melinda was more direct. "You've obviously paid for your mistake."

Mallory laughed without humor. "My editor doesn't see it that way yet. But then, I guess I can't really blame him since he got taken out to the woodshed along with me."

Barry Daniels had been allowed to keep his editorship, but per the terms of the settlement, the *Herald* was required to print a front-page apology and retraction. It didn't get much worse than that for a journalist.

"He must not be too angry with you. You still have a job," Laurel pointed out. The look on the young woman's face said she regretted opening this particular can of worms.

Oddly, Mallory was almost glad Laurel had. She glanced at Logan. In addition to telling him about the baby, there were other things that needed to be said, confessions to be made. Now was neither the time nor the place, but she felt compelled to admit, "I've been trying to get back into his good graces, remind him of my abilities by producing a killer story, but it's hard to come up with anything worthy of page one when my assignments aren't even as meaty as the stuff I wrote as a freshman for my college newspaper."

"I don't know. I seem to recall a riveting piece you penned on that speech I gave last month," he teased.

His mother smiled indulgently. "I clipped it out of the paper after reading it."

"Yeah, and it's still on the refrigerator," Laurel inserted with a roll of her eyes.

"So is the letter announcing that you made the dean's list last semester," Melinda reminded her. "As well as the starred review a food critic did of Luke's portabella mushroom burger." To Mallory she confided, "I don't believe in playing favorites. I'm proud of all of them."

Of course she was. They might be adults, but each was successful in his or her own way. And each could count on Melinda and Douglas's unending support. Lucky, Mallory thought again. So damned lucky. Her last call with her mother had been punctuated with nagging and complaining.

"You should write more stories about Logan," Laurel said. "People, and by people I mean women, love to read about him. He *is* the city's sexiest bachelor or some such nonsense."

Mallory's gaze connected with his across the table. He was smiling. The mood around the table was no longer tense. But she hoped he understood that she meant it when she said, "I'm going to leave stories about your brother to someone else to write."

* * *

It was just after midnight when Mallory and Logan left the Berkley Grill. Technically the restaurant closed at eleven, but even after the customers had gone and the wait staff had called it a night, the Bartholomews had stayed, sipping wine and coffee and sampling food. Mallory had stuck with water and avoided anything too spicy.

She was impressed with the fare and utterly awed by the affection she'd witnessed. With her deadbeat dad and bitter mom, she'd forgotten families could be like this: warm and close. Would her baby be so lucky?

"Your folks are really great," she told Logan as they walked hand in hand to his car. "And the rest of your family."

"You'll get no arguments from me. I even like my kid sister most of the time."

"Come on, you love her."

He shrugged. "That goes without saying. We're family."

"No, it doesn't go without saying," Mallory objected, thinking of her father. "Love isn't automatic just because you're related to someone."

"You're right. It's not."

"Half a dozen times tonight, I found myself thinking how lucky you are. I hope you know it."

"I do. I'm sorry about your dad, Mallory. Sorry not only for what he missed when you were young, but what he's missing out on now." They had arrived at his car and now stood at the passenger door. Instead of reaching for the handle, Logan reached for her. "You're an amazing woman," he whispered into her hair.

If she hadn't already known she was in love with him, she would have figured it out then and there. She still wasn't sure what to do about her emotions or where their relationship was heading, but she knew one thing for certain. She and Logan needed to talk.

CHAPTER TEN

LOGAN sat pitched forward on Mallory's couch, his right foot tapping on the polished hardwood floor as he waited for her to return from the kitchen, where she was getting them both a beverage.

Something was up.

He'd gotten that feeling on and off all evening. He might have attributed it to meeting his family or the awkwardness of his sister's questioning, but Mallory had been acting odd even before they arrived at the restaurant. And then on the way home she'd uttered the words that no man wanted to hear: "There's something I need to tell you."

He'd narrowed her bombshell—and he didn't doubt what she was gearing up to tell him was going to rock him back on his heels—to one of two things. She was either preparing to tell him she didn't want to see him anymore or she was going to tell him she was falling in love with him.

Logically, neither was a stretch. She'd met his entire family tonight. Things were getting serious between the two of them, which might just scare Mallory enough to make her cut and run. Or it might just give her the courage to declare the depth of her feelings for him.

Either possibility had his mouth going dry.

Logan didn't want to lose Mallory. He might not be ready for what was happening between them, but he wasn't a fool. These past couple of months with her had been nothing short of incredible. She had reawakened in him feelings he'd denied for a long time. But love? It was a big word that tended to lead to an even bigger commitment, one he wasn't sure he ever wanted to make again.

"Here's your wine," she said, smiling nervously when she returned. He noticed that she'd stuck with water. Keeping a clear head?

She handed him his glass and set hers on the end table. Before sitting next to him on the couch, she slipped off her shoes and tucked her bare feet up under herself. Even so she looked anything but relaxed.

He sipped his wine and waited. It was a moment before she broke the silence. When she did, it was with the benign comment: "I really enjoyed myself tonight."

"Good. I'm glad. I did, too."

"Do you get guys together often? As a family, I mean?"

Even as he wondered where the conversation was heading, he nodded. "Not as often as my mom would like since we're pretty busy these days. But we aim for Sunday dinner at my folks' house at least once a month."

"Who does the cooking?" She cocked her head to one

side and her expression verged on wistful. It was a sight to behold considering mere weeks ago *jaded* was an adjective his agent had used to describe Mallory.

"My mom, although she puts us all to work in the kitchen when she needs help."

"Even your dad?"

"Especially my dad." He laughed.

"That's nice." She smiled and reached for her water. "I have a confession to make." Uh-oh. Here we go. "I thought that since your folks are well-to-do they would have live-in help."

Okay, that wasn't exactly the confession Logan was expecting Mallory to make. He relaxed a little. Thinking about his family tended to have that effect. "When I was a kid we had a housekeeper who came in once a week, but generally speaking my mom prefers to do the cooking and what she calls 'homemaking.'" This time his smile was wistful. "My mom is proof there's a real art to keeping a nice and well-ordered home, raising children and arranging schedules to maximize together time."

"Did she ever work outside the home?"

He nodded. "She still does, after she retired from an accounting job she started volunteering at the Clearwater Project."

"I've heard of that. It promotes environmental responsibility, right?"

"Yes. My mom's new favorite color is green." Because their conversation was taking on the characteristics of an interview, he decided to ask some questions of his own. "What about your mom? What does she do?"

Mallory's expression was no longer wistful. "Well, she was the quintessential stay-at-home mother before the divorce. She used to bake cakes from scratch. She was a regular Martha Stewart but without the entrepreneurial flair. She was pretty meticulous about the house being clean, things being orderly.

"I used to think that was why my dad worked late so often. He didn't want to be nagged about where he'd taken off his shoes or how he'd forgotten to hang up his clothes." She shook her head and he wondered if she knew how sad she looked when she added, "It turned out he was spending his evenings with someone who didn't care in the least that he left his clothes on the bedroom floor."

"Sorry." He'd said that already once tonight in reference to her father.

She shook her head now. "I understand why my dad stepped out. It was wrong and I'm not making any excuses for his behavior, but I understand. What I don't understand is that my mom knew and she put up with it. Ultimately, he was the one who had to file for divorce."

"It sounds like financially it made sense for her to stay in the relationship, even though it wasn't a good one."

"I know, but—" Mallory shrugged "—my last boyfriend cheated on me. It was over as soon as I found out. I didn't wait for explanations. I didn't want any."

"Actions speak louder than words," he agreed.

"I know about your fiancée."

Logan hadn't seen that coming. Was this what she wanted to talk about? His tone cautious, he asked, "What do you know?"

"That the two of you were engaged to be married a decade ago, and a fall wedding was planned. Felicia married someone else, though."

"Did my mom tell you that the one time I excused myself to go to the men's room?"

Mallory's expression turned sheepish. "No. I did some digging on my own. It was just after you'd invited me onboard your sailboat the first time."

Mere weeks ago and yet it seemed an eternity.

"I see," he said evenly, though his blood pressure began to rise and his heart to sink.

"No, I don't think you do."

"You wanted a story." This time his tone wasn't even. It was crisp with anger—directed at her, but mostly at himself. How many times had his agent warned him that's what Mallory was after? Yet he'd trod boldly ahead. At first he'd claimed he knew what he was doing: keeping enemies closer than friends and all that baloney. Then, as things between Mallory and him had shifted, deepened, he'd insisted to himself that she wouldn't use him, she wouldn't betray him.

Well, he was paying for his hubris now. He sighed inwardly, felt the knife of disappointment pierce him. Had he really thought he could separate the woman from her profession? Especially knowing how important her job was to her.

He didn't really care that his broken engagement could become public knowledge. Let all of Chicago read about it and snicker over how he'd been played for a fool. What bothered him now was the fact that Mallory had dated him, slept with him, claimed the things he told her were off the record when apparently she'd considered him a story all along.

"Logan—"

He swore richly, cutting off her words. "Is that the best you could do?" he demanded. "You mentioned tonight that you're trying to get out of the doghouse at the newspaper. I doubt this is the type of story that is going to help you much. My ex-fiancée tossed me over for another guy." He shrugged, even though at one point that fact had all but lanced his soul. "I'm hardly the first man to suffer a broken heart."

"I'm sorry."

Logan finished off his wine and set the glass aside before rising to his feet. "What did you do to find that out? Run my name through a data base or something?"

"Nothing that high-tech. I just had to weed through some old newspaper clippings."

He stuffed his hands in his trouser pockets, concealing clenched fists. His tone was mild when he said, "That sounds time consuming."

"It took a few days."

"What made you look in the first place?"

Mallory shrugged. "I don't know. You just seemed, well, too perfect to be single."

"That's an interesting comment."

"Interesting or not, it's true."

"So you couldn't resist," he replied.

"I—"

"Don't get me wrong. What man doesn't want to be irresistible? It's just I'd prefer to be considered such for different reasons. But then you are a *reporter*." He spat out the word. "So…what? You put two and two together when you didn't find a wedding announcement?"

"Yes." Mallory cleared her throat and clarified, "Well, not for you."

"Ah." Turning away, he pulled his hands from his pockets and shoved the hair back from his forehead. He'd never felt this angry or this exposed. His voice was deceptively calm when he said, "You found the announcement for Felicia and what's his name?"

"I'm sorry," she murmured again.

Logan wasn't sure if Mallory was apologizing for snooping into his past or for the heartache he'd experienced at the hands of his ex—a heartache that felt minor in comparison to what he was feeling right now. He couldn't believe that once again he'd fallen for a beautiful woman's lies.

He was older now, wiser. Or so he'd thought. In addition to feeling betrayed, he felt like an absolute idiot. Usually he was insightful, astute. He was a trained professional with a degree that had taken him years to earn. It didn't sit well to learn that he had a blind spot a mile wide where Mallory was concerned.

When she'd told him they needed to talk, Logan hadn't seen this particular revelation coming. He'd worried over endings or possible new beginnings when apparently all she'd wanted was a damned interview.

Well, he'd give her one.

"So, what now?" It took an effort to keep all of the bitterness from leaching into his tone. "What else do you need to know to turn this rather mundane piece you're working on into something juicy?"

"It's not a story."

"Not yet it isn't," he agreed calmly. "You've got to throw in the stuff about me questioning my current career path, and the information about my television show contract will spice things up, too."

"Both of those things were said off the record," she replied, looking bewildered.

"We didn't agree to that till the revelations had been made. I'm sure that's some sort of loophole in your favor."

"Logan—"

He glanced away, determined not to be swayed. "Do you need a quote from me?"

"No. No!" she shouted and rose to her feet. He gave her points for looking both sincere and outraged. "I'm not asking for a damned quote, Logan."

Far from feeling relieved when she shared this news, he braced for the worst. "Is that because you already have one? Have you been in touch with my agent?"

Nina was going to read him the riot act if Mallory had called her.

"No."

"Felicia or her family then?" That possibility had his gut clenching.

"I haven't spoken to Felicia."

"Well, sorry, but I can't help you there. She left town not long after she married and she never gave me a forwarding address. I have no idea where she lives these days, and I haven't been in touch with her family to ask." He raised his brows and waited a beat before adding, "For obvious reasons."

"Actually, I know where Felicia is."

Mallory's bold pronouncement cut through his sarcasm with the force and effectiveness of a machete blade. Afterward, he felt laid bare.

"You…you know where…where Felicia…. Of course you do." He laughed humorlessly as he collected himself and then shook a finger in her direction. "Pit bull. Right. How could I forget?"

Mallory winced. Once upon a time she had relished that description. Hell, she'd gone out of her way to foster it. But she was ashamed of it now. Just as she was haunted by the way Logan was looking at her, even though a hundred other people whom she'd interviewed for stories for the newspaper during her career had looked at her in the exact same way: with utter contempt.

In the past she hadn't cared in the least. What did their opinions of her matter? Some of them—for that matter, most of them—were only getting exactly what they deserved. Their dirty little secrets deserved to be exposed and the public was better off for it. Right now, though, nothing—and certainly not a story—was as important as making Logan understand. He had to believe her. He had to trust her.

He had to *forgive* her. If he couldn't or wouldn't, how was she going to tell him about the baby?

"I know where Felicia is, but I haven't contacted her."

"Yet."

"Don't, Logan. I've finally decided to stop selling myself short. Don't you start now." When so much was at stake. "I have no intention of calling Felicia for a quote or anything else."

He said nothing, but the rigid set of his shoulders told Mallory that he didn't quite believe her. She reached out a hand to him, but he was too far away to touch…physically as well as emotionally. The heart she'd worked so hard to gird from breaking suffered its first fissures and began to ache.

She pressed ahead. "Weren't you listening tonight at the restaurant when I told you that I wouldn't be writing any stories where you're concerned? I meant it."

"Why?" he asked.

"I think you know."

"Spell it out, Mallory." His tone was barely above a whisper as he made the command. "Be clear."

"There are a few reasons. One is that doing so would be a conflict of interest."

His brow wrinkled as he studied her, and he crossed his arms over his chest. "A conflict of interest? How so?"

"Isn't it obvious?"

"I said to be clear," he reminded her, though neither his tone nor his stance was quite as rigid as it had been just a moment earlier.

"I… I…" It was a big word for an even bigger emotion. She took a tentative step in his direction, gathering her courage when he didn't back away. "I love you, Logan."

He didn't say anything at first, but he blinked a couple of times and swallowed. She was pretty sure she'd thrown him with that revelation, and even though she wanted to hear him say it in return—God, how she wanted that—it wasn't fair to put him on the spot.

"I'm not expecting you to say anything right now. I just…" She clasped and unclasped her hands. "I just wanted you to know."

"Anything else you want me to know?"

I'm having your baby.

But she decided to keep that information confidential. Sharing it now, with this other big issue unresolved between them, would only complicate matters. Mallory shook her head.

"When I asked you to come with me tonight, I can honestly say I didn't think the evening would end this way," he said after a moment.

"No." Was he saying goodbye? Neither his expression nor his body language gave his intent away.

"I'm sorry, Mallory."

It wasn't exactly what she'd hoped to hear. Arms crossed over her waist as if to protect the life growing inside her from rejection, she braced for his farewell.

"It's all right." The words cost her.

"No. It's not." He closed the distance between them, lifted her chin with his finger. "I'm sorry for doubting you, for jumping to conclusions. Forgive me?"

He was asking for contrition?

"I don't understand. I thought…I thought you were going to say that things between us are over."

"I may be a fool, but I'm not that big a fool."

"I should have told you about the information I'd found. I didn't mean for it to be a secret. It's just that I gathered it before anything had really taken place between us and, well, afterward, when I decided you were more important to me than any story…"

"Because you love me." He looked pleased now.

"Yes."

"Well, I have a scoop for you, and I don't care who knows it." His hands found her hips and pulled her close. Just before he kissed her, he said, "I love you, too."

CHAPTER ELEVEN

THE next few weeks passed in a wondrous haze. Mallory couldn't recall ever being so happy or feeling so complete, which was odd considering she was still writing intern-worthy fluff for the *Herald*'s Lifestyles section and having to put up with Sandra's snide comments whenever their paths crossed at work. Lately Sandra wasn't only snide, she seemed smug. Mallory dismissed it. Her colleague was the last person on her mind.

Indeed, work in general continued to take a back seat. She spent less time at the office, putting in the standard number of hours and no more, unless specifically asked by the features editor. Where a few months earlier she would have spent most of her waking hours breathing in newsprint and combing through wire service stories, she now spent her evenings with Logan at her home or on his sailboat or in his upscale condominium, where he was attempting to teach her the rudiments of cooking in his gorgeous gourmet kitchen. She was learning a great deal, not only about sautéing, basting and frying, but about herself. As she'd told him that night in her apartment, she'd stopped selling herself short.

Mallory liked who she was when she was with Logan. She felt no need to be perfect or to cloak herself in a mantle of toughness. As flawed as she was, he enjoyed spending time with her. He said he loved her. Even so, she still hadn't told him about the baby, whose existence had now been confirmed by her doctor.

Though she told herself not to be, she was a little scared. What would his reaction be? She had to believe he would be happy and supportive despite their circumstances. And surely he would be the polar opposite of her father in every way. A lifetime of hurt, however, was not easy to overcome. Besides, she had time. She was barely two months along. And everything between her and Logan was so new, so perfect. She wanted to give them both time to adjust to being a couple before introducing the fact that they were to become parents.

Mallory was bustling around her apartment rounding up a change of clothes and trying to remember what she'd done with the white chef's apron she'd bought, when the telephone rang. She assumed it was Logan since they were eating in at his condo tonight. He was going to teach her how to make an authentic Chinese stir-fry.

She grinned as she picked up the receiver. "Be patient, lover," she said on a laugh.

"Mallory? Is that you?" On top of the usual agitation in her mother's voice, Maude sounded perplexed.

Mallory sorely regretted not consulting the Caller ID readout. Not only was this conversation bound to be a downer, it was guaranteed to be long.

"Yeah, Mom. Sorry about the greeting. I thought you were someone else."

"That much I gathered," Maude said dryly and with a touch of censure.

"I'm…I'm just on my way out the door, Mom. I have someplace I need to be and I'm already running a little behind. Can I call you back later?"

"By later I assume you mean tomorrow." Not a touch of censure now, but a slap of it, and that was before Maude added, "I thought you'd sworn off men after the last one. What was his name?"

Mallory didn't bother to supply it. The past was irrelevant. "I've met someone special, Mom."

"Oh, no." It wasn't exactly what a woman wanted to hear from her mother in response to a statement like that. "You sound like you think you're in love."

"I don't think it." Mallory left it at that, already regretting mentioning her relationship with Logan. Thank God her mother was clueless about the baby.

"Don't fall into the same trap I did," Maude warned before launching into her old rant. "I wasted fourteen years of my life waiting on your father, making a home for him and putting his needs ahead of my own. You know what I had to show for it when he left me? Nothing."

You had me, Mallory wanted to say. You had a daughter who felt deserted by not one but two parents.

But she knew the futility of trying to rationalize or argue. Maude wanted sympathy and agreement. Mallory couldn't bring herself to offer either, so she substituted them with silence.

Her mother seemed not to notice. "You make a good living at the newspaper," she went on. "You have a career, money, a purpose, all of the things I should have had and would have had in my twenties if I hadn't let your father talk me into marriage and letting him provide for me. I thought I was in love back then, too."

Again Mallory had to bite her tongue, since if her parents had never met she wouldn't have been born. Her mother's bitterness had blinded her to how insulting and hurtful her comments could be.

"You have a good life, Mallory. I'll be very disappointed in you if you let some man ruin it," Maude finished.

This wasn't a new tack her mother took. She'd been saying much the same thing since Mallory's first date at age fifteen. For the first time, though, instead of rolling her eyes and letting it pass without remark, Mallory got angry. Angry enough to break her cardinal rule and argue.

"A good life, Mom? Is that what you think I have?" Until recently, it had been so pathetically empty, so work focused and one dimensional. Spending time with Logan, falling in love with him, made her see that clearly. "Just because I'm single doesn't mean my life has been good."

The rebuttal—the words as much as their crisp

delivery—must have thrown Maude. Mallory pictured her mother's mouth working soundlessly on the other end of the line. It was a wonderful moment, an amazingly liberating one, especially since Mallory hadn't even realized she'd been as tethered to the past as her mother.

But all good things must come to an end, and her mother's silence was one of them.

"That's the way you talk to me? After all of the sacrifices I've made through the years to see to it that you could have everything I didn't and couldn't?"

Mallory almost apologized, not because she felt contrite, but because she could wind up the conversation that much more quickly if she gave in, gave up. A glance at her watch showed that she was already going to be late arriving at Logan's condo. Well, whether a little late or a lot, this couldn't wait. For once, she was going to set the record straight.

"I appreciate your sacrifices, Mom. I always have. What I don't appreciate is the way you've used them as a battering ram, trying to ensure I would always feel beholden to you. You did what a parent is expected to do and, okay, more since Dad skipped out on his obligations after he left."

"After he left!" Maude spat the words. "He wasn't much of a father while he was still in the home. You have no idea the sacrifices I made," she said a second time.

Mallory decided to try a different approach. "You could have more now, Mom. You could go back to school, take some courses so you could get a job you actually liked."

Maude snorted. "At my age?"

"You're fifty-four. That's hardly ancient."

"He's really turned your head, hasn't he? This fellow you're rushing off to see." Her mother sounded disgusted.

"He's a good man." The very best. And he was going to be a good father. She would believe that. She wouldn't let the past poison the future.

"They all start off that way."

"No. They don't." The truth struck Mallory with enough force that she leaned against the kitchen wall for support. "None of the guys I dated in the past started off treating me very well. Maybe that's what I wanted," she murmured, half to herself. "Maybe, after what happened between you and Dad, I didn't want to be tempted to have a serious relationship, one with long-term possibilities."

She was tempted now. More than tempted, she decided. And the baby growing inside her wasn't the only reason.

"Mallory—"

Her mother was gearing up for another depressing diatribe, but Mallory had heard enough. Nothing she'd said to Maude had changed her mother's mind, but at least Mallory had had her say and experienced an epiphany of her own.

"Mom. I've got to go. Logan is waiting for me."

* * *

"You look different," Logan said as she stood chopping a red bell pepper at the kitchen counter.

She was using the Santoku knife the way he'd taught her, keeping the tip of the blade on the cutting board and levering the rest of it up and down to cut the vegetable. She'd already given the same treatment to an onion and a couple stalks of celery for the shrimp stir fry they were making.

"It's your fancy lighting." She used the knife to point to the trio of amber-glass pendant lights that hung above the counter, but a panicky part of her wondered if he could tell she was pregnant just by looking at her.

"No." His eyes narrowed speculatively. "It's more than that."

"You're making me feel self-conscious," she warned when he continued to stare at her. "I'm liable to slice off a finger if you keep inspecting me like that."

He wasn't deterred by the prospect of bloodshed. "You look...lighter."

Mallory blinked at that before setting the knife aside and crossing her arms over her chest. "Are you saying you thought I was fat before?"

He chuckled. "Not lighter in that regard. Lighter in spirit I guess is what I mean."

She made a tsking noise. "Watch it. You're coming awfully close to analyzing me."

"Not close. I am." He plucked a piece of red pepper from the cutting board and popped it in his mouth. "So, what's happened?"

Where to begin, Mallory thought. She unfolded her

arms and decided to keep to the most recent event. "I talked to my mother just before coming here."

"Oh." He nodded. "Is that why you were late?"

"Yes." She wiped her hands on the front of her white chef's apron, not because they were dirty, but because her palms suddenly felt moist.

"Is she okay?"

"Yes." Then Mallory shook her head. "No, not really. I feel sorry for her."

"How so?"

Logan was all doctor now, but Mallory didn't mind. She'd come to appreciate this side of him. His calm assessments and keen insights. She offered some of her own. "My dad did a real number on her, but it was years ago."

"Sometimes the passage of time is irrelevant if the hurt was substantial enough." When she frowned, he said quietly, "I let ten years pass before I found myself in another serious relationship."

"Because of Felicia."

He nodded and the revelation caused Mallory to swallow. They had talked about a lot of things since that night in her apartment, but by unspoken agreement, they'd steered clear of this topic.

"A little ironic, huh?" His expression turned sardonic. "I counsel people on relationships, on moving forward with their lives despite adversity or after heartache. Yet I spent the better part of a decade in emotional limbo."

"You're not in limbo now." She rose on tiptoe and kissed him.

"Nope." He nipped at her lower lip.

"You've moved on with your life."

"Full steam ahead," he agreed. Then he sobered. "You know, I'm still not sure if I prefer what I'm doing to being in private practice, but for the first time since I went on the air, I no longer feel like a fraud."

"I'm glad."

"So, what happened with your mom?"

"She needs to move on. Forget limbo. The woman is in purgatory and she's only too happy to try to drag me there, too. She's lonely and bitter and absolutely determined to remain that way."

"Have you accepted that her unhappiness is not your fault or your responsibility?"

"Oh, I accepted that a long time ago. What occurred to me today when she began lecturing me on the evils of men and relationships—" when Logan's brows lifted, Mallory inserted "—yes, my mother finds your species to be without redemption. Anyway, when she trotted out the same old saw today, I got so angry that I actually argued with her."

"You've never argued with your mother before? You?" he said again, his lips beginning to twitch.

"Are you insinuating that I'm contrary?"

He leaned forward to drop a kiss on the tip of her nose. "I wouldn't dare. Now, go on with your story."

"I've argued with my mom about plenty of things,

but not about men in general or my dad in particular. I've always just let her have her say," Mallory admitted.

"Avoidance," he murmured.

"Maybe. Probably." She shrugged. "But I didn't think I'd put any stock in her words or that they'd had any impact on my life. Until today."

"What changed?" he asked softly and reached for her hand. His fingers weaved through hers, a symbol of the bond that had formed between them. It gave her strength and Mallory smiled.

"I changed. I realized that until recently I was a work-aholic. I didn't just enjoy my job, I'd made it the focus of my life to the exclusion of all else. Well, except for loser guys."

"Present company excluded, I hope."

"Definitely. The men I dated in the past were…so wrong for me. I knew that, on a subconscious level at least, but I didn't want to get serious with anyone. I didn't want to chance a repeat of my mother's life." She shook her head slowly. "The funny thing is I was already living her life. Sure, the circumstances were different— no jerky ex-husband, no child to raise without support." Her heart thudded at that, but she pressed on. "No mediocre job to toil away at because I didn't have a college degree or marketable skills—but I had become every bit as lonely and jaded."

"Wow." He nodded appreciatively. "No wonder you look so light. You shed a ton of baggage."

"Yeah." She smiled. "I did." They both had.

"And you did it all by yourself." He pretended to

frown. "You know, if more people could do what you just did, I'd be out of a job."

"But I'd still need you, Logan." She raised their linked hands to kiss the back of his. "Thank you."

Logan's smile was gentle, his steady gaze mesmerizing. "For what?"

"For not being a jerk."

He laughed. "Thanks, I think."

"I'm starving." She released his hand, but instead of going back to chopping vegetables, Mallory began to untie the apron strings.

"What are you doing?"

Instead of answering his question, she asked one of her own. "Ever made love in a kitchen?"

"This kitchen?" His voice was hoarse and his gaze darkened when she tossed the apron aside and started undoing the buttons on her blouse.

"Or any kitchen."

"No."

"Neither have I." Her blouse joined the apron on the floor. Her bra was new, a sleek and sexy number that created cleavage with the aid of an underwire. Her stomach was still flat, but her breasts were a little fuller, so she looked good wearing it as well as the matching pair of panties that were under her skirt. She unhooked her cotton skirt and let it slide down her legs. If she'd had doubts about her appearance, one look at Logan's expression would have dispelled them.

"Ask me again in an hour." He tugged the tails of his shirt free from his blue jeans and began to unfasten the buttons. She caught a glimpse of his muscular chest and the hair that covered it.

"An hour, huh? That's a long time. You must be feeling pretty confident."

Logan moaned. "I'm feeling a lot of things."

While she was nearly naked, he was mostly clothed.

Mallory appreciated the fact that Logan liked to take his time when it came to intimacy, but his progress with his shirt was much too slow for liking. She nudged his hands aside and made fast work of the remaining buttons.

Need was building, arcing dangerously between them like the current from an exposed wire.

"A lot can happen in an hour," he said as she pushed the shirt off his broad shoulders.

"That's what I'm counting on."

"A reporter from the *Herald* is on the telephone. She insists on speaking to you," Logan's secretary informed him just after he wrapped up his morning show. "Should I take a message?"

"No." He smiled, recalling the scene in his kitchen a couple evenings earlier. And the scene in his bedroom later that same night. And the scene in the shower the following morning. If they kept this up they were liable to kill each other. But what a way to go. "Put her through."

"I was just thinking of you," he said in lieu of a greeting.

"Really? That's a surprise."

And so was the voice on the other end of the line. It didn't belong to Mallory.

Logan straightened in his seat. "My apologies. I thought you were someone else," he replied stiffly.

"Obviously. I think I know exactly who you mean. I'm Sandra Hutchins. We met briefly at a charity dinner a couple months back."

"I remember. Why are you calling?"

"I'd like you to confirm some information for me," she began. "I recently learned that you were engaged to a Felicia Grant ten years ago."

Logan had a sick feeling, but he managed to keep wariness from his tone when he said, "Yes. So?"

"You didn't marry."

"No, we didn't."

"Why?" the woman had the audacity to ask.

"You know, I don't really see how that's your business, Miss Hutchins."

"Infidelity, I believe, was the culprit," she went on as if he hadn't spoken. "Miss Grant married another man mere months after your wedding was called off."

"Old news," he said nonchalantly.

"Perhaps." The gleeful note in her tone worried him. "I assume you understand perfectly the reason Miss Grant divorced her husband less than a year after their marriage?"

"I wasn't aware she'd divorced. She left town almost immediately after they got married, and I saw no reason to keep in touch with her family."

"Really? No reason?"

Something was off here. Way off. Mallory had dug up this very same information, but Sandra was acting as if she had a huge bombshell to drop. Logan couldn't imagine what it might be.

"I'm sorry to hear Felicia's marriage fell apart. Contrary to what you apparently think, I harbor no ill feelings for her, especially after all this time."

And especially now that he'd fallen in love with Mallory. The past was the past. It was the present and the future he wanted to concentrate on now.

"What about your son? What feelings, if any, do you harbor for him?"

CHAPTER TWELVE

LOGAN couldn't breathe. He sucked air in through his mouth, but it didn't seem to make it all the way to his lungs.

"What are you talking about?" he managed after a lengthy pause during which he pictured Sandra smiling gleefully on the other end of the line.

"Little Devon Michael Getty. Well, he's not so little now. While Felicia's ex was kind enough to provide the boy with his surname, it's obvious you provided the DNA. He bears a striking resemblance to you, Dr. Bartholomew."

A child? A son? No. It wasn't true. It couldn't be. Could it?

While nothing made sense at the moment, one thing was clear: Logan was not going to continue talking to a reporter on the record, especially when he didn't know what he was talking about.

He gathered his scattered wits and managed to sound authoritative when he snapped, "This conversation is over."

Even before he cleared the radio station's lobby, he was on his cell phone with his agent. Briefly, he explained the situation, hoping Nina would offer some words of wisdom. Her response was anything but reassuring.

"I knew your getting mixed up with Mallory Stevens was a bad idea."

"This has nothing to do with Mallory."

"It's a different reporter who called you today, but from the same paper. Don't be naive, Logan. Mark my word, she had a hand in this. What have you said to her regarding your former fiancée?"

"Nothing. Well, very little. She admitted a while ago that she knew about Felicia and was aware of our breakup. She never explored it further. That was the end of it."

"*She* didn't," his agent stressed. "She handed it over to someone else."

Logan swore. No. He wouldn't believe that. "This isn't about Mallory. For that matter, it's not even about a damned news story."

"The one in question could very well cripple your career, not to mention cost you the nationally syndicated television show," Nina reminded him. "The contract has been signed, but the fine print clearly allows them to yank the plug under certain circumstances. I think this would qualify."

His agent was paid to think about business and his image, which is why he'd called her. Let her perform damage control. Logan had bigger issues to worry about. My God, what was Mallory going to think when she heard this news? Another thought struck like a blow. Had she already?

"Do whatever you think needs to be done, Nina. I'll be in touch later. I've got to get to the bottom of this," he said, hanging up even as his agent was still sputtering in outrage.

Did he have a son, a boy old enough to be just as confused and hurt by his defection as Mallory had been by her father's? He needed to find the truth. For that he had to talk to Felicia. Unfortunately, Logan didn't know where to find her.

But Mallory did.

Despite the rain, Logan stood on the deck of his sailboat, waiting for Mallory to arrive. After the cryptic phone call he'd left on her office voice mail, he would have understood if Mallory hadn't come. He must have sounded unbalanced, asking her to meet him, to bring her notes on Felicia, and not to tell anyone at her office where she was heading. He spied her jogging along the dock under the protection of a polka-dotted umbrella and sighed in relief.

Mallory didn't know what to make of Logan's desperate-sounding message or their clandestine meeting. But she never questioned going. They had tickets for a Sox game that evening, but he wouldn't have asked her to break away from work in the middle of the day to meet him on his sailboat without a good reason.

When she reached him, she noted that his hair was wet, his oxford shirt soaked through. Something was troubling him, though his manners were unaffected. He helped her aboard the *Tangled Sheets* and ushered her below deck.

"My God. You're drenched." Even so, she didn't protest when he pulled her against him. He needed her. That much was clear.

"Sorry," he mumbled as he pulled away. "Now you're drenched, too."

"Don't worry about me."

"Don't worry about you?" He cocked his head to one side. "I can't help worrying about you. It comes with the territory, you know." His expression was fierce when he said, "I love you, Mallory."

"I know. I love you, too."

"Remember you said that."

She frowned at the odd request. Some of the old doubts whispered in her head. The voice sounded suspiciously like that of her mother. Though the voice wouldn't be silenced, she refused to listen to it. "Logan, you're scaring me. Please, tell me why you asked me to meet you here."

"You haven't spoken to Sandra, then."

Her stomach heaved. It had been doing that ever since she'd retrieved his phone message. She wasn't sure if stress or pregnancy was the culprit.

"Sandra Hutchens? I go out of my way to avoid her. What does Sandra have to do with this?"

"There's something we need to discuss."

Mallory couldn't agree more. She'd already decided she wanted to confide in him about her pregnancy. She'd planned to do it tonight, after the ball game. It was time he knew. She was growing more excited by the day. She wanted him to share in it. Besides, he was an astute man, a doctor by training. He'd figure it out soon enough if she continued to avoid alcohol and munch on saltine crackers to calm her nausea. He'd have every right to be angry with her then.

"You brought your notes, right?"

"Yes." She reached into her satchel and pulled them out. Other than her editor, no one was privy to what was inside the small spiral notebook. She didn't hesitate, though, before asking Logan what he needed.

"Felicia's contact information."

Mallory must have stumbled back a step. The next thing she knew he was holding her by the arms. "You want Felicia's number?"

"I wouldn't ask if it wasn't important. Something's come up." He laughed harshly. "Actually, Sandra has brought something up. I need to find out if it's true."

"What…?" She let the words trail off and fought the urge to pepper him with questions. Now was not the time to turn on her reporter mode. Instead she ripped a piece of paper from her notebook and handed it to him. "Here."

"Just like that?"

She swallowed, nodded. "No questions asked."

He kissed her hard and quick. "I'll let you ask all of the questions you want…later. Right now I have to get to the bottom of some things. It might take a while."

She nodded, determined to stay strong. "That's all right. I've got to get back to the office, anyway. Can you meet me at my apartment this evening?"

"I'll come by right after I finish with my lawyer."

"Lawyer! Are you in some kind of trouble, Logan?" Without waiting for him to reply, she offered, "What can I do? What do you need?"

"I need you," he said quietly. "See you later?"

"I'll be waiting." We'll both be waiting, she added silently.

Mallory didn't get much work done after returning to the office. How could she? Briefly she'd considered contacting Logan's family. As close-knit as the Bartholomew clan was, surely his parents or one of his siblings would know what was going on. But she refrained. She could wait till this evening. Logan would explain the situation, and together they would figure out how to deal with whatever it was that was causing him so much distress.

She was staring at her blank computer screen when her phone rang. It was the editor.

"I need to see you in my office."

In the past being summoned to Barry's office hadn't filled Mallory with trepidation. Heck, she'd barged in without an invitation often enough when she was working on a good story. Today, between nerves and the baby, she felt downright nauseated, and her queasiness intensified when she spied Sandra sitting to one side of his desk.

"Shut the door," Barry told her.

Mallory had the odd feeling that her fate was being sealed as it closed.

"What's up?" she asked, striving for casual.

"Sandra is working on a story, one that will be an exclusive if we can wrap it up quickly."

"How very enterprising of you," Mallory remarked. "What does it have to do with me?"

"She's dug up some rather damning information on a local celebrity. The facts are pretty solid, but our lawyers are demanding we ensure every *i* is dotted and every *t* crossed. They've become a little gun-shy these days."

Mallory's heart had begun to pound so loudly that she had to strain her ears to hear what Sandra was saying. "Let's just cut to the chase, shall we? I need an interview with Logan Bartholomew and, given how chummy the two of you have become lately, I figure you can help me get it."

"Why do you need an interview with Logan?" But she knew. Felicia. It was all starting to make sense.

"You can read the answer to that in the paper when the story breaks."

Mallory stiffened her spine. "You think I'll help you?"

"We're all on the same team," the editor inserted.

"Sandra has offered to give you credit for contributing to her report in a tagline at the end the story."

Did they really think Mallory was holding out for credit? Perhaps the old Mallory would have. The one who put work above everything, including personal relationships.

"Sorry. I can't help you."

The response had Sandra cursing and the editor blowing out a breath. "Fine," Barry said after a moment. "I'll spring you from features."

It was what she'd wanted when she'd pursued Logan in the beginning. She couldn't help but think she was partly to blame for his current mess. Whatever juicy tidbit Sandra had managed to unearth, Mallory was the one who had started the digging.

Ignoring the editor's offer, she turned to her rival. "I have to hand it to you, Hutchens. You're brighter than you look. You saw me riffling through the files that night in the morgue and actually put two and two together."

"I hope you're not going to accuse me of poaching your story." Glancing at the editor, Sandra said, "I merely picked up where she left off, since it didn't appear she was going to do anything with the information."

"I made it pretty easy, even for someone with your poor instincts," Mallory snapped.

Sandra ignored the insult. "You signed out all those clip files in my name and then took your sweet time turning them in." Her smile was both malicious and triumphant. "It made me wonder just what you were up to. Then I saw you with Logan and remembered seeing you reading his engagement announcement."

Mallory was the one who swore this time. "Well, I can't help you out any further."

"Can't or won't?" Sandra asked. "I need to speak to him."

"Sorry." She lifted her shoulders.

Sandra turned to the editor. "I want an exclusive! For the paper, of course."

"Of course," Mallory muttered. Had she really been as driven as Sandra? As blind to everything and everyone around her?

"The lawyers want us to include a response from either Bartholomew or someone authorized to speak on his behalf," the editor said. "Sorry, Sandra. I'm not willing to stick my neck out again." His gaze slid to Mallory before he added, "It still has ax marks on it from the last time."

A moment ago Mallory had been offered a way out of the doghouse, but Barry was letting her know that unless she helped them, she would remain in it.

Sandra stood, braced her hands on his desk and leaned forward. The pose was menacing, but her voice verged on whining when she said, "But, Barry, we can't wait much longer. If we do, one of the other news outlets is bound to scoop us. It's just a matter of time as it is till the news breaks, especially since Venture Media has offered Bartholomew a syndicated television show."

So, they knew about that, too. Mallory tried to

downplay the situation. "What's the big deal? So the guy was dumped by his ex and then had a hard time trusting women. He may be a psychiatrist, but he's also human."

Sandra turned, her eyes lighting up with almost maniacal delight. "He hasn't told you. My God, you, journalist extraordinaire Mallory Stevens, are in the dark." She clapped her hands together. "I love it! I absolutely love it!"

"Sandra," Barry began, looking uncharacteristically uncomfortable as he divided a look between the two women.

Sandra ignored him. "Please, Barry. At least let me break *this* story."

"What are you talking about?" Mallory demanded through clenched teeth.

"Your darling doctor is a daddy. The deadbeat variety."

If she hadn't been sitting, Mallory's legs would have buckled. "What?"

"You heard me. Logan has a son. A nine-year-old boy he fathered with Felicia, and I have it on good authority that he's never seen or so much as tried to contact the kid, much less paid any child support."

Mallory shook her head, unconsciously covering her abdomen with one shaking hand. "You're wrong. Logan doesn't...and even if he did he wouldn't... You're mistaken."

"No. I'm not. Unless the birth certificate is wrong.

You're not only a sloppy reporter, Mallory, you're a damned fool."

Sandra sailed out of Barry's office then, leaving Mallory shell-shocked and reeling. Her humiliation was complete when her stomach heaved and she was forced to wretch in the editor's wastepaper basket.

Barry offered the box of tissue rather than any sympathy.

"I won't even ask about half the stuff Sandra just said, all I want to know is if you're going to help."

She wiped her lips, would have killed for a breath mint. She settled for a stiff spine. "No. I thought I'd already made that clear."

"Come on," he cajoled. "We both know you did half the legwork on this story. Help Sandra finish it and you can get back to doing what you do best."

Hard news. Real stories. Meaty pieces about scandals, lawbreaking and deceit. She was a journalist. She would always enjoy breaking news. But she wouldn't exploit her relationship with Logan to do it, especially since she didn't consider this to be on par with government bribes, police cover-ups or accounting irregularities at city hall. If what Sandra claimed was true, it was Logan's private hell, and she had to believe he had an explanation. He wasn't a deadbeat. He wasn't anything like her father. He'd given her nothing but reasons to trust him. She wouldn't start doubting him now when he needed her most.

"No," she told Barry.

When Mallory rose to her feet, he asked, "Where do you think you're going?"

To tell the father of my unborn child how much I love him. To help him through his current crisis. She wasn't going to walk away from him now, and she certainly wasn't going to play an active role in the effort to destroy his life.

"Mallory," Barry shouted when she reached his door. "I asked where you're going."

"Home. I don't feel well." But she knew what to do to make herself better.

It was nine-twenty when Logan knocked at Mallory's door. Logan was wiped out emotionally and physically, his adrenaline used up. He'd contacted Felicia and spent a couple of hours on the phone with her, and later with her parents. It made him feel marginally better that they hadn't known Devon's true paternity. Like everyone else, they had assumed that Nigel Getty was the child's father. Apparently only Nigel and Felicia had known the whole truth. That she'd discovered her pregnancy after breaking off her engagement to Logan.

Nigel and Felicia had gone ahead with their wedding, both hoping the child would turn out to be Nigel's. But almost immediately after Devon's birth it became apparent he favored Logan. Their marriage had lasted a year. Ironically, while Nigel had had no problem becoming involved with an engaged woman, the idea of raising a son he had not fathered had proven beyond his ability. When a paternity test confirmed that Devon was

Logan's, Nigel filed for divorce. At his insistence, the birth certificate was changed to reflect the boy's true parentage. But neither Logan nor Devon was ever told the truth.

Logan was angry, bitter. He felt betrayed all over again by Felicia, but it was worse this time. He was a father. He had a son. And they were absolute strangers.

Weighing almost as heavily on his mind was what Mallory's reaction was going to be to the news. Would she believe him? Would she accept that he'd had no idea of Felicia's pregnancy when they'd parted ways? Or would she view the situation through the filter of her past and come to the same assumption Sandra had: that he'd happily walked away from his responsibility.

Just as Mallory's father had all those years ago.

Logan tried to smile when the door opened. Mallory's face was ashen, but her shoulders were squared. Something in her expression told him she already knew what he was going to tell her. More than anything he wanted to hold her. He needed her understanding as much as he needed her comfort and support. But he held back, waiting for some sign that she would offer them.

"I was getting worried," she said.

"Sorry. It took a little longer than I'd anticipated."

After his conversations with Felicia and her family, he'd spent time with his lawyer. There would not be a custody battle. Logan and his son were strangers. It would be cruel and traumatic to try to wrench the boy away from Felicia, even though Logan had every intention of being an involved father. A visitation schedule would be worked out as well as financial support.

"Come in," she said.

Stepping into the well-lit foyer, he could see that Mallory was pale and looked drawn. "You look like I feel. Everything okay?"

"The editor summoned me to his office after I returned to the newspaper."

His heart sank. "I think I can guess why."

"Sandra was quite gleeful about the whole matter."

"Yeah, I got that feeling when she reached me at the station the other day and dropped the bomb." He wondered if the shrapnel wounds would ever heal. "Mallory, about the boy—"

"You didn't know."

Her tone held absolutely no equivocation. And here Logan had thought he couldn't love her more than he already did. Given her past, Mallory had every reason not to believe him. But she did. She did.

"Thank you for that. I was worried that you'd think—"

She stopped his words with a kiss. "No. I'm done living in the past, remember? They want a quote from you, by the way, and they want me to get it." She tilted her head to one side. "Sandra said she'd give me a bit of credit in the story tagline. The editor was more generous than that. He offered to spring me from the Lifestyles section."

"If I have to talk to someone, I'd rather it be you. And if you get your old beat back in the process that will make it worthwhile."

Mallory frowned. "You think I agreed to do it? I just told you I'm done living in the past. My job is no longer my life, Logan. I won't use you to get back into the newsroom. It's not worth it."

"I wouldn't mind."

"I would. I love you."

"I love you right back." He kissed her and Mallory smiled.

"See, no job can do that."

As relieved as he was at the moment, Logan was also a realist. They had more to discuss, more decisions to make. He led her to the couch and pulled her down next to him.

"My life is about to become a three-ring circus," he began. "My agent informed me on the way here that the contract for my syndicated show has been nullified."

"Sorry."

"I thought I would be, too. But I'm not. It wasn't the direction I wanted to go professionally. They'll be releasing a statement to the media since the rumors of a deal were already circulating. It's going to get really complicated."

"Are you trying to give me an out?"

"Just for a little while. I don't want you to get struck by any of the mud that's about to get flung."

"That's sweet, but I'm not going anywhere. We're in this together, Logan."

"I was hoping that was what you'd say. I need you, Mallory." He shoved a hand through his hair, his composure crumpling. "My God, I have a son. A son. He's nine years old and he doesn't know who I am, and I don't know the first thing about him or, for that matter, about being a father."

"You'll be a great dad."

He appreciated her conviction, but his voice caught when he said, "I've missed so much stuff that I shouldn't have missed. Forget walking and talking, he's already riding a bike, playing baseball. I can't believe Felicia kept this from me all these years."

Logan's pain was plainly visible. Mallory's heart ached for him. "I'm so sorry."

"Felicia and I talked for a long time. I can't believe she did what she did, especially keeping Devon from me even after she knew the truth. But what's done is done. Arguing about it now won't solve anything."

"So what will you do?"

"Felicia was already considering returning to Chicago. Her business in Portland is failing, and now that I know about Devon she doesn't really have any reason to remain there. After I meet Devon and get to know him well enough that he's comfortable spending time alone with me, we're going to work out a visitation arrangement. So part of the time it won't be just the two of us."

Mallory had planned to tell Logan about their child tonight, and part of her still wanted to, but it wouldn't be fair. He had so much on his plate right now. Her news would keep. For another day or a couple weeks at most. Just until Logan caught his second wind.

* * *

Two weeks passed. Not surprisingly, the media, both in Chicago and nationally, had a field day as the story of Logan's nine-year-old "love child" leaked out.

The tabloids and some Internet blogs questioned Logan's claims that he hadn't known about his son, despite Felicia's statements supporting that version of events. Mallory could only imagine what would be written if anyone was privy to news of her pregnancy. She was still keeping it under wraps. She hadn't even told Vicki, though her friend had raised her eyebrows when Mallory had ordered a virgin margarita at their last get-together.

Logan had to be the first to know. And he would be. Very soon.

He was returning today after a weekend in Oregon. He'd met his son for the first time yesterday. He'd called Mallory last night so full of heartache and hope that she knew she couldn't keep the news to herself any longer. The timing might not be perfect, but it was right.

She was on her way to the airport now and she had it all planned. After she picked him up, she was going to take him back to her apartment where a candlelight dinner waited. She'd cheated on the meal, calling Luke to cater it. She wanted everything to be perfect, and her cooking skills were still iffy at best.

She spied Logan the moment he came through the gate at O'Hare. He looked tired but oddly energized. She greeted him with a hug. When she would have pulled away, he hugged her tighter and finished with a kiss that had her toes wanting to curl.

"I think you missed me."

"I did, indeed. And it got me thinking."

"Yeah? About what?"

"I'll tell you when we get to my place." He bobbed his brows.

"If you're not too tired from your flight, I thought we'd go to my apartment instead. I have dinner waiting and a little surprise."

"That's fine. I have a little surprise of my own," he said with an enigmatic wink.

The last thing Mallory expected Logan to do the moment they entered her apartment was pull a ring box from his pocket and drop to one knee. He'd said he had a little surprise for her. Talk about an understatement. The diamond winking back at her from the box appeared to be all of three carats.

"Wh-what are you doing?" she asked.

"You can't figure it out? You're usually pretty quick." He grinned.

"You…you want…"

"To marry you." He nodded and caught her in his arms when she sagged. They both wound up sitting on the floor. "I love you, Mallory. I want to spend my life with you. If you want to take your time answering, that's okay. I know things are a little crazy right now and they will be for a while yet. I can be patient."

"I don't need to take time. Yes! Yes, I'll marry you." She cupped his face, kissed him soundly and then sighed as he took over and lowered her onto the floor.

It was several moments before he helped her to her

feet. "Dinner smells good," he said. "Hey, didn't you say you had a little surprise for me, too?"

She nibbled her bottom lip, but then smiled. It was too early to feel the baby, but she swore she felt something wonderful flutter inside of her. "Yes, I do."

EPILOGUE

Three years later

"WE'RE having a baby?" Logan was smiling as he asked the question.

"The doctor says I'm due the first week in October." Mallory grinned in reply. "She could arrive on our third wedding anniversary."

"That would be quite a present." He put his arms around her and dropped a kiss on her lips. "And from your reference to the baby as a she, I see that you're hoping for a girl this time."

"I love the men in my life, but with you, Devon and little Patrick, there are too many of you. It would be nice to have another female in the house."

Devon had been coming to stay with Logan on alternating weekends and holidays since he and his mother moved back from Portland six months after the story of Logan's paternity first made headlines. The arrangement wasn't ideal. No child custody arrangement ever was. But they were making it work.

Of course, it had been rough on all of them in the beginning. Not surprisingly Devon had been angry, hurt and confused. He'd lashed out at everyone, with his father the prime target. Even when Logan had been devastated by his son's animosity and pain, he'd remained patient and, with Mallory's help, hopeful that eventually the boy would come around.

And he had.

It had taken Devon more than a year before he called Logan "Dad." Mallory thought it was apropos that the boy did so the same day Patrick uttered his first Da-Da. Things had gotten easier after that, and a real relationship had begun to form. None of the awkwardness that had accompanied their get-togethers during those first months was present now. She wouldn't say things were perfect, but they were close.

"What are you thinking?" Logan asked, pulling Mallory from her musings.

She meant it when she replied, "That I'm the luckiest woman in the world."

The World of Mills & Boon

There's a Mills & Boon® series that's perfect for you! There are ten different series to choose from and new titles every month, so whether you're looking for glamorous seduction, Regency rakes, homespun heroes or sizzling erotica, we'll give you plenty of inspiration for your next read.

By Request

Relive the romance with the best of the best
12 stories every month

Cherish™

Experience the ultimate rush of falling in love.
12 new stories every month

INTRIGUE...

A seductive combination of danger and desire...
7 new stories every month

Desire™

Passionate and dramatic love stories
6 new stories every month

nocturne™

An exhilarating underworld of dark desires
3 new stories every month

For exclusive member offers go to
millsandboon.co.uk/subscribe

Which series will you try next?

Awaken the romance of the past...
6 new stories every month

Medical Romance

The ultimate in romantic medical drama
6 new stories every month

MODERN™

Power, passion and irresistible temptation
8 new stories every month

MODERN tempted™

True love and temptation!
4 new stories every month